RETRIBUTION

Steffen Jacobsen is an orthopaedic surgeon in his native Denmark. He was first inspired to write fiction by Roberto Saviano's non-fiction book, *Gomorrah,* about the Comorrah, and by his travels around Italy. *Retribution* is his third novel.

Also by Steffen Jacobsen

When The Dead Awaken
Trophy

RETRIBUTION

STEFFEN JACOBSEN

*Translated from the Danish
by Charlotte Barslund*

Quercus

First published in Denmark in 2015
First published in Great Britain in 2016 by

Quercus Editions Ltd
Carmelite House
50 Victoria Embankment
London EC4Y 0DZ

An Hachette UK company

A CIP catalogue record for this book is available
from the British Library

PB ISBN 978 1 78429 154 9
EBOOK ISBN 978 1 78429 153 2

10 9 8 7 6 5 4 3 2 1

Typeset by CC Book Production

Printed and bound in Great Britain by Clays Ltd, St Ives plc

The shattered body of the martyr smells of musk.

Hamas commander, Gaza

PROLOGUE

17th September
The year of Makkah 1434

Nabil had seen his mother so clearly, sitting among them in the stranger's living room. He had asked for her forgiveness for what he was about to do, but she had cried out that he must think of mankind's capacity for mercy. Enough people had died.

His resolve had wavered under the pressure of his mother's pleas until Fadr shook him awake.

'Who are you talking to?' he demanded to know.

His friend had grown a sparse moustache to hide his cleft palate, which had never been properly fixed.

'No one,' Nabil said.

His mother was a mirage who existed only in his mind. He had barely eaten these last few weeks and they had told him that hallucinations were to be expected.

After a mortar attack that had destroyed half his childhood street in Damascus, he had dug out the bodies of his parents and his sisters, Basimah and Farhah, from under the rubble in the family's courtyard garden. Together with Sufyan, the imam, he had washed and swaddled them and said *salat al-janazah*, the funeral prayer, over them.

From that day Nabil had been with the militia. While tens of thousands of his countrymen were killed and millions made homeless, the EU, NATO and the USA kept behind their own red lines, vetoed to death by the UN's Security Council. Oil, natural gas, trainers and Putin's ego were more important than Syrian lives, and Nabil hated them all.

With his twenty-four years, Samir was the oldest of the three men in the flat on Nørrebro. He left the lookout post by the window, kneeled in the early morning light between Nabil and Fadr and turned his palms towards the sky.

'Nabil, cleanse your soul of unclean things. Forget all about what we call the world and this life; the time between you and your marriage in heaven is now very short,' he said.

'*Subhan' Allah*, God's honour,' Nabil and Fadr mumbled in unison.

Fadr placed something in Nabil's hands. He unfolded the black scarf with golden characters. Drops of sweat fell from his close-cropped hair and left tiny marks on the fabric.

'*Al-uqab*, the Eagle,' Fadr said solemnly. 'The flag of Saladin. Mohamed al-Amir Atta carried it with him to the towers in New York.'

'I will carry it with honour, *insha' Allah*, if God be willing.'

Nabil folded the scarf.

'I should go and wash,' he said.

The bathroom was filled with feminine scents. In order to respect the home and hospitality of their unknown host, they had not opened a single cupboard or pulled out a single drawer in the flat. There was little by way of decoration in the living room: a map of the world and a poster of a black cat drinking absinthe from a tall glass. The only evidence to suggest that the owner belonged to the network was the Koran on the bedside table, bound in red leather, which, after having been touched by many hands, had eventually become as soft as kid gloves.

Food had been set out for them when they arrived and the only one who had left the flat was Fadr, who had gone to buy more cigarettes from the kiosk across the street.

Nabil washed his face and dried it with a towel that also smelled of the owner of the flat, turned off the light, opened the window to the courtyard and looked up at the sky above the rooftop opposite.

'*Aldebaran, Alnath, Alhena,*' he mumbled.

He had looked at the same stars from the deck of the ship as she sailed up through the Øresund between Denmark and Sweden, to bring them to this small country. When she had dropped her anchor, Samir had paid off the captain with a fat bundle of euros. Then they climbed over the bulwarks and down into the dark-grey rubber dinghy waiting for them on the calm, black water. Samir and Fadr had paddled the dinghy towards the shore, guided by flashes from a torch, while Nabil sat in the stern with the suitcase containing explosives and detonators between his knees. They had let the waves carry the rubber dinghy up onto the beach, then they had pushed it back into the water and walked across the wet sand until they were met by a figure that had stepped out from between the trees.

Samir had exchanged a few words with the stranger. There might have been a brief embrace before they walked, single file, up a steep slope. The figure had moved softly and sure-footedly and Nabil had concluded that it must be a woman. They were taken to a white van in a deserted car park. Samir took the front passenger seat, while the other two sat on the floor in the back with their suitcases and rucksacks.

He heard a mobile ring in the living room. When he came out from the bathroom, Fadr and Samir looked very solemn. Fadr put the mobile in his pocket and Nabil's knees nearly buckled beneath him.

'Be strong, *shaheed*,' Samir said as if he could understand what Nabil was feeling. 'Do not say of those killed in the name of Allah that they are dead. No, they live like shadows among us, but we do not see them.'

The mobile vibrated in Fadr's pocket and he read the new text.

'The car is downstairs.'

It was cold and the three of them sat close together in the back, swaying in unison every time the van turned a corner.

Samir found a Thermos flask, unscrewed the top and sniffed the contents before passing it on.

'Tea?'

Nabil nodded. In the grey light of dawn he studied the white, star-shaped scar on Samir's temple, half hidden by his friend's long black hair. The Syrian would touch it from time to time when he was agitated or deep in thought. He had never explained how he got it. A 'miracle' was all he would say. It looked like a gunshot wound, but how could anyone survive a gunshot to the temple?

The young men had met each other three months ago at a training camp in Iran, and Fadr and Samir had become the closest Nabil had to a family. It was the custom that a believer walking the path of the martyr, *as-shaheed*, recorded a message or read aloud a statement to a video camera. Later, the family could show the recording to friends and neighbours and post it on the Internet. But although this mission constituted a mighty attack on this warmongering and blasphemous small country, his family was with him right now and so Nabil had nothing to say to a camera.

He was not surprised that he had been chosen. Since his childhood, it had been both natural and necessary for him to turn to God. Sufyan, the imam who had taken him in when the civil war broke out, had recommended him to mufti Ebrahim Safar Khan and the network, and sworn to his piety and suitability.

Finally the van came to a stop; the driver pulled the

handbrake on and turned the engine off. The door on the driver's side opened and shut with a bang. They heard light footsteps that faded away – then nothing.

During the next few hours they dozed while the world outside grew lighter. They could hear voices in many languages, hurried footsteps, children, bicycles, car and bus engines, crashing gear changes and squealing tyres.

The tea had failed to take away the dryness in Nabil's throat. One moment he would freeze, the next shiver feverishly. Groggily, he watched the second hand on the watch on Fadr's tanned wrist, which quickly, far too quickly, completed its journey around the clock face.

At ten thirty exactly, the other two sat up and Nabil buried his face in his hands. He sat for a few seconds with his gaze aimed at the floor of the van before he squatted on his haunches and held out his arms.

The suicide vest was as heavy as the sins of mankind. Four rows of slim, rectangular blocks of Semtex had been stitched into canvas pockets on the front and back. The heaviest parts were the flat plastic bags with ball bearings taped around the blocks: tens of thousands of steel bullets would leave Nabil's body in a spherical cloud of death when he detonated the vest. There were additional explosives in his shoulder bag.

Samir attached the vest around his waist with sturdy straps, steel wires and padlocks, so that no heroic ticket inspector or police officer who found him suspicious would be able to remove it without setting it off. Meanwhile Fadr checked the detonators, the batteries and the wires on his back.

Then Samir helped him put on a loose-fitting, light-coloured anorak and zipped it up to his neck. With shaking hands, Nabil placed a blue baseball cap on his head. He had closely cropped hair and no beard; he wore a pair of orange Nike trainers and a pair of faded Levi's jeans. He looked like thousands of other young men in Copenhagen.

They embraced each other.

'*Assalamu alaikum*,' Samir and Fadr said, both speaking at once.

'*Walaikum assalam*,' Nabil returned the centuries-old greeting.

'I'm proud, and I envy you,' Samir said. 'Next time, God be willing, it'll be me or Fadr who will plunge the sword into the belly of Denmark, or another crusader country that murders our people.'

'*Insha' Allah*,' Nabil mumbled.

'Do you have the map of the park?' Fadr asked.

Nabil nodded and patted the inside pocket of his anorak, but he would not need a map. Anyone could identify the target simply by craning their neck.

Nabil got out and turned to the other two.

'The woman will let me in?' he asked.

Samir nodded.

'*Ma'assalam, fi aman Allah*, go with God,' he said. 'The woman will be there. And we'll be there. You're not alone.'

Nabil straightened up and started walking at a fast pace, keeping his eyes on the pavement. It was easy now. Soon it would be over. He felt as if he were observing himself from above, moving diagonally across a wide street with heavy traffic, walking towards the eastern end of the amusement park.

He wiped his forehead with the sleeve of his anorak and pressed the brim of his baseball cap further down over his eyes as he approached a small, barred entrance gate. The sun was high in the sky; it was very hot and bright, but the shade provided by the trees was deep and cool. Nabil saw a woman's figure behind the fence and heard a click from the lock. He slipped inside and found himself in a narrow passage between a restaurant and an amusement arcade, out of sight of the surveillance cameras in the park. The smell of food coming from the restaurant and the flies buzzing around the waste containers made him feel hollow and nauseous. But the scent of the woman was fresh. He guessed her to be the same age as him. She was wearing a white, short-sleeved shirt, black trousers and had a long white apron tied around her slim waist. The name of the restaurant was embroidered in green above her left breast. She wore no jewellery and her hair was uncovered. It was put up in a bun at the back and held together with two crossed, yellow pencils. Nabil felt vaguely ashamed on her behalf, but understood why it had to be this way: whether or not she belonged to the network, she had done what she was supposed to do. Opened the door to Paradise for him.

He wondered if she was the same woman who had picked them up on the coast, if they had stayed in her flat these last few days, if she had driven them to the target. Did she know Samir? He felt a stab of jealousy, but suppressed the emotion immediately. Jealousy belonged to this world.

'My name is Ain,' she said in Arabic.

Nabil nodded but made no reply, and she promptly took his wrist and fixed a paper strip around it. He was too taken aback to resist her cool fingers. He could not remember the last time he had felt a woman's touch.

'This is a multi-ride ticket,' she said. 'You can go on all the rides in the park without paying. All you have to do is show them this wristband.'

'Rides?'

She smiled.

'Yes, they're fantastic. This is a great place.'

'Will you be staying here in the restaurant?' he asked her gravely. 'I mean, right here? Working?'

'Yes.'

'Then stay in the restaurant, do you hear me? Don't go anywhere.'

'I promise,' she said, seeking out his eyes under the baseball cap. 'Why is that so important?'

'It's important to do your job well,' he said, as if he were much older and wiser than her.

She brushed a strand of hair behind her ear and adjusted the bun at the back of her head. Her breasts strained against her white shirt and Nabil stared at the ground.

'Very well, very important, then I had better get back,' she said with a smile. 'By the way, are you cold?'

'Eh?'

'Why don't you take off your jacket?'

'I've come straight from a desert. I think your country is very cold.'

He shivered as if he really did feel cold.

'Which desert?'

'Just a desert, all right? Sand, snakes and dust. Sun.'

'Okay. When you get hungry just come back and knock on that door over there. I'll give you some food. You won't have to pay.'

He looked past her.

'I will, little sister. *Walaikum assalam*, Ain,' he said, but there was something in his voice and posture, something he could not control, which made her smile freeze on her lips. Then she turned and went back inside the restaurant.

Nabil sighed. His nostrils expanded. That scent again. It was fleeting and intangible, but he was convinced that he recognized it from the flat. He walked towards the door to the restaurant and opened it. Between steel tables chefs dressed in white were busy with steaming pots and dishes piled high with meat, fruit and bread, but no one appeared to take any notice of him.

Ain was putting glasses on a tray, but turned when he called out. Again her hand tugged the hair behind her ear and she came towards him, walking between the tables.

Nabil stuck his hand into his heavy shoulder bag and found the scarf with the holy characters. He stepped backwards out into the alleyway as she held the door open for him.

'Ain . . .'

'Yes? By the way, what's your name? You must have a name?'

'Nothing. My name is nothing. Nabil, perhaps.'

He pressed the folded scarf into her hand.

'Thank you,' he said. 'Thank you so much.'

'What for?'

He pointed to the band around his wrist.

'The rides.'

She made to unfold the fabric, but he clasped her cool hands.

'Wait,' he said. 'And promise me you'll stay in the restaurant?'

'I will, but—'

'Goodbye.'

Nabil was carried off by the slow stream of people moving through the park. They had told him that everyone who visited Copenhagen in the summer would come here.

He walked north-east. *Don't look people in the eye, don't look at their faces*, they had told him. They are nothing. They are shadows walking in the valley of death, but they do not know it. They are *kufr*, infidels. Non-humans, Nabil.

The air was heavy with the saccharine scent of sweet shops, candyfloss stands and ice cream parlours. He could almost feel the sugary crunch between his teeth and looked with contempt at the spoiled, fat people around him.

He stayed at the edge of the crowd and could see that in three hundred paces he would be standing right under the target: the eighty-metre-tall steel construction which had the peculiarly apt name the Star Flyer, northern Europe's highest carousel.

There was room for twenty-four people on the carousel. Passengers were carried skywards by strong, pneumatic pumps and whirled around for a couple of minutes in seats attached to long chains.

Nabil wondered if some of the bodies would end up in the streets outside the amusement park. The Pakistani engineer who had shown them the construction blueprints, the technical photographs and a model of the Star Flyer, had identified the steel mesh tower's northern plinth as the target. When this section of the carousel's tower collapsed, the concert hall, several restaurants and amusement arcades would lie right in the line of its fall.

He waited outside the railings until a group of visitors had left the steps leading down from the tower and a new group had taken their seats. The pumps squealed and the large platform started to rise. Nabil glanced at a young, blonde woman in a glass cubicle, who was operating the pumps. She kept her eyes on the platform while her hands were busy moving the levers. He straddled the low fence, pushed a couple of children aside and scaled another set of railings.

Someone tried to restrain him, but he wriggled free and ran underneath the construction. He pressed his cheek against the cold steel of the girder, embraced it as he listened to the squealing people high above him as the Star Flyer at the top of its tower flung them through the blue skies above Copenhagen. The steel vibrated against his cheek.

He saw two ticket inspectors come running towards him, saw them comically retreat when he unzipped his anorak and they spotted the vest, the yellow wires and the blocks of explosives.

Then he smiled at the blonde girl behind the glass. She had a walkie-talkie pressed to her ear. He thought about his mother, his sisters – and the girl, Ain. He hoped that she had stayed inside the restaurant.

Nabil grabbed the detonator in the pocket of his anorak, closed his eyes to the sight of human faces and his ears to their screaming.

'*Allahu' Akbar*, God is great,' he whispered as he pressed the button.

I

1

The lecture theatre at Copenhagen Police Headquarters was packed to the rafters. People were sitting on the floor, along the walls and around the desk housing the technician, his projectors and computers.

It was one of the few advantages of being a superintendent, thought Lene Jensen, who was sitting in the middle of a row of chairs. She was certain to get a seat, even though she had recently crashed down spectacularly through the ranks.

She was with colleagues from Rigspolitiet (Denmark's national police force), the Danish Emergency Management Agency, various government departments, PET (the Danish Security and Intelligence Service) and FET (the Danish Military Intelligence Service). The ranks and salary levels that mattered sat in the front row.

The American on the podium was the most recent terror expert to be invited to Copenhagen to explain to the authorities what had happened that September day in the Tivoli Gardens last year – from a retrospective and informed perspective.

He was tanned, tall and sinewy and had the shoulders of an officer. He was dressed in a neat navy-blue suit with sharp creases, shiny black shoes, a white shirt and a discreet grey-striped tie, but looked as if he would have been more comfortable in uniform.

The microphone howled and the American held it further away from his lips.

'What you have to understand is that no one in the Middle East can – or wants to – break the cycle now. Violence is inevitably paid back with more violence, creating more orphans with a deep hatred of the West and Israel. Let's take, for example, the massacres in the Palestinian refugee camps Sabra and Shatila in Beirut in 1982. The night of the 16th September, Christian Phalangists and units from the Lebanese army moved into the camps and started massacring women, children and old people. They carried on doing so without interruption, for two days.'

Behind him old press photographs showed piles of mangled bodies of children, brickwork shot to pieces, burning tents and corrugated iron huts. The earth between the huts was red, as were the puddles in the tyre tracks.

'After the invasion of Lebanon, the Israeli army was officially entrusted with maintaining security at the camps, but they did nothing to protect the refugees. On the contrary, they fired flares above the camps so that the attackers could work at night, and no one – no one – escaped.'

The face of the American was devoid of expression. He sipped some water before he carried on.

'Everybody knew that Yasser Arafat had been evacuated to Tunisia a month earlier with his young PLO fighters and some of the children, and that there were no armed "terrorists" left in Sabra and Shatila. There were no angry young men with Kalashnikovs in the camps, but that counted for nothing: the purpose of the massacres was to send a message to Yasser Arafat from Elie Hobeika, the intelligence chief of the Lebanese army, and from Ariel Sharon, Israel's defence Minister.'

The American let his gaze glide across the front rows as photographs of Sharon and Hobeika appeared on the screen.

'Between the 16th and 18th September, the Phalangists killed approximately three thousand five hundred people. Roughly the same number as were killed during the attacks on the World Trade Centre and the Pentagon in 2001. You will obviously note the coincidence between the date of the Tivoli bomb last year and the dates of these massacres.'

Obviously, Lene thought. The question was whether it was significant or just coincidental. No one had yet claimed responsibility for the Tivoli bomb, which was unusual. Although everyone had expected that every organization from Al-Qaeda to Ansar al-Islam would have claimed victory, no one had sent a letter or video to the international press agencies and no footage had been uploaded to YouTube from the tribal territories in north-west Pakistan or the Yemen.

The screen turned grey.

'After Sabra and Shatila, the American Embassy in Beirut was attacked and sixty-three young people died. Later, the US Marines' barracks were bombed and another two hundred and forty-one young Americans lost their lives. The Middle East is a chronic, political epicentre. An animal that eats its young and that of others. Someone has to break that cycle, ladies and gentlemen, or history will judge all of us harshly. Any questions?'

A muscular man to Lene's far left got up, raised his hand and was handed a microphone. Lene did not recognize him, but he looked like your typical intelligence agent: early forties, fit, wearing jeans and a black T-shirt. His sleeves were pushed up over impressive biceps but his lean face was burdened, his eyes raw and sunken, and his short dark hair prematurely greying. A vein throbbed slowly in his neck.

'Deputy Chief Superintendent Kim Thomsen, PET,' he said. 'If we, or anyone else, are to break the cycle, surely we have to put the attack into a meaningful context, no matter how twisted that context is. That's quite difficult when no one has claimed responsibility.'

The PET agent's body language was perfectly controlled, but a certain fatigue in his voice suggested that he had been personally affected.

As had practically everyone in this tiny country, Lene thought. Everyone had known, been related to or heard of someone who had been in Tivoli on the 17th September. The bomb had dealt an almost fatal blow to a country that history had otherwise treated so gently. The Danes were unprepared, they had never experienced anything like it, and they had no idea how to respond.

Her mobile vibrated against her thigh. She shifted in her chair and ignored it. Her eyelids were leaden. She could not remember when she had last slept without the help of sleeping pills, red wine or vodka – or a combination of all three.

The American nodded.

'I don't think anyone familiar with the Middle Eastern scene today would not place responsibility for the Tivoli attack with a jihadist terror cell. The fact that no one has claimed responsibility for this act of terror is in itself a kind of signature. Al-Saleem from Tehran and Sheikh Ebrahim Safar Khan from ... God knows where ... but probably Amman, have made it their trademark never to claim official responsibility for their actions. Both of them head small but well-organized units of dedicated young men and women.'

The PET agent with the microphone did not appear to have any comments to make, so the American continued.

'These terrorists are highly educated, but more than that, they are patient. They are fighting for a global caliphate and view the extermination or the conversion of all infidels as a necessity. But they are also men and, perhaps even more so, women who to some extent live in the Middle Ages, while we, the Western intelligence services and police forces with all our satellites, drones, listening stations and computers, are from the future.'

He gestured towards the audience.

'To them, you're *all* science-fiction creatures. We live in two parallel but separate timelines, and it's unbelievably difficult to bridge the gap, track them down . . . and liquidate them. We in the West are incredibly vulnerable because no one can defend themselves against a determined man or woman who doesn't care about dying. It short-circuits our whole way of thinking because we would never choose death, and certainly not for a "cause".'

The man who had introduced himself as Kim Thomsen looked confused, but the American smiled supportively.

'As a rule they don't use mobile phones, but when they do, they use prepaid burners and just say a few words or send a text message before destroying the phone. They know each other's appearance, each other's clans, families, dialects and accents, and they have proved their loyalty. They have all executed a bus full of Shia Muslims on their way to a market, blown up a school for girls, blinded a woman who claimed that she had been raped, or beheaded a homosexual. We can't infiltrate them because we can't ask our agents to disfigure or kill little girls. They don't claim responsibility for their missions, and they no longer behave like rock stars – like Ilich Ramirez Sánchez, better known as Carlos the Jackal, did.'

The American stared into the air.

'The ideological hardcore today might consist of young, well-educated women, which makes the threat scenario much more complicated. They don't need specialist training just because they're women. They're discreet; they're excellent liars and they're generally far better at keeping secrets than men.'

A predictable murmur erupted among the female members of the audience and the American waited patiently for it to die down.

'We all know it's men who forget to log out of Facebook, leave the G-string in their pocket, who come home with lipstick on their collar, conspicuous long hairs on their jacket or who forget to delete breathless text messages from their cell phones when they have been with their mistresses. These women are motivated by personal tragedies. They may have lost husbands, brothers, sisters, children or parents or their country and inheritance, and they blame the West and Israel for their loss. They don't wear burkas or niqabs or walk twelve paces behind a man. They smoke cigarettes, they drive cars, they drink mojitos, have premarital sex and listen to Rihanna. They are allowed to do this because it serves a higher purpose: destabilizing the West.'

The man had a point, Lene thought.

'But why now? And why Denmark?' the PET agent asked.

The tall American shrugged his shoulders and pinched the bridge of his nose with his thumb and forefinger.

'Well . . . it's no secret that we, your allies, have wondered about the relaxed attitude with which Denmark in the 1970s and 1980s offered political asylum and granted permanent leave to remain to the world and his wife, including active Muslim fundamentalists and demagogues. You welcomed them because you thought they were being persecuted by the Egyptian dictatorship, even though that is the risk you run when you plan to kill your own head of state. You felt sorry for them. Secondly, there are the Mohammed cartoons, which refuse to die and are resurrected whenever the mullahs want people out in the streets. And last but not least, you joined the coalition forces in Afghanistan and Iraq as our time's version of Christian crusaders. Plus there could be any number of reasons that we don't know yet. For example, a modern Islamist cell might have been set up here in Denmark and it's testing its strength.'

'So you're saying that we only have ourselves to blame?' the PET agent said angrily.

The American looked exasperated.

'Of course not, and the truth is I have no solid facts on which to base a good answer,' he replied after a pause. 'Perhaps it was just your turn or you were too easy a target. We have to face the fact that the attack on Tivoli was particularly successful. You need to think and act differently if you want to prevent a repeat. Post-Tivoli, Denmark has been confronted with a new reality. The question is, are you prepared to intensify the surveillance of civilians, monitor their communication, arrest them without charges, apply physical pressure during interrogations, use truth serum, lie detectors or extraordinary rendition without warrants? Are you willing to turn yourself into a police state to prevent this ever happening again?'

People shifted uneasily in their chairs. Again? The possibility did not bear thinking of.

Lene saw her boss, Chief Superintendent Charlotte Falster, get up. The slim woman with the immaculate grey bob turned and stared hard at the PET agent until he sat down. Then she marched up to the podium, smiled and thanked the American. They were facing the audience and someone photographed their handshake. Charlotte Falster was a master of detail.

Lene's eyelids began to close again, but when her superior's next words struck a chord, she forced them open.

Charlotte was in the process of introducing the next speaker and used words such as doctor of medicine, international Arabic studies, educational books, Harvard and Oxford, special adviser to PET.

Consultant psychiatrist Irene Adler.

Every head in the auditorium turned as if pulled by the same string. Irene Adler had that effect, Lene thought. If you wanted to know what real charisma was, then you only had to meet Irene. Her long golden hair was gathered in a plait as thick as a man's wrist and it reached the studded belt around the tight black jeans. The plait swung rhythmically across her slim lower back with each footstep as if the simple act of putting one foot in front of the other gave her pleasure; she looked like a model on the catwalk.

The only person who appeared not to take any notice of the psychiatrist was the PET agent at the far end of the row. He sat with his forearms resting on his knees, staring at the floor.

Charlotte Falster started saying something about the recruitment of terrorists, the manipulation of their minds and the social backgrounds of suicide bombers, but Lene was no longer listening. The nausea she felt at the sight of Irene Adler brought her to her feet. She pushed her way out between the rows of chairs and quickly walked up the centre aisle and out of the lecture hall.

She could feel the psychiatrist's eyes on her back the whole time.

2

Lene crossed the famous flagstone courtyard of Copenhagen Police Headquarters with her hands stuffed into the pockets of her leather jacket, glad to be outside. It was too soon. She could not handle people being so close to her. She felt that they penetrated her defences, merged with her. When she heard rapid footsteps, she turned around and spotted the gloomy PET agent. Kim ... Thomsen? He did not appear to have noticed her, but strode across the courtyard and slipped into the front seat of a dark-blue Ford Mondeo. The car left with squealing tyres and the blue flashing lights were switched on before the first street corner.

Lene continued around the building and up Otto Mønsteds Gade while she contemplated going for a cup of coffee at the patisserie at the Glyptoteket Museum. It was bound to be tranquil there. Perhaps she should spend the rest of the day wandering around the cool exhibition rooms, the sort of thing normal people might do.

The yellow building cranes carved up the sky above Tivoli in broad segments. The clear-up was still continuing inside the amusement park.

Her mobile vibrated again, and she wondered how many text messages she had received by now. She took it out and looked at the display.

'Ain . . .?' she mumbled and swore softly under her breath. Lene frowned. She had previously spoken to the young Arab woman in her capacity as a volunteer with Livslinjen, an anonymous telephone counselling service for the suicidal, but as far as she could recall the most recent time had been a couple of months ago. She did not even know if Ain was the girl's real name, and she had no idea how Ain could have got hold of her private mobile number, but Lene had now received four text messages and two voicemails from her; the second more pleading and incoherent than the first.

She rang Ain back immediately.

The young woman was panting and her voice was almost drowned out by background noise.

'Ain?'

'Lene? Lene . . . Thank you! You have to help me. I'm sorry.'

The girl's tone of voice automatically made Lene's feet accelerate and she jogged towards her car, which was parked outside Glyptoteket.

'How did you get my number? Never mind . . . I can barely hear you, Ain. Where are you? Can't you find somewhere quieter? What's going on? What's wrong?'

'I think someone is after me. No, I know they are . . . Hold on . . .'

'Where are you?'

'Nørreport Station.'

The signal disappeared and Lene stomped her feet in frustration. She tore open the door to her car, dropped her mobile near the pedals and found it with shaking hands. She was about to call back when the display lit up.

The girl was sobbing.

'They're coming after me, Lene!'

Lene took a deep breath and tried making her voice sound calm. Livslinjen-calm.

'They're *not* coming after you, Ain. Nobody is after you! Now calm down . . . You're being para—'

She was about to say paranoid, but stopped herself. She could hear metallic loudspeaker voices in the background, the sound of many people gathered together; an echoing roar of voices.

'I'm not paranoid, Lene. I'm really not. I am not ill!'

'Of course you're not, Ain. You're not ill. But who are *they*?'

The young woman suddenly sounded strangely calm, which was much worse. An inexplicable pause arose in the infernal racket that surrounded her and the little hairs on Lene's forearms rose when she heard the other woman's childish sobs.

'It's my own fault, Lene. I deserve it. I did something terrible, something absolutely awful. It was me who . . . and now I've dragged you into it as well . . .'

'What do you mean? What do you deserve? Listen, I'll come pick you up and we'll find a place to talk, okay? Okay, Ain?'

Lene managed to start her old Citroën and stepped on the accelerator. A man with a dog ran for dear life when she ran a red light at H. C. Andersens Boulevard, and a bicycle messenger banged his fist on the roof of her car when she forced him up onto the kerb.

'Talk to me, Ain!'

Lene could hear the girl's rapid, high-heeled footsteps clattering across the hard surface of the platform.

'Yes, Lene . . . Are you really coming? I can see him. He's down here.'

'I'll be there in two minutes.'

'Thank you . . .'

Lene could see Nørreport Station ahead of her, but the road was blocked by traffic. She had her mobile pressed against one ear and was steering the car with the other hand. Again she could hear loudspeaker voices, the sound of a train arriving. Ain had stopped talking, but Lene could hear her frantic breathing.

'It's no use, Lene, I—'

Lene heard a loud gasp and the next second someone screamed; loud, high-pitched female voices.

'Ain!'

Lene heard a crash as the mobile hit the platform that nearly shattered her eardrum. The crash was followed by the sound of numerous running feet. The screeching, high-pitched squeal of the train brakes sounded very close and Lene's eyes started to mist over.

She stopped at a pedestrian crossing and saw the street fill with people, pouring out of the station.

The loudspeaker announced laconically that there had been an accident involving a passenger.

Lene next heard slow footsteps approach. Someone picked up Ain's mobile, a man said *hello* a couple of times in a controlled voice before the connection was cut off.

3

The train driver sat leaning against a wall while a couple of kneeling colleagues tried to comfort him. He rested his elbows on his knees, his head slumped forward as he ran his palms mechanically across his pale, shocked face. He stared at the tiles and there was a puddle of vomit between his legs.

Early retirement, Lene thought automatically as she passed the middle-aged man. That man will never drive further than Nørreport Station again.

The empty train stood motionless with all doors open, lit up, abandoned next to the long, echoing platform as if the rest of humanity had been evacuated from the planet. The only sound was a restless whistling from the air brakes.

She walked up to a group of police officers and paramedics standing near a covered stretcher. As she came closer, she could hear crackling radio voices. Two paramedics were walking up and down the tracks with yellow plastic sacks in their hands. One of them bent down, picked something up and dropped it into the sack. It looked heavy.

White ambulance blankets covered a barely recognizable

human form on the stretcher. The blood had already soaked through the blankets where the head ought to have been. The body was unnaturally shortened, and it took a moment before Lene realized that the lower legs and feet were missing as well.

Lene flashed her warrant card at the nearest police officer.

'I think I knew her,' she said to the young dark-haired woman with a ponytail, who looked as if she would rather be anywhere else.

'We have a name,' the police officer said, showing Lene a purse. 'And we found this.'

She held up a shapeless shoulder bag. The leather was torn and stained with blood.

'Ain?' Lene asked. 'Was her name Ain?'

She glanced up at the white CCTV cameras.

The young police officer nodded. 'Ain Ghazzawi Rasmussen. We found her driving licence.'

'Was there a note?'

'A note?'

'A suicide note. Anything?'

'No.'

The young police officer looked at the stretcher.

'As you can imagine, it's difficult to identify her. The body is in a very bad state.'

Lene looked at the driving licence. A cautiously smiling, dark-haired young woman. Ain Ghazzawi Rasmussen lived to be twenty-three years old. She had a scarf around her neck, a pretty mouth, high cheekbones, dark slanted eyes and she looked decidedly Middle Eastern. The driving licence had been issued by Copenhagen Police four years ago.

The two paramedics climbed back up on the platform and shook their heads at the Head of Operations.

'There's nothing more,' one of them said.

Lene looked up at the sound of fresh sirens. The blue flashing lights were reflected on the walls of the nearest stairway.

She handed back the driving licence.

'Did you know her?' the police officer said.

'Not really,' Lene said. 'No.'

She opened the dead woman's purse. A health insurance card, a few banknotes, credit cards. No photographs. There was a business card from a restaurant on Østerbro behind the health insurance card: Le Crocodile Vert.

Lene handed back the purse and the handbag.

'We also found this on the platform,' the police officer said, holding up a white smartphone.

'Have you examined it?'

'Not yet.'

Lene took the mobile and turned it over in her hand. It would appear to be still working, but the screen was locked.

The paramedics rolled the stretcher to the steps and one of the police officer's colleagues placed a hand on her shoulder and muttered a few words.

'We'll take her away now,' she said to Lene. 'I don't know if you would be willing to . . .'

She sent Lene a pleading look. She would probably have been overjoyed if the superintendent had offered to accompany her to the Institute of Forensic Medicine, or to inform the dead woman's next of kin. The superintendent undoubtedly had experience of such matters.

Lene hesitated, but then felt revolted by it all. She could not cope with any more deaths.

'You'll be fine,' she said. 'You'll get used to it.'

'You have?'

'No.'

When Lene rummaged around for the key to her letter box at the bottom of the stairwell, she discovered that she had popped Ain's mobile into her jacket pocket and swore under her breath all the way up to her flat on the fourth floor. She had lived in this peaceful street on Frederiksberg ever since her divorce from Josefine's father when she was thirty-nine and her daughter seventeen. Soon she would be forty-five, and she thought that people lived too long.

She put the newspaper on the kitchen table and made her usual trip to draw the curtains in the living room. She opened the windows to the clear blue afternoon sky, draped her duvet over the balcony railings, and spent a long time looking at the overflowing laundry basket in the bathroom. She didn't have the energy to load and start the washing machine. Then she checked Josefine's old room. The room had been empty since her daughter had moved in with a friend from her physiotherapy course, but for some reason Lene still had to look inside it every day.

She made herself a cup of Nescafé and sat down on the

sofa with today's paper. Since the Tivoli bombing the newspaper had been printed with a slim black border around the front page. It would remain there for 1,241 days: one day for each person killed.

A wintry sobriety had descended upon the Danish media since the disaster. Gone were the endless food programmes and no one appeared to miss them. The faces of the studio hosts were restrained and their voices subdued. Weather forecasters announced sunny days with a tortured sense of guilt, and even the commercial TV channels had weeded out brain-dead reality shows and had started showing serious history documentaries and movies from the Danish golden age. Half the politically correct left wing had been silenced, confronted with a truth which they might have heard about but had never seriously believed, while the other half, with a kind of twisted Schadenfreude, thought that it was Denmark's own fault and that the Danes had to see the situation from the terrorists' point of view: that Denmark got what she deserved because of her neo-imperialist foreign policy driven mainly by the Conservative government. Denmark should have settled for sending exercise books, tree surgeons and traffic wardens to Kosovo and Iraq, and built bicycle paths in Afghanistan – things which Denmark was a global champion at, and could rightly take pride in.

The Danes started looking inwards and upwards. Churches reported an increase in attendance for the first time, and anyone who had done a weekend course in Gestalt therapy or mindfulness made an absolute fortune by treating people for their traumas and anxieties. Denmark's prime minister sacked her old political advisers and hired a talented speech-writer instead. After the attack she gave a much-lauded speech, which was shown in its entirety on CNN. She lowered her voice half an octave and looked, for the first time, as if she shared the world inhabited by her fellow Danes. The polls predicted that she would be re-elected.

But unsurprisingly, the terror attack had also breathed new life into neo-Nazi, anti-Islamic and racist factions usually led by eccentric old men. Several Turkish and Lebanese greengrocers and restaurant owners had had their windows smashed or their vans covered with racist slogans. A fourteen-year-old Jordanian girl had been attacked and sexually assaulted in a pedestrian underpass in a ghetto on Vestegnen by presumed neo-Nazis.

The fallout was predictable, but everyone from immigrant communities to residents' associations called for calm and moderation. Volunteers had started patrolling the ghettos, day and night.

Lene flicked through the newspaper, incapable of reading a single article from beginning to end. She looked at the white smartphone on her coffee table, but did not touch it.

How many times had she spoken to Ain? Five times? Eight? The first conversations had been cautious, as they often were when someone pulled themselves together and called Livslinjen. The young woman had sounded perfectly coherent, her conversations with Lene had rarely lasted more than fifteen minutes and they had usually ended on a constructive, optimistic note.

Ain hadn't revealed many personal details, but had approached her issues obliquely, which was normal. She had had a chaotic childhood as an orphaned Palestinian in a refugee camp in Tunisia, but had been adopted by Danish husband and wife doctors who worked for Médecins Sans Frontières, and had come to Denmark at the age of eight. She spoke unaccented Danish, appeared to live her life just like any other young Danish woman and she had never mentioned problems relating to bullying, ostracizing or discrimination. Ain had talked about her anxiety and loneliness and Lene had suggested that she see a psychiatrist or psychologist. Livslinjen had a list of psychiatrists and psychologists who could start treating patients at short notice, if they judged that a suicide attempt was imminent, but she did not know if Ain had ever taken her advice.

There had been a period of five or six weeks where she had heard nothing from her, and Lene had hoped that the girl had begun treatment or started feeling better of her own accord; that she had fallen in love, or been promoted. That perhaps talking to Lene had actually helped the girl.

Her high hopes were dashed one evening in Livslinjen's offices when another volunteer signalled that Ain was back on the line.

The girl sounded breathless and frightened. There were

long pauses where Lene could only hear white noise, then Ain would return with a sentence or two. Her words were largely meaningless, and Lene sat with her hands pressed against the headphones and her head bowed in deep concentration so as not to miss anything. Ain said that she had discovered that she had done something terrible. Something that could never, ever be forgiven. She wept quietly and her voice grew thick and strangled. She had started going out at night. She could not bear to be at home, or be in any familiar place. Instead, she would walk in the woods or along the beaches north of Copenhagen.

Lene had looked out into the darkness behind the office windows and thought about the girl wandering alone through dark parks and forests or on the beach, and her stomach had lurched. She could vividly recall the feeling of Josefine being out late, wondering where she was and why the hell she did not answer her mobile.

For the next hour Lene had looked for a way into the conversation, something solid and mundane. Was Ain in treatment, did she pay her bills, did she eat properly? Was she working? Did she see her family?

But everything bounced off. Ain was terrified of something with no name, shape or size; some evil and almighty power. She said that someone had used her. She believed people had been in her flat while she was at work or out on one of her lonely walks. They were listening to what she was saying and they watched what she was doing.

'Yes, but who are they, for Christ's sake, Ain?' Lene had finally shouted, as at the surrounding tables the heads of other volunteers popped up like corks. She lowered her voice, knowing that before the next shift she would be summoned to a friendly-sounding extra supervision session and reminded of the organization's policies. Counsellors working for Livslinjen were expected to be empathetic. They were not supposed to give a suicidal person a bollocking.

'Who, Ain?' she had whispered.

There was no reply. Only a quiet sobbing. Lene thought she could hear a click, some music and a low male voice saying a few words in the background before the weeping became the only sound once more.

'I deserve to die,' the girl said at length.

'Of course you don't. No one deserves to die, Ain.'

'Yes! I deserve to die, not once, but more than a thousand times,' the girl had said, then hung up.

Lene went across to the living room window and looked down into the street. When had they had that awful conversation? A few months ago? Since then Ain had rung once again with more of the same. She was taking medication, but it didn't help, she said. Everything was getting worse and worse. People looked at her strangely, they talked about her behind her back. She only went out when she had to go to work, and she always went straight home afterwards. Could Lene come to her home?

It was impossible, Lene had said. Out of the question.

Sadly. This was not how it worked. The girl was inconsolable and Lene decided at that moment that tonight was her last shift on Livslinjen. She ended the call right in the middle of the girl's crying, got up, took her jacket and handbag and left the room with a feeling that everyone was looking at her.

Christ!

Lene went out into the kitchen, looking for the bottle of wine she knew had to be there somewhere. Could she have done more for Ain? She thought about the figure under the white, blood-soaked ambulance blanket and her hands shook as she peeled the foil off the bottleneck, taking three fumbling attempts to uncork the bottle and fill her glass to the brim. She drained it and filled it up again.

She took the glass with her to the sofa, sat down, and stared at the white mobile phone. Then she covered it with her newspaper. She looked at her own mobile, but the display was blank. No text messages or calls. No one would appear to be missing her. Not even a cold caller.

She snoozed for half an hour, until the sound of train station announcements and squealing train brakes made her fling open her eyes with a gasp.

She got up, went over to the bookcase, lifted the lid from an old cardboard box and put a videotape in the video recorder.

The footage lasted a couple of minutes and had been recorded by her ex-husband, Niels, during an end of season performance at Svenningsen's School of Ballet. Josefine was fourth in the line of thin, nervous-looking girls aged twelve or thirteen. She was just as straight-backed and tall as the others. Her long blonde hair was scraped back tightly and gathered in a bun at the top of her head. It extended the neck, Mrs Svenningsen said. The camera zoomed in clumsily when it was Josefine's turn and Lene could hear herself reproach Niels. Their daughter pirouetted across the stage on the tips of her toes. Her limbs were long and slender, her wrists straight. She leaped and smiled a dazzling white smile as she arched her back mid-leap so that the bun on her head almost touched the back of her leg. Her short tutu stuck out like a disc and her arms floated smoothly and high up through the air.

Lene heard herself clap a little too loudly and a little too close to the camera's microphone as her daughter danced off into the wings.

She lay for a long time just staring at the sky as it slowly turned a darker shade of blue above the rooftops across the street. In a few hours the sun would go down in an archipelago of orange, red and violet clouds.

She wondered when Josefine had stopped ballet. Was it when she started sixth form college? Lene had tried persuading her to do tae kwon do or kickboxing instead. She thought ballet was too girly, but her daughter had loved it. Tae kwon do isn't *graceful*, Mum, she argued.

And ballet isn't just about art, Mum, but artistry, her daughter had then informed her.

5

The wine bottle was almost empty when Lene got up. She went to the bathroom and swallowed a couple of sleeping pills although it was only seven o'clock in the evening. She preferred to live in a dreamless doze and during the day she took Diazepam to get through it without feeling anything.

Physically, Lene had always been in great shape. She weighed the same as when she was twenty, her bottom was in exactly the same place as when she was seventeen, and she had always exercised frequently, the last few years by boxing at the Police Association's Sports Club. But these days she got out of breath just walking up four flights of stairs. Her green eyes were still in good working order, though they had acquired another expression, but her chestnut hair and milky-white skin were unkempt and dull.

She brushed her teeth and sat down on the sofa, where she half-followed a news programme until the sleeping tablets dissolved and deposited calm and indifference inside her. She channel-hopped to DR News whose main story was the return of two Danish merchant sailors after almost three years of being held hostage by Somali pirates on the godfor-saken Horn of Africa.

For three years the shipping company had dragged out their release, claiming it could not afford to meet the kidnappers' demands. A tabloid newspaper had displayed photographs of the able seaman and the captain on its front page for 1,133 days until the defence minister, uncharacteristically for a Dane, finally had enough and decided to do what should have been done long ago: buy a subscription to the British and American intelligence traffic in the area, which in no time at all and with an accuracy of a few metres had pinpointed the location of the exhausted and ill Danes.

Two American Black Hawk helicopters landed with a unit from the Danish Jægerkorpset a few kilometres from where the hostages were being kept and waited until the Danish Special Forces had won a not terribly impressive fight and liberated the seamen along with three German nuns.

The rescue went according to plan and the prime minister turned up to welcome the sailors, who were wearing orange overalls, as they were helped down the steps of the Danish Air Force's Challenger aircraft at Copenhagen Airport. They moved gingerly down the red carpet towards the welcoming committee and a forest of microphones. They wore big sun-glasses even though the sun was about to go down.

The prime minister was ecstatic. Her long blonde hair flapped in the wind, and her round blue eyes sparkled.

Lene watched the screen without really taking anything

in. Her eyes were about to close when something made her open them and lean forward. The freed men walked slowly across the landing strip, the prime minister waiting, her blue dress clinging to her long legs, when an officer wearing the wine-coloured beret of the Jægerkorpset on his grey stubble leaned forward and said something to her. She smiled and nodded. The camera zoomed in on the freed men's long matted hair and starved faces. A group of well-dressed bureaucrats were standing in the background and Lene took them to represent the Foreign Ministry.

But her attention was drawn to a solitary figure behind the hostages. The man leaped nimbly down the short gangway from the plane and crossed the tarmac while chatting to one of the pilots. He had nothing on his head, he was in his mid-forties with short black hair and a side parting, good posture and quick, economical movements. He was slightly above average height and of athletic build. His broad face turned briefly to the welcoming committee and the press presence behind the prime minister. He scanned the political extras indifferently, retrieved a pair of sunglasses from his chest pocket, put them on and lost himself in conversation with the pilot.

Michael Sander.

Lene froze the screen with the remote control and replayed the short sequence from the start, using the cable TV box's hard drive. There was no doubt. It *was* the secretive, exclusive, private detective – or 'security consultant', as he preferred to call himself. Lene fast-forwarded the feature.

Michael had left the pilot and was now standing lost in his own thoughts under the looming wing of a Hercules plane.

She had not seen or spoken to the man for almost two years, but for a few brief, intense days they had been closer to each other than many people ever experience in a marriage.

Lene had investigated the presumed suicide of an ex-soldier, and the amiable but cynical Michael Sander had been hired by one of the richest women in Denmark to find and punish her late father's deviant hunting friends who had pursued young people to their deaths in some of the most remote corners of the world. Their investigations had merged and they had themselves become the prey in a grotesque new hunt, which they had barely survived.

Since then Michael had called her several times, but she never answered or returned his calls.

Now she saw him stand as large as life next to a military aircraft, which had presumably flown the Jægerkorpset to friendly Djibouti, after which the American helicopters had taken over transportation of the unit.

The prime minister spoke and kept on speaking, with a compassionate hand on one of the hostage's skinny forearms. The man was swaying: from relief, exhaustion or hunger – or a combination of all three. In the background Michael Sander took out a mobile and entered a number.

Lene's own mobile started ringing and she raised her head with a jerk, rummaged frantically around the sofa cushions, found it and pressed *accept*.

'Yes? Hello?'

'Lene?'

'Yes. Who is this?'

'Michael. Michael Sander. How are you?'

She saw him bow his head over the mobile, while in the foreground the prime minister continued her congratulating and well-wishing. It was surreal.

'I can see you,' she grunted.

'What? Sodding telephone!'

He walked under the wing and the setting sun glowed behind his dark figure. It was a beautiful and dramatic image, she thought. Hollywood could not have done it better.

'I can see you on the television,' she shouted and had an idiotic urge to wave.

Michael turned around, shaded his eyes with his free hand and spotted the welcoming committee and the cameras. He grinned from ear to ear, raised his arm and waved like crazy.

Lene's resistance melted away. She too raised her hand and waved to the television. For some reason her eyes filled with tears.

'How are you?'

'Fine. I'm fine,' she said.

'You're lying.'

'Yes, I'm lying.'

'I'm in Copenhagen for a couple of days,' he shouted. 'If you fancy meeting up . . . talking?'

Lene did not reply. Her mobile grew heavier and heavier.

Michael started saying something, but the roar of an aircraft engine drowned his voice out.

'Go home, Michael,' she said. 'Go home to your wife and children, do you hear me? They miss you.'

'What?'

'Go home, God damn you!'

The two hostages were escorted away from the red carpet. The prime minister headed for her black Audi and a protection officer opened the door for her. She waved regally once more to her fellow countrymen and folded herself into the back seat.

There was only static crackling from Lene's mobile.

Michael shook his mobile before putting it in his pocket. He looked gravely towards the television cameras until the producer cut to a female studio host. Lene turned off the television.

The remote control slipped out of her fingers, and her last, conscious thought was about the man at the airport. She thought that she might have a small, reluctant smile on her lips. Michael had that effect on her.

His presence at the airport was not difficult to explain, she thought sleepily. Wherever there were sensitive private concerns, a lot of money and the reputation of important people at stake, you would usually find a man like Michael Sander deploying his special skills. He was an ex-soldier, a former captain with the military police, an ex-police officer and an ex-consultant in one of the biggest multinational security companies in the world, Shepherd & Wilkins in London. He had excellent contacts in the shadowy world of Special Forces. Perhaps the shipping company had promised a reward for information about the location of the seamen held by the Al-Shabaab terrorists . . . Perhaps . . .

Lene fell asleep, but with a final, lingering feeling that maybe she was not quite so desperately alone as she had felt a few hours ago.

6

It was an achievement in itself to reach Rigspolitiet's office building in Glostrup, where the Tivoli investigation was based. Following new security regulations, the nearest car park was fifty metres from the main entrance and the area outside it was barricaded with concrete blocks and steel posts.

Staff parked in a fenced-in car park, but had to get out of their cars whatever the weather, while specially trained Labradors sniffed the inside for explosives, and guards armed with machine guns examined the boot and the undercarriage of the car with mirrors and cameras mounted on long aluminium poles.

Once inside, they then had to queue while their bags were X-rayed and searched before they passed through metal detectors, chip card readers and iris scanners that rarely worked as they were supposed to. Often they triggered piercing alarms that sounded as if a nuclear reactor was on the verge of a meltdown.

Lene was exhausted by the time she reached the Mosaic

Hall on the second floor. Here, twenty-five patient men and women, most of them retired police officers, had spent months reviewing hundreds of thousands of digital photographs and footage from every tablet, camera and mobile phone in Tivoli on the 17th September last year.

People from all over the world had uploaded recordings to a special portal set up by Rigspolitiet, and all the films and photographs were formatted, time stamped and placed in a gigantic, three-dimensional model of the Tivoli Gardens. It was a painstaking and monumental task, the biggest of its kind in the history of criminology. The hope was to find footage of the suicide bomber and his or her accomplices. Identifying that one face among the thousands of faces in Tivoli that would match the international directories of known or alleged terrorists.

Lene glanced briefly at the long tables laid out with computers, printers and light boxes. The walls were covered with faces and architectural drawings, the tables with 3D models of Tivoli. A few images had been enlarged and marked with a red cross because they were of the 1,241 victims. Some showed a calm, carefree face, others had been taken from above or below, crooked or shaken. Some had been taken in the second before the photographer themselves was turned into a living torch by exploding gases, ripped apart by the pressure wave, hit by steel bullets from the suicide vest or crushed under the twisted, crashing steel girders of the Star Flyer.

They had found mobile telephones and cameras close to Point Zero: the area immediately below the Star Flyer. The devices were often smashed up or burned, but the technicians were able to recover intact digital pictures with astonishing frequency.

As far as Lene knew, they had yet to identify the suicide bomber, but she had been taken off the central investigation due to her chronic mental exhaustion. She was thoroughly fed up with the job she had otherwise loved for eighteen years. The spark had been snuffed out, and she could no longer blow life back into it. She had always been hard-working, brimming with initiative and enthusiasm. She had always given her best. But it was all gone, and Lene knew that she was showing every textbook symptom of being burned out: the need for isolation, her short temper with everything and everyone, sleep problems and alcohol dependency, along with an overwhelming sense of futility. One of the ways she had tried fighting this was to volunteer for Livslinjen, but her heart had not been in it.

She continued through the hall to the small office she had been allocated for her new subsection: Borders and Access. She was now in charge of a shapeless technician called Bjarne, whose all-consuming hobbies were the Maritime and Coastguard Band and model aeroplanes. He was lonely, shy, sweaty, socially awkward and, in Lene's opinion, semi-autistic. Their remit was to discover how the suicide bomber had entered the country – presuming, of course, that he or she was not from Denmark.

The two of them spent their days reviewing reports from the Danish Maritime and Coastguard Agency, local marinas, the pilot service, organizations such as BELTREP and SUNDREP that monitored traffic in internal Danish waters, reservations for planes, trains or cars, flight schedules from private planes and reports from traffic police, from campsites and hotels from July to September of last year. It was ultimately a total waste of effort. Following the Schengen Agreement, Denmark had become a wide-open country. Anyone could wander in across Denmark's border from Germany without being stopped, catch a ferry from Helsingborg to Helsingør, drive across the Øresund Bridge or fly in from Bornholm. The person in question could do so without leaving a trail.

Lene opened the door to their small cubicle, hastily constructed in a corner of the Mosaic Hall with plasterboard walls and a door. She was greeted by a loud clapping noise and managed to duck just before she was struck by a remote-controlled helicopter.

'Turn it off, Bjarne,' she said.

The helicopter executed a perfect landing on the IT technician's desk, and the engine died.

'Sorry,' the fat IT technician mumbled. 'Coffee?'

'Yes, please,' Lene said. She hung her leather jacket over the back of a chair, put her shoulder bag on the floor and sat down.

Bjarne had created a small kitchen in a corner with a

coffeemaker, a kettle, a tiny fridge and a microwave oven. He never went to the canteen. He squeezed milk from a small cardboard triangle into Lene's mug and put it in front of the superintendent. She blew steam off the surface and took a sip.

'Any news?'

'There's a coordination meeting today,' he said, pushing a slim file across the desk. 'I've written a report about our progress.'

'I didn't know we had made any progress.'

'It's only half a page.'

'Super.'

Lene skimmed the text, which was no longer than the verse of a psalm.

'A Polish ship?'

Bjarne nodded. His fingers twitched nervously between a confusion of electronic gadgets, cables, switches, tension gauges, dropped cheesy Wotsits and the scorched insides of various mobile phones. The man had a universal and uncomplicated talent for anything electronic.

'The *Kazimierz Pulaski*, registered in Gdansk,' he said. 'It's an old bucket of 2,300 tons. She sailed from Kaliningrad to Oslo on the 12th September, with a cargo of graphite.'

'And?'

Bjarne wiped his forehead with a handkerchief, which his mother had embroidered with an elegant, slanted monogram as if he were of noble birth. He performed all right as long as she did not pressure him or speak to him harshly, but Lene had never managed to make eye contact with him. It would seem as if he had learned from an early age not to expect anything good from the rest of humanity.

'She dropped her anchor off the coast of Vedbæk on the night between the 13th and 14th September, according to SUNDREP. The ship broadcast on channel 16 that they had engine problems, but that they could manage it themselves.'

'So what? That could happen to anyone.'

Lene closed the cover of the file and pushed it aside. Nothing. As usual.

'It sailed on after half an hour,' he said wearily. 'That's very quick, in my opinion.'

'Is it? Perhaps the problem just wasn't serious. Anything else?'

'We need to check the final campsites, and that'll be that, I think.'

'Fantastic.'

At the coordination meeting Charlotte Falster would undoubtedly look at her with her usual disappointed smile, as if Lene was a dog that had failed to return with the stick yet again.

She found Ain's white mobile in her jacket pocket, placed it on the desk and twirled it between her fingers while Bjarne shuffled over to the kettle in his noiseless Mao shoes to brew one of today's many cups of lemon tea.

'Bjarne?'

'Hmm.'

'I found this mobile on a bus, but it needs a passcode. Do you think you can open it?'

'Of course.'

The office chair groaned under the weight of the IT technician. He took the mobile, plugged it in and opened a programme on his computer. Lene watched rows of green, rapidly changing groups of numbers. A few seconds later, the mobile's display lit up and Bjarne returned it to her.

'2246. Probably the last four digits of the owner's civil registration number. It usually is.'

Not this time, thought Lene, who knew Ain's civil registration number off by heart.

'Thank you.'

Bjarne had turned his back to her, lost in visitor lists from camping sites on Sjælland.

There was only the odd saved text message on the mobile; a couple of 'How are you, darling?' from 'Mum', and the same from a worried 'Dad'. There were a couple of reminders about the birthday of somebody called Laura, and invitations to drop by for a chat, had she made plans for her summer holidays or did she want to join them at their holiday cottage? They missed her.

And Lene read Ain's vague, non-committal and at times even rude replies, which she recognized only too well from her own daughter, Josefine. She smiled wryly at the thought. They could have been twins. The message between the lines was the same: 'Mind your own business, Mum', 'Leave me alone' or 'Get a life, why don't you?'

A list of incoming and outgoing calls showed that the day before her death, Ain had tried to call someone called 'Nazeera' without success. The last attempt had been made half an hour before Lene had spoken to her at Nørreport Station.

She clicked on the Photos folder. There were remarkably few pictures: late afternoon images from a deserted beach. The sun hung low and the sea mist stretched far across the black water. There were pictures from a wintry-looking jetty, decorated with long icicles and thick blankets of ice hanging from railings, with steps leading down to the water. And there was a single selfie of a carefree, smiling Ain, who Lene recognized from her driving licence. She was standing with her arm around another woman's shoulders. They wore identical white shirts, black trousers and long black aprons. They were standing in front of a popular chain of Copenhagen restaurants, which had had a branch in Tivoli. In the background, she could see part of a tree with slender twigs and new, pale-green leaves. A spring picture. The woman was older than Ain; in her early thirties, perhaps. She was approximately ten centimetres taller, attractive like a Playboy model, and of Middle Eastern appearance. She had clear green eyes the same shade as Lene's own, light skin and a smiling, sensuous mouth. She had black hair, wore discreet make-up and was just as slim as Ain. Lene zoomed in on the badges: Ain and Nazeera.

The double portrait oozed friendship and carefree times. Ain had the same open and trusting smile as Josefine.

The tears started burning behind Lene's eyelids. Everything conspired to remind her of Josefine. Bjarne stirred nervously even though he was sitting with his back to her. Like many people who have been subjected to intense bullying from an early age, he was equipped with a finely tuned seismograph for any mood change around him.

She frowned at the last pictures in the folder and felt the blood leave her face: the camera on the mobile had caught a woman in her forties leaving a supermarket. She held a yellow carrier bag in each hand, one of them clearly filled with bottles – probably that week's special offer of six bottles of Chilean or Australian red wine. The woman looked stony-faced. A young man with a pram had politely stepped out of her way on the pavement. Standing next to the man, a child in a blue snowsuit closed a red mitten around the handlebar of the pram. The child looked gravely up at the woman, who saw nothing.

The next photograph showed the same woman getting out of a small blue car and on the third and last, she was withdrawing cash from a cashpoint on Strøget. And finally there was a series of well-lit and sharp photographs taken inside Frederiksberg Church.

Lene put down the mobile and closed her eyes. She recognized that woman. Her face was the first thing she saw in the mirror every morning, and she was in the habit of entering churches and sitting there for half an hour listening to the silence and the occasional organ or choral rehearsal.

'Shit ... shit!'

Bjarne turned his chair around.

'What?'

'Nothing. It was nothing, Bjarne.'

'You sure?'

'Yes.'

How long had Ain been following her? And why the hell had she not noticed? Lene regarded herself as a rational human being, but eighteen years of hard police work had developed in her both a sixth and a seventh sense. She always knew when someone was lying, and she had always, always known if she was being followed. It resulted in an unmistakable sensation at the back of her head; a light pressure or discomfort. She had never been wrong. She had evidently deteriorated more than she had feared, and made up her mind on the spot to do something about it. Quitting drinking would be a start.

She checked the mobile's contact list and found her own name and address listed among a dozen others. She recognized the name of a Jesper Horn with an address in Grønnegade and a telephone number. Horn was one of the psychiatrists to whom Livslinjen would refer suicidal callers.

She deleted her name and Ain's pictures of her from the mobile.

'Don't forget your meeting,' Bjarne said.

'Sure,' Lene mumbled without knowing what she was agreeing to.

'Incidentally, that phone is being tapped,' Bjarne said.

Lene stared at the mobile while the information slowly sank in.

'What did you just say, Bjarne?'

He pointed to a list of monitored telephone numbers on his computer screen. A list that had exploded after the Tivoli bombing.

'The number is flagged up. Three months ago, the public prosecutor in Copenhagen applied for a warrant to monitor and it was granted by a judge.'

Bjarne flinched automatically when Lene rose to look at the screen over his shoulder. He reacted to physical proximity by shrinking.

'Who the hell asked for that?' she demanded to know.

'You'll have to ask the public prosecutor. Or the Telecommunications Centre at Bellahøj, but they won't tell you anything. They're not allowed to.'

Lene straightened up and folded her arms across her chest. She glared at the innocent-looking white smartphone lying silent and turned off on her desk. Had they been listening to her? Had they heard her speak to Ain before she threw herself in front of the train? Had they recorded her calls to Livslinjen?

'What's the status of the court order?' she asked and made an effort to keep her voice steady.

Bjarne looked around the menus.

'A request to terminate the tap was made last night at 20:32,' he said.

Of course, she thought. By then Ain was dead. Why would anyone bother bugging a dead person's mobile?

The office started to contract and she could no longer breathe. She snatched her jacket from the back of the chair, grabbed her shoulder bag and stuffed Ain's mobile into her pocket.

'Don't forget that meeting,' Bjarne reminded her miserably.

'Yeah, yeah. See you later.'

Lene took his report and was about to put a reassuring hand on his shoulder when she remembered that he did not like being touched.

She marched through the Mosaic Hall, but her resolve wavered when she reached the stairs. She should be making her way up to the next floor and humbly taking her place at the end of the conference table, but instead she ran down the stairs, exited the building and crossed the car park. She got into her car, leaving the door open. There was a sewer grid cover by her left foot. The white mobile would plunge into the depths and disappear without a trace. She would make Bjarne swear that he had never seen or heard anything. The loyalty of the IT technician knew no bounds.

She fished the mobile out of her jeans pocket, pinched it between two fingers, looked around the empty car park and bent forward.

Then she remembered the two young women outside the restaurant underneath the branches of the beech tree. Their joy of life. Pure and unadulterated happiness. Not a cloud in the sky. A spring picture.

Before she was quite aware of what she was doing, she had pressed *Call* under the picture of the beautiful dark-haired woman with green eyes.

7

'Who is it?'

In the background Lene could hear the sound of people and the clattering of china, cutlery and glass.

Lene cleared her throat.

'Ain? Is that you?'

The woman's voice was dark and tense.

'My name is Lene Jensen. I work for Rigspolitiet. Are you Nazeera?'

'Who is this?'

'Lene Jensen, Rigspolitiet. You're listed in Ain's mobile phone directory. She tried calling you several times yesterday.'

'Yes, I'm Nazeera. Why? What's wrong? Who did you say you were?'

There was a sharp intake of breath at the other end. She was moving through an echoing space, and a door slammed behind her.

'Has something happened to Ain?' she asked in the sudden silence.

She spoke almost without an accent.

'Are the two of you related?' Lene asked.

'No, but she's a really good friend. A very good friend. What has happened?'

'The two of you work together?'

'Yes! Now tell me what has happened. Please!'

'I'm afraid that Ain is dead, Nazeera. I'm sorry. She died yesterday.'

'Dead?'

'I would really like to talk to you,' Lene said to her own considerable surprise.

Up on the third floor she watched people take their places around the table in the conference room. Chief Superintendent Charlotte Falster leaned to one side and said something to the person next to her.

'Do her parents know . . .?'

'I'm quite sure they do,' Lene said.

'I don't understand . . . She is dead? How?'

'Can we meet?' Lene asked. 'Now?'

'Of course . . . I just need to talk to someone. Of course we can . . . I just can't understand it.'

Lene closed the car door and started the engine. She was freezing cold all the way to her bones and turned up the heating to max.

'Nazeera, I think we should do this in private, okay? I promise to explain everything.'

'All right . . .'

'Are you at work?' she asked.

'Of course.'

The woman gave her an address at Østerbro: restaurant Le Crocodile Vert on Marskensgade.

'I'll be there in half an hour,' Lene said.

Lene and Nazeera made eye contact immediately. The slim dark-haired woman was standing behind the bar in a busy, bistro-style restaurant. She wiped her hands on her apron and waved her closer.

Lene followed her down a narrow passage, which led past a chaotic, noisy kitchen. The woman trailed an invisible pennant of sensual perfume as she moved. She opened the door to a quiet office where an old grey computer was humming on a messy desk. She removed a pile of ring binders from a chair so that Lene could sit down and looked around before dropping the ring binders on the floor.

'Busy?' Lene asked as she stuck out her hand.

The other woman nodded and pressed the tip of her fingers.

'Last week we got five stars, so now we're trendy. Authentic Parisian mood, the critics wrote, even though not a single person here speaks a word of French.'

'Congratulations.'

The woman sat down behind the desk and swept her glossy black hair behind her ears. She looked down at her hands, which were folded in her lap. Her nail polish was deep red, unchipped and shiny, and her nails were beautiful ovals.

Lene looked at her own bitten claws and stuffed her hands into her jacket pockets. Michael Sander had once said that he divided new acquaintances into head or body people. He could tell from the way they moved if their joints were well oiled or dry. It was all in the pelvis and the hips, he said. There was absolutely nothing wrong with Nazeera's pelvis or hips, that was for sure, Lene thought. She radiated a direct, animalistic sensuality so thick you could practically slice it.

'So Ain is dead,' she said and looked at Lene. 'How?'

'She jumped in front of a train at Nørreport Station yesterday morning. She called me right before she did it. In fact, I spoke to her just as she did it.'

'Why?'

'Why what, Nazeera? Why did she do it? I have no idea. She said that she deserved it. That someone was following her. Was someone following her? Did she deserve it?'

The woman twisted a necklace angrily between her fingers and looked past Lene. She snorted with derision.

'Deserved it? Ain? If you had known her, you wouldn't ask that question. She was as innocent as a newborn baby. Why was she talking to you?'

She looked straight at Lene, who recognized a competent and unswerving human being when she saw one. The woman's voice was rock steady. She had the natural suspicion of someone who has spoken to police officers or other people in authority many times and has never been impressed. Or intimidated, for that matter.

'I used to volunteer for Livslinjen,' Lene said. 'It's a—'

'I know what it is.'

Lene fell silent and blinked. She was seriously out of practice; in her heyday she had been regarded as one of Rigspolitiet's best lead interrogators. Get your act together and take the initiative, she ordered herself.

'Right, Nazeera. She was unhappy ... I don't know why exactly but, as far as I can gather, she grew up in a refugee camp, she never knew her biological parents and had a rough childhood.'

Nazeera narrowed her eyes and looked through a small, filthy window overlooking a dreary courtyard as if she wanted to either polish or smash it. She shrugged her shoulders. Who hasn't had a miserable childhood?

'Now, of course you don't need to have a specific reason to be unhappy or depressed,' Lene said quietly. 'How did you meet her, Nazeera?'

'You don't have to say my name all the time. I know what my name is.'

'I'm sorry.'

The woman found a packet of cigarettes in the pocket of her apron and lit one before looking at Lene through the pale-grey plume of smoke slowly flowing from her red lips. She turned her face to the cool light from the courtyard. Her profile was clean with a high, intelligent forehead and fine black down curling from her temples down in front of her ears. She wore a row of silver earrings up through the side of one ear and had a small silver lizard in her pierced nose. She did not ask if it would bother Lene if she smoked. She simply chewed one of her perfect red nails lightly and looked down.

'I think that many people who were in Tivoli that day and survived feel guilty about it,' she said at length. 'We ask ourselves if we could have done anything to prevent it and why we survived when so many other, good people died, do you understand?'

Lene nodded. *I deserve to die, not once, but more than a thousand times*, Ain had said.

'So you were both in Tivoli that day?'

'We both worked at Restaurant Picasso, and we were at work on the 17th September. The Star Flyer was at the opposite end of the gardens. Nothing happened down our end. Yes, of course the windows were blown in, but apart from that nothing happened to us.'

Lene frowned.

'What could you have done?' she asked.

The woman shrugged her shoulders. You would only understand if you had been there.

'Nothing,' she said. 'Did she leave a note? Was there anything for me?'

'I don't think so. Did she change after Tivoli?'

A tired half-smile lingered on Nazeera's lips. She shook her head and looked down.

'Yes! No! What do you want me to say? It's possible that

she changed. Perhaps. She was an Arab, but Danish. She was adopted by lovely Danish people, but she was still an Arab. A Palestinian. How easy is that? It isn't easy for any of us. We don't know where our loyalties lie. She was trying to find out who she was, don't you see? We all have to. Did she believe in God or in Allah? Did she want to marry an Arab or a Dane? Did she want to have a dog and eat roast pork and drink herself senseless every Friday night, or wear a scarf and be invisible and modest and study the Koran while waiting to marry a cousin from back home and have six kids with him? Should she travel to Syria to fight?'

'You don't wear a scarf,' Lene pointed out.

The woman smiled. The tip of her pink tongue slipped out between her white, even teeth and moistened her lower lip, before returning to her mouth, and Lene felt a faint sense of physical unease. If she had been a man, she would have found Nazeera irresistible, she thought. She had large breasts, long legs and a narrow waist; the skin on her neck was smooth and golden.

'I'm a sinner,' the woman said. 'I'm not like Ain.'

'But you were good friends?'

'I'm eight years older than her. I know where I come from. I know who I am, okay? I'm from Jordan and my father is from Jordan. My brother and sister, uncles and aunts are from Jordan. My parents came to Denmark when I was fourteen years old. My father is a professor at the University of Copenhagen, and my mother is a chemist who works for

Novo. They were not refugees; they were invited to come to Denmark because my father will one day be awarded the Nobel Prize, or something like it. He can do something no one else understands. They don't believe in God or Allah at home, but in elements, organic chemistry, Darwin, coincidences and the Big Bang. There are no problems.'

'And what do you believe in?'

'Freedom and money.'

'But not Allah?'

'That's my own private business, okay? But if I do, it's certainly not something my parents taught me.'

'Was Ain trying to be like you?'

Nazeera blinked in surprise.

'Yes, but I wouldn't let her. She was worth much more than me. She shouldn't be anyone else but herself. She just had to learn that being Ain was more than good enough.'

'Where did you meet her?'

The cigarette was squashed into an overflowing ashtray and the woman folded her arms across her chest.

'You and I are heroes. I try to help Muslim girls, you try to help would-be suicides.'

'Not any more,' Lene said.

'Well, I'm still trying. I volunteer at a club for Muslim girls in Møllegade on Nørrebro. They go there to talk and drink coffee and take off their fucking scarves. They can watch television, dance or do aerobics without their brothers or fathers or uncles watching their every move and the boys in the street calling them whores because they don't wear the hijab.'

'Do they call you a whore, Nazeera?'

The smile disappeared from the woman's face.

'I've never heard that.'

'Okay. So Ain would come to the club?'

Nazeera looked at her watch, a man's Rolex with a steel bracelet – too expensive, surely, for a waitress, Lene thought. She wore sturdy Doc Martens boots and was a strange mixture of a young Monica Bellucci and Lara Croft.

'Yes, she visited with a friend, two or three years ago. I liked her. We talked a lot. We travelled to Venice together. We . . . were together . . .'

A faint blushing coloured her cheekbones.

Oh God, Lene thought. Ain and Nazeera had been lovers.

'I understand,' she said softly.

The other woman looked straight at her. Then she nodded and gulped. Her eyes grew moist.

'I need to go now,' she said.

'Of course.'

Lene got up and looked out of the narrow window. There was a kind of courtyard behind the restaurant. An animal the size of a calf was standing in the middle of a patch of grass with its legs astride, watching her without blinking. The beast wore a wide, black leather collar with studs.

'Is that . . . a dog?' she asked as she pointed.

Nazeera smiled indulgently.

'Rudy. Rudolf. Half Rottweiler, half Hells Angel. It guards everything around here. Including me.'

'It's yours?'

Nazeera shrugged.

'He's mostly his own. But I feed him. And only me.'

'It looks lethal,' Lene said.

'He *is* lethal. You asked me just now if those useless ghetto dickheads call me a whore. Well, they don't when Rudy is around.'

'I guess not,' Lene mumbled.

The dog stared at her for a few more seconds, as if to memorize her face for later use. Then it turned its massive body and lumbered into the shadows under a garden bench.

Lene followed the Arab woman into the restaurant. A fat man pressed keys on a till and looked morosely at Nazeera. He made an impatient gesture towards the packed room.

Nazeera tossed her head.

'I'm here. Take it easy, Tomasz!'

She turned to Lene.

'Moron,' she whispered. 'I don't know her parents very well, but I would like to go to Ain's funeral. If you find out anything, please would you call? If, for example, she left a note?'

'I'll call you when I know more,' Lene said.

'Thank you.'

The hardness and cynicism were gone. She put a light

hand on Lene's arm by way of goodbye, smiled warmly and turned to the fat owner.

'How far have we got?' she asked.

The man rolled his eyes.

'Far! People are only waiting half an hour for their starters,' the man said in a strong, central European accent.

'We're in no hurry. Remember, we're French, Tomasz. The longer people wait for their food, the better they think it is.'

She smiled at Lene again, who returned her smile.

8

A young woman searching for her identity, who had given up on that and everything else, had jumped in front of a train. She had been in a relationship with the older and more experienced Nazeera, who reminded Lene of a cat with razor-sharp claws.

Leave it alone, for Christ's sake, she told herself, as she drifted with the slow traffic down Østerbrogade, knowing perfectly well that she could not. For the first time this year, she felt there might just be a purpose to her existence. That she was almost alive. Or at least not comatose. She checked her watch. The meeting in Glostrup was over. She didn't feel bad. Bjarne didn't really need her to be there.

A Polish ship . . . God help us . . .

Lene stopped for a red light on Dag Hammarskjölds Allé and stared at Ain's mobile phone on the passenger seat until the van behind her sounded its horn to signal that the lights had changed. In her rear-view mirror, she gave the driver the finger and made a highly illegal U-turn back down Østerbrogade. The van driver sounded his horn with indignation behind her.

Lene smiled. Then she noticed a long dark-blue saloon car imitating her hazardous manoeuvre in her rear-view mirror. The chaos-inducing metro expansion work was turning the traffic in central Copenhagen into Bangkok; car drivers and cyclists all broke the law equally.

She turned on the car radio to avoid having to think and sang along to an Abba song, while she let her subconscious take her wherever it wanted to go. She turned left down Øster Allé, past Fælledparken and looked across to the tower of Rigshospitalet and the low buildings in front of it, which housed the Institute of Forensic Medicine and where the body of Ain Ghazzawi Rasmussen lay in a steel tray behind a white fridge door, waiting for the undertaker. Did she jump or was she pushed? Lene thought she already knew the answer.

She slowed down outside number 102 on Jagtvej, pulled over by a kiosk and looked across the road and up to the fourth-floor windows to the left, where Ain had lived. There was a French balcony with a couple of empty terracotta pots and the white curtains were open. She got out of the car, went into the kiosk and bought two Snickers bars, a packet of chewing gum and a bottle of mineral water.

Through the shop window, she saw the red front door to the stairwell open and a middle-aged couple step out into the street.

'Thirty-five fifty,' said the girl behind the till.

Lene held up a hand without turning around.

'Hang on.'

The man was tall and lean, with unruly grey hair, bushy eyebrows, a small goatee and rimless glasses, while the woman was smaller, slim, well dressed – and distraught. She blew her nose and stared down at the tarmac without speaking. Her eyes were red. The man supported her as they walked to an older, light-grey Volvo. The woman turned around and threw a last glance up at the building before she got in. He held the door open for her and looked up towards the top windows as well before he closed the door and walked around to the driver's side.

'Will there be anything else?' the girl asked.

'Do you think you could shut up for a minute,' Lene hissed.

The Volvo drove off towards Tagensvej.

A young man emerged from the back room. Indian or Pakistani. Very dignified. He looked at Lene.

'Listen—' he began.

'What?!'

The three of them looked at each other. Then Lene looked away and muttered something. She put 50 kroner on the counter, took the water and the chocolate and left. She tore the wrapping off one of the Snickers bars and devoured it in a couple of mouthfuls. She became irritable and aggressive when her blood sugar was too low. The Volvo indicated left at the next set of lights and Lene looked up at Ain's windows a second time. Were those the adoptive parents? Lene recalled the woman's deflated expression. The age was right, and those glances up to the fourth floor spoke more than a thousand words. The man had had a cardboard box under one arm.

Lene made a note of the Volvo's registration number and called the Vehicle Registration Office for the name of the owner and the address: Helge Rasmussen, Violvej in Værløse. A doctor. She got into her car and drank the water in small, pensive sips.

She felt like a peeping Tom. An uninvited stranger who stuck their nose into other people's tragedies. For the tenth time at least that day she questioned her own motives. Deep down, there was no reason to carry on. Only a vague sense of guilt at not having saved the girl and talked her out of it; she wished she had met Ain when she had asked her to, but the fact was that Ain had not sounded like someone about to jump in front of a train. Far from it. She had said that she would wait for Lene and she had said it as if she meant it.

Then there were her old instincts, which had been dormant for so long that she had almost forgotten their existence. They had been reawakened now and were flashing merrily. She looked down Jagtvej, which lost itself in blue exhaust fumes in the distance.

That road led to Frederiksberg – to Kong Georgs Vej – her home. Home to what? Bottles, emptiness, pills, futility, old videos of Josefine?

Lene swore and shook the steering wheel.

Then something made her look up and to the side. The

two people from the corner shop were watching her. Lene sent them a pale smile and started her car.

One last thing, she thought. Then she would forget about Ain and everything she represented. She would chuck that blasted mobile in a bin and go home. She was just tying up a loose end. A quick chat. That was all.

She opened the girl's mobile and called Jesper Horn, the psychiatrist. Lene spent a couple of minutes arguing with a staunch secretary before she managed to speak to the psychiatrist in person. It was inconvenient he said. Very. But the superintendent could have fifteen minutes of his time. In fact, he would skip lunch for her sake.

She ended the call and put Ain's mobile into her glove compartment. According to Bjarne, the mobile was no longer being tapped. Even so, she felt annoyed that she had not made the call from her own phone.

9

The psychiatrist was younger than Lene had expected. He was slim and athletic, wore a white linen shirt with no collar, and tight jeans. He had rings in both ears and tattoos on his muscular forearms. Straightaway, Lene had him down as a popular spiritual adviser for young urban women with mental health issues on the lighter end of the neurotic spectrum. She thought it unlikely that any dark, knotted depressives or agonized schizophrenics had ever sat in the spacious, bright consulting room which was furnished with three light Italian chairs, French blinds and a spotless, paperless floating glass desk on which a silver MacBook was admiring its own reflection. A large painting depicting a vast, deserted coastal landscape had been hung behind the psychiatrist's handsome, tanned head. The artist was Maria Horn. Presumably the doctor's creative wife, who was a stay-at-home mum, Lene thought. That was one scenario she had no trouble visualizing.

Jesper Horn took a seat behind the glass desk and gestured to the chair opposite. He meshed his fingers in front of him and sent her a light smile.

'You're from the police?'

'I am. And you treated Ain Ghazzawi Rasmussen. She came here, I mean?'

The fingers were raised to the psychiatrist's upper lip and the smile died away.

'Do you have any ID?'

Lene slid her warrant card across the desk. Jesper Horn studied it carefully before he handed it back to her.

'Are you next of kin, so to speak?' he asked.

'No, not officially. But I spoke to her several times when I was working at Livslinjen as a volunteer. It was me who suggested that Ain contact you. You're on our list.'

'Because she expressed suicidal thoughts?'

'Not directly,' Lene said. 'She felt guilty. What about, I don't know. She said that she deserved to die, but I don't know if you would class that as a suicide risk.'

The doctor nodded.

'You're right. I spoke with her a couple of times during last November and December. She didn't turn up for half of her appointments and the other times she would just come here and wait until I had finished with my other patients.'

The psychiatrist checked the MacBook.

'The last time I saw Ain was the 21st December. It wasn't a good session; she asked to be referred to someone else.'

'Who was she?' Lene asked.

'Was?'

'She jumped in front of a train at Nørreport Station yesterday. She's dead.'

The doctor pushed back his chair and got up. He walked across to the window, opened the French blinds and stood for a long time. The shiny parquet flooring reflected his shape like an underwater doppelgänger. If there was one thing that could shake a psychiatrist's faith in his own powers, it was a patient's suicide, she thought. It was understandable.

'Is this an official investigation?' he then asked her.

'No, not at all. It's private. I think I feel . . .'

'Responsible?'

'Yes.'

'Don't,' he said.

'Thank you. I'll bear that in mind. I was on the phone to her when she died. I just happened to pick up her mobile and stick it in my pocket on the platform and later I found your number.'

He turned to her with a smile: 'You just happened to pick up her mobile? Or did you do it because you're a cop?'

The psychiatrist had a nice smile, Lene thought, the kind where the eyes joined in.

Jesper Horn sat down and stared past her. Suddenly he looked older. In the bright daylight she saw that his stubble was grey. She had misjudged his age by a decade. He was in fact the same age as her, perhaps a little older.

'Livslinjen . . . What were you doing there? And do the police bug those conversations?'

Lene stared at him with knitted brows. Could paranoia really be infectious?

'I'm not paranoid, if that's what you're thinking,' he said, 'but you can't imagine how busy we've been since Tivoli. The world has literally gone insane. After the World Trade Centre and the Madrid and the London bombings, all those countries registered a steep rise in suicides, attempted suicides and mental health admissions, and the same is happening here in Denmark. Acts of terror affect the minds of our fellow human beings more than we would like to think. One day you're in the wrong place at the wrong time for one second and your life is snuffed out like a candle. It goes without saying that challenges us to our very core. Everything becomes relative, doesn't it? We've all visited Tivoli and we can easily relate to those who were killed that day, because they were exactly like us.'

'True.'

'Many of us have been there lots of times. For most Danes Tivoli is synonymous with happy memories. It's a national treasure and a symbol of everything that is Danish, of innocence and nostalgia. I have a daughter who used to dance ballet at the Pantomime Theatre in the Tivoli Gardens every summer. She was meant to have danced on the 17th September, but had sprained her ankle. Six of her friends were killed. All of them thirteen years old. Now, whenever she sees a pair of ballet shoes or hears ballet music, she just wants to throw up. It makes her ill. She has started playing handball instead.'

'Ballet?'

'Yes . . .'

'Why?'

'Nothing. Ain worked as a waitress in a restaurant in Tivoli,' Lene said. 'I have spoken to one of her friends who was also in Tivoli that day. She mentioned a kind of survivor guilt.'

The psychiatrist nodded.

'Exactly. Like I said, a catastrophe with so many victims challenges us. Especially in Denmark, because we have never experienced anything like it. For some, the tragedy becomes an incentive to value life more, enjoying the now. For others, it becomes a negative reinforcement of their mortality and the futility of it all. You can see it in subcultures: Goth and death metal concerts have become extremely popular. Perhaps it's how we process it.'

'I presume that Ain belonged to the latter category. Those convinced of the futility of it all,' said Lene who had, indeed, noticed that many young people had started looking like 1980s punks. She herself had sported a green mohican once, worn black lipstick and listened to the Cure, Dead Kennedys and the Sex Pistols – the sole teenager in Vordingborg to do so.

Jesper Horn leaned back and shook his head.

'Yes and no. She wasn't psychotic – that's to say, insane. But she was a practically complete catalogue of every other psychiatric condition. If you wanted to write a textbook about identity issues in young adults, she would be the only case study you would ever need.'

'Can you give me some examples?'

'Everything!'

The psychiatrist had started relating to her as a kind of equal, Lene noticed.

'Ain was shy and had difficulties with her sense of self,' he said. 'She was an older child when she came to Denmark from a refugee camp in Tunisia, but she was originally a Palestinian refugee from one of the occupied areas in Israel, the West Bank or Gaza. So there had been many changes early on in her life, which, not surprisingly, gives you a default setting of impotence – you believe you have no control over your own destiny, that you're an object moved around by other people's whims. I don't think she ever really felt at home anywhere. Besides, she was confused about whether she was a Muslim or a Christian. Whether she was heterosexual, bisexual or homosexual. She experimented quite a lot with that side of her personality.'

The psychiatrist threw up his hands in despair.

'These were just some of the questions she constantly asked herself; her past and the world around her alone would have been difficult enough for anyone to cope with.'

'So she was an easy target for manipulation?'

'An easy target for anyone who showed her a little kindness. Went to bed with her, for example. She was far from innocent in sexual terms, and actually prided herself on her promiscuity, her courage to experiment, even though in my opinion it was anything but liberating. It's not difficult to find people from the Middle East with cracks in their personalities, as some people call them. Those cracks can be filled with twisted ideology by manipulative fundamentalists, for example. It acts like a kind of glue, it holds together the way they view the world. They give young people, adrift or orphans, what they long for. Meaning, norms, a family, a fellowship with other young people who are just like them. The indoctrination and the preparation for suicide bombings happen systematically in some Koranic schools and mosques. They get a sense of purpose and a mission, even if that mission is to blow up a café in Jerusalem or blow a bus in the West Bank to bits. Coffee?'

'I beg your pardon?'

'Coffee? All I have is Nescafé.'

'Thanks. That's fine.'

Jesper Horn left his office. Lene looked after him. He was the most energetic and fast-talking person she had met for a long time.

He returned a few minutes later with two mugs of coffee and a bowl of English biscuits, and put one mug in front of Lene.

'I've cancelled my next patient,' he said, taking a small handful of biscuits.

'I didn't mean to mess up your diary.'

He dismissed her apology with a wave of the hand as he munched.

'That's okay. Besides, he's more of an old friend than a patient. In fact, I talk much more than he does. I talk too much, I'm perfectly aware of it. Not very clever when you're a psychiatrist.'

Lene smiled and sipped her coffee.

'So he's cured, then?'

Jesper Horn grinned.

'Cured is a completely unscientific and undocumented state, Superintendent. And not one worth striving for. Let's just say that he's in a stable period, which has now lasted several years.'

'Did Ain ever express radical political convictions?' she asked.

'God, no. She was far too self-obsessed to feel indignation, or to adopt a basic political ideology. Ain was a narcissist through and through. And when I say self-obsessed and narcissistic, I'm not actually being derogative. Most of her time and energy were spent keeping chaos at bay.'

'So you were not treating her with drugs?'

'Why would I do that? She didn't suffer from anxiety and she wasn't clinically depressed. She wasn't delusional nor did she experience any debilitating phobias. And besides, it wouldn't have helped one jot.'

'She told me once in January that she was on medication,' Lene said. 'But that it didn't work, that it only made her feel worse.'

'I didn't prescribe it, and it sounds irresponsible.'

The psychiatrist seemed ill at ease. He cleared his throat and opened his mouth, only to close it again. Took a couple of biscuits and offered the bowl to Lene, who shook her head.

'Why did you ask me if I volunteered for Livslinjen in a professional capacity?' Lene said.

'Ah . . .' Jesper Horn got up and started pacing up and down his office.

'Now maybe I *am* getting a little paranoid,' he began, 'but about three months after the terror attack we – I mean privately practising psychologists and psychiatrists – were given the option to refer patients showing symptoms of post-traumatic stress to a new centre at Rigshospitalet. Huge grants had been made available and the plan was to gather the expertise under one roof.'

He smiled thinly.

'It was the nature of these things that the centre was mostly interested in speaking to Danes with a Middle Eastern background going back one, two or three generations. If, for example, such individuals had experienced bullying or discrimination because other people thought that they were responsible in some way.'

'So you referred Ain to Rigshospitalet?'

'No. I couldn't see what she would get out of that. Her ethnicity was only one aspect of her problems, and not even the most important one. The whole initiative seemed odd to me and I can't help but think that the real aim was to screen patients or their next of kin for political radicalism. That they wanted to identify people who might potentially be of interest to a terror network.'

Lene looked down at her coffee mug.

'Do you have any evidence of this?' she asked. 'That the treatment centre was something other than what it claimed to be?'

'No, but the last time I saw Ain, she showed me a brochure from the centre. Very nice. Beautiful people – models, no doubt. They certainly had great teeth. The doctors promised potential clients group therapy, care, understanding and affirmative togetherness with young people from similar backgrounds, table tennis and Friday café. It was irresistible to someone like Ain. I tried talking her out of it, but she got furious when I expressed doubts about the project.'

'Why?'

'If the clever doctors at Rigshospitalet managed to identify her ethnicity as her main problem, then everything would be oh so simple, wouldn't it? Her private misery would, in fact, be a social issue. An external conflict which no one could do anything about, and which meant she would never have to take responsibility for her life.'

'I can see that,' Lene said. It sounded plausible.

Her mobile rang in her pocket.

'Sorry.'

She looked at the display. Chief Superintendent Charlotte Falster. Lene had been expecting the call and wondered why it had not come sooner. She pressed *Ignore*, set the mobile to silent and slipped it back in her pocket.

'There's something else,' the psychiatrist said in a low voice.

'What?'

'The person behind the initiative is Irene Adler, someone I don't like, even though she's highly respected and has an illustrious career. And no, I'm not jealous.'

'Of course not,' Lene said.

'She knows all the right people,' he continued. 'And she has been awarded all sorts of honours and undertakes a vast amount of research. But she's also a special consultant to PET. She's interested in terrorists. She bloody loves them! She would keep them as pets if they would let her. Very early on in her career she received a grant to study in the USA, where it would seem that she developed an interest in suicide bombers. Her first articles about the psyche of terrorists were published by a university on the East Coast. Some people have claimed that the CIA provided the finance for that part of her research.'

'The CIA? Of course!'

'I know that it sounds like something from the lunatic fringes of conspiracy theories, but I'm sure that Irene has received training in military psychology. You can tell just by listening to her.'

'What was she taught?'

'Fucking with people's heads. She has learned how to

make people think that white is black and black is white. There is actually a precedent in Denmark. The CIA funded LSD experiments at Frederiksberg Hospital in the 1970s; they were looking for a wonder drug that would control people's behaviour and thoughts. Several of the subjects became permanently psychotic and some committed suicide. They never resurfaced, but were forever trapped in some sort of raw subconscious.'

'Is she married?' Lene asked pensively.

'Irene? I believe that's far too conventional for her. I don't even want to think about her private life,' he grunted. 'I'm sorry, I know I sound totally unprofessional, but there's something about her which quite unscientifically gives me the creeps.'

Lene studied him more closely. Something was clearly bothering him; this collaboration between PET and Irene Adler, and Ain's fate. Perhaps he was even pleased to have the opportunity to talk to someone like her. When you always took the part of the listener, working as a priest or a psychiatrist, you probably needed to offload onto someone else from time to time.

Jesper Horn continued.

'Rumour had it that she wanted to convert to Islam. To get closer to the individuals she was studying, I presume. Or perhaps she had actually started believing.'

'And has she?' Lene asked.

'Not a clue. She speaks Arabic like a native and she has

worked at universities in Egypt and in Jerusalem. She's always in the Middle East.'

'When does she sleep?'

'On the plane, I guess.'

'Okay. But Ain? It sounds as if she was properly fucked up, to use your expression,' Lene said.

'It was in response to your earlier question,' Jesper Horn said. 'I didn't treat her with psychoactive drugs. If anyone did, it was either her GP – which I doubt, because in Ain's case, it would have to be done by an expert in mental health – or it was another psychiatrist.'

'Such as Irene?'

'Yes. Do you know her?'

'Why do you think that?'

'The way you say her name. Your facial expression.'

Lene folded her arms self-consciously across her chest and stared down at the shiny floor. Was it really so obvious?

'Nothing. It's nothing.'

He tilted his head slightly to one side and smiled.

'I have a duty of confidentiality, you know,' he said. 'Out with it. If you want to.'

She closed her eyes and nodded harshly.

'All right, then.'

Lene gulped and kept her eyes shut.

'Irene treated my daughter, Josefine, for severe depression,' she said in a loud, clear voice. 'She was admitted to a secure psychiatric ward at Rigshospitalet for six months.

Irene discharged her to an outpatient clinic, even though I thought it was far too soon. She wasn't ready at all. A week later she went to my flat and shot herself through the head with my service pistol. She had wrapped a towel around her head. Just like when she used to wash her hair . . . She was always thinking of others, my beautiful, beautiful girl. She was twenty-three years old, and it was me who found her.'

10

Was it really her own voice? So steady and unforced?

Jesper Horn said nothing. The psychiatrist sat, tiger-striped by the sunlight falling through the blinds.

Lene folded her hands over her knees to stop them from shaking.

'Of course it wasn't only Irene who was responsible for Josefine, but I disagreed with her completely. I thought Josefine was too ill to be discharged. I hated Irene. I happened to see her yesterday, and she walks around as if nothing has happened. While Josefine . . .'

'. . . is dead,' the psychiatrist said. 'And that was a misjudgement on her part. But possibly not an error. Do you understand the difference?'

'Yes.'

'Was it the first time your daughter had been admitted to a psychiatric ward?'

'Yes. A couple of years ago she was assaulted by some criminals I was investigating. They kidnapped her to stop me. She was badly injured when she was found, but I was convinced that she would pull through. She had a bright mind and was very strong. Very healthy.'

Lene tried swallowing something that refused to be swallowed. Something big and warm expanded in her chest and she tried again. Then she gave up and started crying, even though she hardly ever cried.

It went on and on.

He was obviously used to despair, she thought, in a moment of clarity – until the next wave of grief washed over her.

Jesper Horn pushed a box of Kleenex across the glass desk, but it took a long time before she could use them. She blew her nose, tried to get her breathing under control, threw back her head and looked up at the ceiling before the crying finally ebbed away.

She felt no relief. She felt nothing.

The psychiatrist smiled. Then he got up, walked around the table and placed his hand lightly on her shoulder, before resuming his favourite position by the window.

'Are you all right?' he asked.

'Perhaps. Thank you.'

'Ain is someone else's daughter, Lene. She's *not* Josefine. And you had no way of knowing that your daughter would be assaulted.'

'I know. I know.'

'I presume that was why you volunteered for Livslinjen?'

'Of course.'

'I'm surprised that they let you,' he said.

'I bullied them into it. To begin with they refused point-blank. I should never have done it. It was a kind of outlet, but it wasn't healthy and it didn't bring Josefine back. I was no good at it.'

'So, are you going to leave the case alone? Ain, I mean?'

She looked at the clock above the door to the front office. It was much later than she had imagined. Jesper Horn must have communicated with the secretary in the front office somehow, to make sure they were not disturbed.

'I don't think I can,' she said.

'Why not?'

She studied the toes of her scuffed boots.

'It wasn't a suicide,' she said. 'It was murder, and that's the only thing I'm good at. Really good at.'

'Murder?'

'Yes. She wanted to meet with me. She didn't say, "Good-bye," or, "See you in the next life," or, "Take care," or, "Say hi to my parents!" She didn't sound like someone who was about to throw herself in front of a train halfway through the next sentence. She didn't leave a note. Nothing.'

'Perhaps it wasn't planned,' he said. 'It might have been a spur-of-the-moment thing. She saw the train, gave up . . . Perhaps she was in a dangerous, unstable mood.'

'Perhaps. But I don't think so.'

'So you'll carry on?' he asked. 'Is that for her sake or yours?'

'I think I owe it to her.'

'So it's for your own sake.'

'Yes.'

Lene got up and headed for the door. Jesper Horn said something she did not quite catch.

Lene turned around and watched him suspiciously.

'What did you say?'

'That I would like to see you again.'

'Here?' She giggled nervously. 'My boss has tried sending me to various . . . experts. Psychologists. Coaches. I think I probably wore them out. Drove them crazy.' She tried striking up a cheerful tone: 'I believe the last one drives a cab now.'

'I didn't mean here, and certainly not as a patient,' he said.

Lene stared at him blankly. She ran her fingers through her hair. Her ponytail was a mess and she knew that tears and mascara had drawn clown stripes down her face. What was wrong with the man? Did he get off on losers?

'I meant a date,' he said.

'A kind of date? Why?'

'A date, not a *kind* of date. A cup of coffee, for Christ's sake . . . a glass of wine. Or you can use me as a punch ball.'

She looked at the painting behind his chair. The colours had grown darker and seemed to merge. Maybe it was not a coastal landscape after all.

Jesper Horn followed her gaze.

'My sister, Maria. It's a kind of arts subsidy. I buy most

of her paintings and our parents buy the rest. My father uses them to insulate the attic – without her knowledge, obviously. She's very productive. Believing yourself an artist while you have no talent is a true tragedy, don't you think? I'm a single dad with a daughter. My wife died from breast cancer seven years ago.'

'I'm sorry,' she said. 'Were you serious about the date?'

'Of course I was.'

He walked towards her and she retreated as if he was a stuffed Bengali tiger that had suddenly come alive. She heard a telephone ring in the front office. Jesper Horn's grey eyes lay in shadow under his strong eyebrows. His body was slim and light. Lene took another look at the earrings and the tattoos: he wasn't her type at all.

He produced a worn wallet from his back pocket and found a business card.

'My mobile number is on the back,' he said. 'Think about it.'

She had one hand behind the small of her back. It was fumbling about for the door handle.

'I will,' she said. 'Thank you.'

He nodded, reached behind her and opened the door.

Lene rushed through the front office with the secretary's eyes on her back. She opened the door to the stairs and glanced over her shoulder. Jesper Horn smiled at her from the secretary's desk, and she nearly tripped over the threshold.

She didn't start breathing until she was safely back in her car. She turned over the thick, ivory-coloured business card in her hand. Then she pulled down the sun visor and studied her face in the mirror. It was much worse than she had feared. What was wrong with him?

She snapped back the sun visor with a bang and found the number for the psychiatric ward at Rigshospitalet in her phone.

Doctor Adler was currently taking part in the department's afternoon conference, the secretary informed her. Lene remembered her as a skinny joyless woman who had probably been chosen by Irene Adler in order to emphasize her own glamour.

'I'm happy to drop by and wait until she has finished,' she said.

'Who did you say you were, Madam?'

'I'm Superintendent Lene Jensen. My daughter was once a patient of yours, but that's not why I'm calling.'

'I see. I'm afraid Dr Adler is busy.'

'After the meeting?'

'There is another meeting. She's terribly busy at the moment. So I'm afraid . . .'

Clearly hell would freeze over before Irene Adler had time to speak to the superintendent.

'She can't actually refuse,' Lene said at length. 'This is a police matter, so either you find me some time with her today, or I march into that bloody conference room in ten minutes and arrest her for obstructing a police investigation. And, yes, I know where it is.'

The line went dead.

Lene stared at her mobile in disbelief.

She rang back.

The line was busy.

Bloody woman!

She tried a few more times before her call was finally answered.

'Hello!' she shouted.

'Irene Adler's secretary.'

Lene took a deep breath.

'It's me again. I don't know if I made it quite clear to you that I really need to speak to Irene Adler?'

'You did, Madam. There was no confusion.'

'And?'

The woman hesitated.

'I did try, Superintendent Jensen, I went up there, but I was told that Dr Adler had left the ward.'

'So where the fu— Where do you think Doctor Irene Adler might be right now?'

'I really have no idea. I think she's going abroad.'

'Where to?'

'I *don't* know! I'm sorry, but she doesn't tell me where she's going. She travels all the time.'

Lene closed her eyes and saw Ain's still figure under the blood-soaked ambulance blankets. Why was she wasting her time scaring the life out of some middle-aged secretary who was only doing her job?

'No, I'm the one who should apologize,' she muttered. 'Forget it. It's all right. I'll think of something.'

'I do want to help you,' the secretary said in a conciliatory tone of voice. 'I remember Josefine . . . your daughter . . .'

'Goodbye,' Lene said.

11

It would appear that for once she was keeping up with Irene Adler. Lene slumped further down into the driver's seat of her Citroën as the psychiatrist's black Audi TT bounced over the speed bumps on the narrow street in Østerbro. The doctor owned a rustic town house in Kartoffelrækkerne.

The tall, elegant figure extricated herself from the low car, swung the strap of her bag onto her shoulder and walked up the flagstone path.

Lene massaged her forehead and made a failed attempt at improving her appearance with a hairbrush, a wet wipe and an elastic band. Hopeless. She gave the psychiatrist five minutes before she got out of her car, walked through the small front garden and let the doorknocker fall hard three times against the brass plate.

Up close, Irene Adler's beautiful face was strangely naked and defenceless. She wore no make-up and tried to shut the door, but Lene wedged her shoulder against it. The psychiatrist gave in and flung up her hands.

'Very well, then, come in,' she said.

'Thank you.'

'I think we should have had a conversation about Josefine long ago, Lene. I just don't understand why it has to be right now, and there's no need for you to frighten the living daylights out of my secretary.'

'This isn't about my daughter,' Lene said. 'I'm actually here on police business.'

There were beautiful Arabic woodcarvings on the walls and an ancient Persian carpet on the floor.

Lene spotted a travel bag with a plane ticket sticking out of the side pocket.

'Going somewhere?'

Irene Adler followed her gaze.

'A stunning piece of detective work. My taxi will be here in half an hour and I happen to be in a hurry.'

'Where are you going?' Lene asked distractedly, while she looked around.

'What do you want?'

'Are we going to stand here in the hall?'

Irene Adler made a sound that was a cross between a sigh and a groan and opened a white door to two interconnected living rooms.

The living rooms were furnished like a Bedouin tent with low, beaten brass coffee tables, leather pouffes and cushions, a hookah, beautiful, antique rugs and several more wood-carvings on the walls.

'Where do you keep the camels?' Lene said.

'What do you want?'

Lene didn't reply. She walked slowly around the room because she knew it would irritate the other woman. There was an elegant desk below the window, overlooking a small courtyard. Lene picked up a long, engraved antique silver syringe from the blotting pad. At one end it had a needle screwed on. The tip was still sharp.

'What's this?'

'An embalming syringe. It was used for injecting formaldehyde or other embalming fluids into the veins of the deceased. I use it to open my letters. Please would you put it down? It happens to be valuable.'

Lene returned it to the desk and slowly continued her inspection.

There was a bureau up against one wall. Lene approached it and discovered that it was in fact an illuminated glass display cabinet; a suitable home for the antique Koran, which was opened on the centre pages and handwritten with the most beautiful Arabic calligraphy. The pages had yellowed and were delicate like butterfly wings. Each one was embellished with hand-decorated illustrations. The book had to be ancient and was undoubtedly priceless.

'Are you done?' the psychiatrist asked.

'It's beautiful,' Lene said.

'Thank you, it represents countless working hours and much truth for me.'

'I'm sure,' Lene mumbled, without understanding what Irene Adler meant.

The psychiatrist gestured to a Moroccan pouffe and Lene sat down accompanied by a series of cracks from her lower back. Irene Adler sank noiselessly and nimbly down onto another pouffe, as far away from her as possible, and folded her hands in her lap.

'Ain Ghazzawi Rasmussen,' Lene said.

'Who is that?'

'She is, or was, a young orphaned woman of Palestinian heritage, who was treated at your new centre.'

'So, a patient?'

'Yes.'

'I can't talk about my patients, Lene, and you know it. We're wasting one another's time. You need a warrant. Do you have a warrant?'

'She's dead. She jumped in front of a train at Nørreport Station yesterday. She said she was on medication, but that it didn't help. She was frightened, isolated and believed that she was being followed. She was twenty-three years old. Ain Ghazzawi. Ring any bells?'

The psychiatrist pulled a knee under her chin and folded her hands around her ankle. She was calm and collected, sitting still like a statue.

'It's sad, of course,' she said. 'What makes you think I was treating her?'

'She received counselling from a psychiatrist in town,

Jesper Horn, but discontinued her sessions last December, and demanded to be referred to your new centre instead. She had your brochure.'

Irene Adler shrugged her shoulders.

'The name doesn't mean anything to me. We have lots of girls with lots of problems. You don't need a referral to come to us, all you have to do is turn up. Several of our patients want to be anonymous and we respect that, of course.'

'She was working in a restaurant in Tivoli on the 17th September last year,' Lene said.

'As were dozens of other young, non-ethnic Danes. Some of them got ill. I don't know them all.'

Lene nodded and took out Ain's mobile. She clicked on the spring photograph of Ain and Nazeera and showed the psychiatrist the display.

'It's her on the right.'

Irene Adler did not take the mobile, but kept her fingers interlaced around her ankle. Her face was immobile, but her pupils slowly expanded. Lene watched her.

'I have never seen her before.'

'And not the other one either. Nazeera?'

'No.'

She was lying. Lene was sure of it.

She felt an overpowering urge to get up and slap the psychiatrist hard across the face; smash the woman's restrained, perfect façade. Instead, she glanced up at the ceiling when a floorboard creaked above her.

'Are you on your own?'

'Not that it's any of your business, but yes, I am. I like being on my own.'

Irene Adler unfolded her long body and rose to her feet, while Lene pointedly stayed where she was.

'So you didn't treat Ain Ghazzawi with, for example, psychoactive medication? Some drug that made her delusional and paranoid?'

The psychiatrist smiled.

'Do you seriously expect me to answer that question? Goodbye, Lene. I have a plane to catch. It has been absolutely great talking to you, but I think you should find something other than a suicide to investigate. And is this official? Does Charlotte Falster know that you're running around harassing people?'

Lene got up eventually and walked out into the hall. She stopped in the middle of the floor and looked up the white staircase winding its way to the floors above. She closed her eyes and sniffed. There was a scent of another woman in the house.

Irene watched her with an indulgent and slightly mystified smile, but for the first time Lene told herself that she could see something other than cool superiority in the psychiatrist's face. A shadow of anxiety swam across the bottom of her blue eyes.

'Have you converted?' Lene asked just as she opened the front door.

'I beg your pardon?'

'Have you converted to Islam?'

'That's none of your business. And you're leaving now.'

The other woman's voice had taken on a new, raw edge. Lene smiled. She had an innate talent for getting on people's nerves.

On the doormat she turned around and looked at the psychiatrist.

'One last thing . . . Irene . . .'

'Get out!'

'If I find out that you lied to me, if I find out that Ain was your patient and that you and PET used her as a guinea pig or drove her over the edge of that platform, I will not rest until you are all made to take responsibility, no matter how good you think your contacts are and how many accolades you have won. And you can consider that a promise.'

She smiled sweetly.

'Understand?'

The door was slammed shut with a loud bang that made the blue tits on the feeding tray in next door's garden take off.

Lene looked up at the first-floor windows and thought she saw a shadow behind the curtains. Then it disappeared.

She considered asking Bjarne to check the passenger lists for planes departing from Copenhagen Airport, but abandoned the idea. Irene was undoubtedly attending a conference in Brazil or Tobago. Somewhere with beaches, palm trees. Wasn't that what doctors did all the time?

12

Lene was sitting in a café on Kongens Nytorv, staring vacantly at a club sandwich. It looked like a strange fossil.

Although she had loved cooking for Josefine, and had actually been quite good at it, these days food was just fuel for her. She had been about to order a glass of red wine, when she remembered her vow of just a few hours ago to quit drinking.

She carved off a corner of the sandwich and was about to steer the fork into her mouth when her mobile rang. She stuck the food in her mouth and answered the call.

'Hello?'

Lene chewed, swallowed and drank a mouthful of water.

'Hi, Charlotte.'

'Are you eating?' Her boss sounded outraged.

'Er, yes. I eat, you know, food.'

'We missed you at the coordination meeting.'

'Didn't Bjarne go?'

'Oh, yes. He was there. Thanks, Lene. He mumbles and sweats, grinds to a halt and loses his train of thought, even though there is no train of thought to begin with. A Polish ship with engine trouble? Is that really the best you can come up with?'

Charlotte Falster should try sitting next to Bjarne for eight hours a day, day in and day out. Even today's pollen count was more inspiring.

'It is for the time being,' Lene said. 'Sorry.'

'What are you really doing?' the chief superintendent asked. 'Apart from eating, I mean.'

Lene could visualize Charlotte Falster behind the neat and tidy desk, the silver triptych frame with pictures of her top civil servant husband and their two successful children – one a lawyer, the other a vet – placed in front of her.

The two women had never liked each other, and had known it from the moment they first met. It was an instant, chemical reaction. Lene thought that her boss was a heartless bureaucrat and Charlotte Falster thought that Lene was an anarchic individualist, a dinosaur in a modern age that valued teamwork, organization, consensus, documentation and endless meetings. But they had learned to respect each other, and during the investigation into the human hunt, they had grown close.

Charlotte Falster and her husband had attended Josefine's funeral and Lene had been granted all the leave and time off she could want, without any questions being asked. But since then their relationship had cooled professionally and personally to almost absolute zero. Lene no longer performed or delivered, and after the Tivoli bomb, the pressure on Charlotte Falster had grown close to suffocating. Everyone – politicians, the media and the public – demanded results; not now, not tomorrow, but yesterday. Or she would be crucified. It was not a question of if but when she would be replaced, unless something happened soon that could satisfy the public's and next of kin's demand for justice. In police circles this was known as Olof Palme Syndrome: following the murder of the Swedish prime minister, one head of investigation after another had been replaced, ridiculed or accused of incompetence or corruption, often with tragic consequences for the individual in question and with absolutely no benefit to the investigation itself.

'We'll try to make more of an effort,' she mumbled.

'I hope so. I really do. For your sake. And I hope that you understand how important this is. More important than spending your time on private investigations, for example.'

Lene put down her knife and fork.

'What do you mean?' she asked in a low voice.

'Nørreport Station. Ain Ghazzawi Rasmussen. What were you doing down there? Or rather, what did you think you were doing?'

Lene lost her rag.

'Listen, Charlotte. I don't see why I have to account for what I do in my spare time, and I have no intention of explaining my private life to anyone, dead or alive. Who told you?'

'We're not talking about your spare time, Lene! You were on duty and you're supposed to be finding out how the suicide bomber and his accomplices crossed Denmark's borders, who they knew here, how they were organized, who they paid to sail, fly or drive them into the country. That's what you should be spending your time on!'

The chief superintendent's voice had grown shrill.

Lene stared at her mobile in disbelief. Charlotte Falster was the most measured and imperturbable person she had ever met. She *never* lost her temper.

'The girl was about to kill herself!' Lene screamed. 'In fact, she *did* kill herself, or someone pushed her in front of that bloody train. I'm more inclined to believe the latter. She called me, Charlotte! I was the last person she should have wanted to talk to and yet I was the last person to listen to her . . . Don't you understand? This is real life! You should try stepping outside your air-conditioned office for once! What was I supposed to do? Hang up? Tell her I had to listen to yet another lecture on *salafi* terrorism and that she could call me from St Peter's switchboard? Or could she please jump in front of the next train? What would you have done? She was twenty-three years old! Exactly the same age as . . . as . . .'

There was total silence at the other end, and the words died on Lene's lips. There was also total silence in the café, and she became aware that she might have been shouting a little too loudly. She signalled to the waiter and ten seconds later the bill was on the table. Lene placed her credit card on the silver tray and again she could hear Charlotte Falster's rapid breathing.

Have I just been sacked? she wondered, and felt an unexpected and unspeakable sense of relief at the prospect.

'You're not sacked, if that's what you're hoping,' her boss said. 'Unfortunately, I need you, although I wish I didn't. Pushed? What do you mean? Are you sure?'

'No,' Lene said wearily. 'I'm not sure of anything right now. But I promise to be a good girl and to sit on my perch with Bjarne tomorrow.'

'Good. Because if you're near a television, I suggest you turn it on. NATO and the Danish government have announced that Denmark, France and the Netherlands will deploy combat troops to Mali and Niger. The Danish Parliament is in agreement. Two F-16 squadrons, the Royal Life Guards and Spejderkompaniet will be sent in. And we haven't even got the last military instructors out of Afghanistan yet.'

Lene blinked. *Afri-Ghanistan*, as the press had dubbed the new front in the global war against terror in the sparsely populated void of West Africa. Brilliant.

Charlotte Falster continued.

'The first Danish armoured personnel carriers have just arrived in Mali. The embassy in Cairo is under siege. People are throwing Molotov cocktails over the walls and setting fire to the Danish flag. I presume you know what that means, Lene?'

'The threat level has been raised,' she mumbled.

'Not just raised. It's red hot.'

'I understand.'

'Are you going to help us?'

'Of course.'

'Then I expect to see you tomorrow,' Charlotte said. 'Oh, and one more thing. Stay away from Irene. She has made a formal complaint. Not just that, she's taking it further. She went to school with the justice secretary.'

'What?! I never—'

'She says you called her four times today, that you bullied her secretary and triggered a migraine and that you behaved in a threatening manner towards her in her own home.'

Had she behaved in a threatening manner? Lene thought about it. Had she really? She probably had, towards the end. She might have been a tiny bit hostile, but then again she was only human.

'I don't think I did,' she said. 'Not at all. Or . . . perhaps a tiny bit. She's so . . . so bloody . . .'

'It doesn't matter what she is, Lene, and in private and just between the two of us, I might completely agree with you, but stay away from her! That's an order, just to be clear. Everybody knows that you complained about your daughter's treatment. Perhaps you had good cause, I've no way of knowing, but she's an essential part of the investigation into the Tivoli bombing, whether you like it or not. And she has connections throughout the Establishment.'

'Of course. Fuck. I promise to stay away from the bitch.'

Lene's credit card was returned and she got up. Slowly she headed for the exit, while she contemplated three things: who had told Charlotte Falster about Ain, why her boss had not asked her who the young woman was, and what her connection to Irene Adler was.

She walked across to her car, tore the parking ticket which had been slipped under the windscreen wiper into tiny pieces and let them flutter down into the gutter.

In her office in Glostrup, Chief Superintendent Charlotte Falster put down her mobile on her desk. For a couple of minutes she sat in reflection before she did something she would once have thought she would never even contemplate. She submitted a request to the public prosecutor for a warrant which would make it legal to tap Superintendent Lene Jensen's phone and to have her followed. Then she faxed the sensitive document to a case worker at the public prosecutor's office.

A television in the corner showed disturbances at Tahrir Square in Cairo and demonstrations in front of the Danish embassy in Hassan Sabry Street. An effigy meant to depict the Danish General Secretary of NATO was in the process of being set alight outside the gate.

Charlotte turned off the television before she, for the second time that day, carried out an act she would previously have dismissed as unthinkable.

She dialled a long, international telephone number.

13

Lene truly hated this place.

She felt nauseous and her head was aching, but she did
not know whether it was due to the smell of formaldehyde
or withdrawal symptoms. The night before she had drunk
only tea – and taken the usual two sleeping tablets. Her
hands were trembling.

Bjarne had been even more introverted and timid than
usual, and Lene wondered if Charlotte had had words with
him. She could just imagine it. Bjarne shyly stepping on his
own toes, while the cool, formidable chief superintendent
cross-examined him about Lene. Perhaps he had been told
to watch her and report back? It looked like it, because he
would lift his head and ask where she was going even when
she was just nipping to the lavatory. At three thirty she
had grabbed her bag and her jacket and left without saying
goodbye, although she knew it would reduce him to despair.

Now she was standing in the cold-storage facility outside
an autopsy room below the Institute of Forensic Medicine,
together with a young, female medical examiner with a gap

between her front teeth, whom she knew from previous cases.

They waited while a square-set, hairy attendant by the name of Jesus located the right shelf. He opened the door and pulled a steel gurney out onto a hydraulic trolley. Then he rolled it into the autopsy room on noiseless rubber wheels and transferred the gurney with Ain on it onto the dissection table. There were brown stains on the sheet covering the body.

'Can you take it from here?' he asked.

'If not, I'll call you,' the medical examiner said.

The attendant waddled out of the room. He wore large gold earrings and looked like something from a pirate movie, Lene thought. As he left, he stuck the white earphones of an iPod into his ears.

'Jesus,' she muttered.

The medical examiner smiled. Then she looked at the table, and her smile faded away.

'Are you sure?'

Lene nodded. 'Unfortunately, yes.'

'All right, then.'

The doctor quickly removed the sheet and Lene took a step backwards. She made a sound and covered her face with her hands.

'Oh, God . . .'

'Yes,' the medical examiner said. 'It's really very bad. It's my opinion that her head must have landed close to one rail and her knees on the other. Is that her?'

'I think so . . . Yes, it's her. For God's sake, cover her up,' Lene said in a strangled voice as she turned away.

'Why don't we go to my office?'

There were two noticeboards in the medical examiner's office. One was filled with technical photographs of injuries – stab wounds with rulers next to them, defensive lesions on victims' forearms and hands – and the introverted, closed faces of the dead. The other was covered by drawings produced by her three children. Lene had never understood the woman's choice of profession, but the medical examiner had once muttered something about not letting them get away with it. That was important.

'Coffee?' she offered.

'No, thank you.'

The medical examiner sat down behind her desk and looked at Lene.

'Ain is being buried the day after tomorrow at Værløse Church,' she said.

'Thank you.'

'What's going on, Lene? Is this an official investigation? As far as I'm aware, the police are saying no such thing. Will I get into trouble?'

'What do you mean?'

'You know exactly what I mean. It's going to be somewhat difficult for me to explain why you called me at home last night to ask for a full tox screen of a girl who jumped in front of a train; a girl nobody else appears to be interested in.'

The doctor leaned forward and placed her elegant, slim hands on the desk. They picked up a letter opener of carved ivory and moved it to a new position next to a ceramic mug with the word 'Mum', filled with ballpoint pens and pencils. Lene watched the beautiful hands in silence.

'So I haven't,' the medical examiner said.

'You haven't what?'

'Told anyone.'

'Thank you.'

'Who is she? Come on.'

'I used to volunteer for Livslinjen,' Lene began. 'I spoke to her a couple of times. She was sad . . . for countless different reasons, I have discovered, but she thought that she was being followed. She also expressed guilt, although she wouldn't tell me why. She received counselling from a psychiatrist for a short while. Jesper Horn. Do you know him?'

'No.'

'Well, anyway, she quit counselling because she thought she would receive better treatment at Rigshospitalet, at a new unit specializing in issues specific to immigrants after Tivoli. Discrimination, hate crimes . . .'

'I've heard about it.'

'I spoke to her just before she died. In fact, I heard it happen.'

The other woman nodded lightly.

'She was depressed. She was an Arab. Adopted as a child, wasn't she? She felt persecuted. And guilty. The train . . . So what's the problem?'

Lene flung out her hands.

'She didn't sound like someone who was about to kill herself. She was twenty-three years old, for fuck's sake, and I was on my way to meet her. If she had only waited five minutes, we could have come up with something.'

She looked at the medical examiner.

'You don't believe me, do you? You think I'm getting her mixed up with someone else, don't you? You think I'm—'

'Insane?'

'Yes,' Lene whispered wearily and looked at her hands in her lap, which were still trembling, even though she was trying to keep them under control. She was also developing a tic under her right eye. A nerve was firing constantly under her skin, and she knew she was blinking compulsively like a village idiot, although she felt anything but amicable.

The doctor studied Lene's chaotic face with fascination. Then she withdrew her gaze with a shake of the head and clicked instead on some menus on her computer screen.

'Are you aware that I made two lab assistants work all night on analysing blood and tissue samples from Ain Ghazzawi Rasmussen? And are you aware that they're now entitled to a ridiculous amount of time off in lieu of the eight hours of overtime they've just worked? And are you aware that I stood up my husband for our first cinema trip, just the two of us, since we were twenty-one, which was sometime in the previous century? No, the century before that.'

'I'm sorry,' said Lene, hoping she sounded suitably contrite.

'No, you're not,' the medical examiner muttered while she scrutinized a series of codes on her screen. 'But anyway, I don't think you're insane. If that's any consolation.'

'It really is. Why not?'

'Because something *is* wrong. Right here.'

The medical examiner highlighted a curve. The otherwise smooth graph showed noticeable spikes.

'What's that?' Lene asked.

'I haven't seen it before and that in itself is unusual. We found a kind of D-lysergic acid diethylamide in Ain's blood – that's LSD. It's undoubtedly a new designer drug.'

'A *kind* of LSD?'

'A new and improved version,' the medical examiner said. 'A couple of sulphur groups have been attached to the active molecule. My guess is they make the drug work more quickly, for longer and more strongly. And it's undoubtedly hugely addictive.'

Lene could no longer sit still. She got up and walked across to one of the windows where she eased apart the plastic blind. From the institute she had a view of the low buildings that housed Rigshospitalet's psychiatric wards.

'How do you take it?'

'She had no needle marks. But you can take it as a tablet, inhale the substance or consume it in liquid form. It doesn't actually matter. It's easily absorbed from the gastrointestinal system or through the lungs.'

'What does it do to people?'

'It opens the trapdoor to their subconscious – and leaves it open. Colours are distorted and intensified. Everyday objects look weird or menacing. It's the strongest hallucinogen known to man. Some never recover.'

'Paranoia?'

'Oh, that goes without saying. It's practically the same alkaloid also found in ergot and thorn apple. In ancient times the Oracle at Delphi was in fact a priestess who spoke in tongues after inhaling vapours from burning thorn apple twigs. It makes you go insane. And increases paranoia, of course.'

Lene turned and folded her arms across her chest.

'It sounds to me as if that poison was the last thing Ain needed,' she said.

'Perhaps she didn't know she was taking it.'

'Come again?'

'You can't taste or smell it. You could slip it in someone's drink, or tell them it's something else. If you have the authority. If, say, you're a doctor.'

'Seriously?'

'Yes.'

'But why would anyone want to do that?' Lene asked.

For a while the doctor looked pensive.

'I'm no expert,' she said at length. 'LSD was accidentally

synthesized by a chemist at Sandoz in Switzerland in 1938, and the CIA became very interested in it in the 1950s because they thought it could be used as a truth serum. There was a chemical arms race between the USA and the Russians during the Cold War. The Soviet Union used the drug during show trials of dissidents, most commonly in Hungary after 1956 and in Czechoslovakia after 1968. Footage shows highly intelligent and principled politicians and scientists behaving like zombies. All dignity and resistance have been burned out of them. They confess to everything, give up their deepest convictions, and denounce friends and children to the KGB.'

'Could it be back in fashion?' Lene asked. 'Because of the war on terror, for example?'

'I've no idea. It's weird that they've added sulphur groups to the active alkaloid. It's not something you cook up in your kitchen, and it suggests that somebody has been developing it. So who was she, Lene?'

'Do you know something, I think I will have that coffee after all,' Lene said. 'Do you have any cigarettes?'

'I didn't think you smoked?'

Lene shook her head.

'I smoked until I was twenty-five. Sometimes I wish I had never quit.'

'Well, I haven't.'

The medical examiner switched on an electric kettle and spooned Nescafé into two plastic cups.

'Sugar?'

'Yes, please.'

'I haven't got any. I only offered to be polite.'

'Super.'

Lene sipped her coffee.

'I'm not saying that Ain was special,' she said at length. 'Confused and overly sensitive, perhaps. I don't think she found life easy, which is what you would expect from someone who grew up in a refugee camp. Did the tests show up anything else?'

'No.'

'Have you heard about it? Recently, I mean? LSD?'

'In my line of work you hear the odd rumour. Even though we're scientists, the most interesting part of any conference is always the informal chats over coffee breaks. I've always liked toxins. There's something romantic about poison.'

Lene stared at the other woman, and the medical examiner blushed.

'Small green bottles with a skull and crossbones. Am I right?'

Lene nodded slowly. It struck her that you never really knew people as well as you thought you did.

'I guess so,' she said. 'So what do your colleagues talk about during coffee breaks?'

'That the Obama administration no longer favours waterboarding, the simulated drowning of terrorist suspects. They have learned their lesson after Abu Ghraib, Guantánamo, and Bagram.'

'So they're looking for an alternative to beating people half to death or drowning them?' Lene asked.

'Exactly. They're still desperate for the information. And now I hear we're about to go into Mali. So my colleagues talk about truth serums. It's possible that those given it have no recollection afterwards of what they've said, and perhaps that's the most frightening aspect of all.'

Lene pointed towards the low buildings.

'Do you know Irene Adler?'

'She's a star. She has one of the biggest research budgets here at Rigshospitalet. She's charming and looks stunning at receptions and award ceremonies. Do you know her?'

'She treated my daughter. What's her area of research?'

'Let's have a look.'

The young woman looked up PubMed.com, the biggest Internet database of published medical science articles, then she leaned back in her chair.

'Two hundred and thirty-six articles!' she muttered. 'That's unbelievable . . . *Clinical Psychology*, *Journal of Terrorism Research*, *Nature* . . . It goes on and on.'

She looked up.

'At first glance, I would say that she's trying to identify basic traits in people who choose to become terrorists, in particular suicide bombers. She's a busy girl. She wrote her first papers while she was still a medical student.'

'Choose?'

'There's choosing and then there's choosing. You're right.

How many of us ever really choose anything in this life?'

'Where does she get the money from?' Lene asked.

'My guess would be that she employs at least two full-time fundraisers who do nothing but write funding applications. Once this kind of thing starts rolling, it tends to snowball. She's carrying out sexy, relevant, modern research.'

'The USA?'

'The USA, the EU, private money too, of course. Have you spoken to her?'

'I tried,' Lene said. 'It didn't go very well, to put it mildly. She called my boss and accused me of having threatened her.'

'And had you?'

'What with? Messing up her hair or stealing her Gucci bag? I don't know. My memory isn't good these days.'

Lene drained her cup and tossed it in the wastepaper basket. She put on her leather jacket and picked up her shoulder bag from the floor.

'Are you in trouble?' she asked the medical examiner.

'Only if you say something, Lene.'

'You can be damn sure I won't. But save those files somewhere secure, won't you? On a USB stick in your dog's collar, for example.'

The medical examiner smiled.

'Point taken. Incidentally, have you watched the footage? Of course you have.'

'What footage?'

'Nørreport Station is packed with surveillance cameras,'

the doctor said. 'Passive safety measures for girls catching the train alone, late at night. But perhaps they're not even connected.'

'Bollocks,' Lene said, annoyed with herself. 'It did actually cross my mind when I was down there. So why haven't I? You should be doing my job.'

The doctor shuddered.

'Thanks, but no thanks.'

14

From an anonymous dark-blue saloon car two men watched the superintendent cross the car park behind the Institute of Forensic Medicine and get into her own car. She started the engine, turned on the headlights, but the car did not move.

'What's she doing?' asked the younger of the two men, the one with the ponytail.

'She's thinking, or taking a nap,' his partner replied.

The ponytail glanced furtively at his colleague in the driver's seat, Deputy Chief Superintendent Kim Thomsen. Kim had insisted that they were not replaced. That they stayed put. They had slept and eaten in the car for two days and it stank like a student campervan. The ponytail thought that Lene Jensen and his sleepless, tortured colleague were like two peas in a pod. Both fanatics with no thoughts or considerations for anyone other than themselves, with a purpose for which they would sacrifice everyone. He strangled a yawn. But then again, he pondered, that was how the source of the Nile was discovered, and America, and the grave of Tutankhamun . . . by someone with an obsession.

Lene Jensen was a blurred shape in her small Citroën fifty metres away.

A green LED light blinked on a special app on his iPad, and he put on his headphones.

'She's making a call,' he said.

'Who to?'

'Hang on . . . Nazeera. Again.'

He could feel the other man's eyes on him and heard a squeak from stretched vinyl when his colleague tightened his grip on the steering wheel.

'Isn't that the fifth time today?'

'At least.'

'Does she pick up?'

'Of course not. Only the usual: *Hiya, it's Nazeera, leave me an important message or a cute one . . .*'

'And what does she say to that?'

'*Nazeera, my name is Lene Jensen. Call me back. It's about Ain,*' mumbled the ponytail, whose name was Christian Erichsen. 'And her telephone number, even though that must surely show up on the display.'

He took off his headphones and looked up at the medical examiner's office. The doctor walked past the window, put on a black beanie over her short, blonde hair and turned off the desk lamp.

'What have they discovered?' he asked.

'Sweet FA,' Kim said.

'Can that drug be traced?'

'Of course not.'

Kim started the engine the moment the superintendent's Citroën reversed out of the bay and left the car park, even though it was more professional to wait a short while.

Christian heaved a sigh.

They tailed Lene Jensen to Østerbrogade. The superintendent parked, got out and crossed the street deep in thought – and was nearly hit by a taxi. The two men held their breath. The taxi sounded its horn continuously until it was several hundred metres away. The driver had undoubtedly had a shock. The superintendent stood motionless in the street, looking vaguely in the direction of the taxi. Then she continued to the other side and entered a McDonald's.

'Bloody hell,' Kim exhaled.

'Yes, that was close,' Christian said. 'Phew!'

Kim looked down, clenched and unclenched his fingers. He took a deep breath and Christian closed his eyes. He knew what was coming. Yet another pep talk. The third one today. As time went on, Kim appeared increasingly consumed by the urge to convince him – and possibly himself – of the importance of their mission.

'Christian, you know it's happening right now, don't you?' he began. 'I mean right now. Not tomorrow or next week, but right now. Do you understand?'

'I understand,' Christian said and stared into space. Previously his partner had not been totally devoid of a sense of humour, but during this surveillance it had evaporated completely.

Kim continued in the same monotonous tone of voice.

'Right now someone is risking their life for us. For all of us. For Denmark. Right now someone is doing everything they can to make sure that Tivoli never happens again.'

He swallowed something, and Christian shifted uneasily in his seat. Yes, I know, he thought. Stop it, Kim. Please.

'I know!' he said harshly.

The other sat for a while in silence.

'Okay. Then you also know that I'll never, ever allow that lunatic woman over there to ruin everything.'

'What do you have in mind? You can't just shoot her. She is actually on your side.'

'Not mine. She's not on my side.'

'Please stop it.'

Kim smiled a ghostly smile and placed his hand on Christian's thigh. He left it there long enough for it to leave a warm imprint.

'But you're on my side, aren't you?'

'Of course,' he said. And he actually meant it.

There was no way back. They had managed to place a mole exactly where they wanted it: at the very entrance to the cave of mufti Ebrahim Safar Khan, the mass-murdering scholar from Amman, whom they were fairly certain was the architect behind the Tivoli bomb and half a dozen other attacks in the West, and was number two on Barack Obama's kill list. Right now the mole was taking the final steps into the theatre of war that was the Middle East. Right now, as they sat here in Østerbrogade, a Danish spade was making the first stab at digging the grave of Ebrahim Safar Khan. No one had dared to dream about this before.

And it was solely down to Kim's efforts. His persistence and hard work had triumphed over the chronic doubters and conventional thinkers in PET.

The mole, whose codename was Zebra, was Kim's brainchild. He had scouted for the talent and recruited her, nurtured her and trained her. She was a natural, with ice in her veins. And Kim was indispensable. Unstable and fanatical, perhaps, but indispensable. The mole could not be instructed, contacted or handled by anyone else, and everything was too sensitive right now to even think of deploying another lead officer.

The superintendent cleared her tray and headed for the exit.

Christian hoped sincerely that Lene Jensen felt that she had done enough damage for one day; that she would drive home and go to bed so everyone could get a bit of peace and quiet. But one look at the long-legged, determined figure now standing outside the burger bar extinguished his vain hope. Suddenly she looked wide awake.

'Where is she?' Kim asked.

'She's crossing the street.'

'I can bloody see that, Christian! I was talking about Zebra.'

'Sorry . . .'

He clicked on a map on his iPad and zoomed in on a small red cross in the middle of the screen, which currently showed a section of a large, international airport.

'Queen Alia Airport in Jordan. She's not moving. She's probably queuing for passport control.'

Kim nodded. In a few minutes the mole would rent a locker at the airport and deposit all her electronic or mechanical items: her wristwatch, a small FM clock radio, her mobile, which was currently giving them the location of the airport south of Amman, her laptop and even her credit cards, if they were fitted with a chip.

If Ebrahim Safar Khan's bodyguards found anything that could even remotely be interpreted as a GPS tracking unit, she would be tortured, raped, shot. One day Jordanian police would discover her charred remains in the burned-out wreck of a car, or someone would find her on a skip when the dogs had torn the plastic bags off the body.

'Good luck,' Christian muttered, as his partner started the engine and followed the superintendent's car.

It took her only a few minutes to drive down Jagtvej, cross Vibenshus Runddel and head into the city centre. The small Citroën reduced its speed and squeezed in front of a box van outside a kiosk opposite the flat of the late Ain Ghazzawi Rasmussen.

Christian did not dare to look at his partner.

15

The dilapidated medical clinic on Omar Al Mokhtar Street in Amman served as Ebrahim Safar Khan's reception. The set-up was simple. Either you convinced staff that your intentions were honourable and that you therefore deserved to leave the building by your own efforts, or you ended up in the back, swaddled and placed in a cheap pine coffin with a fake death certificate nailed to the lid – the diagnosis usually being heart failure, which two bullets to the chest would indeed induce.

Zebra had never found it easy to undress in the large, tiled room while the fat woman in the filthy medical coat exchanged quiet and apparently humorous comments about her trimmed pubic hair with the ever-present young men in jeans, leather jackets, sunglasses and machine guns. It had not become easier for her to tolerate the woman's probing, gloved fingers in all her bodily orifices, after which she was ordered up onto a truly disgusting examination couch where she was scanned with a dangerously crackling, antique X-ray machine. But she had learned to go inside herself, to find a safe place.

The fat woman expressed sadistic disappointment when she found nothing suspicious on or inside Zebra. She threw her clothes on the tiles in front of her and Zebra got dressed, while the guards politely turned their backs. She almost succeeded in ignoring the solid wooden chair with leather straps, bolted to the floor in the centre of the room, covered in dark-brown trails which could only be dried blood that refused to be scrubbed off.

She followed the men outside. The dusty, battered Toyota that had picked her up at the airport had been replaced with a yellow Mercedes that looked as if it had been in service since the Flood. The driver could have been Noah's grandfather. The three young men got into a battered black van behind them.

A withered, ancient hand gestured Zebra closer. The car radio's din of atonal, Arabic music filled the quiet street. She opened the back door, threw in her bag and got in the passenger seat at the front. The geriatric with the goatee put a pair of enormous sunglasses lined with black felt over her eyes.

'You okay, miss?'

Her few possessions had been searched outside the airport and every seam in her clothes checked. Her new, expensive Tom Ford sunglasses had been tossed into the gutter and crushed under a heel. New safety precautions.

She nodded and pulled her scarf closer together at her neck and over her lower face.

'Period?'

'It's all right, you can talk Arabic to me,' she said.

The man continued in his broken English. Perhaps he was proud of it.

'Period, miss?'

'Period?'

She sensed movement in the air. Perhaps his hands were miming a shape; it was utterly futile as she could not see a thing.

'Moon?'

It was unbearably hot inside the car, even though Zebra had noticed a ridiculously small whirring fan on the dashboard between the prayer beads dangling from the rear-view mirror. The sun was hammering down on the yellow metal roof. At last she realized what the old man meant: was she menstruating? In which case that would be awkward for the mufti, the holy Sheikh Ebrahim Safar Khan, and the manner of the visit would have to be changed. The holy man could not be in the same room as an unclean woman.

'No moon. No period,' she mumbled.

'You sure?'

'Yes! Can we go now, please? I have to catch a plane out of here in three hours.'

'Water?'

'From a sealed bottle?'

'Sure.'

She heard the cap being twisted off and felt the cold

plastic neck against her lips. She drank greedily. Her stomach rumbled and she pressed her fingers against her abdomen. The diesel engine started with a cough and the taxi was put into first gear with a clatter.

'Not far,' the old man shouted to drown out the music and the engine.

'Great,' she muttered.

It was never the same place, but always the same kind of place; low, square houses with flat roofs, a courtyard with whitewashed concrete walls, where the ever-patrolling young men cast black shadows. White plastic garden chairs. At times, a babbling fountain. And children. The everyday voices of women, whom she never saw, from the living rooms nearby, and the smell of food.

This was home more than any other place in the world. There was always a television turned on somewhere, but never, ever a ringing telephone. The skies over Jordan were stuffed with spy satellites and drones. A few careless words spoken by the mufti or one of his trusted staff on a mobile phone would trigger a short, unstoppable sequence of events: in an air-conditioned control centre in Langley, Virginia, a signal officer would identify the voice using specialist software and a Predator drone would fall out of the sky over Amman like a small, lethal metal splinter. In a matter of seconds its thermal cameras would zoom in on its target and a Hellfire missile would swallow up Ebrahim Safar Khan and all his women, children, advisers, dogs, donkeys, neighbours and guards in a fireball with the same core temperature as the sun.

She did not react when she heard the wheelchair stop near her head. She focused all her attention on the Persian carpet's intricate red and blue pattern when the brakes were engaged. She was not the first person to kneel here. Where Zebra's forehead touched the carpet, the thread had almost been worn away. She bowed even deeper until she heard the squeaky geriatric voice above her.

'*Assalamu alaikum*, little daughter. You're here. That is good. You have come, you have come, my daughter. Your visits are all too rare, which only makes it so much better to see you, daughter.'

'*Walaikum assalam*, learned father.'

'Let me see you,' Safar Khan said, and she knew that there were no other women in the room.

She rocked back on her knees and removed the scarf from her face. She did not look straight at Khan, obviously, but she could smell peppermint on his breath.

'Look at me,' he said.

She blinked and looked up. Ebrahim Safar Khan's white beard reached the third button of his red waistcoat, a couple of hands' widths above the rhino horn handle of his dagger. He wore the white crocheted skullcap of the believer on his head and thick, smoke-coloured glasses, which concentrated the gaze in his dark, cold, runny eyes. Frequent use of the hookah had left yellow stripes in his beard.

Khan scrutinized her face. Then he nodded.

'Sit down, my daughter.'

He gestured towards a low stool. Sitting in the presence of Safar Khan was the ultimate favour. She smiled and sat down, but took care that her face remained reserved and respectful.

The mufti folded his long hands in his lap. From a corner, one of Khan's adjutants watched her with burning eyes: a mullah who undoubtedly viewed her as an amoral whore because she bared her face among men, even if it was at Khan's own order. Zebra ignored him. She knew his type. God, how she knew it.

Outside the window openings a couple of guards were watching her without expression.

Safar Khan leaned forward as if to ease his sore lower back.

'All is well?'

Zebra nodded.

'All is well, learned father.'

'And no one suspects anything? You live your life?'

'I live my life, father, and no one suspects a thing. It's the shadow life which you have taught me, but I live it because it is necessary.'

Khan aimed a remote control at a plasma screen leaning up against the wall. Like most buildings in Amman the house had two satellite dishes, one facing east and one west. He clicked it in vain. The adjutant gently took the remote control from the old man's hands and found Al Jazeera, the pan-Arabic TV channel.

Zebra watched the screen. NATO's Danish Secretary General was standing behind a lectern in the organization's headquarters in Brussels with the blue four-pointed compass star in the background. He accounted for NATO's joint military deployment in Mali and Niger against the holy warriors of Al-Qaeda, who were once again spilling in from the desert and threatening oil and natural gas installations in the vast, sparsely populated desert states. The camera cut to a dusty desert road somewhere in Mali where armed personnel carriers sent up columns of dust in the blue, stagnant air. Weather-beaten, camouflage-clad soldiers were sitting or lying on the beds of the trucks and the Dannebrog, the Danish flag, fluttered from a long antenna.

The adjutant swore into his sparse, black beard, while the mufti sat without moving. He nodded and the plasma screen turned grey and then black.

Safar Khan looked at her.

'As you can see, our work is not yet finished,' he said.

'Our work is not yet finished because the Danes have not learned the dangers of spilling the blood of Islam.'

'How is the mood in your little country?'

Zebra smiled.

'They have no leads. They fly in Americans and Israelis to tell them what to do, to train them, but it's hopeless. They have only the faces we give them, father, and those faces lead them nowhere.'

The mufti appeared content. He made a signal to the

young mullah, who left the room. Lost in his own thoughts, Safar Khan filled a small brass cup with coffee as viscous as syrup and sipped the black drink. He pulled a face and pressed his hand against his stomach.

'I should not drink coffee. It gives me acid indigestion. And I should not smoke so much sweet tobacco either, but it's hard to change your habits when you're old.'

Zebra nodded. She was overcome by the urge to put her hand on the knee of the mufti to show sympathy, like a good daughter would have done, but that was obviously out of the question.

'Are we waiting for anyone, great Khan?' she asked.

He looked past her and had turned his wheelchair to face the courtyard, when two young men entered and kneeled on the cheap, cracked tiles. They pressed their foreheads against the floor. The adjutant placed a worn leather bag behind them and resumed his position by the wall.

The mufti held out his hands to bless the new arrivals and asked them to sit up so that he could see their faces. There was music in the old man's voice, as if they were two favourite sons who had returned home after a too-long absence. The mufti rolled his wheelchair closer so that they could kiss his hands. Then he deftly turned the chair one hundred and eighty degrees so that he could look at Zebra at the same time.

'You know Samir and Fadr,' he said.

Zebra smiled at the two young men. Samir, the elder,

was handsome. His long, black hair reached his shoulders; his eyes behind the dense eyelashes were golden and large, and his facial features masculine and even. The only feature marring his appearance was a strange, star-shaped scar to his left temple, white against the dark, smooth skin. He returned Zebra's smile, then averted his eyes.

'*Assalamu alaikum*,' he muttered.

Zebra closed her palms in front of her chest.

'*Walaikum assalam*, Samir. Are you well?'

'I'm well, sister.'

Fadr with the flimsy moustache over his cleft palate nodded and smiled, and they greeted each other like brother and sister.

Safar Khan wheeled his chair behind the two kneeling men, who kept looking straight ahead. The adjutant picked up the bag from the floor and placed it in the lap of the mufti.

Khan looked gravely at Zebra across the kneeling men's heads.

'Our movement is small but lethal, like a newborn cobra. It is lethal because we know each other, and because no outsiders can endanger us. We are strong because we believe, because we are pure, because we live, concealed and hidden, in the shadows of centuries. We fear nothing because we see ourselves as of the next world. We are chaste. We do not fear Israel or the Christian Crusaders. We are trusting like children in the assurance that we are loved by God.'

He leaned forward and placed a hand on Fadr's shoulder. The boy jumped and frowned and he looked at Zebra as if searching for something in her face. She shook her head lightly while the mufti continued.

'Chastity, Fadr. Does that mean anything to you?'

The boy smiled.

'Of course.'

The mufti opened the bag on his lap and let a handful of DVDs cascade to the floor in front of the young man. The movies scattered across the tiles and Zebra leaned forward. *Rocco Ravages Ibiza*, *Teen Gangbang*, *Double Anal Penetration* . . . A mosaic of female orifices, all straining with huge, glistening dicks.

'Father—' the boy began.

'Silence!'

This was the true voice of Safar Khan, Zebra thought; no longer squeaky or rusty, but clear like the sound of a bell. It was a voice schooled to travel across the roofs of a city and call the faithful to prayer.

Fadr buried his face in his hands. Behind him, the paralysed mufti rose miraculously from his wheelchair. Something long and gleaming was passed through a window opening, and the old man clasped the handle of the sabre with both hands and raised it high. Fadr's fingers slipped away from his face and again he looked at Zebra. His lips moved, but made no sound.

Then the blade swooped through the air and cleaved

his head, from the top of his scalp halfway down to the eyebrows, with the sharpest, driest sound in the world. The boy's arms and legs straightened out electrically, for a second he squinted at the half-metre of arched steel sticking out from his forehead, then he slumped forward without a sound, while Zebra screamed loudly on his behalf. Samir kneeled beside her to restrain her. She tried freeing herself, but he was too strong and held her easily. Then she gave up and the last few seconds replayed in her mind.

This had to be impossible. Before Ebrahim Safar Khan became the most skilful puppet master of suicide bombers in the Middle East, he had been a professor of Middle Eastern Studies in London, and dozens of photographs and recordings existed of him from the university. Pictures of him teaching, as well as from conventions and conferences in which he had participated. He had walked on his own two feet until a traffic accident in 1998, but never since then. Everyone knew that. She knew it better than most.

When the terrible blow fell, Zebra's gaze had brushed Samir's face. He had not even blinked when his friend's skull was cleaved. Samir had known it was going to happen, she thought. Perhaps he had found the films; perhaps he had betrayed his friend. She must not underestimate Samir. He was much more than a pretty face. Safar Khan had looked at the young man with genuine devotion, even respect.

'Sit up, my daughter.'

Once again, the mufti was back in his wheelchair, resting

his thin hands on the arm rests. For a while he looked at the floor with regret, before he gave a signal. Young bodyguards carried the boy out into the courtyard, where a modern hospital stretcher was waiting. A couple of uniformed paramedics placed electrodes on Fadr's chest and quickly, and with expert skill, inserted a specialized plastic tube down his throat and established intravenous access. One of them started resuscitating the boy with a black rubber balloon while the other connected the electrodes from his heart to a monitor.

The scene was demonic and surreal, and the bile rose up in her throat. Now she remembered that in the seconds before the execution, she had heard the distant siren of an ambulance. An elderly man with gold-framed spectacles and wearing a clean white hospital coat arrived and quickly whittled the sabre out of the boy's head. The cut was bleeding surprisingly little. They applied a temporary, tight bandage with thick, blue gauze compresses. The doctor shone a light into both eyes, and walked across to the window opening. He greeted Khan reverently with his palms on his chest and forehead.

'*Assalamu alaikum*, my sheikh. A masterly blow. The boy is dead, but not dead.'

'You're sure?'

'I am but human, Safar Khan, but that is my assessment. His heart is beating.'

'Good. Then take him with you and get him ready.'

The doctor bowed deeply and the stretcher was rolled to the waiting ambulance.

Zebra pulled herself together. She knew that she was being watched and judged.

'Samir, remove the films,' Khan said.

Samir picked up the films, tossing them into the leather bag as if they were tainted, and put the bag on the windowsill from where invisible hands took it away.

Safar Khan scratched his beard and looked at Zebra. He made an apologetic gesture towards the courtyard.

'It wasn't the films, my daughter. As such. I understand the films. They are vile, but Fadr is young and it is the way of the world and man's desire, wouldn't you agree?'

She nodded and Khan continued.

'I was young once. I was of this world. What was unforgivable was that Fadr bought the movies in Copenhagen.'

'In Copenhagen?'

'In the kiosk opposite the flat. Samir told me that Fadr left the flat once—'

'To buy cigarettes,' Samir interjected.

'It is normal to buy cigarettes, but fifteen pornography films?' Khan asked. 'Hardly. He'll be remembered by the owner and might have been seen by cameras in the shop. Don't you agree, my daughter?'

'Yes.'

Khan smiled faintly.

'Fadr will be infinitely more useful as a dead shell with a beating heart than he ever was alive.'

Zebra smiled enthusiastically.

'And you can walk, great Khan! It's a miracle. Allah be praised!'

At first she thought that she had gone too far. Much too far. The young mullah who had returned to the room and was standing once more like a pillar of salt at the furthest wall watched her with a gaze that ought to reduce her to ashes. Even the much more level-headed Samir narrowed his eyes as if he was in pain.

The old man winked. Then he threw back his head and laughed with a cackle and revealed a fortune in gold teeth. She could feel the whole room expanding in relief.

'Never show anyone who you are, my daughter, not the living or the dead, your friends or your enemies. Never! Remember that. It's more important for you now than it ever was.'

'I will remember that,' she said.

16

Khan invited his advisers to the table. A woman brought fresh coffee, sherbet and fruit. Once more he rose from his wheelchair, stretched and wandered noiselessly around in his goatskin slippers.

'Samir, did you find what I asked you for in Russia?'

Samir opened a black sports bag. He placed two objects on the tiles: vests with pockets stitched on, the pockets wider and flatter than usual, and the charges not connected with visible cables. The vests were made from dark-grey neoprene, the same material used for wetsuits.

'They were expensive, Khan. But worth the money, I think. Modern. They take up much less room than the old Semtex vests. You can wear this under a jacket without anyone being any the wiser. The explosive is isopropyl nitrate. There isn't a sniffer dog in all the world that can detect it, and the trigger is built into an ordinary mobile phone.'

He pulled a flat, transparent plastic bag filled with balls the size of peas out of the pocket and handed it to Safar Khan, who massaged the bag pensively between his fingers.

'The bag is armoured and very strong,' Samir said. 'The balls are made from glass, but are just as effective as lead or steel bullets at a distance of fifty metres.'

Safar Khan passed the bag with the miraculous glass balls to his sombre-looking adjutant.

'Excellent,' he said. 'So the vest can pass through a metal detector?'

Samir smiled.

'Of course. It's invisible. The wearer is able to move about freely. The explosive cells are connected with fibre-optic cables. There's no metal in the cables. Only silicon, mirrors and . . . light.'

Safar Khan clapped his hands in delight.

'Light! The Prophet loves you, Samir!'

The young man smiled and bowed his head modestly. Zebra tried to keep her face neutral and her eyes aimed at the floor because she knew that the smouldering jealousy she felt must not be revealed under any circumstances. Her hunch had been correct: Samir was the chosen one. Not her. Samir would carry out Khan's orders and be the sheikh's extended hand and brain, and she had to obey.

She breathed deeply a couple of times and then risked looking up. Samir calmly met her gaze. There was no triumph in his expression, but she knew that he was aware of her disappointment.

'The question now is when and where,' Khan said.

'Perhaps our sister can contribute?' Samir suggested in a friendly voice.

She flashed him a brief, frosty smile.

'I have several suggestions, father, with your permission?'

He nodded graciously and Zebra reeled off dates, times, guards, media presence and access.

The adjutant placed a hookah next to Khan's wheelchair and lit it for the old man. A spicy aroma of tobacco and apples wafted across the room under its low ceiling, while the mufti listened to her without interruption.

Then he nodded pensively.

'You mention several good targets, my daughter. But we have very little time to plan, am I right?'

She could feel the blood rise to her face.

'I know, father. But the quicker the better, in my opinion. And with the new vests—'

'But why this haste?'

'They're catching up. Soon they'll have finished checking the photographs from Tivoli. They will find a lead and then my position will be difficult. If it's to be in my country, then I think we should strike as soon as possible. The borders are better guarded now and it won't be so easy to get into Europe next time.'

She fell silent and the hookah bubbled.

Khan looked at her, then shifted his gaze to Samir and nodded one millimetre.

Zebra knew that this was her cue.

'Give me your blessing, father.'

She kneeled down.

'You have my blessing. I will think about what you have said.'

He placed his hand on her head for a second.

'Samir . . . would you?'

The young man accompanied her outside to the waiting taxi. The driver appeared to be asleep or dead, and Samir stuck his arm through the side window and sounded the horn. The old man jerked and swore out loud.

Samir held open the door for her.

'Your ideas aren't bad, little sister,' he said as he closed the car door after her. 'Not bad at all.'

'Thank you,' she muttered dryly.

She could still hear the swish from the sabre when she closed her eyes.

'We were expecting them to be guarding their borders better. It won't be as easy next time,' he said.

To her enormous irritation, Samir's smile was rather patronizing. She believed she had proved her worth just as much as he had.

'We'll think of something, *insha' Allah*,' he said. 'Be ready. We'll find a way in.'

Zebra stuck her hand out of the open side window and Samir studied it for a moment before he carefully took it. She let the tips of her fingers glide lightly over his palm and moistened her lips at the same time. She was sure that he noticed the tip of her tongue.

'Goodbye, little brother,' she said and looked right at him.

He blushed under her gaze. She knew she could still have anyone. Except for the mufti and his young, fanatical adjutant, of course. And yet. If they had urges, she could have them.

'Airport, miss?'

With a great effort the old man turned around in the driver's seat and looked at her. There were small, yellow clumps of sleep in the corners of his eyes.

Zebra flashed him a smile.

'Yes, please. And turn the music on!'

She opened her handbag, found her make-up compact and studied her face. She inflated her cheeks slightly and observed the effects. The lips could be made fuller, the nose slightly wider. The hair colour was no problem. She knew exactly which target she herself would pick in Copenhagen. The rest was merely preparation.

17

Lene's heart was beating surprisingly fast as she stood on the landing outside Ain's back door, and she had to convince herself again that it was her right and duty to be where she was and do what she was about to do.

The door was fitted with an old-fashioned lock and there were no painted-over cables along the skirting board to indicate an alarm system. Behind the neighbouring kitchen door a dog was barking, a child was screaming and a woman was trying to silence them both.

Lene tried the handle on Ain's kitchen door, but it did not budge. She had seen Michael walk through doors as if they were air, armed with his lock picks, but she had no tools. She started counting in her head to pass the time and had got as far as thirty-five, when the neighbour's kitchen fell silent. Then she took a step backwards and kicked the woodwork under the handle, hard and with precision. The door sprang open with a short, splintering crash.

She could make out black-and-white floor tiles in the dark kitchen. She froze, listening out for any reaction to the noise from next door, but could hear only the dog and the sound of a television being turned on.

Then she closed the door behind her, turned on the ceiling light and looked around; a fridge humming faintly, a stale smell, impersonal. There were a dozen fridge magnets on the fridge, but no pictures, reminders, postcards or unpaid bills. Perhaps Ain's adoptive parents had taken them. She removed the ice cube tray from the freezer compartment, pulled out kitchen drawers and opened cupboards at random without finding anything that was not normal, neat, tidy and like millions of other homes. She ran her fingers behind the cupboards, explored every nook and cranny using her small torch. Nothing.

A heavy-footed resident was wandering around, coughing above her head. The dog next door started barking again, but it was quiet in the girl's flat. On a row of pegs in the hallway there was a dark woolly beanie, a pink pashmina and a pretty suede jacket. There was a cupboard with a Hoover and cleaning materials and next to the cupboard there was a large mirror on the wall. She continued through to a bedroom, which was bare and cold like a convent cell. The iron bedstead was narrow and chaste and covered with a white, crocheted blanket. There was not a single picture or poster in here; only the bed, the white walls, a bedside table and a wardrobe.

Like a welcome, the inside of the wardrobe and the clothes themselves gave off a fresh citrus perfume she did not recognize. Lene opened a drawer at the bottom of the wardrobe and held up a handful of knickers, bras and G-strings as delicate as cobwebs. There would appear to have been a limit to Ain's modesty, she thought.

Again she looked at the narrow bed and then at the lingerie.

There must have been another side to the neurotic and tormented girl: a confident young woman, proud of her body.

She kneeled down in front of the bedside table and opened the door. There was nothing in there she would not have expected to find in the home of any other modern young woman – except for a five-centimetre-long strip of tape on the back of the door. A certain type of 3M tape which Lene had seen countless times at various crime scenes, because crime scene technicians across the globe used it to lift fingerprints from hard surfaces.

She pulled the tape off the wood, folded it and stuck it in her pocket.

Lene was in the living room, looking at a poster of a tipsy cat drinking green absinthe when someone tried the front door.

A man coughed on the landing outside.

'Ain?'

The letter box clattered like a guillotine.

'Ain?'

Lene held her breath.

'Open up, damn you!'

With her heart in her throat, she ran on tiptoe through the kitchen, turned off the ceiling light, stepped out onto the dark back stairs and straight into something round and hard that smashed into her abdomen with great force. A figure loomed in her diminishing field of vision. Lene was about to fall backwards when large hands reached out and kept her upright.

The man said nothing while Lene was overcome by an uncontrollable burning urge to curl up around the huge, empty pain in her stomach.

After what seemed like an eternity, she managed to get a little air into her lungs and, at the same time, became aware of the body of another attacker behind her. Her head was forced backwards as the attacker behind her grabbed a handful of her long hair and yanked it hard.

'But,' she whispered in a thin, strained voice. 'I . . . fuck . . . hey, listen . . .'

A sack was pulled over her head, and Lene could not remember ever being so blind and disoriented. A cord under her chin was tightened, and she started pleading on her last exhale, convinced that they were about to strangle her.

She could smell the attacker behind her and guessed his location. She launched a final, desperate counter-attack by flinging her head back hard, and felt the top of her skull make contact with something simultaneously soft, firm and yielding . . . like a face, for example.

The attacker behind her screamed out loud, but the arm

remained in place around her neck and her head was jerked backwards again until her vertebrae started creaking and sliding. She arched with the movement while at the same time kicking out with all her strength at the attacker in front of her.

She heard a stunned, anguished roar as she recognized the rubbery, bouncy feel of a man's genitals against her instep. It was not the first time she had kicked a man in the groin, but every time it was strangely satisfying.

They put her on her stomach on the small landing, her hands were twisted behind her back and she felt the cold plastic of a cable tie slide around her wrists.

She tried protesting from the absolute darkness of the sack, but received a hard kick to the back of her head. Time stood still and a bottomless darkness opened up.

18

Otto Jarl Falster, permanent secretary at the Interior Ministry, could not remember when he had last enjoyed an uninterrupted night's sleep. Previously he had always slept like a baby; he lived an ordered life and ate healthily, his wife of twenty-eight years saw to that. He drank only in moderation, did not smoke, detested business dinners and protracted official lunches, played thirty-six holes of golf every week and cycled both summer and winter from their home in Hellerup to his office on Slotsholmen.

But ever since he got a new minister two years ago, and especially since his wife had been appointed to coordinate the police and intelligence investigations into the Tivoli bombing, every single night had been interrupted by countless telephone calls for his wife and stomach-acid-inducing worries about his own minister's inadequacy.

The young woman was quite simply hopeless. Her qualifications were essentially her gender, her youth, a relatively photogenic face and her descent from a left-wing political dynasty. A dynasty that had supplied members to Denmark's parliament for several generations and at this point was suited for little else, like a family of circus acrobats. The minister's only contact with the real world had been her time as head of the student council at a provincial sixth form college, and three years reading PPE at university.

These days the permanent secretary was sleeping like Nero, the family's cat: on tenterhooks, lightly, and always with one eye half open. Listening to the darkness.

Tonight, his wife's mobile rang at one-thirty and the permanent secretary opened his eyes and watched the stuccoed ceiling when the light on his wife's bedside table was turned on.

Otto Jarl Falster placed a pyjama-clad arm over his eyes and heaved a sigh. He had already aired the possibility of converting a redundant nursery into a separate bedroom, but his wife would not hear talk of it. 'Then we would never see each other, Otto darling,' she said, with a veiled reference to their active and varied sex life.

He decided to raise the subject again as soon as the next opportunity arose. But not right now; his wife sounded unusually agitated.

'What?!' she cried and fired off questions with the speed of a machine gun. 'Where? Who? NOW?! In her flat? Do nothing, do you understand? I'm on my way.'

'Christ on a bike,' he groaned as he felt stomach acid burn his throat.

The cat leaped down from the end of their bed, where it

normally spent the night, and walked off with a wounded expression.

He closed his eyes and felt the weight in the bed shift as his wife swung her legs over the side and got up. He heard an angry, static crackling as she pulled a blouse over her head, and the short, whirring sound of a zip.

'Who was it?' he asked. Not because he was terribly interested, more to show a kind of empathy.

'No one,' she mumbled.

'What do you mean no one?'

'Please be quiet, Otto. I actually mean no one.'

'Then come back to bed.'

'You know I can't, darling.'

She muttered to herself while pulling on her boots. 'What is going on? Just what *is* going on? Has everyone gone completely insane?'

He thought about his minister.

'I couldn't agree more,' he said. 'Let's emigrate to French Polynesia.'

She leaned across him and he picked up the scent of Cerruti 1881. He loved it and tried to grab her.

She slapped him across his fingers and kissed him lightly on his forehead.

'I really do have to go.'

'Are you really the only one who knows which way is up these days? For God's sake, Charlotte, you're the boss. Did they blow up Parliament?'

'Not yet, but you would like that, wouldn't you?'

Otto Jarl Falster toyed with the idea. A deep feeling of peace and warmth spread through him.

'That would be wonderful,' he said. 'Only if nobody got hurt, of course.'

'Of course.'

The permanent secretary turned onto his side and gazed after her. His wife was still slim and upright although she had given birth to two children, and her movements were quick and focused. They had met at Mahout, the old fencing club. He was a beginner with the foil and she had shown him no mercy and sent him home with bruises all over his chest.

He heaved another sigh, rolled across the mattress and turned off her bedside light.

19

Lene did not know how long she had been unconscious, and
she had no wish to wake up again. Why would she?

When she came round the next time, she discovered that
the cell's furnishing consisted of a black mattress covered in
rubber. A sharp, white light came from an armoured fitting
in the ceiling, out of reach. There was a stainless-steel toilet
bowl in a corner, but the toilet roll dispenser was empty.
The cell stank of vomit and urine. The walls were tiled and
graffiti-proof.

Lene crawled across the floor and threw up.

She stretched out and slowly staggered to her feet, while
she looked down herself. Someone had removed the plastic
ties around her wrists and the hood over her head. She
unbuttoned her shirt and discovered a broad, tender blue
bruise across her abdomen and lower ribs. She rubbed the
back of her head and winced when her fingers made contact
with a longish swelling at the base of her neck. Then she
discovered a cut to her scalp where the hair was matted
together with blood. She remembered head-butting one of

her attackers and that someone had subsequently kicked her in the head.

The cell door was a grey steel surface. She pressed her ear against it, but could hear only her own heartbeat.

'Hello? . . . HEY?! . . . FUCK!'

Lene slammed the palms of her hands against the door, but it did not budge one millimetre. She kicked it, but only succeeded in hurting her toes. Then she sat down on the mattress with her back against the cold, tiled wall and covered her eyes with her hands.

She had no idea where she was or what time it was.

She was stretching out her legs when she remembered the fingerprint tape in her jeans pocket. She found the sticky strip and held it up against the light. At least that was real. She curled up on her side with the tape between her fingers as if it was a small beacon in a big, dark, hostile world.

She woke up again at the sound of jingling keys. The door was opened and she could hear light footsteps cross the floor. She opened her eyes a little and through the gap saw a pair of high-heeled, black boots right next to her face. The boots led up to a pair of well-pressed, grey trouser legs and higher up she discovered Charlotte Falster's expressionless face.

'Are you able to stand up?' she asked.

'Where am I?'

'PET headquarters in Søborg.'

Lene looked at her blankly.

'PET?'

'Yes.'

'As in the Danish intelligence service?'

'Exactly. Where did you think you were?'

Lene ran a weary hand across her forehead and whimpered faintly.

'Duh, where else . . . obviously.'

The chief superintendent reached down and pulled her to her feet. Even though Charlotte was a head shorter and of a slimmer build than Lene, she was surprisingly strong.

Lene touched her ribs.

'Ouch . . .'

'What happened?'

'I was hoping that you could tell me.'

'I mean, physically?'

'I took a beating,' Lene said.

'Come with me.'

She followed her boss down a sterile, well-lit corridor with grey steel doors. Their heels echoed on the floor tiles. A tap was running behind one of the doors and someone was singing in Arabic.

'You're in trouble,' Charlotte said without turning around. 'Big trouble.'

'Yes, I know.'

'I'm not sure you do.'

Charlotte stopped and Lene nearly collided with her. It began to dawn on her that her boss was absolutely apoplectic with rage. Her eyes narrowed and flashed maliciously; the thin neck muscles over Charlotte's navy-blue suit collar were long and strained.

'Didn't I tell you to stay away from Ain?' she hissed. 'I distinctly remember giving you a clear and direct order to forget about the girl and do your job. I also remember you promising me with all your heart to drop the girl and focus on Borders and Access with Bjarne. Do you know how many people think you're unsuited to any kind of police work now? Or that the cleaners have found that little cupboard where you thought you could hide your empties? Or that everybody regards you as my private and utterly misplaced charity project?'

'Sorry, but . . .'

She did not know what to say.

Lene noticed that the other woman's lipstick had been applied slapdash to her upper lip. Charlotte really must be beside herself.

'But surely that doesn't give them the right to attack me,' she objected.

'Right now they can do whatever the hell they like! PET regards you as a direct threat to their most sensitive operation. You don't know the big picture, Lene, but you're about to wreck it.'

'It was purely vindictive,' she protested. 'Since when is it all right for police officers to attack each other? And what is the big picture? Why don't you tell me? Why the hell is Ain so bloody important that I can't approach her flat without being beaten to a pulp?'

'You'll find out in a moment – even though you don't deserve to know because, right now, the end does justify the means. And that applies to everyone! If, just for once, you could look beyond your own tragedy, you would see that Denmark is in crisis. You're not the only one to have lost someone. The relatives of one thousand, two hundred and forty-one dead Tivoli visitors have lost just as much – and some more, much more. Not to mention the hundreds of people who were maimed or wounded. Perhaps you should use the pitiful remnants of your brain to contemplate that fact.'

Charlotte looked as if she was far from finished, but then turned on her heel and walked away, up an echoing metal staircase.

PET's headquarters were quiet before dawn. Lene spotted a couple of female police officers chatting by the coffee machine. They fell silent when they saw the battered super-intendent and her boss. Charlotte turned a corner, opened a soundproof door and let Lene enter first.

The room was a standard interview room with a wooden table and four uncomfortable plastic chairs that could not be used effectively as a weapon. A couple of microphones had been suspended from the ceiling, a two-way mirror had been concreted into the wall and there was a video camera mounted in each corner. A laptop hummed on the table. Lene's effects – purse, keys, Maglite torch and mobile – lay next to a plastic water carafe.

She had time to think how lucky it was that she had hidden Ain's smartphone under the front seat of her Citroën before she realized that they had company. A young blond man with a ponytail, wearing a blood-stained leather jacket, was pressing an icepack over his nose and lower jaw. He looked at her without smiling. Lene could make out a black shoulder holster and the muzzle of a pistol under his left armpit.

Leaning against the wall was an athletic, prematurely greying man in his early forties with his body weight distributed evenly between his trainers, his legs apart; presumably the man she had kicked in the groin on Ain's back stairs. He was just as motionless as his partner, but his eyes were different. They were empty, black and devoid of pity.

She recognized the PET agent from the American's briefing at Copenhagen Police Headquarters. They had sat in the same row, and the agent had asked the American questions, she could not remember about what. On the way out he had overtaken her and got into a dark-blue Ford Mondeo.

Charlotte placed her hand on her shoulder, gestured to a chair and sat down on the other side of the table.

'The young man sitting down is Superintendent Christian Erichsen from PET,' Charlotte introduced him.

Lene nodded and the man held up a hand.

'You broke my nose and knocked out two of my front teeth,' he said in a thick voice. 'I hope you're proud of yourself.'

'I'm sorry, perhaps you should have told me who you were or listened to what I was trying to say. I don't like being attacked.'

'Perhaps we should have done that.'

He was not as cold as the other, Lene thought.

'And this is Deputy Chief Superintendent Kim Thomsen,' Charlotte said. 'He's heading PET's investigation into Tivoli.'

'You've been following me,' Lene said as several pieces fell into place. She remembered the dark-blue saloon, which had imitated her hazardous U-turn by Trianglen. She hated herself for being so blind, deaf, vulnerable and stupid. 'Why?'

'Because you're poking your nose into things you don't understand.' Kim's voice was low, but icy. 'And because you were about to ruin several years' intelligence work.'

The agent with the ponytail removed the icepack from his face.

'We didn't follow you; we bumped into you when we were monitoring one of Ain's close friends. It wasn't personal . . . not to begin with. You were the one who made it personal.'

'Nazeera?'

'Nazeera Gamil, yes.'

He pressed the icepack to his face again.

'But why?'

'Why what?'

'Why are you watching Nazeera? And why have you checked Ain's flat for fingerprints?'

Lene found the piece of tape with the red iodine powder in her pocket and placed it on the table.

Charlotte leaned forward and studied the tape with a frown. Then she folded her arms across her chest and looked at Kim Thomsen.

'I give you permission to answer, Kim,' she said, loud and clear, for the benefit of the microphones.

'Are you quite sure?' the PET agent asked, looking at Lene as if she was something he had scraped off the sole of his shoe after walking his dog.

'I am,' Charlotte said.

He waddled across the floor, sat down with a groan, turned a laptop towards himself and logged on. Lene got up to look over his shoulder. He smelled of stale sweat. There was a pale band of skin on his left ring finger where his wedding ring used to be.

The PET agent clicked to open a high-resolution photograph on the screen, and pointed.

'The woman in the foreground is Elsa Valerius-Klüver,' he began monotonously. 'She's fifty-six years old and she was standing outside Restaurant Picasso in Tivoli at ten forty-six on the 17th September last year. The photographer is her husband Åke Valerius-Klüver, aged fifty-eight. The couple live in Södertälje in Sweden and were in Denmark on a camping holiday. Do you follow?'

'Åke and Elsa. Camping. And?'

Kim blinked irritably.

'This.'

He highlighted a rectangle to the right of the smiling woman in the floral summer dress and pink Crocs, and zoomed in on the shadows between the restaurant and the adjacent amusement arcade, where two young people were talking. Lene leaned forward. The girl had good posture, a narrow waist and wore a standard waitress uniform: practical black shoes, black trousers, a long white apron and a short-sleeved white shirt. Her face was clearly visible.

'Ain,' she stated.

'Your suicidal friend,' he nodded.

Christian interjected, 'Åke Valerius-Klüver is a civil engineer and, like every other civil engineer I've met, he's an anally fixated pedant. In his spare time he's a keen wildlife photographer specializing in predatory birds and his camera is top of the range. He uploaded a series of pictures on Rigspolitiet's Tivoli portal on the Internet last December, because he's a responsible member of society. These are the original images from the memory card.'

Lene pointed to the other figure.

'Who is he?'

'The bomber,' Kim said.

'What?'

'Nabil Maroun, an eighteen-year-old mass murderer

from Damascus, almost as successful as Mohamed al-Amir Atta,' the deputy chief superintendent said laconically.

The picture quality became grainier when the agent enlarged the highlighted section. A faded blue baseball cap had been pulled deep down over the young man's forehead. He was wearing a light-coloured anorak, jeans and orange trainers. His neck and legs were skinny and his face gaunt, but the anorak was strangely bulky and zipped right up to his neck, despite the sunshine. His eyes, under the shade of the peak of his cap, were sunken and staring, and his mouth sombre, soft and young.

'Fuck,' Lene muttered.

Charlotte had not moved, but stared distractedly at the ceiling. Of course, Lene thought, she has already seen the pictures.

'And you're absolutely sure?' she asked.

Kim glanced at Charlotte Falster.

'Show her,' she said.

He leaned back with his lips close to Lene's ear. 'Stupid bitch,' he hissed under his breath.

'I think you should just do what you're told, Kim,' Lene said out loud. 'And perhaps you should consider cleaning your teeth every now and then.'

The eyes underneath the ponytail, half hidden behind the icepack, smiled at her.

20

The sky above the desert was pure blue, like a robin's egg. Far, far below the camera she could make out the tiny, dark, aerodynamic shadow of the drone. The unmanned craft flew swift and straight like an arrow. The details were incredible. The shadows of the mountains were carved in black ink. Lene saw the occasional, withered mounds along the dried-out river. Three long-haired, motionless goats were standing behind a craggy rock.

White numbers at the bottom of the screen dated the recording to 2013-04-17, 11:23:56 UTC, followed by changing coordinates. The drone's altitude was listed as 5,400 feet. The small, silent machine flew over a cluster of gloomy-looking trees which miraculously had found both footing and nourishment on a steep slope, a tarmac road almost covered by sand and a dirt track which led to some godforsaken destination between the barren, jagged mountains.

The drone caught up with and hovered above a slow-moving dirt-brown truck fighting its way up the mountain road. You could almost hear its protesting engine and crunching gearbox. The truck caused a broad fan of dust to rise behind it, which lingered for a long time in the stagnant air. Then the drone rose vertically above the truck. The altimeter flickered and settled at 13,600 feet, more than four kilometres, but the details of the recordings remained razor sharp.

'Kuh-e Sar Tangal,' Kim said. 'Or at least that's the nearest named place. I doubt if the area itself is called anything at all. Only scorpions, terrorists and goats live there.'

'Where is it?' Lene asked.

'North-eastern Iran. The Iranians and Hezbollah have a habit of locating their secret training camps in the region. It's very peaceful.'

He pointed to the truck.

'That's the weekly truck bringing food, water, orders, new recruits, diesel for the generator and a hell of a lot of ammunition for the shooting range.'

In a dip between the two ridges, she could see two irregular rows of tents, a couple of corrugated-iron sheds and a cleared plateau with a kind of assault course.

The drone slowed down and regained altitude, while the camera effortlessly zoomed in on the training camp.

It had to be unbearably hot down there, Lene thought. You could probably fry eggs on the corrugated-iron sheds. A machine gun position set up at the outskirts of the camp controlled the only access road. A torn scrap of canvas stretched out over a couple of poles, and leaking sandbags offered the crew their only chance of a bit of shade.

Kim clicked to fast-forward the film. The drone was now so shockingly close to the ground that Lene could not help but pull her head back. It was worse, or better, than anything she had seen in a Hollywood movie. The camera found the camp's inhabitants, froze individual faces in separate rectangles, gathered them up and enlarged them. It was unique. Everyone in the camp was identified in a matter of seconds, both the heroically strutting young men dressed in an irregular mixture of desert uniforms, jeans and T-shirts and the young women in the same casual clothing, but with their hair covered.

Some ten recruits on the shooting range were emptying Kalashnikovs into distant, perforated cardboard cut-outs which undoubtedly depicted Navy Seals or Israelis. A small group was doing push-ups supervised by a bossy instructor, while others relaxed in the shadow of their tents.

'The photo from Tivoli was step one,' Kim said in a neutral voice.

The hostility had temporarily disappeared from his face and voice. Once more he was the objective, highly skilled analyst from the intelligence service, and Lene realized that the deputy chief superintendent was probably brilliant at his job, when he wasn't . . . deranged.

'When we received the recording from Åke Valerius-Klüver, we asked the CIA to match Nabil Maroun's face against their databases.'

He clicked until he came to a gunman sitting on a box

of munitions on the camp's main thoroughfare. The boy took a sip from a felt-covered drinking canister and when he lowered his hand, she could clearly see his clean-shaven face. The canteen was raised again. Perhaps he had just finished exercising, Lene thought, because there were fresh half-moons of sweat under his armpits, and his neck gleamed with moisture. The drone continued its distant orbit in a circular, anticlockwise movement, and she could see the boy from all angles. A comrade of roughly the same age was squatting on his haunches in front of him. He was resting his forearms on his knees and flexing his legs as if he had cramps. His face was gaunt and very young. Lene could see long front teeth disappear behind a sparse moustache and concluded that he had been born with a cleft palate that had not been reconstructed altogether successfully.

'Who is the boy with the cleft palate?' she asked.

'We don't know.'

He's lying, she thought.

Lene poured herself a glass of water, drank it and wondered whether someone was sitting on the other side of the two-way mirror.

'That drone,' she said. 'According to the date stamp, it was in the air above Iran a year ago, am I right?'

Kim leaned back, touched his groin and nodded.

'That's correct.'

'Okay. So why the hell didn't it blast the whole lot of them to smithereens while it was there? Girls, boys and instructors. It's fitted with missiles, isn't it? If it had done that, then Tivoli would never have happened.'

Christian put the icepack on the table, and Lene felt a dart of guilt when she saw the handsome young man's ruined nose.

'The drone was American,' he said with a nasal twang. 'It was unarmed, tiny, practically invisible and equipped with the latest in camera sensors. The system is called Argus, and it can span all of Copenhagen in a single frame. The training camp is in Iran. Iran is an independent, sovereign nation—'

'So are Pakistan and the Yemen,' she objected. 'But that hasn't stopped the Americans using their drones on all and sundry down there—'

'Pakistan is an ally of the USA, to some extent. You can't exactly say that about Iran, can you? The problem is that nobody knows how far they have got with their nuclear programme, and no one feels like starting a countdown sequence and watching Tel Aviv disappear in a mushroom cloud. No one gives a toss about the Yemen. They haven't received enriched uranium from North Korea, and even if they had, they wouldn't know what to do with it.'

'I see. So how come you know his name, and how do you know that he's from Damascus?'

Kim and Charlotte exchanged glances once again. The agent had an almost pleading expression in his eyes, but the chief superintendent nodded harshly.

He clicked reluctantly on a fresh file, this time from a

camera monitoring the passport control in an American airport. Passengers were queuing in front of a large black woman with Afro hair, dark-blue uniform and a large revolver on her hip.

'Newark Airport, just over three years ago,' he said, pointing to a hunched, tall figure in a suit creased from travel in the middle of the queue.

'Hassan Maroun from Damascus, aged forty-seven, wholesale trader and importer of Western delicatessen goods. Sunni. He travelled on a Syrian passport, but was originally a Palestinian refugee from Araqa on the West Bank.'

'Was?'

'Hassan, his wife and two young daughters, Nabil's sisters, were later killed during a mortar attack in Damascus. Only one member of the Maroun family survived.'

He pointed to a skinny dark-haired boy with soft, almost feminine facial features, standing in front of the older, slouching man. The boy turned and said something to his father, who smiled back, placed a hand on his shoulder and said a few words. Then he continued looking straight ahead with the dogged patience of a lifer.

The queue moved on towards the obligatory photographing and fingerprint scanning. The boy's face filled the screen. Personal data, passport number and a print from his index finger came up below his unsmiling face.

Kim looked at Lene.

'Now do you believe me? He was in Tivoli on the 17th

September; he was in the training camp in Iran. Name, passport number, fingerprint. If you're still not satisfied, we can go through it all over again.'

Lene pressed her fingertip against the tape on the table and picked it up.

'And you found his fingerprint in Ain's flat, I presume?'

'Yes.'

'So why are all those poor people still beavering away in the Mosaic Hall, if you've already identified the bomber?'

'It's called intelligence work, sweetheart. We want everyone to think that we have no leads.'

Lene wished that she had kicked him even harder.

'Thanks. I suppose that he wasn't acting alone, so where are the others?'

Charlotte shrugged her shoulders.

'Of course he wasn't acting alone. He had two accomplices. One bought a carton of cigarettes and fifteen porn DVDs in the kiosk opposite the flat. People tend to remember you if you buy fifteen porn DVDs. We don't know anything about the third one. We only have his fingerprint. We also found a kind of scarf, a black flag, in Ain's flat. *Al-uqab*, also known as the Eagle. It's a copy of the flag of Saladin. It has only one meaning, according to the experts: holy jihad.'

'So you were monitoring her phone and watching her flat?'

'Of course,' Christian said.

'Why didn't you just arrest her?'

'Because she didn't get us anywhere! She visited the mosques in outer Nørrebro, she frequented an immigrant club for young women in Møllegade, where she made friends with Nazeera Gamil, but we don't know all of her contacts.'

He stared at Lene.

'Perhaps she was only a brain-dead groupie, a star-fucker. Personally, that's what I'm inclined to believe. Or maybe she was a hardcore fundamentalist. What the hell do I know? Perhaps she thought it was exciting to screw young suicide warriors. Give them a proper send-off. Or perhaps she was looking for a family or the road to Mecca or Paradise. It really doesn't matter. We were watching her. Of course we were. To discover who her friends were, who she spoke to and who she went to bed with.'

'Did you find out?' Lene asked.

At this point Kim jumped to his feet. He stared at Charlotte.

'And that's all the information you're getting from us, do you understand? I'm not giving you anything else!'

You could have heard a pin drop.

Lene watched, mesmerized, as red spots emerged on Charlotte's cheekbones. She was expecting an explosion, but it never came. Things were too sensitive, she thought. Everyone needed each other. Breaking off the partnership between PET and Rigspolitiet right now would be a mortal sin which would never be forgiven.

It was the well-balanced and diplomatic Christian who defused the tension.

'I have to say that I agree with Kim, Charlotte, even though he could have chosen his words more carefully. I think we've shown considerable cooperation in order that Lene can be at peace with herself – although being at peace with yourself around here constitutes something of a luxury. I really hope that's what she feels. But she doesn't need to know any more. It's unnecessary and it's dangerous. For everyone.'

He smiled at Charlotte, but his blue eyes sent her a warning that could not be mistaken.

Kim had sat down again. He was not looking at the two women.

'I think that was our cue, Lene,' Charlotte said, getting up.

'So do I.'

She rose as well. She was about to say something, but fell silent. Then she looked at Christian.

'You know that day Ain died?'

'Yes.'

He looked at her steadily over the icepack.

'Where were you? I know where Kim was, but I don't know where you were, Christian.'

Charlotte placed her hand on her elbow, but Lene shrugged it off. She studied Christian and waited.

He looked at his partner, then back at Lene.

'I really don't know. I guess I was at home. Sleeping.'

'Christian was at home,' Kim said. 'Now get the hell out of here.'

21

Charlotte opened the curtains and turned on the coffee-maker, which was now bubbling away quietly in her office. The two women sat at opposite ends of the sofa. They had driven from Søborg to Glostrup in Charlotte's car, and neither of them had uttered one word along the way.

Lene was half lying down, balancing the heels of her boots on the floor. She was dog tired, and everything hurt. Her neck was seizing up and emitted flashes of pain whenever she turned her head. It was as if the vertebrae in her neck had somehow been displaced.

'Paracetamol?' her boss offered.

'Yes please.'

Lene gathered her leather jacket around her throat. Charlotte pointed to a rug and she draped it over her legs. She got her painkillers and washed them down with warm coffee.

'Are you satisfied?' Charlotte asked.

'Satisfied?'

'With the explanation.'

'I guess so. Thank you. Why did you do it? You didn't have

to give me an explanation. You could just have suspended me or left me in that cell.'

The chief superintendent stretched her thin arms towards the ceiling and rotated her wrists, which cracked in protest. She looked past Lene and at the morning sun, which plaited delicate and transparent yellow, red and purple ribbons across the eastern sky.

'Oh, but I am going to suspend you,' she said.

'What?' Lene stared at the other woman in outrage. 'You can't do that!'

'I can and I will. Partly for your own sake, but possibly more for mine. I can't keep covering up for you, Lene, and I know that you won't stop. It's in your nature. You're like the scorpion in that fable about the frog, the scorpion and the river. Besides, Kim is definitely going to lodge a complaint about you. He has many supporters in the higher echelons of the system and I simply don't have the time or the energy to watch your back, Lene. I'm sorry.'

Lene got up. 'That's it, I'm leaving.'

'Sit down!'

Lene ignored her.

'Sit down, woman!'

She stopped in her tracks as abruptly as if she had walked into a glass wall. It had been a night like no other. Charlotte's badly applied lipstick and drill sergeant's voice, for starters, in addition to being attacked and beaten up by her own colleagues. And now this!

Lene perched on the edge of the sofa as far away as possible from her boss, who pressed a tired forearm against her eyes. Slim gold bracelets jingled down her wrist.

'Tell me what you know,' Charlotte asked her calmly. 'About this Ain.'

'What I know? She wasn't who they said she was,' Lene began tentatively. 'She genuinely feared for her life. She thought she was being watched, and now it turns out that she was being watched by those two pillocks from Søborg. But I, being the idiot know-it-all that I am, kept telling her that she was paranoid ... cracking up. But she wasn't, she really wasn't ...'

Her voice grew faint and ebbed away.

'Go on.'

'Why in heaven's name would she contact me if she was a hardened terrorist? It makes no sense. Why did she stay in Denmark after Tivoli?'

'Possibly to help with the next attack? Besides, I don't suppose she knew what you did for a living.'

Lene nodded. 'No, but why then kill herself in the middle of everything, rather than contact the network and go into hiding?'

The chief superintendent shrugged her shoulders.

'She was young, inexperienced and desperate, I'm happy to concede that. But Ain might also have been a revolutionary romantic who had found a kind of family in the organization. Many of the young women in Red Army Faction and the Red Brigades were middle-class girls with good school reports and nice manners. They had learned to embroider, arrange flowers and discuss Picasso's blue and pink periods respectively before they kicked off against mummy and daddy and their own inherited privileges and started reading Che Guevara. Perhaps it took a long time before Ain realized that real, living people – women, children, people her own age – had been killed in their hundreds because of something she had done. Perhaps that was why she started calling you.'

Charlotte poured them both more coffee. The mugs were made by a well-known ceramic artist, Lene could not remember who.

'No,' she said.

'No, what?'

'It's too neat, can't you see it? Drones, passport photographs, fingerprints, tourist snapshots from a Swedish wildlife photographer who takes razor-sharp pictures just as Ain and this Nabil Maroun happen to be talking to each other. How much time did they spend together? A couple of minutes, maximum. The key to it all is a poor, confused girl who kills herself on cue, before PET have time to arrest her? That guy Kim ... Christ, the man is borderline insane.'

Charlotte's gaunt cheeks inflated. She let the air escape in a long, thin stream.

'But who set it all up?' she demanded to know. 'We don't

need conspiracy theories right now. We actually live in the middle of a conspiracy. What would PET have made up? The drones? The camp? Father and son in Newark Airport? The Swedish photographer? It makes no sense.'

'Listen, Charlotte, they found a new type of LSD in Ain's blood. That's another fact. I can give you the number of Helle Englund, the medical examiner. You already know her. Bright girl. People don't remember they've been given it, and they can't remember what they said and to whom. It's a kind of truth serum.'

'The medical examiner? Tell me, just how many people have you involved in this top-secret, eyes-only investigation?'

'No one,' Lene said angrily. 'But she did have LSD in her blood, and only Irene Adler could have administered it. That woman lives and breathes terrorists, isn't that right?'

Charlotte pulled an exasperated face.

'And next you're going to tell me that she planned the Tivoli bomb. Can you prove that it was Irene Adler? You do remember that old-fashioned legal concept, don't you? Evidence?'

'I remember it well. And no, I can't.'

'And you won't find any, either. Because like I said, I'm suspending you.'

Charlotte rose and started pacing up and down.

Then she stopped in front of Lene. 'Kim. How well do you really know him?'

'All I know is that he's a high-grade psycho who beats up

his own colleagues. I wouldn't want to know him. PET always keep to themselves like they're Freemasons, elevated above all of us mortals.'

'He might have been a little overzealous,' her boss conceded.

'Overzealous! If his partner hadn't been there, he would have driven me to Nordhavn and tossed me in the sea with a bench tied around my neck. Who gave him permission to follow me in the first place? Who does he report to?'

At that very moment the only possible conclusion dawned on her, and she scowled at Charlotte through narrowed eyes. In the growing daylight the chief superintendent looked extremely uncomfortable.

Lene nodded slowly.

'Of course,' she muttered. 'Who else? You're the big cheese. Did you put a whole team on the assignment, all because of little me? All I can say is, they have my sympathy because my life is arse-numbingly boring.'

'I do what I find optimal with the resources available to me, Lene, and I do not have the time or the inclination to consider people's wounded feelings. They're not relevant. What is relevant is that terrorists are heading this way again, and you're about to destroy our only chance of preventing the next attack. Because there will be another attack. More victims. Many, many more. I had to have somebody keeping an eye on you.'

She started pacing up and down again while her words slowly sank in.

'Is that something you know?' Lene asked.

'Yes, it is, and I deeply regret having told you. As always, you put me in an impossible situation, Lene. Something for which you have a fabulous knack.'

Charlotte walked up to the window and looked down at the empty car park.

'If you ever breathe a word of this to anyone, I don't know what I'll do to you, but it will be something memorable, you can be absolutely sure of that.'

'You asked if I knew Kim,' Lene said. 'Why? And why does he have this incredibly high level of support you just mentioned?'

'You lost Josefine. He lost everything.'

'Everything?'

'Everything. Anne, his thirty-six-year-old wife, and their two daughters, aged ten and twelve, were waiting to go on the Star Flyer on the 17th September . . .'

'Oh, God,' Lene muttered.

She remembered Kim's eyes. She should have recognized them. She saw the same eyes in the mirror every day.

'So you've both lost someone,' Charlotte said slowly. 'I'm prepared to accept that he comes across as unstable, but anything else would be surprising. What we're subjecting him to is actually inhumane. But for the time being, there are no options other than for him to carry on as best he can, while the rest of us try to make it as easy for him as possible. And that includes you.'

'He should never have been assigned to the investigation,' Lene exclaimed. 'It's irresponsible, unethical and bloody unprofessional. He reacts emotionally to everything, and thinks he's entitled to pursue his own agenda.'

Charlotte did not appear to be listening to her. She drank her coffee and stared into space with her thousand-kilometre gaze. Then she looked at Lene.

'Like I said, there are no other candidates available right now. He's the only PET agent who has completed three postings: Baghdad, Kabul and Islamabad. For most people one is more than enough. He has seen more out there than any human being should ever see.'

Lene watched Charlotte's face furtively across the rim of her mug. So they knew that the terrorists would return to Denmark. Charlotte had just said it, and there was only one thing which could explain the PET agents' fixation: they had managed to infiltrate an informant, an agent, and Lene had got close to this person during her investigation into Ain's death. Fresh suspicions started tumbling around inside her brain.

She sipped her coffee and remarked casually, 'You said just now that they were coming back? Are you saying you know for sure that they're on their way here now?'

'Forget it.'

Lene smiled.

'I promise I won't tell anyone. Cross my heart and hope to die! But you said it yourself, so in for a penny, in for a . . . '

The other woman was unshakable.

'More coffee?'

Lene was about to say no, but changed her mind when she detected a hint of doubt behind the lenses of Charlotte's spectacles.

'Yes please. Let's pretend, purely hypothetically, that they were planning a new terror attack in Denmark. What's the timeframe we're talking about?'

Charlotte heaved a sigh.

'"We" are not talking about anything, Lene. There is no "we". You're suspended and you're out. Totally out.'

Lene racked her brains. Denmark's official policy was not to be affected by terrorism, so the Danish government had continued doing business as usual, as if Tivoli had never happened. For example, the former British prime minister, Tony Blair, would be the main speaker at the annual conference of Socialdemokraterne, the Danish Labour Party, at the end of next week. But Lene dismissed that event: former politicians were rarely, if ever, the primary target of terror organizations.

Then there was the meeting of the EU's foreign ministers in Copenhagen, due to take place in two days. Controversial items on the agenda included Israel's settlement policy and the failed uprisings in Tunisia, Libya, Egypt, the Yemen and Syria, and the Council of Ministers would debate NATO's involvement in Mali and Niger. The eyes of the world would be firmly on the Danish Foreign Ministry, more specifically on Eigtveds Pakhus, a converted warehouse on the waterfront, which was notoriously difficult to secure. Targeting the ministerial meeting would be sensational enough for even the most ambitious terrorist.

'What are you thinking?' Charlotte asked her suspiciously.

'Lovely coffee,' Lene muttered. 'Colombian?'

'No idea. It's just coffee.'

'The meeting of foreign ministers?' Lene asked casually. 'Is that it?'

Charlotte flapped her hand, as if dismissing a fly.

'It's a clear and obvious target. You don't have to be Einstein to work that out. But there are other options. In two days Professor Ehud Berezowsky will be presented with an international peace prize in the Festival Hall of Copenhagen University, where he will be made an honorary doctor. The chancellor, the University Court, members of the government and representatives of the royal family will be present, along with prominent members of the Jewish community in Denmark. Berezowsky is a professor at the University of Tel Aviv and has for decades argued for Palestinian rights and the abandonment of new settlements in the occupied territories. An ultraorthodox Jewish sect has tried to kill him twice, once with a letter bomb, the second time with two bullets fired at his chest during a demonstration in Tel Aviv—'

'But that makes him a kind of ally,' Lene objected. 'They're fighting for the same thing!'

'And would thus attract even more media attention. He's

controversial and famous, and that's what they're going for. Anything spectacular.'

'But they've never claimed responsibility for Tivoli,' Lene said.

'No, but everybody knows who did it: Al-Saleem in Tehran, or Sheikh Ebrahim Safar Khan in Amman, and everyone takes to the streets to cheer the martyrs and the "white sheikhs", who are behind it all. The puppet masters.'

Lene nodded. Adrenaline was brilliant at removing dust from her addled brain. She noticed, for example, that Charlotte had said that Ebrahim Safar Khan lived in Amman, while the American speaker had not been so sure. He had merely suggested it as one of several possibilities.

'Berezowsky will be arriving with his wife and his Mossad close protection officers,' Charlotte said. 'He would make a fine target.'

She got up and checked her mobile. Lene had heard a dozen text messages and emails arrive already.

'So what am I going to do?' she asked.

'What do you mean?'

Lene flung out her hands.

'You fired me. Ten minutes ago.'

'I suspended you, I didn't fire you,' Charlotte corrected her absent-mindedly. 'What are you going to do? I really wouldn't know . . . Go to Paris, learn to paint watercolours or redecorate your kitchen, who am I to say? I wish it was me. Incidentally, I'm going to have to throw you out now.'

'Of course.'

Charlotte walked her to the door.

'And are we agreed that you'll stay away from Ain, from her friends and family, and her flat?'

'Please can I at least attend her funeral?' Lene glanced at her watch. 'It's in four hours.'

'I suppose so. I can't see what difference that would make.'

'Thank you.'

Charlotte Falster closed the door; Lene leaned against it for a moment and took a deep breath.

Now what? Ain's funeral? It was the last place she wanted to be, but she had to go.

She turned around the corner, but caught sight of Bjarne's shuffling figure in brown polyester trousers ahead of her. Lene retreated and found another way out.

Most days there would be a couple of taxis waiting on the other side of the expanded security zone, but today she looked for one in vain. Typical. And a cold rain had started to fall.

She realized just how much she loved and missed her little old blue Citroën. It had faithfully carried her to and from this suburban hell, surrounded on all sides by motorways, ring roads and endless, godforsaken industrial estates where the only signs of life were to be found at petrol stations or takeaways.

Lene pulled up her collar against the wind and started looking for the pedestrian exit while she briefly wondered why Charlotte had not asked her to hand over her warrant card and service weapon. Wasn't that what you did when you suspended someone?

She also thought, with a dash of compassion, about the bitter and sleepless PET Deputy Chief Superintendent Kim Thomsen, about a Jewish civil rights activist and Europe's foreign ministers.

From her office Charlotte watched her suspended superintendent plod across the car park in the rain. The low, grey clouds looked as if they touched the roofs of the hideous buildings opposite. Lene was limping on one leg, and Charlotte held her breath when she tripped down a grassy slope near the ring road. Then she got back up and hobbled on slowly, strangely unsteady.

Charlotte picked up her mobile and looked at the display with a sigh. Fifteen new messages within the last ten minutes, each one more urgent than the next: the Danish Emergency Management Agency, the Air Force, the Danish Airport Authority, PET's close protection officers, the Interior and the Foreign Ministries. The press.

Lene was out of sight.

Charlotte started with Kim.

2 2

'Was that Falster?'

'Eh?'

'Was that our great helmswoman calling?' Christian said.

His lips were the size of woodland snails, and he struggled to pronounce words of more than one syllable. He looked glumly at his desk, which was close to collapsing under the weight of maps, logistics plans, timetables, aerial photographs, reports and requests from the intelligence services in every European country with a foreign minister going to Copenhagen. They all culminated in the same, implied question: did PET really think they could handle security arrangements during the top summit, or were they outnumbered?

Kim was lost in silence after his brief telephone call. He had interlocked his fingers behind his neck and placed his dirty trainers on the desk. Sometimes his fingers would release their grip when he fell asleep, and his head would bounce back and forth like a watch spring. Christian could not remember when he had last slept himself, but it was a long, long time ago. He was just as tired as his partner, but the pain from his broken teeth kept him awake.

'How are your balls?' he asked.

'Oh shut up,' the other man whispered, without opening his eyes.

Eventually Kim staggered to his feet, shuffled to the coffee-maker and gazed sadly at the empty pot. He took the lid off the coffee tin, only to discover that it too was empty; instead, he went to the windows where he studied the gloomy view.

'It was Falster, and my balls are okay, thanks for asking. Actually, no, they're not, they're the size of avocados. Fucking bitch!'

'Which one of them?'

'Both of them.'

'What did she want?'

'They found that new substance in Ain's blood and brain tissue,' Kim said, without turning around.

Of course, Christian thought with resignation. Of course they had. He had never believed what it said on the label. They had brought down Lance Armstrong and Alberto Contador, hadn't they? So they could probably find traces of truth serum in a young, dead woman. He had never believed that they should use it. There were other ways.

Christian regarded himself as more civilized; he wanted nothing more than to do his job following the same, quietly heroic, old-fashioned and fundamentally decent principles which he tried to live his life by. He did not trust information obtained through torture or pharmacological persuasion. He preferred the long, protracted game with the detainee where you exhausted him or her and eventually identified inconsistencies and contradictions. It took time, but it was fair. In time, if you were lucky and skilled, you could make your opponent see you as their best friend. Or at least their last good hope in this world.

'Who found it?'

'Helle Englund. The medical examiner. We're not to do anything. That's an order. She said it five times. We'll be crucified if it comes out.'

'I thought everything was permitted these days. That they needed people to hammer in the nails, not just someone to hang on the crucifix. She said so herself.'

'Apparently not when it's discovered by anyone, and especially not when Falster didn't know anything about it.'

'But you said it was necessary not to tell her, in order to protect her,' Christian said angrily. 'So she could deny all knowledge of it, should it come out.'

'Try telling Falster that.'

'So that crappy substance was traceable after all.'

Kim started pacing up and down. He avoided looking at his partner.

'I've always thought you had a soft spot for that woman, Kim,' Christian went on. 'Irene Adler is using you to get her precious Nobel Prize. You supply the guinea pigs and she screws them up until they no longer know their own name, or they jump in front of a train.'

'It's called science.'

'Oh, I'm sure it is. And I presume you also screw each other in an exquisitely scientific style, with Arabic music in the background?'

Kim stared at him with eyes that were nothing but black, enlarged pupils. Slowly, his face darkened with rage and Christian thought that he had crossed the line.

To his dismay he discovered that he did not care. He no longer believed in the project. They did not have a hope in hell of averting a new disaster. They simply did not know enough.

'Go home,' Kim said. 'Sleep.'

Christian got up, wondering when the dental surgery by Oslo Plads opened.

'What are you going to do?' he asked. 'I'm starting to wonder if I can leave you alone these days.'

'Of course you can. I'm fine.'

Kim yawned, his shoulders relaxed and he summoned up the shadow of a smile, but Christian knew that he was faking it. His partner was close to burning out.

'You know the day Ain died?' he asked.

'Yes?'

'What were we really doing?'

'You were at home brewing your fancy barista coffee, as always, and I was listening to a deadly boring lecture at Police Headquarters.'

'OK. If you're sure . . .'

'Of course I'm sure! I have approximately three hundred witnesses. Now go home, get some sleep and take a shower. You stink.'

'See you later.'

'Yeah, see you later.'

When his partner had left the office, Kim sat down again. He buried his face in his hands and sat for a long time without thinking anything at all. His mobile buzzed with incoming text messages, but he ignored it. He was not hungry, not thirsty, he was nothing. He could not feel anything. A secretary knocked and carefully placed a pile of papers by his elbow. She was young and new and lingered for a moment. He wondered if she was about to put her hand on his shoulder and prayed that she would refrain. She smelled of fresh coffee and a morning shower.

'Thank you,' he said, without looking up.

'More papers,' she said. 'I'm sorry that you—'

'It's okay. Thank you.'

'Do you want something? Coffee?'

I would like you to leave and close the door behind you, he thought. I would like the world to stop turning. For time to go backwards, so that everything will be like it was, so that I took leave like I should have done last year after Islamabad, and that we had spent six months travelling around New Zealand with the girls in the auto camper, like we always said we would.

That we were not in Denmark when those bastards arrived.

'No thanks,' he said.

He felt warmth and expected her palm to land on his shoulder. But her hand continued hovering above his shirt, the warmth disappeared and the secretary's shoes squeaked as she walked lightly across the linoleum floor and closed the door behind her.

His mobile rang with the mournful trumpet solo from Outlandish's 'Warrior//Worrier' that announced Zebra. The ringtone had been her suggestion. He did not know if there was a hidden message in it. Perhaps she knew him better than he thought.

'Any news?' he asked.

'No.'

'Access routes?'

'Not yet. Of course not. I'm told half an hour before I need to be somewhere to pick them up. They'll get into the country a different way this time. How, I don't know. They haven't lowered their security measures, quite the contrary. They even smashed my sunglasses at the airport.'

'Names?'

'One name. Samir.'

'Surname?'

'No. Twenty-five years old max. White star-shaped scar on his left temple. Looks like a gunshot injury. Shoulder-length black hair, light brown eyes. Quite handsome. Syrian. A fighter.'

'And you have no pictures of him?'

'No.'

He pondered it. Apart from that scar, Samir could be anyone. The name meant nothing to him.

'Are you all right?' he suddenly asked, and there was silence at the other end. Mutual concern was not something they normally spent time on.

'Forget it,' he mumbled.

'Are *you* all right, and are *you* ready? It's about to happen, you know that, don't you?' she said.

'I know it, and I'm fine,' he grunted and tried forcing some enthusiasm into his voice.

'Lene Jensen. Has she been taken out of the equation?'

He looked out of the window.

'I think she has got the message by now, although she took a lot of persuading. She has been suspended, but is at large, so to speak. If you bump into her, then make it as short and sweet as you can. Get rid of her, but don't lie. She'll know.'

'Okay.'

'Call me the second you hear something, won't you?' he said unnecessarily and ended the call.

He smiled faintly; the fatherly pride he always felt when he had spoken to Zebra. She was unique. The best retriever and operative he had ever heard about or met. She did not appear to have a nervous system. He had watched her sleep as peacefully as a child in a glowing hot, unventilated fleapit of a hotel room in Karachi after she had watched ten hours of hard, physical interrogation, waterboarding, and the punishment and humiliation of young men suspected of belonging to Al-Qaeda, who had arrived in cages from Waziristan.

Did she not hear the screams, the heavy thuds when cricket bats hit flesh repeatedly, the projectile vomiting and the sounds of the prisoners when a filthy towel was placed over the victim's face and soaked with a thin stream of water? The man under the towel lived through mankind's most basic fear. Did she not feel for them when they were put in dog collars and dragged across the floor, ordered to bark like the most unclean animal their faith could imagine?

Everyone broke at some point and told their torturers what they believed they wanted to hear, plus a little bit they didn't know – rarely of much use. ISI, the Pakistani intelligence service, knew most of what there was to know. Everyone ultimately collapsed into sobbing, incoherent shadows of what they once were. It was not a matter of spiritual strength, maturity, religious faith, responsibility or dignity. These respected and desirable features were a thin veneer which cracked before being swallowed up by the pain. It was simply a question of biology. You could not take the animal out of a human being.

The days in the basement below the headquarters of the Pakistani intelligence service would occasionally ignite her complex sexuality. Several times after a long day in darkness, accompanied by the stench of vomit, urine and faeces, she had tried getting Kim into bed. He had usually declined, but would occasionally succumb to the temptation. It was inevitable; they were out there for months at a time and only had each another. Besides, she was extraordinary.

After a few hours' sleep, she would often disappear in her search for satisfaction, only to return just before dawn. She would let herself quietly into her room, while Kim lay awake sweating in the adjacent room, studying the strange stains in the ceiling, unable to fall asleep until he heard the bed springs squeak under her.

She was an impossible combination of equilibrium, quick thinking, detachment and sensuality, which could entrap anyone.

His mobile rang again and he frowned with a terrible premonition when he saw the caller's name: a senior legal officer from DSB, the public transport network, whom he had been buttering up as part of his preparations for the top summit of EU foreign ministers. She was single, childless, pedantic, loved opera and she thought Kim was a kind of working-class Siegfried. A rough diamond she would love to polish.

'Hi, Grethe,' he said in a neutral voice.

'Good afternoon. I'm just calling to make sure that I haven't done anything wrong. It was a somewhat unusual request, but it was double-checked by my line manager and greenlighted twenty minutes ago. But then again, he's young and it's a little too late to worry about it now because the footage has already been sent to Glostrup by taxi. But, as far as I was concerned, sending the files to you once was enough. If we have to send everything to you twice, we're never going to—'

Kim felt like screaming.

'What request, Grethe? And I can't believe for one moment that you've done anything wrong. Not you. What files are we talking about and who requested them?'

She told him, in great detail, and along the way he experienced hallucinations and watched absent-mindedly how his left hand started shifting sideways along his desk as if it had a mind of its own and had received instructions the rest of him could not access. He pressed his hand hard against the desk, but to no avail. He could not feel it.

Lene Jensen, of course. Again.

Did hate have a taste? Kim thought hate tasted of iron, earth and gall.

'So you did send them the CDs?' he asked.

'Yes. Was that wrong?'

His jaw muscles ached.

'Of course not, Grethe. We're working in partnership with Rigspolitiet on this investigation, but obviously you don't have to do everything twice. That would be pointless. We already have the footage from Nørreport Station. I've got a copy of it right here in front of me. I'll talk to him. Bjarne Poulsen, did you say? Lene Jensen's partner?'

'Yes. We can't just delete the footage. That's out of the question. People would think that was strange.'

'Not a problem. Thanks for calling.'

'You're welcome. But listen, I happen to have two tickets

for *Aida* – with Anna Netrebko and the Copenhagen Phil-harmonic, you know – and my friend has fallen ill, so I was wondering if you—'

He turned off his mobile and watched his hand, which had reached the edge of the desk.

It pulled out a drawer and placed a large blackout-fabric hood on the table. It was a souvenir from the Pakistani intel-ligence service. Every interrogation leader ought to have at least one, they had told him, and they had been deadly serious. Kim switched on the desk lamp and carefully turned the hood inside out; dried flakes of Lene Jensen's blood were stuck to the bottom and a few long red hairs had been trapped by the fabric.

He put down the hood and again interlaced his fingers behind his neck. He could easily imagine the headlines:

PET AND RIGSHOSPITALET PSYCHIATRIST IN ILLEGAL ALLIANCE
SUSPECTED TERRORIST SYMPATHISERS TREATED WITH LSD:
SEVERAL BECAME PSYCHOTIC
THE OMBUDSMAN AND HEALTH MINISTER TO INVESTIGATE

He could not allow it. He had to stop her. For Zebra's sake. She would be exposed, and everything would be lost. No one would be able to prevent the next attack and he would never, ever find the people responsible for the death of Anne and the kids. He had to make them pay. It was the only goal he had in this life.

II

23

Michael Sander spotted Lene a long way away. She was limping on her left leg and kept touching the back of her head. She walked with her mobile pressed to her ear, she was wet and looked as white as a sheet, and she nearly bumped into a man out walking his dog. The dog jumped playfully up at her, but she stood completely still, like a robot without power, not looking at the two of them. The man reined back his dog as he passed the eccentric woman.

Identical bungalows from the 1970s lay either side of the broad residential road. A silver wedding neighbourhood, Michael thought. The owners had paid off their mortgages, the children had left home and every chance to paper over the cracks in their marriage and their lives in general by building conservatories, carports, topiary, fancy terraces and buying slightly-too-expensive cars had long since been exhausted. There were no children's bicycles or prams. Only a frozen silence.

He thought of the sleepy market town on South Funen where he lived with his wife and children. Coincidence or necessity? He did not know. Sara, his wife, ran an antiquarian bookshop on the high street; one of the town's livelier businesses, which spoke volumes about the slow strangling of the outskirts of Denmark. These days, pretty much everything outside the five major cities was regarded as being marginal.

He turned off his iPad and yawned. He had followed Lene from PET's headquarters in Søborg to Glostrup and waited patiently opposite Rigspolitiet's building until she appeared. He had lost sight of her when she executed an unexpected U-turn down by the ring road, but found her again via her mobile.

It had become ridiculously easy to track someone remotely. From a chat room Michael had downloaded a small program with the ominous name *Your-Cell-Told-Me* which transformed any kind of mobile into a GPS transmitter. If you knew someone's mobile number, and if the mobile was turned on, you could follow that person on every smartphone, tablet or computer from the comfort of your own home.

He opened the car door, got out and waited on the pavement. Lene was no longer talking on her mobile, but staring at the ground while her feet mechanically propelled her forward. She was about to walk around him when he interrupted her by putting a hand on her shoulder. Her feet stopped moving. Then she slowly raised her head and looked at him.

'Michael?'

She squinted, as if she was not quite sure that it really was him.

He grabbed her by the elbow and led her to his brand-new, customized Mercedes. He kept hold of her as he opened the passenger door because he knew that she would otherwise carry on towards the horizon like a lab rat that has just escaped.

She sat down in the passenger seat and folded up her long legs.

He got into the driver's seat and turned up the heating.

'Music?' he asked.

'Eh?'

He leaned back and rested his hands in his lap. They sat in silence for several minutes, measured out by the clock on the dashboard.

'How did you find me?' she asked at length.

'Your mobile.'

'How was Somalia?'

'Do you honestly want to know?'

'Yes.'

'That country belongs on another planet,' he said, pensively. 'Like Mars. Or in a nightmare. I think something down there made me ill. Perhaps I caught some tropical bug. I'm bloody freezing all the time, and my urine is brown despite the fact that I swallowed malaria pills like a madman.'

She glanced sideways at him, and her left hand started to move. Perhaps she might momentarily have placed it on his knee in an expression of sympathy, but her hand changed its mind halfway and returned to its partner.

It was not going according to plan. Clinical, competent and detached. That had been his job description for as long as he could remember. Emotions could be fatal; they were useless and distracting. He barely knew her, and he had no particular reasons to have fond memories of her. On two occasions she had come close to shooting him, and she was an oddball. A stubborn, quarrelsome, contrary redhead.

'Why are you avoiding me?' he asked. 'I've called you dozens of times.'

'You're probably busy keeping the rich and mighty in power and in control of their ill-gotten gains,' she said. 'Why would you care about someone like me? I'm nobody. But I'm flattered, of course. I'm okay. I really am.'

'You look like shit,' he said. 'You don't look like someone who is okay.'

'Gee, thanks.'

She raked her hands through her matted hair in a futile attempt to comb it. Then she gave up and let her hands fall down. Her clothes started to steam, causing condensation to form on the windows.

'Have you been home since Somalia?' she asked.

'No.'

'Why not?'

He made a gesture towards the windscreen, towards

the grey, watery world, as if the view offered some kind of explanation.

'What are you doing here, Lene? I mean, right here?'

'I've been suspended. After eighteen years. Thrown out. Dropped. I'm a pariah. And I couldn't find a cab.'

'Why have you been suspended?'

'That's a really long story, Michael,' she said wearily and looked out of the side window. 'A long and bloody miserable story.'

'Tell me,' he said. 'I have all the time in the world, and I love tragedies.'

He leaned forward, turned on the car radio and happened to come across Chrissie Hynde singing the most appropriate song imaginable: 'I'll Stand By You'. He decided to see it as a good sign.

'You knew all along, didn't you?' she said out of the blue.

'What?'

'What would happen to Josefine. You knew it. Thank you for the wreath, incidentally, it was beautiful.'

Michael looked straight ahead.

'I've seen it before,' he said.

'Where?'

'Are you sure you want to know?'

'I really want to know.'

'I once tracked down a young woman who had been kidnapped, mutilated and raped for several days. Her kidnappers demanded a ransom for her. I found her for her father, a rich

Dutchman. She ended up in a clinic in Switzerland. She became insane. Smeared herself in her own faeces to keep people away. Especially men, of course.'

'Thank you,' she said.

Michael turned off the radio.

'So what do you think of my new car?' he asked.

She smiled faintly and for the first time, her eyes joined in.

'It's gorgeous, Michael. Really nice. Is it yours, or did you nick it from outside the Sheraton Hotel?'

'It's mine. Start talking.'

At length her waxen face took on a pink glow from the heat, she stopped trembling and her voice became more assured.

'It all started with an Arab girl, Ain. I spoke to her on Livslinjen. She worked in a restaurant in Tivoli and felt the bombing was her fault. There are several photographs of her outside the restaurant where she's speaking to a young man, Nabil Maroun from Damascus, who has been identified as the bomber by PET. I've seen the photographs. They also found his fingerprints in her flat.'

'Who sent him?'

'Ebrahim Safar Khan in Amman. At least that's what I think.'

Michael nodded.

'I've heard of him. He's clever and very dangerous. He was a professor in London before he became a mass murderer.'

'The identification of Nabil Maroun is not in dispute,' she

said. 'It's an impressive piece of intelligence work. However, the girl called me five minutes before she jumped in front of a train. She had time to tell me that someone was following her. The medical examiner found a new type of LSD in her blood. Something which makes people crack up. They become psychotic, paranoid, they kill themselves. Have you heard about it?'

'It just so happens that I have,' he said. 'It's the latest thing in advanced interrogation methods after the Obama administration took over. These days there are more civil rights lawyers than prisoners in Guantánamo. They have to use Hello Kitty watering cans to waterboard anyone and they have to say sorry afterwards. They're closing down secret CIA interrogation centres one after the other, and they attach more and more importance to electronic surveillance instead of sitting with the natives around the campfire, recruiting informants, old-school style. They no longer promise political asylum, citizenship and a trip to Disneyland to anyone, and they prefer droning them rather than interrogating them. In my opinion it's a crappy solution – what do they do when they've eliminated the last person on their list? So one alternative is this truth drug – LSD, for example – which is smuggled into the victim's toothpaste or bedtime drink along with Propofol, which means they can't remember talking to you afterwards. It wipes your short-term memory. But who would want to start doing this in Denmark?'

'Irene Adler,' she said. 'She's a psychiatrist at Rigshospitalet and ambitious as hell. She has lived in the Middle East for years and is the hottest name working in the new subject area – the study of the psyche of suicide bombers. She thinks she can walk on water, and that she's invulnerable because she has shaken hands with the Queen and Nelson Mandela.'

'She treated your daughter, didn't she?' Michael asked, and could have bitten off his own tongue.

Lene spun around in her seat, eyes blazing.

'It has nothing to do with that, do you hear me, Michael?!'

He interlocked his fingers in his lap and made sure his face took on its most humble expression. 'Sorry. But as far as Irene Adler is concerned, it sounds like career suicide. Stuff like that always comes out. There are too many people involved for a civilian experiment: carers, lab assistants, medical students or PhD students.'

'You've been away from Denmark too long. You don't know what it's like these days,' Lene said. 'Things we would once have rejected out of hand because we associate them with the worst fascist police states have become commonplace. Half the population's mobiles are being bugged. They put CCTV cameras up everywhere, and you practically have to walk through a metal detector before getting on a bus or entering a library. Everything is going to hell in a handcart.'

'Was it Charlotte Falster who suspended you?'

'Of course. She's in charge of everything now. PET bumped into me when I tried to talk to one of Ain's friends, a woman called Nazeera Gamil. Thirty-one years old, single, no children. She has lived in Denmark since she was fourteen, and her father is Jordanian, a senior professor in Economics at the University of Copenhagen. She was also Ain's lover and is very attractive – captivating, in fact. I guess they're interested in her because of her background.'

'Probably,' he said. 'Or it's just coincidence. Perhaps they're checking her out as a matter of routine.'

'Perhaps. Anyway, two PET agents decided I was getting too nosy and started following me. I spoke to Ain's psychiatrist and tried getting a comment from Irene Adler. She complained. Then Charlotte told me to stop poking my nose in where it didn't belong or—'

'What did her psychiatrist say?'

'He suggested a date,' she said with a half-smile.

Michael stared at her.

'He asked you out? Why?'

He held out a hand, but it was too late.

'Sorry,' he mumbled.

She bashed his hand aside. Hard.

'You're right. The idea of any man wanting to spend time with me is obviously ridiculous. There's no need for you to apologize.'

'No, I meant what I said. I don't think I view psychiatrists as human beings. That was the point I was trying to make. You're still—'

'Oh, shut up, Michael. You really are an idiot.'

She yawned, leaned back into the soft, warm leather seat, and her eyes started to close. He shook her by the shoulder.

'What?' she grunted.

'This Ain, why did she call you? Did she leave behind a letter, write something in lipstick on her mirror? A message? A confession?'

Lene rummaged around her shoulder bag and found a blister pack with round, white pills. She clumsily pressed one out of the foil and popped it in her mouth.

'Water?' she asked.

He found a bottle of water in the glove compartment and she grimaced violently as she swallowed it.

He nodded towards her bag, which she closed with some effort and placed, like a shield, on her lap.

'What's that?'

'Something to calm me down.'

'To calm you down? For Christ's sake, you're half asleep already!'

'No. I . . . I can't sleep. It's impossible. This is just . . .'

'Throw them away,' he said. 'Go cold turkey.'

'Then I wouldn't be able to cope.'

'All right, then. Did she write a letter?'

'No.'

'Did she jump or was she pushed?'

'Pushed. I'm sure of it.'

'Are you? Why?'

'She didn't sound like someone who was about kill themselves,' she said.

Michael did not argue with her. He had always believed that Lene's judgement was sound, even if she was currently a pale imitation of her former self.

'So what was she, Lene, your unhappy Arab?' he asked.

'I don't know, but I intend to find out, no matter what they say and how suspended I am. But what are you doing here? I can't afford you. I believe your daily fee is 20,000 kroner?'

'It's 64,000 kroner, actually, thanks to the financial crisis. People really do get up to a lot of strange things. I hope it never ends.'

'Are you looking for a secretary? I think my future in the police force is fairly limited. I believe they think I've already gone as far as I can. Downwards.'

'Perhaps. Then what was she?'

She thought about it.

'I don't think she *was* anything. I think she was unlucky. I think she was shafted by people she trusted. They used her. She had no idea what she was doing. She was a naive fool. She had no political convictions, she had far too many personal problems to be interested in complex Middle Eastern conflicts, justice or injustice. That's what her psychiatrist told me, and I think he read her well. She was just Ain. Sweet and not particularly intelligent. She just wanted to make everyone happy, but someone managed to convince her that she was to blame for what happened in Tivoli. *I deserve to die, not once, but more than a thousand times*, she said. And one thousand two hundred and forty-one fatalities are more than a thousand, aren't they?'

'Yes.'

'She felt responsible for every single one of them.'

'She did speak to the bomber,' Michael pointed out. 'And he was in her home.'

'Yes, perhaps she helped him. And perhaps she had no idea who he was. She didn't contact the psychiatrist until November. That was two months after the bomb.'

'And then PET beat you up to indicate that you had over-reached yourself?' Michael asked.

She nodded.

'Who are they?'

'One is a deputy chief superintendent called Kim Thomsen. He lost his wife and two daughters in Tivoli. To the best of my knowledge, he's fanatical and unhinged. The other, Christian Erichsen, is normal but loyal. They have this unbreakable buddy code. Kim has been stationed in Kabul, Baghdad and Islamabad. No one has ever achieved that before, so he's regarded as something of a hero.'

She told him about the meeting in Søborg.

Michael nodded and drummed his fingers on the steering wheel.

'There can only be one explanation. They've managed to place a mole near Safar Khan, and it's Kim's informant. Otherwise he would have been taken off the case long ago.

He's the agent's handler, and this agent can and will only communicate with him.'

He looked at her.

'Am I right?'

'Yes.'

He leaned back in his seat.

'If this is true, perhaps you ought to leave them alone, Lene. You really risk blowing their operation. It's a huge responsibility. Enormous.'

'I know I risk ruining everything,' she mumbled. 'Charlotte said the same thing, and that was why she suspended me, to keep me away. I know she only did what she had to do, but . . .'

'But?'

'It all fits together too nicely. I know I could be wrong. I just think I ought to find out if Ain committed suicide. It matters to me. I can't think about hundreds of victims, Michael. I can only think of one victim. I'm probably very small-minded and . . . stupid.'

'Of course you're not,' he said. 'I can easily imagine them wanting to come back. To them Denmark is a defenceless fatted pig waited for a skilful man with a knife. Let's assume they're coming back. Target?'

'There's an EU meeting for foreign ministers starting the day after tomorrow. There will be maximum security measures with helicopters, snipers, Frømandskorpset – the Danish Frogman Corps – guarding Copenhagen Harbour,

Jægerkorpset in the air and all manhole covers for miles around welded shut. Then Tony Blair has been invited to speak at Socialdemokraterne's annual conference. Moderate security. And finally there is an Israeli professor who has been a persistent critic of Israel's settlement policy. He's being awarded a prize at the University of Copenhagen and given an honorary doctorate. Jewish activists have tried to kill him twice. I don't know the security level during his stay, but I doubt that Israel lets him travel alone, and I don't suppose anyone is better at guarding him than them. Chief Rabbi Bent Lexner will be present, as will the royal family, the chancellor and the University Court.'

'What's the name of the professor?' he asked.

'Ehud Berezowsky.'

He nodded.

'A likely target. Forget about Tony Blair. He's not important.'

'And the top summit for the EU's foreign ministers?'

'Of course! It would be spectacular. A Mount Everest for every ambitious suicide bomber. The Middle East would be in a frenzy of joy.'

Michael was about to light a cigarette when Lene's mobile rang.

Bjarne was well past hysteria and heading for disintegration. He sounded as if he was about to have a heart attack and his voice was as shrill as a girl's.

'He's trying to get in, Lene. He's trying to get in right now!'

She heard a splintering crash in the background and a deeper, furiously incandescent voice roaring orders at 'that fat sack of shit'.

'Who, Bjarne?'

'LENE! Help!'

She threw a glance at Michael, who had already released the handbrake and put the German wonder in drive. She placed her hand over Bjarne's falsetto squeal.

'We're going back, Michael! Rigspolitiet! Now!'

She removed her hand and heard a meaty slam like a baseball bat hitting a watermelon.

She heard the helpless technician whimper as his attacker ordered him to hand over the fucking CDs from Nørreport

Station, before he got a beating so bad even his own mother would not be able to recognize him.

She lowered her mobile while her vision blackened with hatred.

Kim.

Again.

And why should *she* stop, when *he* never did?

Lene chewed her lower lip anxiously and stared at Michael, who with cool virtuosity sent the long, silver vehicle into controlled slides through the rain-soaked residential roads until they reached the ring road. He pressed down hard on the accelerator and the eight turbo-charged cylinders reacted with an offended roar. They cut out right in front of a hooting Dutch articulated truck on the slip road. Lene was pressed back into her seat, pushing her arms against the dashboard. She was too shocked to even scream. As if in ultra HD, she could make out every single detail of the truck: the mud-stained front bumper, a filthy sticker for a brake supplier in Apeldoorn. The numbers and digits on the registration plate were the size of house walls.

There was room for no more than a banknote between the shiny right front wing of the Mercedes and the Dutch mastodon.

'*Miiiiiichael . . .!*'

He glanced at her.

'What?!'

She closed her eyes.

'Nothing. This thing does have airbags, doesn't it?'

The speedometer needle quivered over 180 km/h as they headed down the slip road to the ring road. The colossal articulated truck grew smaller in the wing mirror.

'Of course it has airbags. Why do you want to know that?'

Carefully she let go of the dashboard. The road ahead was clear, though it appeared narrow like a tunnel.

'Do you want to tell me what's going on?' he asked.

'I asked my colleague, Bjarne, to request copies of the CCTV footage from Nørreport Station on the day Ain died and now Kim, that crazy bastard, is trying to kill him.'

'But that's insane,' he said.

'I know! The man is borderline certifiable.'

'It's his asset,' Michael muttered. 'He'll do anything to protect his asset. I understand him. If he – or she – is someone he has nurtured for years and he has managed to smuggle this person into Safar Khan's inner circle, then that's unique, amazing, laudable . . . and incredibly lucky.'

Lene nodded.

'I wouldn't disagree, but Bjarne is a harmless nerd who collects *Star Wars* chewing gum cards and lives with his mother. He has never hurt a fly. He's a victim of bullying. This is going to destroy him.'

The car moved sideways onto an exit road, as if all four wheels could turn simultaneously.

'One minute and twenty seconds,' Michael declared with a certain amount of pride. 'Do you want me to come with you?'

'Yes, please, but I have no idea how to get you in. This place is like Fort Knox.'

'Oh, we'll think of something,' he said optimistically, and for the first time in months Lene no longer felt completely alone. Michael was the missing piece in all the puzzles she was trying to solve, she thought. Including some she really did not want to know about.

They parked in one of the civilian parking spaces and dashed through the rain. Michael's coat-tails flapped about his legs. The rain had increased and lashed icily at their faces. They took the steps three at a time and then strolled at a regular pace through the lobby to the reception counter. Lene did not recognize the officer on duty, a young woman with dark-brown hair. Her uniform shirt was newly pressed, and she carried her pistol holster over her left hip with the butt poking out.

'He's a guest,' Lene said, showing the officer her warrant card.

The girl looked at Michael, who offered her his best smile. It would appear to have no effect whatsoever, so instead he placed a press card on the counter.

He was bound to have at least ten different identities in his wallet.

'From *Berlingske Tidende*,' Lene said. 'He's here to interview Charlotte Falster. It has just been arranged.'

The girl nodded and waved him through a metal detector. Lene watched nervously, but no alarm was triggered and the red light remained off.

'I had better ring her secretary and check the appointment,' the girl said.

Lene looked at the stairs, expecting any minute to see a triumphant-looking Kim Thomsen appear with a stack of CDs in his hands.

Michael smiled sympathetically. 'Of course. Only we're terribly short of time if Falster wants an official statement about an imminent terror attack in the newspaper tomorrow . . .' He glanced at his watch. 'We need time to write it as well. We could wait for the TV channels, but then it won't be in the printed version of the paper tomorrow. But of course, you have your rules, I understand that, absolutely.'

The girl looked at him.

Lene just wanted to punch her lights out, but forced herself to relax and produce a smile. She read the girl's ID badge.

'Nanna, I'm quite sure that Charlotte won't hold you personally responsible if Jesper here misses his deadline. We'll find some other way. Don't you worry about it.'

The young officer quickly handed a visitor's badge to Michael, who snatched it from her hand.

A gathering of greying retired police officers and technicians, some of them absorbed in an indignant but fruitless discussion, had gathered in front of their little office in the corner of the Mosaic Hall, while others had mobilized past skills and were hammering on the door and the partition walls.

Lene had time to think that all their efforts were utterly pointless. Nabil Maroun had already been identified and they were wasting their time. On the other hand, they had been given a renewed sense of purpose late in life.

A woman with a razor-cut grey bob and narrow green spectacles turned angrily to Lene.

'We keep calling security, but they don't come. He's gone completely berserk in there.'

The tip of her tongue moistened her pink narrow lips in an agitated manner.

Lene heard loud squeals coming from the small office, like a boar being castrated without the luxury of anaesthesia. The woman made a powerless gesture. Her cheeks were suffused with colour and she probably had a fine story to tell at her next bridge party.

Lene turned to find Michael, but he had already moved past her. Without taking much of a run-up, he kicked a hole in the partition wall beside the door frame. At first she thought that he had missed his target, but then she realized the point of his action: the hole was big enough for him to stick his hand through and unlock the door from the inside. He was first through the open door, with Lene following right behind.

The office looked as if hordes of marauding hooligans had been through it. Computers, scanners, printers, tables and chairs, along with Bjarne's model aeroplanes and helicopter lay helter-skelter, smashed and trashed.

A furious Kim stood bent over the defenceless technician, who had curled up in a foetal position by the wall and
placed his arms protectively over his head. The deputy chief
superintendent screamed threats at Bjarne and beat him
steadily across his back and buttocks with a broken table
leg. He turned and glared at the new arrivals with strangely
unseeing, cloudy eyes. Bjarne, too, turned his tearstained
face towards them, and Lene felt a volcanic rage surge inside
her at the sight of the middle-aged man who was now back
in the seventh circle of his childhood hell.

'You miserable bastard—' she began, looking around for
a suitable weapon.

Kim's face was deathly pale from anger. His mouth moved,
but the words were incomprehensible. The strange membrane disappeared from his eyes and he recognized her, but
it made him no less murderous. On the contrary, he started
moving towards Lene, who could only find a ridiculous
wooden ruler with which to defend herself.

Michael pushed her calmly out of the way, and she looked
at him in surprise. As far as she was concerned, this was her
battle and she could handle herself without any difficulties.
Bjarne was her responsibility. But Michael's face was stripped
of every emotion; he did not look directly at the PET agent,
but moved steadily through the broken furniture.

Lene knew that Michael had a brain like a computer
behind his high, smooth forehead. The rest of him was
anything but unmarked. She had seen him naked from the

STEFFEN JACOBSEN • 228

waist up only once and the sight had scorched itself on her mind. Michael's upper body looked like an aerial photograph from a battlefield, covered with uneven skin grafts and tight, crinkled scar tissue where the transplants had failed to take. Across his lower back there was a cluster of scars which resembled volcanic atolls; projectiles had entered to the left of his navel and exited through his back. There was also a long, irregular scar from a temporary colostomy, which had probably been inserted because the bullets had destroyed his intestines.

You could not look at that body without experiencing intense compassion for the man, no matter how much you otherwise disliked him. But his face was miraculously unscathed and, apart from the cigarettes, she knew that Michael kept very fit. He used to say it was a kind of life insurance.

Kim's blow with the table leg was parried, and that was pretty much the end of it.

Lene blinked.

Kim was now lying on the floor next to Bjarne, who was scrambling to his feet. The PET agent lay with his knees pulled up, his arms hanging limply along his side, his eyes aimed at the ceiling, seeing nothing. He gulped and gurgled, struggling to get his breath back. Lene had seen Michael's lightning-quick, hard and accurate blow with the hollow between his thumb and index finger towards Kim's larynx. It had looked effortless.

'Is he going to die?' she asked.

Michael studied the prostrate PET agent. His face was starting to turn blue. Kim Thomsen sent him a pleading look as if Michael could do his breathing for him. There was white foam at the corners of his mouth.

'No,' he said. He thought about it and took a closer look at the man. 'At least I don't think so,' he clarified.

He dragged Kim across to the wall and made him sit up. The PET agent gasped for breath like a fish out of water and finally got the first mouthful of air into his lungs, making long, forced squealing sounds as he crouched forward and managed a second inhalation.

Meanwhile Lene tried to comfort the technician, who was hiccupping and sobbing from shame and physical pain.

He stared at her with moist, desperate eyes.

'I didn't tell him anything, Lene. I didn't tell him anything.'

'Of course not, Bjarne. I knew you wouldn't. You did well. You did really well. I'm so proud of you.'

The technician shivered as he wheezed.

'Are you?'

'Yes, really proud of you.'

His face regained a little colour, his eyes a tiny spark of life. He looked at the PET agent, but he spooked and quickly withdrew his gaze.

That bastard, Lene thought impotently. That evil, despicable bastard. What little confidence her technician had managed to acquire – a sense of self he could live with, and which helped get him through the day in one piece – had now been shredded by this cursed incarnation of the ultimate playground bully. She was sorely tempted to kick the incapacitated deputy chief superintendent in the face, or invite Bjarne to do it himself, even though she knew he could never bring himself to.

Michael positioned himself next to her and Bjarne looked at him as if he were God. He put his hand on the technician's shoulder and asked if he was okay. Lene could have hugged him, but had no idea how that would have been received: with an exaggerated, self-deprecating shrug and a sarcastic remark, probably. No, definitely.

Kim Thomsen had got up and was heading for the door without looking at them, his hands pressed against his throat. The retired police officers and technicians stepped aside. Michael looked quizzically at Lene, who shook her head.

'Let him go. Where are they, Bjarne?'

He pointed. 'In your secret cupboard.'

Lene pulled aside the upturned water cooler and opened a small panel in the wall. Behind a half-empty bottle of Stolichnaya vodka and a couple of empty blister packs lay a stack of grey and official-looking CDs held together by a rubber band. She passed them to Michael, who popped them into his coat pocket.

'Bjarne, I have to go now. I'm really sorry, but I have to,' she said. 'Are you going to be all right?'

The technician nodded wretchedly, but brightened up a

little bit when the older, fearless woman with the bob and the green spectacles put her arm around him.

'I'll look after him,' she said.

She whispered a few words to him which Lene could not hear, but he looked at her with gratitude.

She patted his arm and left.

They trundled across the wet tarmac.

'Who the hell taught you that?' she asked.

'What?'

'That thing you just did?'

She imitated, without particular skill or speed, the blow to an imaginary opponent's larynx.

Michael grinned.

'My baby sister,' he said.

'Your baby sister?'

'Yes.'

'Are you taking the piss?'

'Not at all. She joined a kibbutz in Israel after doing her A-levels and never came back. Now she lives in Haifa and has a teenage son with her husband, who is an eye specialist. She's an Israeli citizen and . . .'

'And what?'

He gave a light shrug.

'She's incredibly good at fighting. She was in the army. They have to do that all the time. I'd never stand a chance against her, if we fought for real. I'm serious. Now what?'

Lene glanced at her watch.

'I need to be at a funeral in Værløse in twenty minutes,' she said.

He looked her up and down.

'Are you sure there isn't someplace you could tidy yourself up first?'

'Where would that be?'

'Well, at least sit at the back. It's a church, not a dole queue.'

Lene was somewhat taken aback. Usually the private security consultant was a casual man of the world to the tips of his fingers: ironic, well informed and witty. But every now and then another side would pop up: prudish, conventional and remarkably Puritan.

25

Michael had offered to accompany her, but Lene did not think it was a good idea. Instead, he leaned against his car, smoking.

Værløse Church was geometrical and modern and he did not think much of it. It had little in common with the solid, low medieval church that looked as if the landscape itself had given birth to it, where his father had been the vicar and where Michael had grown up until his father was sacked. The male members of the parish council and the female bishop had agreed. The charges had been conduct unbecoming and drunkenness, but the truth was that Michael's father had cuckolded most members of the parish council. He had shagged everything in the parish with a pulse. He had broken Michael's mother's heart in his protracted, obsessive and self-destructive downward spiral, and yet Michael had always forgiven him.

He took out his mobile and looked at it. The display was blank. He had not been at home for six weeks and had not spoken to his wife or children in the past week either. He kept putting off making the call – and Sara undoubtedly did the same. With each hour it grew more difficult and he was starting to feel like a stranger in his own life.

Perhaps it was a sad fact that by now he had quite simply seen too much. It made everything so relative. Death, life, faith, love and innocence became a question of random circumstances or bad timing and the chasm between his assignments and the calm, provincial life on South Funen only widened. In the last five years he had really only made occasional visits. Normality had become increasingly exotic, bizarrely irrelevant and unreal. Perhaps he was finally turning into one of those highly paid, ruthless, hollow adrenaline junkies; the mission bums he knew from private security companies who seeped into Afghanistan, Iraq and the Balkans as military instructors and bodyguards when the coalition forces withdrew. He had felt sorry for them. Perhaps it was time he took a long, hard look at himself instead.

As if to underline his thoughts, the church bells started tolling mournfully. He took out a small pair of binoculars and scanned his surroundings. He had parked the car in a clearing by Hareskoven Forest, but in the last hour he had only seen a couple of yuppies with motorbikes, and two skinny female runners absorbed in effortless conversation. He thought about the embittered PET agent. Michael recognized the type: people who never gave up. As the man had passed him, Michael had caught that distinct glint in his eyes: this was merely the first half, those eyes had told him. You haven't won. You'll never win. And if Kim was the handler for a mole inside the terror network of Ebrahim Safar Khan himself, of course he should be allowed to continue.

Michael rubbed his face hard. It was one hell of a dilemma. Who was right? The demented and stubborn Kim or the equally demented and stubborn Lene? Neither, in all likelihood. Or possibly both. Had he really incapacitated the wrong person? Should he have let Kim walk off with the films? Then again, to Michael, it sounded utterly improbable that PET had succeeded in infiltrating Khan's cell when every major Western intelligence service had tried and failed for years.

The female vicar appeared on the steps; the mourners started filing out of the church and headed for their cars. Michael focused on the last mourners to leave: a slim grey-haired woman dressed in black, supported by her husband. Lene had described Ain's parents to him. The woman was weeping quietly and dabbing her eyes with a handkerchief. They spent a while saying goodbye to the vicar outside the entrance to the church, before getting into a grey Volvo and driving off.

He had agreed with Lene that she would get Ain's friend Nazeera out into the open so that he could photograph her. The two women walked around the corner of the church, deep in conversation, and stopped at the foot of the tower. They were roughly one hundred metres from his position, but through the zoom lens of the camera he could count every eyebrow hair on their faces.

Lene was right, the woman was sensational.

A light-grey woollen dress clung to her beautifully curved hips, and it was pressed against her model-length, straight legs and slim waist by the light breeze. Her hands were stuck into the pockets of a dark trench coat. Her shoulders were relaxed, her neck long, her skin perfect, her eyes large and green and the same shade as Lene's. When she smiled, she revealed every dentist's dream, or worst nightmare, depending on whether the yardstick was the achievements of their profession or their profits. Her cheekbones were high and her forehead clear and unblemished. The thick blue-black hair was gathered with an ivory hair slide at the back of her neck. She wore long black boots that made her slightly taller than the superintendent. Occasionally, her hands would leave their refuge in her pockets and gesture expressively. She moved like a dancer. She had a habit of running her fingers through her hair.

Lene was the complete opposite. Her face was pale, battered and contorted. Her make-up and hair were a disaster and her clothes bloody and torn. She moved gingerly to protect her various injuries and her hands seemed glued to the pockets of her leather jacket. It was like looking at a thoroughbred walking next to a stray dog, and yet Michael caught himself zooming in on the tired face of the red-headed superintendent.

It was baffling. It was . . . he could not explain it, but the two women were separated by irreconcilable qualities of soul and character.

They continued around the church, and disappeared from his field of vision before reappearing in the church forecourt. Here they exchanged a few final remarks. Nazeera Gamil and Lene embraced, and the Arab woman headed for a new black BMW. Michael frowned. As far as he was aware, she worked as a waitress in a bistro on Østerbro. Perhaps the car belonged to her father?

He also noticed that the smile had vanished from the face of the Arab woman. She looked neither to the right nor the left, but drove quickly out of the car park. The whole time, he had been able to see an immobile figure behind the tinted windows in the back of the car, and had taken it to be a human companion. Now he realized that it was an enormous black dog.

The mechanical quality of Lene's movements had disappeared. She walked briskly up the forest road and Michael got back in the car and leaned across the passenger seat to open the door to her.

She put on her seatbelt and glanced sideways at him.

'What do you think?'

'Nazeera? Wow! What on earth is she doing here in Værløse when she could be on the runway for Victoria's Secret in Milan, or be the March bunny in *Playboy*?'

'Down, boy.'

'You did ask.'

'Your tongue is hanging out, did you know that?'

He grinned.

'That's a big dog she's got,' he said.

'It's her bodyguard, Rudy or Rudolf. I've seen it close up. It's the size of a pony.'

'What did she say?'

'Nothing. I did most of the talking. She was somewhat surprised at my appearance. The blood. The bruises. The sleeve that's coming off my jacket. She doesn't miss much.'

'Did she talk to Ain's parents?'

'No, she didn't. I don't think any of the mourners knew who she was. People looked at her, as you would expect, but not as if they recognized her.'

'So the two of them were secret lovers?'

'I think so.'

'And how did you explain your appearance?'

'I said I was investigating Ain's suicide and that someone thought I shouldn't. I asked if she knew why Ain – and I – provoked such an emotional response in people, but she had no idea. She kept saying Ain was just an ordinary, lovely girl. A little wild, perhaps. Confused, but decent. She seemed taken aback.'

'She looked very serious and determined when she left you,' Michael said. 'As if she wanted to ask someone some hard questions. And she looks like a girl who can take care of herself.'

'No doubt about it.'

'Did you speak to Ain's parents?'

'I expressed my condolences. I didn't think somehow that a funeral was a suitable location for an interrogation.'

'You didn't tell Nazeera that PET were taking an interest?'

Lene shook her head. She made to open her bag, possibly looking for more of those blasted pills, but appeared to have a change of heart.

'It wasn't necessary, although I was prepared to tell her. It seemed as if she already knew who was behind it.'

'Now that *is* interesting,' Michael said.

Lene covered her mouth and yawned, then slumped deeper into the seat.

'Christ, I don't think I have ever been so tired in all my life,' she mumbled. 'Even my eyes are hurting.'

She found a pair of sunglasses in her bag and put them on.

They drove slowly down the road. Michael checked the wing mirrors and the rear-view mirror, but everything was calm and there was hardly any traffic on the narrow forest roads.

'Now what?' she asked him after some time had passed.

'You need to disappear from view for a while, Lene. Too many people are interested in you. You need to go to ground.'

She smiled.

'Back to the scout cabin?'

Michael shuddered. During the investigation into the human hunters, they had spent several unforgettable days in a cold and primitive scout cabin in Herfølge. It had been awful.

'I was thinking more of Admiral Hotel,' he said. 'They have hot running water. They change the towels daily, there's electricity, they put a mint chocolate on your pillow every night, there's room service and a minibar.'

She placed her hand on his arm for a moment.

'That sounds lovely, Michael, but I had better go home.'

'No.'

'No?'

'No, Lene. Things are too fluid. People are agitated, they're at breaking point, and they fear a fresh attack and act without thinking of the consequences. Remember Kim and the films. We need to find a quiet spot. Work out who our friends and enemies are, and who the opposition is.'

'*Us* and the opposition?'

'Yes.'

She took off her sunglasses and looked at him.

'That's incredibly nice of you, but I'm sure that you have other, more lucrative cases waiting for you. And you don't need to look after me. I'm a grown-up. Very grown up.'

'My diary is blank at the moment,' he said. 'It's okay.'

'Then go home. You have a wife and children, for God's sake.' She paused and looked at him. 'Or maybe you don't? Has something happened?'

'No, no, not at all. They're fine. Superfine. Brilliant. Fantastic. All three of them. And the dog.'

'So what's wrong?' she demanded to know. 'Are you in the middle of a divorce? Please don't, Michael, it's so depressingly banal.'

He glanced furtively at her. It was like he had never been away, he thought. They had picked up their relationship and it was just as problematic and unresolved as it had been two years ago.

'I'm not in the middle of a divorce,' he said. 'Or at least I wasn't, the last time I checked, but . . .'

'But what?'

'Well, you've tried being married, haven't you? You know that a marriage, any marriage, is the graveyard of conversation. At the start there's nothing you can't talk about or imagine doing together. East to West, from China to Alaska. Everything is permitted and anything is possible, but after a few years all you can talk about is your own tiny island. Somehow the rest of the world has become a no-go area. Together you agreed some goals, but along the way you forgot what they were, or if you haven't forgotten, you now have other plans. That's just how it is! Distance and intimacy. Intimacy and distance! It's enough to drive you crazy.'

He bashed the steering wheel with his hand.

'But to tell you the truth, that's not all it is,' he mumbled.

'What?'

'I don't seem to be able to go home any more. It's bloody difficult. It's like night and day: what I do out there in the wide world in the twisted forecourts of hell. Then at home,

I clean the gutters, do the shopping, go to parents' evenings or barbecues with the neighbours and wonder what to say. The dots don't join up.' He looked at Lene. 'Earlier that *was* my reality, my home on Funen. The kids. Sara. People in the town. Now it's everything out there, outside Denmark's jurisdiction, that feels like . . . not like home, exactly, but more like my natural habitat.'

'I understand, Michael,' she said. 'But I don't think it'll always be that way. I think it will change. We always assume that we'll stay the same, but we don't, do we? We change.'

'Sara doesn't understand.'

'Of course not. She doesn't want to. She can't. It would be the same as giving up and letting go. She has to make it work with you. She has given you two children. She takes care of everything when you're gone, and every day she worries that something might happen to you.'

'Okay, then. But at least give me twenty-four measly hours as your personal guardian angel, so you can get some rest and have some time to think. You need it. People make mistakes when they're tired. Big mistakes.'

He thought about Bjarne, her technician. She should have known that Kim would be tipped off about the films.

'If you insist, then thank you. Admiral Hotel sounds wonderful,' she said wearily. 'It really does. That guy Kim, what did you make of him?'

'He won't give up. Not as long as you won't.'

'He won't give up.'

He smiled. 'From which I conclude that you won't either? You probably don't even know what that means.'

'It wouldn't even cross my mind,' she said.

'But what if he's right and is in fact protecting a very important asset?'

'He might be,' she conceded. 'And if that's the case, I'll help him if I can. I promise. But right now I'm convinced that he can't tell the difference between right and wrong, his own hatred, his hunger for revenge and the overall aim.'

'Very well. But let's do this professionally. Mobile?'

She handed him her new, expensive smartphone. He tossed it out of the window and watched it shatter into a thousand pieces in the rear-view mirror.

'I paid over 4,000 kroner for that,' she said.

'If I could find you by your mobile, so can they,' Michael said. 'Anything else? Tablets? Laptops?'

'None of the above. I presume they haven't fitted my mascara with GPS? You've quite clearly forgotten what they pay police officers these days.'

'I've repressed it,' he said. 'Do you need anything from your flat?'

'Everything! Clothes, make-up, underwear, my gun, toothbrush. I stink, for Christ's sake.'

'I can't smell anything,' he said politely.

'Did you get some pictures of her?' she asked.

He gestured towards the back.

'The camera is on the back seat,' he began, but regretted it immediately. 'Perhaps you should wait . . .'

'For what?'

She flung out her arm and grabbed the camera.

'Wouldn't you rather see them on a computer?'

'What difference would that make?'

She clicked through the whole series, furrowed her brow and went back through the pictures again before she lowered the camera.

'Michael, why is—'

'What? Are you telling me they're not good enough?'

'No, no . . . calm down. They're great.'

She returned the camera to the back seat.

26

Michael walked up and down Kong Georgs Vej nervously watching cars, stairwells and shop fronts for the twenty minutes it took Lene to pack the items she thought she would need.

He hurried across the road and got into the car as soon as he saw her emerge from the entrance door. She had changed her clothing, but had not had time to improve her appearance significantly.

'Was everything okay?' he asked as they drove towards Allégade.

'No one had burned down my flat, if that's what you're asking.'

'Cameras and microphones?'

'I didn't check.'

Half an hour later, they left the car in an underground car park not far from the Admiral Hotel. They crossed Bredgade, passed the Marble Church and walked down Toldbodgade. Michael was carrying her bag over his shoulder.

She nodded in the direction of the hotel entrance. A small

cluster of exiled business people were smoking outside the swing door.

'So I'm Mrs Sander?'

'Petersen.'

'Mrs Michael Petersen?'

He shrugged his shoulders.

'It's just a name, Lene. You can call yourself Maria Callas, for all I care. I know the concierge fairly well. She's very discreet, trained at the finest hotel school in Zürich. I'm actually in love with her, but please don't tell anyone. It wouldn't be the first time that—'

'You brought someone up to your room?'

'No.'

'But not someone your own age, am I right? And not someone who looks like they were dragged under a bus, either. I imagine they were younger models in rabbit fur, black thigh-high boots, short dresses, Ukrainian accents? Charging by the hour?'

Michael sized her up.

'I was talking about clients, Lene. They come in all shapes and sizes. This is my office when I'm in Copenhagen.'

'Of course.'

He stopped in the middle of the pavement and a couple of Japanese tourists had to walk around them.

'Did we get married without me noticing, or when I was drunk?'

'No.'

'Fine, then shut up and stop acting as if we were. I get all the nagging I need at home from my wife.'

'Ah, poor Michael.'

'Yes, now shut up.'

A few minutes of awkward and self-conscious manoeuvrings followed in Michael's large hotel room with the high ceiling and a spectacular view of Copenhagen harbour. Both of them were used to being alone and they kept bumping into each other while he rigged up his mobiles, cameras and portable lap-tops. Lene tried finding space in the wardrobe for her clothing and secured an empty shelf in the bathroom for her toiletries.

Michael ordered a bottle of red wine and some sandwiches from room service. Lene showered. He opened the balcony door and smoked three cigarettes, while he watched the old sailing ships by the quay and the yellow water busses carrying passengers to and from Holmen and the new opera house. A waiter knocked on the door and Michael arranged glasses, cutlery and plates on the small table by the sofa.

The shower kept running in the bathroom.

There were five grey disks with recordings from the surveillance cameras at Nørreport Station on the day Ain died. Someone had neatly registered date, camera number and time on each one. He inserted the first CD into the computer drive. It took a couple of downloads from the Internet to find the official software to read them and when he had opened the files, he copied them into his preferred image editing program.

More and more of his work was spent in front of a computer and by now he had acquired fairly solid skills in digital image editing. The time when he shadowed people, interviewed witnesses and relatives and spent weeks searching through public registers and archives was irrevocably over, and he did not miss it. Nowadays, it was rare for important information to be more than a few mouse clicks away, and his expenditure on bribery had fallen considerably in recent years.

He was about to view the first recording when he heard her behind him. Lene's face glowed after the shower, her hair was wrapped up in a white hand towel. She was wearing one of the luxurious hotel dressing gowns and without make-up looked like a young girl. She had slim calves and pretty feet, and Michael realized that he had practically never seen her wear anything other than faded jeans, boots and a leather jacket. She seemed smaller.

He got up and gestured to the food and the wine.

'Are you hungry?'

She nodded and took a seat by the coffee table. She smelled of bath products, but her eyes were too shiny. He noticed an angry blue-black and protracted swelling at the base of her neck, and she moved her head as if it was welded to her shoulders.

'Wine?'

'Yes, please. Only to keep you company. I've quit, you see.'

He poured wine for her and water for himself.

'Aren't you going to have some?'

'Just coffee for me,' he smiled. 'I want to do some work on those films.'

She bit off a mouthful of a chicken salad sandwich, chewed carefully and looked around the room, turning all of her body stiffly.

'It's nice,' she said.

'It's a converted warehouse. With six-metre ceilings.'

'Do you always stay in the same room?'

'In 408, yes.'

They fell silent.

Michael drank coffee and water, ate a little. His gaze kept returning to the computer while Lene's face was bent over her plate.

They looked up at the same time.

'What?' Michael asked.

She blushed.

'Nothing. I thought you were about to say something.'

'Lene, we're behaving like a couple of teenagers washed up on a desert island after a shipwreck.'

'That's pretty much how I feel,' she said.

'Why? We have slept in the same room before; in scout cabins, cars and tents. And a helicopter, for that matter.'

She got up.

'I'll get dressed.'

He grabbed her wrist as she passed. Her fingers were long and her nails cut short. He could feel her quick pulse under her fingertips.

'It's almost six o'clock,' he said. 'Go to bed. You're knackered. Get some sleep.'

She slowly retracted her wrist.

'I need to go back,' she said. 'Home.'

'Home? Why? It's really not safe. Lene. Here is safe.'

She looked out of the window. Her posture was good; she had folded her arms across her chest and was leaning her head back slightly. Her eyes were brimming with tears.

Then she looked down and let the tears flow. No longer trying to fight it.

'I forgot my sleeping pills, Michael. I'm sorry. But I can't sleep without them, and if I don't sleep, I can't think, and I can't remember when I last slept without them. I simply can't remember!'

She started to cry, and Michael got up. He wanted to give her a long, tight hug, comfort her, tell her all sorts of wonderful fairy tales, but he could not remember a single one, nor utter one single word. He couldn't touch her, either. She looked like a seventeen-year-old with her white skin and freckles.

'Okay. Okay. I'll get them. What's your poison?'

'Imovane. They're on my bedside table. I don't know how I could forget them.'

'I'm not going back to your flat! One encounter with Kim a day is more than enough, thank you very much.'

'That's how I feel. He's like the Duracell bunny, he just keeps—'

'I've seen it.'

He picked up his mobile from the desk, found a number in his contact list and made a call. The conversation lasted less than one minute.

'That was a doctor. A friend . . . I helped him find his cat once. He has uploaded a prescription on the chemist's server, so that I can go and pick up your crappy pills.'

Lene studied her neatly polished, pale-pink toenails.

'Thank you.'

'You're welcome.'

He took her carefully by the shoulders and guided her towards the bed.

'I'll go get your pills. Do you think you could watch a bit of television and rest until I come back?'

'Of course. I will. Where will you sleep?'

'The sofa. It's excellent.'

'It's a two-seater.'

'I always sleep in a foetal position, due to my traumatic childhood.'

'Thank you, Michael. You're so . . .'

'What?'

'Ah, nothing.'

She crawled obediently under the duvet and he handed her the remote control. She looked younger than ever. Vulnerable. Her face began to relax. She started to cry again.

27

The rain was tipping down. Michael found a vacant taxi on Store Kongensgade and was soaked through by the time he reached the twenty-four-hour chemist by Frihedsstøtten. A number of sniffling children, mothers and pensioners were queuing in front of him and he waited forever before a fraught-looking chemist handed him the medication.

He took a taxi back from Copenhagen Central Railway Station and cast a long, pensive look at the stacks of grey Portakabins and yellow construction cranes still barricading Tivoli. He was driven back to the hotel through many odd detours by a Turkish cab driver who played Anatolian ballads the whole way. All of them sounded as if they were about deep but ultimately doomed love.

The female concierge, with whom Michael had developed a mostly wordless but deep friendship during previous visits, had taken over the reception counter. Their communication was just as discreet as their friendship and consisted mainly of nods, looks and the young woman's expressive eyebrow technique. Like all brilliant hotel staff, she knew exactly who belonged and who did not, who was in each room and why, along with an accurate assessment of their relationship to the paying guest of that room.

She was assisting a German couple when Michael passed the counter, and she raised her eyebrow a few millimetres in his direction. Michael took it to mean that she knew about Lene, that there were no messages or enquiries, and that everything was okay.

He hung up his wet coat in the small hallway of his room and walked noiselessly across the thick carpet. Only the desk lamp was on and he approached the alcove with the sleeping tablets and a glass of water in his hand.

Lene was out like a light.

She lay on her side with her hands folded under her cheek like a child, and her eyeballs twitched under thin eyelids. Her lips were slightly parted and her breathing regular.

Michael stared in disbelief at the box of sleeping tablets and the glass of water. His wet shoes squelched with every footstep; he was shivering with cold and was sorely tempted to shake her until she woke up so that he could force those blasted pills down her throat.

Instead, he watched the television at the foot of the bed while he pulled out a chair for himself with the tips of his toes. He drank the water in the glass, and watched a news broadcast about extensive security precautions at selected hotels where the EU's foreign delegations would be staying. It was the biggest security operation in Denmark since Barack

Obama and Oprah Winfrey had visited. The conference would be opened with an official dinner at Amalienborg Palace the following evening. Friday was set aside for discussions in the Foreign Ministry, after which the foreign ministers would hold a press conference the same evening. Everyone would travel home on the Saturday.

Today was Wednesday and Michael evaluated the risk of an attack. He thought it likely. The terrorists had undoubtedly been spurred on by their first success and Denmark was still a prominent member of the new imperialist crusader countries trying to introduce democracy and decadent human rights into ancient Bedouin societies. He tried putting himself in their shoes. The foreign ministers or Ehud Berezowsky? Both? Both would probably be too demanding for Sheikh Safar Khan. His organization was efficient, but small.

He considered checking with his contacts in Israel. He had not told Lene the whole truth about his sister, Ida. Like many Israelis with a mixed background, she was a potential asset. The diaspora was and always had been Mossad's advantage over other intelligence services. They commanded loyal helpers, local knowledge and languages in every corner of the world, and anyone who got the call would obey *Eretz Israel*, the fatherland. Including new citizens such as his sister. Living in a country the size of Jutland with your back to the sea and in a part of the world where all races and governments officially strove to exterminate you and your family was incredibly conducive to patriotic loyalty, although his sister was far from blind to the attacks to which the state of Israel subjected the stateless minority in the region. She would often describe the country as an over-militarized Sparta, but her criticism had no negative consequences: Mossad welcomed differences and disagreement. They said it kept people's eyes open and their senses heightened.

But there was no time. The summit would take place the day after tomorrow. Besides, he doubted very much whether Ida or her friends would have any information about Ebrahim Safar Khan that Charlotte Falster or PET didn't already know.

As if on cue, the bespectacled chief superintendent with the grey bob appeared on his TV screen. Charlotte Falster looked tired, but immaculate. He was about to turn up the volume, but Lene mumbled in her sleep and turned over. Besides, the journalist was bound to ask only the usual questions. Were they satisfied with security measures? Would it be possible for something like the Tivoli bomb to happen again?

Charlotte Falster was smiling and reassuring, but her eyes behind the lenses were anxious.

The feature ended the only way it could: with the Hansson footage which by now must have been seen by pretty much everyone on the planet, and which had long since exceeded every other contender as the most watched clip on YouTube.

Jonathan Hansson Jr was a young tourist from Portland, Oregon, holidaying in Denmark with his girlfriend, Julie, in order to visit the little village on Møn from where the

Hansson family had emigrated a long time ago. The young couple had been in the top gondola on Tivoli's Ferris wheel at 11:13 on the 17th September.

Julie was blonde, freckled and pretty, and an infatuated Jonathan Hansson caressed her face, neck and one bare shoulder with the video camera. The girl squinted against the sunlight. Embarrassed, she tried to push the camera aside and so the viewfinder settled instead on the tall dark-green Star Flyer and lingered on the taut wires and the tiny, remote figures being hurled around in orbit against a high, clear sky over Copenhagen.

Then you heard a sudden outburst from Julie. The camera frame wobbled before discovering the doughnut-shaped explosion which rocked the buildings, stalls and pavilions surrounding the Star Flyer, before they collapsed like houses of cards. Dust and smoke and indefinable objects floated slowly towards the camera and you could hear the sharp pings of ball bearings ricocheting off the steel girders of the Ferris wheel. The gondola braked, stopped and swung back and forth calmly while the young couple screamed.

The tower is collapsing, for Christ's sake! Jonathan Hansson shouted and, with admirable presence of mind, zoomed in on the towering steel construction, which with infinite slowness started tilting to the north. You could hear distant cries from people in the chairs. At first, one chair tore itself loose from its chains and a barely recognizable black shape was flung through the air by the centrifugal force. The rest followed and floppy dark bodies that looked like rag dolls were outlined against the redbrick backdrop of Copenhagen Town Hall. Julie screamed and stood up in the gondola, but Jonathan Hansson reached up his hand and pulled her back into the seat. The Star Flyer was keeling now at an impossible angle, before snapping suddenly and silently under its own weight.

Oh my God, it's gonna crash! Julie screamed and buried her face in her hands. *It's gonna . . . Oh my God, my God! Jon, it's awful, those poor, poor people . . . those poor, poor people!*

The camera followed the tower as it fell and registered the enormous cloud of dust that rose from the amusement park.

It was by no means the only film documenting the bombing, but from a technical point of view it was the most successful. It had the advantage of the unique angle from the Ferris wheel and the pitiful soundtrack of the two terrified youngsters.

The Hansson film had become an almost official documentation of the Tivoli bombing. TV channels, schools and documentary film-makers always used it. It was etched on the world's retina.

28

Ain had died at 11:48 exactly.

There were no delays on the E-line train from Køge to Hillerød that day and there were six active surveillance cameras on the platforms. Three on the northbound platform where Ain was standing and three on the southbound and, as far as Michael could see, no one had manipulated the recordings. There were no odd, jerky pauses and the time stamp flowed continuously.

The young woman was wearing a short, pale leather jacket, jeans and grey Adidas trainers; she had a dark-blue scarf around her neck and a light-coloured leather bag over her shoulder. According to Lene's information, she was 1.73 metres tall and weighed sixty-one kilos. Michael identified her quickly on the northbound platform's three cameras, but the cameras on the opposite platform never picked her up.

He saw Ain from the back, from the front and from the right, from the moment she came down the stairs, until she disappeared. The morning rush-hour was over and the afternoon peak had yet to begin. Most passengers were young, while a few elderly couples moved sedately across the tiled platform floor.

For the first twenty metres the girl walked quickly, unaware of the other passengers. She had her left hand on the strap of her shoulder bag and her right hand pressed her mobile to her ear. She quickly made her way between commuters, looking over her shoulder several times. Her face was pale, but composed. When she was not talking, her lips remained parted. Her eyes were large and dark. She did not look at people's faces, and her gaze appeared to be locked in the middle distance. Her stride was long and confident, and Michael was convinced that she was not under the influence of medication. She was possibly scared half to death, but her central nervous system was functioning faultlessly. She looked very much like a person who expected to remain alive. This was not the introverted, empty face of someone about to kill herself.

There was no soundtrack, but it was easy to read exactly what had happened by observing people's movements. For example, everyone turned around on the opposite platform when the stopping service from Valby arrived at 11:37. The train stopped, the doors opened, and the platform filled with passengers.

The southbound platform slowly emptied while more people arrived on the other side. Ain had nearly reached the yellow line where the front section of the northbound train would stop. Again, she looked over her shoulder and came to an abrupt halt, facing the exit behind her.

Michael clicked through all the images from all the cameras. He was especially interested in people coming down the stairs. A young couple in conversation, a boy pushing a bicycle over the last few steps, a blind man accompanied by a guide dog sweeping his white stick in small, exploring arcs in front of them and . . .

Michael froze the picture.

Someone had stopped at the fourth step from the bottom, closest to the wall. Michael selected the section, enlarged it – and lost all detail.

Ain's face crumbled. It turned deathly pale. She let her hand with the mobile drop down by her side, and walked slowly on. People pushed against each other at the edge of the platform and the young Arab woman disappeared from sight. The train's headlights lit up the tunnel and the cameras quivered when it pulled up.

He found the last recordings of her from the camera located at the platform's northern staircase. A glimpse of her clear profile, her black hair, which was lifted by the air pressure of the train. The train braked, people pushed together and then the crowd suddenly moved away from the place where he had last seen Ain, to reveal an empty semicircle of tiles and the platform edge.

The train was at a standstill while the train driver, an older man, got up and opened the window. People were still retreating from the front section of the train; he opened the side window, placed his hand on the window frame, leaned out and stared into the gap between the carriage and the platform edge. Then his hands moved up to his face and he slumped into the driver's seat. It was twelve seconds before he pushed the button that opened all doors and started the red warning lights flashing.

Michael leaned closer and studied the screen. The stranger's shoes and lower legs were still on the fourth step from the bottom, right up against the wall, even though everyone else was aiming for the stairs, pushing and shoving to get up and away.

At length, the quiet bystander also disappeared in the crowd.

A white mobile was left behind on the tiles. An older man in a cotton coat walked over, picked it up and pressed it to his ear. It looked as if he said a few words before his wife arrived. She grabbed him firmly by the arm and pointed to the tiles. He looked at her, nodded and carefully returned the mobile to the spot where he had found it. The woman dragged him away.

Michael rubbed his eyes and yawned until his jaw creaked. He was exhausted and considered taking a cold shower, but did not have the energy.

It had been a simple one-two manoeuvre, he thought glumly. One pursuer lets the victim spot them, gets their attention and drives him or her forward and while the victim is looking back, their partner appears ahead and carries out the attack.

In his line of work, this was known as the Kansas City Shuffle. Faced with an inexperienced prey – and Ain was one of the most innocent and defenceless victims Michael could imagine – it was bound to work because people instinctively expected danger to come from behind.

A couple of ticket inspectors arrived and looked down at the tracks. One of them threw up immediately. He shook his head at his colleague and the white-faced train driver, who by this point had reversed the train a few metres. Together they supported the shocked driver between them towards the exit, where he could sit up against the wall.

An ambulance, an emergency doctor and some police officers arrived in the course of six impressive minutes. The doctor jumped onto the tracks, squatted down on his haunches and peered under the train before standing up again. He looked at the head of operations, who was a man, and a young dark-haired woman in a police uniform and shrugged his shoulders. As far as Michael could see, he did not say anything. There was no need to. The doctor and the driver disappeared from the station: there was nothing they could do. The paramedics started salvaging body parts from the tracks. Michael closed his eyes and counted to thirty. He opened them again and saw that Ain's body had been placed on a stretcher and covered with white blankets.

Three minutes further into the film, he saw a figure he knew very well: Lene came walking into the field of view of the first camera. She was staring straight ahead. She did not look like a professional investigator about to assess a potential crime scene. She looked like a sleepwalker.

Michael clicked back to the first CDs showing the seconds before the impact. Where the hell was the first attacker? He or she had to be there, right in front of him.

The waiting passengers, who had been the first to surge towards the train, retreated once again, revealing a semicircle of bare tiles on his computer screen. Ain's final action in this world had been making her way through a small group of boys with skateboards sticking out of their rucksacks or tucked under their arms; big jackets, baggy trousers and hoodies. Indistinguishable from one another. She stopped abruptly in the middle of the group and looked up, closed her eyes and quickly moved on.

Two seconds later she was dead.

Michael went out into the bathroom, splashed cold water on his face and glanced at the heavily sleeping Lene, who was slurping in her sleep like a well-fed baby.

He made sketches and diagrams. The position of the train, stairs leading up and down, the location of the cameras. The three surveillance cameras on the southbound platform were useless . . . Or were they?

He had ignored them because they did not show Ain at any time. But perhaps they showed other people of interest? If he had been spearheading a Kansas City Shuffle, he would have avoided the surveillance cameras most likely to show the target, until the opportunity arose where he could cross the platform. Which arose when the southbound train to Køge emptied of passengers.

Perhaps the killer had arrived by train?

For the next half-hour he concentrated on the Valby train and the small cluster of skateboarders. They shuffled across the platform to wait for the train to Hillerød.

The five boys were almost impossible to tell apart in their hoodies, scarves, beanies and puffa jackets. They had only a few metres to walk before they appeared in the cameras Michael had been studying.

A member of their group, a slowcoach, lagged behind the others; big jacket, trainers, baggy trousers, a hood pulled down to obscure his or her face. He took up position on the outskirts of the group when Ain passed and then started pushing towards the edge of the platform as the train pulled up. When Ain was halfway through the group, she stopped, lifted her head and closed her eyes like someone . . . like someone who . . . oh, shit!

Michael got up, opened the door to the minibar fridge and studied the contents critically. Kahlúa. Who the hell drank Kahlúa? He was hopelessly stuck while, at the same time, he had a frustrating feeling that the answer was staring him in the face. Only he was too blind and dumb to see it. He squatted down and fished out two miniature bottles of whisky, poured them into one glass and lit acigarette.

He hoped that the alcohol and nicotine would jump-start

a couple of brain cells. Then he thought about his seven-year-old son who, outside their speed bump in front of their house, had started practising his first tentative moves on his beloved skateboard which Michael had brought back for him from the USA. It had been signed by a twenty-one-year-old Californian idol and his son slept with it every night, Sara had told him.

He raised his head and smiled at his reflection in the dark balcony door.

'Hey, hey, hey, my little friend, where the hell is *your* skateboard?'

He stubbed out the cigarette and carried his glass to the computer. His heart was pounding, but he was sure he was right: he had found the missing piece. The boy in the dark puffa jacket, the slowcoach with the downcast eyes and his face hidden by the hoodie, shuffling at the heels of the others across the platform. Beanie, gloves. But no rucksack. No skateboard.

Michael could easily imagine it. The boy did not belong to the others. He had attached himself to the group on the platform, thinking they could serve as camouflage.

I've got you under my skin / I've got you deep in the heart of me ... Michael hummed a private version of Sinatra's evergreen. Then he heard the bed creak under Lene and settled for miming.

Ain stopped on the platform, raised her face and closed her eyes, before she carried on ... Ain stopped in the middle of the group, raised her face and closed her eyes before she . . . Ain stopped . . .

Like someone listening to a melody or someone picking up a scent which should not be there, Michael thought. She was sniffing. That was exactly what she was doing! Scent. Perfume. Sixteen-year-old skateboarders don't wear perfume. They would rather be buried alive. Perhaps Ain was not even conscious of the anomaly, Michael thought. She was on the run, she was at the highest, animalistic state of alert and all her senses were wide open. Sound, taste, smell and sight were razor sharp.

'You're not a boy, my friend, are you?' he muttered. 'So what are you, then? You're a girl, and you think you're so devious and oh so scary, but I'm smarter than you and I'm much more dangerous than you'll ever be.'

Everything inside Michael calmed down. He experienced that deep sense of satisfaction and serenity he always felt when he had been proved right, when he had found something no one else in the world could find. A killer. The boy/girl. Tall, slim, disguised and ruthless. Like any other clever, young terrorist of the right, deadly material.

He yawned and stretched out. He could rest now. He had earned it.

29

The only sign of life in the narrow street was a young woman. She had a black guitar case on her back; she slowed down and jumped off her bicycle a few houses ahead. She opened the garden gate and pushed her bicycle through it. The light from the hallway fell over the front steps, the girl and the garden path until the front door shut behind her.

He waited another half-hour before he opened the gate and walked up the cracked flagstone path. The house was quiet and the neighbouring houses lay in darkness. The moon had waned to a slim crescent and the night was black and cool.

The doorbell made a low, melodic sound and he heard a door being opened inside.

He closed the front door behind him and stood very close to her. Neither of them said anything. The heat radiated from her body and the hairs on his forearms stood up.

'Are you alone?'

'Of course,' she said. 'Of course. Come in.'

Her arms were bare and he noticed that she was dressed

in a long, flimsy sleeveless kaftan gathered together with a fabric belt, tied in a loose knot. Her nipples were pushed up against the thin fabric. Her pure, beautiful face was tilted and her hair was swept behind one shoulder. She expected to be embraced and kissed, but he walked past her, through the hallway and into the living room.

'Would you like a drink?' she asked.

'Later, perhaps.'

'Have you met her?' she asked. 'Is she going to carry on?'

'She'll stop now.'

'Are you sure?'

'Yes. After tonight. Yes.'

'I've missed you,' she said. 'Come here.'

Coco Mademoiselle, but only a hint. She looked down while she loosened the belt with a well-rehearsed movement and let it fall to the floor. The kaftan opened and in the faint light from the street her nipples were very dark and erect, the rest of her skin pale, smooth perfection. She took his hand and pressed it against her sex, and he slipped a finger inside her.

'Oh, yes,' she whispered.

He pressed her against the desk and their tongues entwined. They swayed together as only lovers can. He found and caressed her clitoris and the purring in her throat grew deeper. His other, free hand fumbled around the desk behind her arched back. Her hips started moving rhythmically against his hand.

He found the long embalming syringe on the desk, exactly where it ought to be. Their mouths released, and he looked deep into her eyes.

'Let's go upstairs!' she pleaded.

'Yes.'

With black despair he stabbed the long, sharp needle hard and precisely into her open, smiling left eye. The eyeball offered no resistance and the thin bone of the eye socket snapped with a barely audible noise. The needle continued deep into her brain.

Her right eye widened in shock. Then she was overcome by intense agony and the eye was firmly shut. She did not scream; he did not suppose that she was able to. He removed his free hand which was pressed over her mouth. She walked slowly around the living room in a large circle. Instinctively she avoided the furniture. She held her head high and blood flowed freely from the eye socket. Not one sound erupted from her mouth. Her blood was black and ran over her chin, spreading down her throat and chest in thin channels.

Her path ended by the desk and him. About fifteen centimetres of the silver embalming needle was sticking out of her eye socket and he bashed it hard and desperately with his flat hand. The needle continued until it hit something in her skull that refused to budge.

Finally the loud, piercing cry and the spasms came, and he pushed her down on the floor and put a cushion over her mouth and nose. Her screams continued, but were now muffled. He placed all of his body weight on top of it, and finally her naked heels drummed hard, but briefly, against the floorboards and she stopped moving. He removed the cushion and watched her right pupil slowly expand from oxygen deprivation. There was no longer a pulse in the arteries of her neck. Her mouth opened.

He sat for a long time by her head, his face buried in his hands, muttering meaningless apologies before he started setting everything up.

The whole process took him less than half an hour.

He exited the house, leaving the front door open, and checked out his surroundings carefully before he walked down the street.

Halfway down the row of houses a dormer window was open, and he could hear the crisp strumming of a guitar.

30

The white, two-engine Lear jet belonging to Trinity Air Ambulance from Amman was given permission to land at 04:36, and the wheels touched down on runway 23A in Frankfurt International Airport two minutes later. The aircraft taxied away from the control tower and across to the private section of the airport. Here, it stopped outside a long, low administration building and the aircraft's engines were turned off. A specialist ambulance and two sleepy, middle-aged Customs officers in a green VW reached the aircraft the moment the disembarking steps were lowered.

Two young men, wearing the smart white uniforms of the freight company, started unloading the reinforced, fluorescent-orange plastic crates from the aircraft's hold and stacking them on the tarmac. They worked skilfully and efficiently. Each box was fitted with an instrument panel and a cooling aggregate, and draped in a fine layer of hoar frost.

The ambulance crew helped them unload the last crates from the hold of the aircraft.

One of the young men from Trinity Air tugged his long

black hair behind his ear, smiled at the older of the two Customs officers and handed him a voluminous ring binder with the loading manifest. He had a relaxed, engaging manner and his English was flawless. The officer noticed a white, star-shaped scar on the young man's left temple.

The Customs officer knew that time was of the essence: fresh, donated organs for the European market were a serious and urgent matter, and this time they would seem to have struck gold. A twenty-two-year-old, perfectly healthy young man had fallen from construction scaffolding in a suburb of Amman.

For once, everything had gone by the book. The young man had been taken promptly to a university hospital, where they concluded that he had broken only his upper arm but suffered serious head trauma and subsequent intracranial bleeding which, a few hours later, had squeezed the life out of him. But his heart had continued to beat and the respirator oxygenated the blood and the organs perfectly.

His parents were modern and sensible. The young man was declared brain dead the same evening, following an MRI scan and extensive neurological examinations, and the transplant team were given full access a few hours later. His heart, lungs, kidneys, liver, bones, bone marrow and corneas were harvested. The corneas and bone marrow were sent to Houston, Texas, while Universitätsklinikum der Johann Wolfgang Goethe in Frankfurt-am-Main was the happy recipient of the remaining organs, according to the International Transplant Register's acute list.

The Customs officer licked his thumb and index finger and compared the cargo list with the orange boxes. All the numbers and codes matched. He was conscious that everyone around him was shifting restlessly from foot to foot. For the staff these transports had an element of routine, but right now terminally ill people in central Germany would be receiving the most important telephone call of their lives, either on their own or on their children's behalf: a donor has been found. You must come now! This instant!

'Only twenty-two years old,' he muttered. 'Poor lad, how tragic.'

The young man with the scar pursed his lips and nodded gravely.

'Very tragic, Herr Zollbeamten.'

The Customs officer's sister had received a donor kidney from Jordan at the prestigious Universitätsklinikum, and thus he had no interest in making things more difficult for the team than necessary. He asked to see the men's passports and papers, but checked them only superficially. He nodded and smiled, and the young man placed a friendly hand on his shoulder. The crew transferred the organs to a specialist ambulance, where the crates were connected to the ambulance's more robust cooling and oxygen systems. Normally the responsibility of the transport team did not come to an end until the receiving hospital had signed for the organs, after which the men would take a civilian aircraft home if the ambulance plane was unable to wait for them.

The doors of the ambulance were slammed shut and the Customs officer muttered a few words into his walkie-talkie, telling the guard at the gate to allow them to drive straight through.

The ambulance joined the E451 and headed north. Samir and his new partner, Adil – a young veteran from the Syrian civil war, originally a citizen of the Netherlands – put their own suitcases in the rear of the ambulance. The cases contained nothing but a change of clothes and toiletries, and they could have passed any inspection. The men took off their white overalls and changed into thick sweaters and leather jackets. Adil also put on a pair of cotton gloves and found the two crates that were marked with a discreet chalk line. He loosened the locking clamps and white smoke from the dry ice wafted towards the roof of the ambulance. He carefully removed the polystyrene tray covered with dry ice and placed it on the ambulance floor. Underneath the first tray were two ultramodern Russian explosive vests with packets of glass balls, armed with the scent-free explosive isopropyl nitrate. Samir helped him pack the vests into a sports bag. They returned the tray with the dry ice to the first box and opened the next. Under the polystyrene were two sawn-off AK-47 automatic carbines, known as baby Kalashnikovs, with four magazines for each carbine, along with two fat envelopes: money for the Polish skipper who, in a few hours, would pick them up at the port of Rostock, and euros and Danish kroner for any unforeseen expenses.

They had finished repacking by the time the ambulance pulled into a layby. One of the drivers went behind some bushes to take a leak. He lit a cigarette and strolled calmly up and down the layby until he was sure there was no one around. Then he returned to the ambulance and slammed his palms against the back door.

Samir and Adil received a brief, ritual embrace and a couple of muttered blessings from the others. They picked up their heavy cases and walked towards an old grey Audi. The ambulance set off for Frankfurt and the waiting university hospital, with its valuable cargo of human spare parts which had once belonged to a young man with a cleft palate.

The car keys had been left in the exhaust pipe of the Audi. Adil got in on the passenger side and started programming the satnav while Samir loaded the bags and suitcases and looked briefly up at the stars.

It was a moment filled with both triumph and sadness. The arrival into Europe had gone exactly as Safar Khan had predicted, and the end of borders as established by the Schengen Agreement ensured there would be no obstacles on their onward journey to Denmark. They would carry out their holy mission, *insha' Allah*, and many important and mighty people would die at their hands. But if they succeeded, if they were skilled and careful, their own lives would also be over.

He got into the car. Adil looked at him without saying anything and Samir nodded, started the engine and headed for Rostock.

31

It was the sound he detested most. His wife's mobile. It continued to ring and Otto Jarl Falster rose on his elbow and stared at his wife's face. Her eyes were wide awake in the dim light, but she would appear to be paralysed. He let himself fall onto his back, reassured that at least she was still breathing. He watched the luminous hands on his wristwatch. Four-thirty in the morning. This was intolerable. Quite simply, intolerable.

After what seemed to him like eternity, her bedside lamp was switched on, she sat up and muttered something into her mobile.

The words eventually became clearer.

'Who?', 'Where?', 'No, no, no . . .!', 'Don't move her. I want a forensic pathologist to attend . . . Dr Helle Englund, perhaps. No, no, not perhaps. I want her.' And finally the inevitably gritted, 'I'll be there right away.'

These days, she was faster at getting dressed than a fireman and was soon standing by the bed, looking down at her husband.

'Don't say anything, Otto.'

'I didn't say a bloody word, for Christ's sake!'

'No, but I know what you were going to say.'

He furrowed his brow.

'You're reproaching me for something you think I'm about to say?'

'Yes.'

'*Bon voyage*,' he mumbled.

'I'd be happy to swap,' she said. 'I'll take your meetings instead.'

The permanent secretary emitted a burst of hollow laughter.

'I don't think you would make that offer if you knew that I have a two-hour meeting with the minister this morning. You would shoot her after thirty minutes.'

A soft expression flitted across her face. Perhaps she could see that he was suffering from heartburn and indigestion.

'Poor you, darling,' she mumbled.

He smiled bravely.

'No, poor you. Has anyone died?'

She sighed and he clasped one of her hands; the one with the wedding ring.

'I'm afraid so. Irene Adler. Someone killed her.'

'Adler?'

He sat up in bed.

'Yes.'

'Poor woman.'

'Yes.'

'Do they know who did it?'

She stared into space.

'I can think of only one person who had a motive and the determination necessary.'

'Who?'

She withdrew her hand.

'Oh, God, Otto. It's impossible . . . Christ, I couldn't bear it if it turns out that . . . that . . . Lene Jensen is an obvious candidate. Irene Adler treated her daughter. A young woman who committed suicide.'

'I was at her funeral, Charlotte.'

He leaned his head against the bedstead and looked pensively at the predawn sky. His wife watched him, and he finally looked at her and rubbed his chin.

'What is it?' she asked.

'Thomas Thierry's committee.'

'The Interior Ministry? What committee, Otto?'

'A top-secret committee. It reports directly to the Interior Ministry and the Ministry of Defence. We coordinate Denmark's intelligence services. All countries have such committees, though not many people know.'

'I understand.'

'I'll be shot if this comes out, Charlotte, but . . . well, it was that committee, I mean the ministry, that allocated money to Adler's centre. I was on it.'

She placed a small, warm hand on his shoulder and he looked searchingly at her.

'We have to do something, Charlotte.'

'Of course.'

'They called the project creative and ground-breaking, but I thought all along that mixing psychiatric treatment with surveillance and intelligence activity was dangerous. There are no real precedents, but we agreed to try it. Perhaps someone in PET thought that the partnership was problematic? The media would have a field day if this was to come out. I'm just asking you to bear that in mind, Charlotte.'

'I will.'

She turned in the doorway and looked him.

'Thank you,' she said.

She closed the door behind her and Otto Jarl Falster opened a drawer in his bedside table and found his antacids. He swallowed three, just to be on the safe side.

The street between the town houses was cordoned off with red-and-white police tape, and the narrow façades were illuminated in flashes by the blue lights from the emergency vehicles. There were not many people in the street, but several residents were standing behind their windows in various stages of undress, watching with interest.

Two white box vans from the Department of Forensics were parked outside number 19. Charlotte got out of her Passat and approached the scene. She shuddered. It was an unnaturally cold April with record low temperatures that refused to lift. She spotted two men in a dark-blue Mondeo parked outside the cordons. A blue emergency light had been placed on the roof of the car, but it was not switched on. She bent down and rapped her knuckles on the driver's window. He did not react. His partner said a few words to him, and eventually the window was rolled down.

'What are you waiting for?' she asked.

She bent down further and Christian Erichsen smiled at her from the passenger seat. He held up a stainless-steel Thermos flask and a clean plastic cup by way of invitation. There was a round thermometer fitted to the side of the flask. Charlotte was aware of his reputation as an amateur barista.

'No, thanks,' she said, and studied Kim behind the wheel.

The deputy chief superintendent looked straight ahead as if Charlotte didn't exist. The furrows and the lines in his face looked as if they were tattooed in black ink, and his jaw was covered by white and grey stubble.

'Irene Adler,' he said, seeming to think that would suffice.

Charlotte straightened up and stuffed her hands into her coat pockets.

'Yes. What a shame. We'll deal with it.'

His jaw muscles worked under the taut skin.

'You won't find shit, as usual,' he grunted. 'There's only one person who wanted Irene dead, and you know exactly who that is.'

Charlotte looked down at him calmly.

'You say that once more, Kim, and I'll make sure that in about five minutes you're forced into early retirement due to your totally fucked-up nervous system, and I'll back it up with psychiatric and work-related medical statements and the whole shebang, even if it's the last thing I do. You'll be lucky to get a job as a traffic warden, and I don't care how far you have your tongue up your boss's arse. If you two psychopaths bother, pester, or harass Lene or any other of my staff, including my IT technicians, the same will apply. Understood?'

She bent down again, ignored Kim and glowered at Christian.

'Please would you translate for the idiot sitting next to you?'

Christian's face had paled, but whether it was due to exhaustion, cold or her speech, she did not know, nor did she care.

'I will, Charlotte. Definitely. Absolutely. Of course.'

'Good. Besides, I would have thought that you had better things to do than sit here watching other people work. As far as I've been briefed, the first delegations will land at eleven o'clock. Perhaps you should go over security measures once more. It would be awfully embarrassing if one of our guests was blown up before they had even reached their hotel.'

She nodded curtly by way of goodbye, raised the cordon over her head and marched up the flagstone path and into Irene Adler's town house.

Charlotte could hear people moving about upstairs and scrambling below in the basement. All the doors were open and the long, narrow rooms were peopled by figures in white nylon all-in-ones and blue shoe covers. One of them handed her a pair and she slipped them over her shoes.

The interior looked like the set of *Casablanca* with dark, ancient, geometrically intricate Arab woodcarvings, desks, thick Persian carpets everywhere, low brass tables and more pouffes and chairs. Irene Adler was lying on her back in the middle of the living room floor; in the total relaxation of death, she seemed to take up most of the space.

A woman dressed in white with short, blonde hair was kneeling by the body and reading something on her smartphone. From her mobile, a white cable wound its way down between the body's slightly parted legs and disappeared out of sight. Charlotte frowned, carefully stepped closer and the woman looked up at her with a smile. Charlotte recognized her as Lene Jensen's special friend: Helle Englund, the medical examiner.

'Is that a new app?' she said.

'There's an app for everything these days. This is a rectal thermometer. It's very accurate, I'll have you know.'

Charlotte nodded and looked at the dead woman's face. Her right eye studied the living room ceiling blindly, while a bent, silver-coloured needle stuck out ten centimetres from the left eye. The mouth was half open, revealing a row of perfect teeth. The blood had formed a river delta across her face, neck and chest. Her nipples were small and dark brown, her sex naked and smooth.

The medical examiner extracted the thermometer from the body's rectum, slipped off a latex sheath, and placed the probe and the cable in a plastic bag. She rose and for a moment they stood shoulder to shoulder, looking down at the beautiful, dead woman.

Charlotte pointed to the murder weapon.

'What is that?'

'I believe it's an embalming syringe. It was used for injecting embalming fluid or formaldehyde into the major veins of the dead. I've seen them at a History of Medicine museum.'

'Ghastly thing.'

The medical examiner nodded.

'It's macabre. But not very effective.'

Charlotte frowned. A certain nausea was stirring inside her.

'Isn't it? I would have thought sticking an object like that into someone's brain would . . . well, short-circuit every-thing immediately?'

'Yes, that was undoubtedly what the killer thought as well,' Helle Englund said. 'But that only works in the movies. In real life there are plenty of instances where people, espe-cially Greenlanders for some reason, have mounted a chisel on a workbench and tried killing themselves by bashing their head against the blade. If you're not lucky – or lucky enough, depending on how you look at it – to hit one of the main arteries in the brain, nothing much happens. Unconsciousness and possibly spasms, but it won't kill you. As an organ the brain lacks sensitivity. It does not react to pain, cold, heat or touch.'

'Then what happens?'

'Some of them just stand there, waiting to be found. Others manage to unscrew the chisel from the wood bench or the vice, go inside the house and call an ambulance themselves.'

Charlotte looked at the other woman.

'Are you taking . . .?'

'I'm not taking the mickey, no.'

The woman smiled. She had a gap between her front teeth. It was really rather charming.

She pointed to the floor.

'There's a characteristic, circular blood trail on the floor which begins and ends at the desk. My preliminary hypothesis is that the blow was inflicted while she was standing with her back to the desk. The syringe damaged the motor cortex, the white substance in the left side of the brain, which controls the right arm and leg. She would have been able to walk, but only to the right, clockwise that is. She has wandered through the living room, but ended up at her starting point. And back to the killer, of course. Perhaps she realized that she had to flee, but was unable to navigate out of the room. She—'

'Stop it!'

The medical examiner looked at Charlotte in amazement.

It might be just as natural for her as discussing the price of milk, or the latest winner of the *X Factor*, but it was not natural for the chief superintendent.

She had been assistant principal and later principal in the Ministry of Justice before she applied for the job with Rigspolitiet. She had a superficial knowledge of the practical side of a crime scene, and crime in general, but compensated for it with her intelligence and imagination. It was one of the things Lene held against her. That she had never worked at the coal face.

She held up one hand and gave a pale smile.

'Thank you. I understand, and I can vividly imagine the rest. So what killed her, if it wasn't that thing in her . . . in her brain?'

She cleared her throat harshly.

'She was suffocated with that,' the medical examiner said, pointing.

A crime scene officer was easing a soft, round leather cushion into a plastic bag.

'There was plenty of blood on the cushion. My guess is that the killer lost patience, got nervous or did not have time to wait, so he or she put her on the floor and pressed the cushion over her face.'

'That makes sense,' Charlotte conceded. 'When did she die?'

'Her core temperature was 26.7°C, and the room temperature is 19.2°C.'

The medical examiner found a chart on her smartphone. 'So . . . around 03:20.'

'Had she had sex with someone? She's dressed very . . . invitingly?'

'There's no semen in her vagina, and no signs of lesions to her groin area, but I need to get her to the institute before I can say for sure.'

Charlotte nodded and looked around. The kitchen would appear to be free for the time being. She frogmarched the medical examiner inside it and closed the door behind them.

'Sit down,' she said, pointing to a chair at a rectangular, rustic table.

The doctor sat down with a puzzled expression.

Charlotte took a moment to reflect. She did not know quite how to begin, so instead she opened the door to the large stainless-steel fridge. It contained nothing but fine, organic foods. A large selection of fruit and vegetables, hardly any dairy products and a couple of unopened foil bags from one of Copenhagen's best fishmongers in Frederiks-borggade, date stamped the day before. And three bottles of Möet & Chandon champagne. Irene was probably used to unexpected, international guests, and Charlotte imagined there would often be new grant allocations or articles in *Nature* or *The Lancet* to be celebrated.

She closed the fridge, sat down opposite the medical examiner and interlaced her fingers on the table.

'Helle . . . May I call you Helle?'

The other woman smiled and nodded, and Charlotte continued.

'Nothing, and I really do mean nothing, which will be said here in the next few minutes must ever be repeated. Do you understand? I'm going to ask you some questions. And I'm going to ask you to answer them as clearly and honestly as you can. It's important.'

'Of course.'

'You know Superintendent Lene Jensen quite well, don't you?'

'Yes. Not privately, of course, but . . . yes.'

Charlotte studied her nails. They needed filing.

'In your professional opinion – and I'm aware that you're not a psychiatrist or psychologist – but nevertheless . . . how does she seem to you? I know that the two of you met recently, and I know that you know her from previous cases. Is she . . . I mean, is she entirely sane? In your opinion?'

The younger woman nodded.

'Absolutely. She's exhausted and grieving. She might even be clinically depressed. Who wouldn't be? After all, she blames herself for what happened to her daughter. And, indirectly, she's absolutely right. That's the problem. That knowledge just won't go away. But she's robust. She's fully functioning, although I understand exactly why you ask. But she's completely focused, and I would trust her with my life, if that doesn't sound ridiculously dramatic.'

Charlotte drew a square with her fingertip on the rustic

tabletop. She wanted to smile, but preserved her expression-less poker face.

'Not at all, Helle. Not at all. It's just possible a lot of people may end up being in that situation. So she's not crazy? Off her rocker?'

'Not at all.'

'Thank you. Now, Ain Ghazzawi Rasmussen. You found a type of reconstructed LSD in her blood, as I understand it? Lene didn't blab. I made her tell me.'

'We did. Not in high concentration, it was mainly break-down products, but that's correct. We found it both in her blood, and in her brain fluid.'

Charlotte frowned.

'Breakdown products? So she was not acutely affected when she was hit by the train? Groggy or disoriented?'

'It's hard to say but, no, not in my opinion. Nobody quite knows what the therapeutic dosage of the drug is, except for the people who administer and produce it, but it was almost out of her body when she died.'

'Who might have administered it to her?'

Helle Englund glanced at the door to the living room and raised one eyebrow.

'Lene thought it was Irene Adler, but I don't think she had any proof.'

'And it acts as a kind of truth serum?' the chief superin-tendent asked.

'Now that's not something which is made public, or

debated openly at our conferences, but several of my colleagues believe that various intelligence services have started using it. It's more discreet than waterboarding or outright torture. It's experiencing something of a revival. After I spoke to Lene, I contacted some colleagues abroad and several have actually come across cases where they suspect LSD had been administered during interrogations. Even in some so-called civilized countries.'

Charlotte rose and held open the door.

'Thank you so much,' she said. 'You've been very helpful. You really have. I appreciate it.'

Charlotte exchanged a few comments with the senior crime scene officer, Arne, who was known for being taciturn, but also for being brilliant at his job and utterly loyal. She told him that if he came across records, lists or computer files of patients who had been treated by Irene Adler's specialist centre at Rigshospitalet, she expected to be informed immediately.

They had not found anything yet, he said, and was about to scratch his neck with a bloody latex glove, but stopped himself at the last moment. In fact, they had not come across a single computer in the house.

'Any sign of burglary, Arne?'

'No.'

'So she knew her killer?'

'Or she was unusually trusting at three-thirty in the

morning,' he said. 'Incidentally, there's no spy hole in the front door.'

Charlotte nodded. It had not been her impression that Irene Adler had been the trusting type.

'Who found her?'

'The guy who delivers her newspaper. This has been his regular route for years, and he has never seen the front door open before. He thought something was wrong and went inside.'

'So the door was open?' she mumbled distractedly.

Arne was about to scratch his neck again. If he had to say everything twice, this was going to take a very long time.

'It was.'

'What about her mobile?'

'It was in the kitchen. No calls since yesterday afternoon. To some scientist in San Diego. And no incoming calls, unfortunately.'

'Thank you, Arne.'

'You're welcome.'

Charlotte walked down the flagstone path. Most lights behind the neighbouring windows had been turned off. The Mondeo with the two PET agents had disappeared. Irene Adler had, as Charlotte herself had pointed out, been very invitingly dressed. And not by chance. She had been expecting a lover, not a killer. So not Lene, clearly.

She heaved a sigh. The psychiatrist's circle of friends and acquaintances had undoubtedly been very extensive.

3 2

Michael was dreaming about Somalia. Or rather, in his semi-conscious state, he was processing several chaotic and painful memories. From the metallic heat, which made the air dance over the endless, low, brown mountains, to the small pack of hyenas he had seen cross the dry riverbed down by the pirates' campsite early one morning. Their heavy, angular heads hung down between their front legs and their coats glowed red in the rising sun.

He was lying very still between some rocks, hidden under a camouflage net three hundred metres from the camp. He had put gauze across the telescopic sight of the rifle so that there would be no reflection to reveal his position.

Michael had been lying there for two days in the silence, interrupted only by the buzzing of insects and a few brief exchanges via satellite phone with a coordinator on a Danish warship in the Bay of Aden. The sun was a constant white, glowing hole in a cloudless sky. He had watched how the young, skinny Somali boys, high on their constant khat chewing, had dragged the Danish seamen and the three

German nuns out from a roasting-hot, corrugated-iron shed and entertained themselves by making them run the gauntlet between the barrels of their Kalashnikov rifles. They forced them to dance while they fired at the ground or made them lie on their backs while they urinated on them. They were young, and these antics rated among the more innocent. Michael had seen so much worse. They were not mutilating the men and they were not raping the nuns. They were just bored.

And they were not the only ones; Michael was bored out of his mind, just like the hostage takers. The water in his camel bags, which he sipped frugally, had grown warm and foul tasting, even though he had tried to sterilize it with a little silver nitrate. Besides, his presence was probably superfluous. He was sure that the Jægerkorpset or their friends from the British SAS or American Navy Seals were present in the small valley, dug in like himself. Invisible. Watching. Michael was just there to assure the shipping company that everything was being done properly.

The insects were driving him crazy. They were everywhere. They lived, grew and hatched under his skin, and he couldn't apply insect repellent to himself because the scrawny dogs down by the fence would smell it.

Ten minutes before daybreak on the third night in the valley, when someone senior and capable of making a decision had arrived on the bridge of the warship, and the analysts had given them the thumbs up, the order was finally given to liberate the hostages.

Up until the last minute, using a restricted frequency of the radio spectrum, they had discussed whether or not to rescue the nuns. The Al-Shabaab pirates had also demanded a ransom for the three German women, religious sisters of the Sacred Heart and thus the responsibility of the Vatican, but Michael had no idea what it was. A fountain, a statue of a knight, a section of the ceiling of the Sistine Chapel? Everyone knew that the three young women would have died of old age before the wise fathers in the Vatican would be prepared to even acknowledge that they had a minor problem down in the Horn of Africa. So the consensus had been that they should take them too.

Michael was wearing night vision goggles when the signal came. He had folded his hands under his chin and was trying to ignore the mosquitoes when he pricked up his ears. He had not heard the helicopters land on the other side of the low mountains, but had spotted half a dozen bulky figures as they made their way over the ridge in the transition between darkness and dawn. Nothing stirred between the tents or the dilapidated corrugated-iron sheds in which the hostages were locked up for the night. Even the dogs would appear to be asleep. The unit spread out in the landscape and five minutes later Michael saw a few blue flashes from the muzzles of their rifles light up the walls and tents. Everything would appear to be going according to plan.

No Somali hostages were taken and no survivors were left behind that morning. So he lifted his head in surprise when a tall, slim figure emerged from the camp's only latrine and escaped between the hills. It had grown lighter by now and he could see the kaftan flap against the figure's long, skinny legs. The sandals raised small clouds of dust in the light morning breeze.

He swore as he spotted something black and square in the hands of the fleeing figure; a radio or satellite phone. The boy slipped through a fold in the landscape and reappeared, leaning, panting heavily against a rock face. He was probably terrified. He crouched forward and started working the device, and Michael quickly pulled out his excellent silenced sniper rifle, flicked down the support legs and removed the lens caps from the long Schmidt & Bender telescope. The figure was squatting on his haunches, pressing the telephone to his ear. The hood of his djellaba was up and Michael had only a section of the throat and the right side of the back in the cross hairs of his telescopic sight.

He released the safety catch and inhaled deeply. There was no time and no choice. If the young pirate called for help, the Danish special forces and the freed hostages would be long gone when the boy's friends turned up. They would be safe and sound in their helicopters, but Michael did not have that luxury. There was no helicopter waiting for him; there might or might not be an Izuzu pick-up built before the pyramids, driven by a young, squinting boy with no wristwatch, with whom he had a kind of agreement.

It was a military as well as a bureaucratic decision. The

Jægerkorpset would under no circumstances take responsibility for the security of a civilian, no matter how competent and experienced this person might be. If his young driver ever showed up, he would hide Michael under sacks of millet and crates of onions on the bed of the pick-up and drive him to a quiet beach north of Hordio where, if the Danish warship's senior commander considered it safe, Michael would be picked up by the Frømandskorpset in one of their speedy rubber dinghies. Training elite soldiers was expensive, and the Danish army preferred using them only for parachute jumps at village fêtes.

The newly arrived pirates would only have Michael to worry about in the narrow, open valley and there could be only one possible ending to that scenario. If he was lucky, they would execute him.

He let out half of his breath and released the shot. The distance was so great that it took almost one second before the dust blew up from the boy's kaftan. The figure slumped forward, ending up in a praying position. Michael watched it for a long time without registering movement. He could clearly see the pink soles of the boy's feet through the telescopic sight.

Six special forces soldiers appeared down by the campsite. They carried two stretchers with the seamen on while the German nuns, who had only been hostages for about a month, were able to half run without assistance. The group disappeared between the hills in the opposite direction to the pirate.

When Michael had packed away his bivouac, he walked briskly down through the valley. It was not the sensible thing to do, he was well aware of it, but from the second he spotted the escaping figure, he had known that something was wrong.

He edged his way through rocks as tall as houses and approached the body carefully from behind, holding his pistol with the safety catch off and the muzzle aimed at the head of the kneeling pirate. When he was one metre away, he returned his pistol to its holster. The bullet had hit the boy in the middle of his back, and had most likely killed him instantly. A scratched Thuraya satellite telephone was lying a short distance away. Michael picked it up and checked it for outgoing calls. The last had taken place two days ago, he noticed to his relief.

He grabbed hold of an arm and rolled the boy onto his back. Then he got up, shocked, as he stared at the face framed by the loose grey hood of the djellaba. The girl could not have been more than sixteen years old. Her black curly hair had been gathered in dozens of tiny pigtails with endless patience and red woollen yarn. A masterpiece of geometry. The girl's right breast was no bigger than half an apple and there was a bloody exit wound above it. Michael pulled aside the stiff, bloody fabric and the girl mewed like a kitten. There was a little bubbly blood from her lungs in the wound. The earth and the rock underneath her were red and brown. Her pretty, slim face was grey under her brown skin.

Her large dark eyes followed his searching hands before

they closed. Her breast heaved, her lungs emptied, and it was over.

She had gathered her hands protectively over her belly and there they stayed while Michael examined her. Then he moved them gently and lifted up her kaftan.

Later, he covered her face with the hood and buried her using all the loose rocks he could find nearby.

He watched the exposed ceiling beams above him and, for a moment, he couldn't remember where he was. He had a fairly insistent hangover and his tongue tasted like a gorilla's armpit. He was alone. He knew it. Lene was gone.

Michael staggered to his feet with a soft groan, stretching out from the foetal position he had assumed on the two armchairs he had pushed together, and fearing he would never walk properly again.

It was seven thirty in the morning and he realized what had woken him up. It was not the American Black Hawk helicopters in Somalia, but police helicopters in the air above Copenhagen.

Lene had made the double bed neatly. He stuck a hand under the duvet, which smelled of her. The mattress was still warm. Her sports bag was sitting on the end of the bed and the bathroom mirror was steamed up.

Michael took a hot shower, which he gradually turned colder and colder until he stood stock-still under the spray with a big repressed scream behind his teeth.

He peed and watched the urine with concern. Today it was browner than ever. Blackwater fever. Wasn't that what they called the final stage of malaria, when you peed blood as your kidneys were eaten up by parasites?

The Dark Continent. It scarred you for life, he had read somewhere. Too true.

He towel-dried himself in front of the mirror and was about to brush his teeth when he heard someone in the hall.

'Lene?'

'Yes.'

He put on his trousers and shirt, swallowed a couple of painkillers and left the bathroom.

She looked surprisingly refreshed and ten years younger. Her hair was clean, brushed back and gathered in a tight ponytail. The many hours of sleep had worked miracles. Her eyes were clear and her mouth relaxed.

She held up a couple of tall styrofoam cups and a paper bag.

'Coffee. Croissants. Cigarettes. I noticed that you had run out.'

'Thank you. But all you had to do was call room service. They're open 24/7, and their coffee is quite acceptable,' he grunted.

She shrugged her shoulders. She was moving her head much more naturally and had covered up the bruises on her neck with a soft grey scarf.

'I needed some fresh air. It's stopped raining. You'd almost think that spring has arrived.'

'When did you wake up?'

'A couple of hours ago. Come on, drink your coffee while it's hot.'

'I was out buying sleeping pills for you yesterday,' he said. She blushed.

'I don't know what happened. I really don't. I feel great. I don't understand it. Thank you so much. I think . . .'

'What?'

'You . . . nothing. It's nice not to be alone, that's all.'

'Thank you.'

They sat down on the sofa. Michael munched croissants and Danish pastries, drank his coffee and started to feel a little more human. Lene read the morning papers. It was really quite cosy sitting in this quiet, unfamiliar way as if they were sharing a train carriage and going somewhere nice.

He walked up to the open balcony door with his coffee and the first cigarette of the day.

'I shot and killed a girl in Somalia,' he said, addressing the empty harbour. 'She was no more than sixteen. I shot her in the back.'

He glanced at her over his shoulder. Lene finished chewing, dabbed her lips with the napkin, which she then folded carefully before saying anything.

'That's awful, Michael. Dreadful. I don't know what to say, but I don't suppose you did it for practice.'

He rubbed his face and the stubble grated against his palms.

'I wasn't practising,' he mumbled. 'I thought she was about to call for help. I was on my own, and knew that I would never get out of that crappy valley if she managed to call for backup. And I thought she was a young man. I mean, I thought she was a boy.'

'Does it make any difference whether she was a boy or a girl?'

'It shouldn't, I suppose, but it does. Especially in this case – she was four or five months pregnant, I think.'

'Is that why you haven't gone home yet?'

Michael frowned and considered it.

'No ... yes, I think so. I don't know. It could be one of the reasons.'

Lene got up, walked over to him and rested her hands on the railing. Then she looked at him without blinking and put one hand on his arm. He could have reached her with a small movement, but instead he edged his way around her and sat down at the desk. He turned on the computer and waited.

'So anyway, while you were lying unconscious in *my* bed, I was hard at work most of the night,' he said. 'Hard and constructively.'

She pulled up a chair next to him.

'Did you get lucky?'

'Ain did *not* kill herself. I'm one hundred per cent sure, so you were right.'

'Are you sure, Michael?'

'Totally.'

Her shoulders relaxed an inch; she placed her fingers on her face and looked at him over her fingertips, which were long and narrow.

'Fuck ... Sorry. I knew it all along, but everybody kept telling me that I was—'

'Unstable?'

'Yes, or worse.'

Michael showed her selected sequences from the footage, including the immobile observer on the stairs.

'This one, he or she, just stands there. Feet slightly too big and shoes too plain for a woman. And it's someone Ain knows and is scared to death of. She kept glancing back over her shoulder while she was on the phone to you. Does that sound accurate?'

'Yes. She was incoherent and very frightened.'

'She's so busy watching the stairs that she never realizes that she has been cut off at the front. The killer has mingled with a group of skateboarding boys. Hoodie, big jacket. Except he doesn't have a skateboard.'

He froze the picture the moment Ain stopped, raised her head and sniffed.

'She can smell something that shouldn't be there,' Lene said.

Michael's face fell. That was supposed to be his insightful observation. He had actually been looking forward to telling her.

'It's a woman dressed as a boy,' Lene went on, deep in concentration. 'But she forgot about her perfume.'

'For God's sake. It took me almost four hours to reach that conclusion. How . . .? I really must be ill.'

She smiled.

'So your mysterious tropical disease has attacked your brain, then?'

He pushed back his chair and got up.

'Yes. I'll end up a vegetable.'

'That's obviously the only possible explanation.'

'It certainly is!'

Lene leaned towards the computer screen.

'But why? Why kill her? She's just—'

'A pawn,' he said. 'They used Ain and knocked her off the board when they no longer needed her. They hid out in her flat and she let them into Tivoli. Perhaps she knew what she was doing, perhaps not. Bearing in mind the things she told you, it seems as if she didn't join the dots until later.'

'But why now? Why did she have to die now?'

'Because they're coming back for more. They knew she had started talking to you, and they knew that you were a police officer.'

'Who killed her?' she asked.

'Well, that's what we're going to find out, isn't it?'

'Very much so.'

He looked at her.

'I mean, it's important to you, isn't it?'

She frowned.

'Of course.'

'Even though you risk wrecking PET's operation? This is no longer personal. This isn't about you and Livslinjen and what you could have done, but didn't do, etcetera.'

'But what if they're wrong, Michael? What if they're protecting the wrong person?'

'You have no reason to think that they're wrong.'

'I know that . . . it's a . . .'

'Hunch?'

Michael stared at her in despair, wondering yet again who to back, and who to stop. The anguished, fanatical Kim, who might very well be in the process of preventing another terror attack in Denmark through skilled intelligence work; or the anguished, fanatical Lene, who had . . . hunches.

'What are you thinking about?' she said, placing her hand on his forearm again.

He smiled faintly.

'More coffee?'

33

'Perhaps they used Ain one last time,' Lene said later. 'I mean, it's just a theory.'

'Let me have it,' he said.

She thought about the American terror expert who, three days ago, had lectured about a new kind of terrorist. Three days? It felt like as many years.

'It's almost impossible to infiltrate a jihadist terrorist network. You might be able to recruit a defector if you promise them asylum, money and a new identity. But you would never be able to trust their information. People will tell you whatever they think you want to hear, won't they?'

Michael looked for something that could serve as an ashtray, and lit a cigarette.

'It's one of their strengths,' he nodded. 'If you know too much and you've been a part of the cell for too long without making your way up the greasy pole, sooner or later someone higher up will point at you and say: *shaheed*, martyr! Congratulations! I wish it were me!'

'So it's better to get one of your own agents to infiltrate the cell?'

'Of course, but that's impossible. The terrorists all know each other, many have grown up together or they've been recommended by someone who has known them since they were babies. Or they pick young orphans from the Koranic schools. The smallest thing would give you away; the wrong accent, the wrong name, the way you kneel, eat, greet or pray, your identity must be one hundred per cent convincing, 24/7. Everyone has tried planting an informant in Safar Khan's group, but no one has ever succeeded. Besides, they'll want proof that you're serious . . .'

'They'll want you to kill someone?'

'Yes.'

'Like Ain, for example?'

Michael looked at her through the restless smoke rising from the cigarette. He flung out his hands.

'Yes, but that's the last part. You need to have everything else in place before that stage. They must believe in you. The killing is just the icing on the cake. A ritual.'

'Perhaps that's what Kim has been doing in Afghanistan and Pakistan,' she speculated. 'Perhaps he has been baking the cake. Perhaps he's the man on the steps at Nørreport Station . . .'

'Danish police officer implicated in the murder of a twenty-three-year-old Danish woman? I know you don't think he's a nice guy, but isn't it a little bit extreme to—'

'It isn't,' she interrupted him. 'He has lost everything. You don't understand! He lost his wife and two children. He has lived in places where human life counts for nothing, and he has worked with intelligence officers for whom the end justifies all means. If he thinks, if he truly believes that he can prevent the murder of hundreds of innocent Danes by taking another life, he'll do it. And perhaps another one, and then another one after that . . . The problem is, in my opinion, that he doesn't know when or how to stop.'

She stared at her hands in her lap.

'When Josefine died, something inside me broke, Michael. I don't know what it was, but I know that I'll never be the same. Everything became so blurred, so utterly pointless. She was here one day, my child, with whom I had spent twenty-three years, and the next day she was gone. It ought to have been me who, having lived many years, died. I can't imagine what it must be like to lose your entire family on one day in Tivoli. I would have gone insane – more insane that I already am – and I wouldn't have cared one jot about one life more or less . . . I'm serious. I don't see why Kim shouldn't feel exactly the same.'

She quickly got up and went to the bathroom, locked the door and looked at herself in the mirror. Something was choking her, something made her gasp for air. She filled the sink with cold water and stuck her face under the surface. Air bubbles floated from the corner of her mouth and nostrils up along her face and she could hear Michael's mobile ring in the other room. The water amplified the sound. The mobile kept ringing until it was finally answered. She heard his low, composed voice.

Lene raised her head and gasped for air. It was a technique she had taught herself whenever grief and fear tightened her throat. It helped.

He knocked on the door.

'Lene? Lene?'

'Let me at least have two minutes to myself, for God's sake. Don't you understand that . . .'

His sigh actually went through the door. She had never met anyone who could heave so deep and expressive a sigh as Michael, except for very old large dogs. The sighs could mean everything from boredom to irritation to exasperation. This sigh meant that he was extremely displeased with her.

'It's actually for you,' he shouted angrily, and she prayed that he had put his hand over the phone. 'It's your boss. Or former boss . . .'

'Charlotte?'

'Charlotte, yes. Shall I tell her that you drowned yourself in the sink or are taking a bath with a toaster, or what?'

'One moment.'

She quickly dried her face and hair and opened the door. Michael handed her the mobile.

'I've tried calling you countless times,' her boss said. 'I thought you had a mobile phone?'

'It's broken,' she said. 'How did you get Michael's number and how did you know that I'm with him?'

'Why don't we take a look at that later?'

Lene looked at Michael, who was drinking coffee by the balcony and pretending not to eavesdrop.

'Perhaps we should put it aside for the time being.'

'Irene Adler is dead, Lene. She was found in her living room early this morning. Someone had bashed a long embalming syringe through one of her eyes and into her brain, and when that was not enough to kill her, the murderer suffocated her with a cushion.'

Lene said nothing.

'I attended the crime scene myself early this morning,' Charlotte said, clearing her throat and giggling with embarrassment. 'You didn't do it, did you? I mean . . . No, of course you didn't.'

'No.'

'Good, but you understand that I had to ask because . . .'

'I understand.'

Again, this completely uncharacteristic, embarrassed laughter.

'So you have an alibi? It's common knowledge that the two of you were not the best of friends.'

'Neither are you and I, Charlotte, but I haven't killed you yet.'

Lene studied Michael. He did look thinner and more sallow than the last time she saw him. Perhaps he really had caught some tropical bug in Somalia? She experienced an unexpected tinge of concern. Why the hell did he not just go home to Funen? Get himself checked out and treated?

'No, Irene and I were not the best of friends,' she then said calmly. 'That is correct. And yes, I have a kind of alibi. Anything else?'

The superintendent inhaled, but the exhale brought no more words.

'What do you mean?' she said eventually. 'Isn't that enough? I would have thought that you—'

'You suspended me yesterday morning, remember? I've signed up for that watercolour course in Tuscany like you suggested. In fact, I'm looking forward to it,' she said maliciously.

'Did I really? I have no memory of that. But if I suspended you, I can certainly reinstate you.'

'I suppose you can,' Lene said after a pause. 'All right, then. Deal. Who is Kim's agent, Charlotte? The retriever? The Messiah?'

Out of the corner of her eye, she noticed that Michael had turned around.

'No way! This is the most blatant form of blackmail I've ever experienced in my life. You have only your wounded vanity, but I'm responsible for thirty foreign ministers, their delegations, and a Jewish prize recipient arriving at Copenhagen in three hours. If – and I repeat, *if* – it's the case that Kim or another PET employee have access to intelligence about a possible terror attack on Danish soil, it is a matter *only* for the head of PET, the handler and me. And that's that.'

Lene could hear that Charlotte was adamant.

'Ain didn't commit suicide,' she said. 'She was pushed. The cameras on Nørreport Station prove it. We believe – Michael and I – that an unidentified woman committed the murder.'

'Are you sure?'

'One hundred per cent!'

'Motive?'

'Ain was a loose cannon. We don't think she knew what she was doing when she helped Nabil Maroun. She worked it out later, evidently, and started calling me on Livslinjen and seeing a psychiatrist. She must have told someone she shouldn't have.'

The word *we* came with effortless ease, Lene thought. It seemed to carry more weight.

'But you can't be sure that she didn't know what she was doing,' Charlotte protested.

'I'm sure. That'll have to satisfy you for now, until I find the evidence that has to be out there somewhere. If I'm to return to my job, I have to investigate this latest development. I knew Ain, and I should have helped her instead of telling her that she was paranoid.'

'What you're saying is that you won't stop until you've found out if Ain was Irene Adler's guinea pig?'

'Exactly.'

Once again Charlotte became her usual clear and logical self.

'But that's impossible with such short notice, Lene, and it would require a commission of international scientists to get to the bottom of her research. She has, to my knowledge, six senior researchers and a dozen PhD students on her team and she supervises God knows how many foreign students. They're loyal to her and they depend on her grants. It would take months – years, possibly – to find the specific figures and the documentation you're looking for . . . you see that, don't you?'

Lene rubbed her forehead. Her gleeful moment evaporated. Charlotte was right. The evidence that proved Irene Adler's illegal LSD experiments was probably encrypted, hidden away in the depths of a hard drive in a distant vault of cyberspace or loaded onto an iCloud server beyond reach.

'I guess you're right,' she mumbled and forced her brain into the first gear of basic police work. 'Any signs of forced entry, broken windows or locks?'

'The front door was open. It was the newspaper guy who found her.'

'So she knew her killer and he or she wanted her found as quickly as possible. That is interesting. Normally the killer would want as much time as possible to pass so that—'

'I'm aware of that, Lene. I'm also aware that you think that my practical criminal knowledge can be summed up in very few words.'

Lene did not contradict her. After all, it was the truth.

'I'll go over there shortly,' she said.

'There's plenty of time for you to drink your morning coffee. The CSOs need at least another hour. I'm glad I caught you. You sound better. Much better.'

'Yes. Thank you. Bye.'

'Give my best to Michael. And, Lene?'

'Yes.'

'I've spoken to Kim. I'm sorry about what happened to Bjarne. He won't bother you again.'

'Thank you.'

'Can I get you to give me the same assurance?'

'Of course,' Lene said warmly and without meaning it. 'Of course he needs space to work. I do understand how important it is.'

'Do you really?'

'Absolutely. Definitely. Bye.'

She handed the mobile back to Michael.

'I've been rehired,' she said.

'Congratulations.'

'Someone has killed Irene Adler.'

'So I gather.'

'What? Yes . . . the strange thing is . . . the strange thing is that I very clearly remember the murder weapon.'

'A horseman's sabre? A halberd? A guillotine?'

'An antique horribly long and sharp embalming syringe which the killer bashed through her brain. I remember it lying on her desk. I picked it up to take a look at it, and she told me to put it back.'

'So your fingerprints will be on that blasted syringe?'

'But I was here, Michael. You know I was here all night.'

She looked at him.

Michael walked over to the open balcony door and lit another cigarette. He slowly exhaled smoke through his nostrils and pointed at her with the glowing tip. The helicopters circled like distant insects under the grey sky.

'Coming from someone who is so incredibly – although only periodically – bright, that is a completely idiotic remark. I'm no lawyer, but the point is that you weren't here!'

'What do you mean? I was!'

'I was asleep and so I can't swear that you actually were here. I woke up and you were gone. Did you take a taxi from the hotel?'

'No. I just went for a long walk.'

'Did you pay for the coffees and the croissants with your Dankort?'

'I had enough cash,' she said.

'Did you speak to anyone in reception when you left or when you returned?'

'The night porter was watching television when I left,' Lene said, thinking until her brain ached. 'And he was busy with a group of Swedish travellers when I came back, so I don't think anyone saw me.'

'Super,' he said.

'But why on earth would I kill her?'

'Because you loathed and detested every atom in her body and blamed her for your daughter's suicide?'

'But . . .'

She buried her face in her hands, but at length she splayed her fingers and looked at him.

'But you believe me, don't you?'

He raised his eyebrows in surprise.

'Of course I believe you, you idiot. Of course I do. I would have known if you had been gone a long time. Your bedding was warm. I could smell that you had . . .' He looked at her. 'The bathroom mirror was steamed up, for God's sake. Besides, you wouldn't do anything so incredibly stupid.'

'Thank you, Michael,' she said quietly. 'I really do appreciate—'

'But I'm not the one who needs convincing. So what do we do now? I think we should split up.'

'I want to take a look at the crime scene,' she nodded. 'There has to be something. There usually is. What are you going to do?'

Michael deftly disassembled his mobile and tossed the parts into the harbour basin through the open balcony door. Then he unwrapped a box and took a new mobile out and found a SIM card in his wallet.

'Write down this number,' he said, handing her a pen.

'Where?'

'On your wrist, for example. Or on your forehead – only then you have to do it in mirror writing, of course.'

'How do I call you? There are hardly any phone booths left.'

'Here you go.'

He found another smartphone box in his suitcase and lobbed it through the air.

'Thank you.'

'There's a SIM card in the box, the number is stored in my mobile, and it's charged.'

'So what are you going to do now? Not that you have to do anything at all. You've done more than enough already. You actually don't look all that well.'

'Don't I?'

'No. Isn't it about time that you took care of yourself? Saw a doctor, got diagnosed, got treated? Like normal people do when they fall ill.'

Michael went into the bathroom, pulled down his eyelids and inspected the mucous membranes around his eyes.

'I'll do it when I get the time,' he said. 'Right now, I thought I'd get some rest, while you're out being the super detective. Okay?'

'Okay. But when all this is over, I'm taking you to the hospital.'

'Of course. Agreed. And watch your back. One more thing, Lene.'

She was in the hall with one arm stuck through the sleeve of her jacket.

'What?'

'If you did not kill Irene Adler, then who did and why?'

'No idea, but I'll find out,' she said with a swagger. Possibly a little too much.

'Watch your back,' he mumbled again. 'And call me right away if you bump into the . . . opposition.'

Lene heaved a sigh.

'The opposition? You mean the rest of the world? Oh, I will.'

34

Truth be told, Michael was feeling dreadful. He was well aware that he was a born hypochondriac, but surely hypochondriacs fell ill sometimes? He considered calling reception and getting them to stock up the minibar with whisky, but instead asked them to bring him a fresh pot of coffee.

His glum thoughts were really his way of postponing the next, inevitable step, which was calling his former employer, the eminent and multinational security company Shepherd & Wilkins, where he had worked for a dozen hard but educational years. More specifically, its trusted archivist, Sandy Huffington – or Sandy the Syndrome, as he was cruelly known behind his back. No one knew how old he was. Unconfirmed rumours had it that Sandy had simply been born and bred in the old building near Oxford Circus, that he had originally been produced as a kind of homunculus in an electrified glass bottle, for the purpose of creating a perpetual archivist who would never need paying. But Sandy had escaped from the petri dish and since then resided behind an enormous, overladen desk which, according to him, had belonged to Lord

Louis Mountbatten, Viceroy of India. Sandy's office, which he seldom left, was a grotto-like, three-storey library in the heart of the building. With nostalgic devotion, everyone still referred to it as 'the telex room'.

The only reason no one had fired him, or had him put down yet, was that Sandy had a photographic memory and constituted an unfailing and detailed source of knowledge about practically everything that had occurred since the world was created. It included who was bedding who in the big company, who was fiddling their expenses, who knew about it and who must not be told.

Now, Michael could, of course, choose to go through the company's official channels. He was still associated with it as a freelancer. But it would take time and cost a fortune. The company would demand that his research and enquiries were treated as a formal investigation, and that would incur a basic fee of several thousand pounds. Michael might be a son of the house, but there was little fellow feeling between members of S&W's extended family, and the company had never been intended as a philanthropic enterprise. From the day Messrs Shepherd & Wilkins set it up after the First World War, S&W had been a success and, to Michael's knowledge, the company had never given a single penny to charity. The directors made Rupert Murdoch look like St Thomas Aquinas as far as the milk of human kindness was concerned.

A nasal voice cut through Michael's thoughts.

'Sandy Huffington, who is calling?'

'Michael Sander. How are you, Sandy? Is life treating you as you deserve?'

'I bloody well hope not. Michael! My dear, dear boy!'

Michael heard a rustling of paper and Sandy crunching pizza. The creature ate pizza three times a day. It sounded as if the base on this latest one was fresh and crisp. Michael waited patiently for Sandy to finish munching. You could not hurry Sandy. Any kind of pleading, urgency, impatience, threats, anger or appeal to human empathy and decency provoked exactly the same reaction: a flood of crude swear-words after which the conversation would invariably be terminated. Everyone, from the chairman of the board to the most recently hired office junior, was treated in exactly the same way. In this respect, Sandy was endlessly democratic and impossible to bribe.

'Do you have a moment?' Michael interjected before the next mouthful.

'Michael! For you? Always. You're in need of my extra-ordinary brain, I presume? The price is inflation linked. As always.'

Michael sighed.

'How much?'

'Two thousand pounds for a basic five-page report. One thousand for each subsequent hour or page.'

'Just the basic report, Sandy.'

'Of course. Fire away.'

'Mufti Ebrahim Safar Khan . . .'

'The white sheikh in Amman? That in itself takes you far, far beyond the basic, Michael, my dear, dear young friend.'

'I don't need a complete profile, Sandy, just the facts about his time in London. Where he lived, whether he brought his family, did he work anywhere other than the London School of Economics, that kind of thing. Street names, for—'

He had been on the verge of swearing, which was a mortal sin when talking to Sandy. If there was any swearing to be done, Sandy Huffington would do it himself.

'Okay. Anything else?'

'Ahem, yes. This one is a little more delicate. There's a woman here in Copenhagen. Nazeera Gamil.'

He spelled the name.

'Her father, Khalid Gamil, is an economist at the University of Copenhagen and the family is originally from Jordan. He's an internationally renowned theoretical economist. It might be a bit far-fetched, but it would be interesting to know if . . .'

'. . . there might be geographical, familial or chronological overlaps between the two Jordanian families?'

'Exactly.'

'Sure. Here's my account number.'

Michael wrote it down on a napkin. He was not Sandy Huffington, who had never made a note of anything in his entire life. He said that he could visualize information: people's passport numbers, height, weight, addresses, eye colour, the receipt from the previous time he filled up his car with petrol. It was always astonishingly accurate.

'You know that I won't do a second's work until the money has arrived, Michael.'

'Of course. Would five minutes be okay?' he asked, with light irony in his voice. He held his breath. Sandy did not like irony either.

'Of course,' the creature squealed magnanimously. 'Fax? PDF? Runes? After all, you *are* in Denmark, aren't you?'

'PDF, thank you.'

'Same email address as last time, Michael?'

'Yes.'

'I remember it.'

'Of course you do, Sandy.'

'And, Michael?'

'Yes?'

'Let me give you some good advice for free. At all times keep at least a continent between yourself and Ebrahim Safar Khan. The man is lethal, and there's nothing wrong with his IQ, either. That means it's far above your own, as I recall from your personnel files, and only somewhat lower than mine. So unless you want to be beheaded in front of a clumsily painted banner on YouTube, surrounded by ecstatically waving jihadists who are also atrocious photographers and surgeons, then stay away, do you hear?'

'Thank you . . . or, you know what I mean, Sandy,' Michael said and rang off.

He clicked on a bank account in Luxembourg opened for this very purpose, and transferred a deposit of £2,000 to the greedy gnome.

He ought to eat something. He called room service and ordered a full English breakfast. It seemed appropriate after talking to Sandy. Part of him missed the years in London. He had been young – or younger, at any rate – independent and had only had healthy, carefree interests: cricket at the Oval, cars, women, weapons, stand-up comedy at the London Palladium, U2 concerts . . . staying alive. That kind of thing.

When the trolley arrived with his breakfast, he found he was unable to eat anything after all, and could only manage coffee, juice and cigarettes. He looked at his watch. Right now Nazeera Gamil was probably at work at the bistro on Østerbro. He did not expect to discover anything significant, but there was no way he could avoid a little bit of old-fashioned surveillance of the beautiful woman.

Michael studied Marskensgade on Østerbro on Google maps and detailed technical maps from Copenhagen City Council. He memorized possible access and escape routes from the restaurant, Le Crocodile Vert.

A couple of quick searches in publicly available databases revealed that Nazeera lived on the third floor of an impressive apartment building on Grønningen, with an expensive view of Kastellet. He searched the property register and discovered that she owned the 175-square-metre residence: a desirable, patrician apartment with high ceilings, with an official valuation of 5.25 million kroner. She had bought the apartment three years ago, and the outstanding mortgage was just 2 million kroner. How interesting. This apartment was clearly not bought on an ordinary waitress's salary, that was for sure. But then again, the Gamil family might be wealthy.

He checked his watch and did another quick Internet search. For a modern young woman, Nazeera Gamil was remarkably non-existent. There was not one photograph of her on Google, nor was she on Facebook, Twitter, LinkedIn, Instagram, Tumblr or any other social network, something which most people of her generation regarded as essential.

Nor was there a college yearbook or higher education enrolment register listing a Nazeera Gamil. In fact, there was nothing.

Michael did not exist either, but that was because his real name was not Michael Vedby Sander. His small business drew as little attention to itself as Nazeera, and only very persistent souls ever found his company's homepage, which was buried in the basement of the Internet, out of range of ordinary search engines. Even if they did, the information was exceedingly sparse. A mobile telephone number, which was replaced at least once a month, was listed under a condensed biography. Nor was there a photograph of him on his homepage. Michael was discriminating in his choice of clients. They usually came recommended by word of mouth among rich, secretive and important people.

However, the Internet was not short of references to Nazeera's father, the eminent Professor Khalid Gamil. There were even pictures of his wife, Judita, who had lectured in Chemistry at the University of Prague before she met a young, handsome Khalid in Cairo. Michael was also able to find the odd image of a young man and woman, who had to be Nazeera's brother and sister. They both looked like super-models. Her brother worked on special effects at a British film studio and her sister was an investment consultant for Barclays bank in London.

Michael started walking up and down the room. Nazeera had been cherry-picked by an organization that had spotted her talent and appreciated her Arabic, English and Danish identities, languages and cultural flexibility. She had the perfect CV from every intelligence organization's point of view. After that the organization had made her anonymous. Lene had suggested Nazeera as the possible mole or retriever, one of the Danish army's typically awkward terms for a person who on behalf of FET – Army Intelligence – obtained information as the first link in the food chain. This was typically done by infiltrating mosques, sports clubs, immigration clubs, subcultures or minorities of dissatisfied immigrants in other countries. Michael had met such young people working for FET. They spoke at least three languages and had two nationalities, but were completely loyal to Denmark.

However, being allowed into the inner circle of one of the world's most effective and secretive terror cells took more than a low-level informant. It was the difference between being Rembrandt and a bog-standard decorator. It required extraordinary stamina, composure and an almost schizophrenic personality. Every day you had to perform at an Oscar-winning level unless you wanted to wake up without your head. Or worse.

Michael forced himself to stop thinking about Nazeera Gamil, although it was difficult, and pursued another train of thought instead: the retired Swedish engineer and wildlife photographer who just happened to be in the right spot at the right time in Tivoli on the 17th September last year with his brilliant, digital camera – and survived the day.

Åke Valerius-Klüver, aged fifty-eight, lived at Tomatstigen 26 in Södertälje. Michael found Åke and his wife, Elsa, listed in local Swedish telephone directories and there were also a few photographs on Google of the couple; mostly from photographic competitions where a proudly smiling photographer was presented with an engraved glass or small silver cups. *Picture of the Year in Fiskörnan 2008.*

The last award ceremony was from May 2011.

To be on the safe side, Michael clicked and found Södertälje on Google maps. He had never visited the town, but it looked as if it had an idyllic location west of Stockholm, surrounded by several rivers, long lakes with many branches, and forests. It looked rather lovely, at least from an aerial view. He found Tomatstigen in a leafy, neatly trimmed area with similar closely spaced family houses. He counted along the road and decided that number 26 had to be the corner plot. The only problem was that there no longer was a house on the plot. There had been a house once, evidently, but it had been reduced to its foundations and fragments of external walls. He zoomed in on the street picture: Google Earth had driven right past with their camera cars, and there were excellent recordings of the scorched remains. In between the other white, well-maintained properties, the sooty ruin stuck out like a rotten tooth in an otherwise perfect row. The satellite recording was dated November last year.

Like a bloodhound on the scent, Michael felt the blood flow faster through his veins. His senses heightened and after twenty minutes of searching, he found the small news-paper cutting he knew had to be there somewhere. It was from *Länstidningen Södertälje*, dated the 20th October last year; eight lines squeezed in between a feature on bridal hairstyles and an article about an excessive lottery win for a nineteen-year-old local girl. A middle-aged couple, Åke Valeri-us-Klüver, aged fifty-eight, and his wife, Elsa Valerius-Klüver, aged fifty-six, were killed in a house fire in their home on Tomatstigen after an electric blanket short-circuited in the couple's bedroom. Fire investigators were unanimous in their conclusion: the fire was caused by the electric defect, not started deliberately.

Michael shut the lid on his laptop and leaned back in his chair, relatively pleased with himself. Whoever uploaded the razor-sharp photographs to Rigspolitiet's Tivoli homepage last December and possibly accompanied the pictures with a short explanation, was most certainly not Åke Valerius-Klüver. At that point, his and his wife's charred remains had long since been put to rest at the local cemetery.

It was really rather beautiful and symmetrical, he thought. Everything slotted neatly into place. He could not remember ever having seen such thorough planning in connection with a terror act. There was quite clearly intelligence behind it, pulling the strings. Perhaps a mastermind such as Safar Khan's.

PET had had their scapegoat served on a plate: Ain in conversation with the bomber Nabil Maroun, documented with excellent digital photographs. They had been given something to play with, like when you toss a puppy a rubber bone so that the grown-ups can work in peace. Ain had been completely screwed over: unaware that her flat had been used as a safe base for the terrorists while they were in Copenhagen, used again as the blue-eyed, naive door opener for the bomber, and finally murdered as proof of the killer's devotion to the cause.

It was genius. Cynical and incredibly repellent. For the first time in a very long while, Michael felt a tiny flame igniting deep inside him. It flickered a little before it grew stronger and more passionate. On behalf of the young woman, he felt that his humanity had been violated, and he got a totally unprofessional urge to hold those responsible to account.

III

35

The deck of the old Polish coaster was loaded to the gun-wales. The crates contained engine parts from an East German cotton mill, which could not compete on the new, open market and as a result had been disassembled and sold as scrap to an enterprising breaker in Göteborg. The skipper had arranged a square to be left empty on the deck between the hatches where the two young Arabs could be out of sight of the crew's prying eyes. He was known for having an easily provoked temper and fast fists, but he was also a reasonable man who asked no questions. Everyone on board knew they would get their fair share of the generous bonus for this voyage.

The two young men had rolled out their prayer mats in the enclosure, they had said their prayers facing Mecca and had drunk water and a little tea which they prepared on a spirit burner, and shared some bread and dried fruit.

Samir was now standing at the starboard rail, watching the flat land and the long, white and green headlands by Falsterbo. They were in plenty of time. The skipper had lowered the speed to six knots and the wake was barely audible below the rusty bows of the ship. The sea was flat and calm, but further inshore the wind whipped up long dark waves and white horses under passing, brief showers.

It was always cold at sea so he opened his thick leather jacket to tuck the ends of his scarf inside to cover his chest, and zipped it up. He did not like the sea. He heard a metallic scrambling from the galley behind the bridge and looked at his watch. The smiling, fat Filipino cook was punctuality itself – the leftovers from the crew's meals were always thrown overboard and, as if by magic, screeching, wildly flapping herring gulls would drop out of the sky. They fought over the food scraps in the air and on the water.

Samir smiled. It was an inexplicable phenomenon. Normally there was not a single bird to be seen for miles around, but as soon as the cook was ready, they would appear.

He had made the call almost five hours ago, before they sailed from Rostock and while mobile coverage was still good. They had used innocent phrases, pretending to be distant relatives agreeing to meet for a few hours in Copenhagen, and yet they had managed to slip in and confirm the few facts needed such as the place and time they would get picked up. Everything was ready. He had listened to his instincts, tried to catch a slight hesitation or intonation which might indicate treachery, but there had been nothing; no sixth sense stirring. He saw the route ahead as clearly as the highway between Damascus and Homs, where he was from, and where he had started fighting with the militia after the first massacres of the town's protesters.

They had ended their conversation and Samir had snapped the SIM card between his fingers. He had inserted a new, prepaid SIM card into his mobile and sent a text message with the new number.

Adil had waved to him from the bows, and Samir had embarked while the crew slipped the last moorings. Half an hour later they were in the Baltic Sea.

The seagulls screeched and fought over the last scraps before leaving the ship. Samir turned on his iPad and clicked until an electronic naval chart appeared on the screen. The coaster was marked as a small boat-shaped icon and he calculated the speed of the ship and the distance to the agreed meeting place. They had enough time, but not too much. Soon the skipper would contact SUNDREP, the Baltic Sea Traffic Control Authority, to inform them of their course, speed and destination, and their onward voyage must not look suspiciously fast or slow on SUNDREP's radars. He returned the iPad to his shoulder bag and rested his elbows on the gunwale, which needed sanding and varnishing. Everything was ready. The weapons, the vests, the ridiculous white uniform which, together with his ID card, would give him access to the target.

Insha' Allah, God be willing.

Samir felt nothing. The fighting in Homs and being held captive by the wild warriors whom President Bashar Al-Assad had conscripted from the Bekaa Valley, had torn out his heart. He never felt nervous or agitated. He believed that his humanity had flown out of his chest like a bird on the day he was taken prisoner, and that it was waiting for him on the other side. He was the last surviving student from his sixth form class, from Homs United FC, from the Liverpool FC fan club. He was the last of all his friends from the street where he had been born.

He had been captured and tortured by the Alawites, the Al-Assad clan from the mountains, and regular Syrian forces. The last morning they had roused him from unconsciousness by chucking a bucket of cold water over him. They had dragged him across the concrete floor of the garage and out into the dawning day along with fifteen other boys aged twelve to seventeen. They had kneeled on the ground, their hands tied behind their backs, and the line started to stink as the first in the row were shot in the back of their heads and their rectal muscles opened. The adjacent, still-living boys started wetting themselves and soiling their pants in fear when they heard the officer's footsteps behind them. The Alawites had pinched their noses and howled with laughter as they mimicked the boys' intestinal sounds.

The officer stopped behind the boy to Samir's right. The boy, whom Samir did not know, had kept his head held high and his back straight, even though he was resting on his knees and had his hands tied behind his back. The officer ordered him to bow his head. The boy refused. He had started praying in a loud voice, and Samir's raw, bloodshot eyes filled with tears of pride. One of the private soldiers walked calmly up to the boy and kicked him in the mouth, so that his teeth glowed white and red in the sand. The boy continued to mumble his prayer as the soldier grabbed his hair while screaming curses at him and forced his face into the dirt. The officer had shot him with the Russian Nagant pistol at the top of his spine and then in the back of his head when he was lying down.

Samir had also come close to wetting himself, but had suppressed the impulse. Behind him, the officer was cursing and sweating from agitation. The private soldier was ready and waiting in case Samir, too, decided to act up. His shadow fell across Samir. The officer had pushed the muzzle of his pistol against Samir's left temple, pressed the trigger, and Samir's head was flung to the side from the impact. But the shot had been a part dud, or the cartridge's powder load was defective, and he opened his eyes and looked up at the private soldier, who in frustration and with the officer still swearing, had kicked him in the face and broken his nose.

Samir lay with his cheek against the cool sand as he heard the officer reload. The pistol clicked and Samir felt quite calm. Today was not the day for him to die. In the distance he had heard the militia's Toyota pick-ups and the heavy roar of the American M-50 machine guns, which the rebels had mounted on the flatbeds of their trucks. Then everything dissolved in an ear-piercing apocalypse and it was not until much later that he and the other surviving boys watched as the figures of the rebels emerged from the dust clouds. Most of them had *shemagh* scarves covering their faces, but the boys could still make out triumphant smiles behind the scarves and sunglasses.

He had not died that day, but lived. Since then he had given his life to whoever might need it in the fight against Allah's enemies, the infidels in the West and the Baathists at home in Syria.

He lit a cigarette and thought about Zebra. The woman was a whore who bared her face, drove cars, went to bed with men and women, smoked cigarettes and listened to rock 'n' roll and blues. She lived with no shame. But she was so much more than that, and she was pure in her love of Islam. Safar Khan treated her like a daughter and had never expressed one word of doubt about her.

He was not immune to her beauty. Far from it. At times she would visit his dreams at dawn in the vulnerable state between dream and awakening, where she caused hard, shameful erections. It was inevitable.

During one of her visits to Jordan, Samir had escorted her on a trip to the Dead Sea one afternoon. On her instructions, they had left the car in a car park above the steep rocks, and walked down to the sea. Far to the west they could make out the low golden mountains on the occupied West Bank. The sun hung just above feathery clouds and the heat was no longer unbearable. They had shared a bottle of water. The woman had sat without moving on a rock with one long jeans-clad leg pulled up so that she could rest her forearms and her chin on her knee. Her foot in the white trainer was naked and Samir studied a small vein, slowly beating under the smooth skin of her ankle. She wore a white, short-sleeved shirt and had a dark-blue pullover draped over her shoulders. He could make out the thin white lace of her bra under her shirt. The woman watched the sea through her sunglasses and Samir followed her gaze. A newspaper-reading tourist with psoriasis was floating weightless on the surface of the water a few hundred metres away.

'Have you been here before?' he had asked.

'Yes. I like it here.'

'But there's nothing here,' he objected, sweeping his hand from south to north. 'Nothing lives here. There's nothing to like.'

'The landscape.'

The landscape was bare and elementary. The surface of the water was grey and smooth, the rocks red and brown. The only thing that changed was the light, which was now scarlet and violet.

'Except bacteria,' he continued, pensively. 'They've found bacteria here, which can only live in the salt and nowhere else.'

'Bacteria? How romantic you are, Samir!'

She had smiled and he had stuttered something. She was very different from the girls he had known in Homs.

With a howl, three Israeli F-16 fighter jets fell out of the sky above the West Bank and settled playfully above the sea. In the exact same fraction of a second they turned over in the air and flew with their cockpits upside down. They rotated again one hundred and eighty degrees and rose vertically in the southern sky down by Ararat before they disappeared out of sight.

'Are they invincible?' she asked gravely.

He had launched passionately into singing the praises of the Arab revolution and the historic inevitability of the caliphate, but stopped after half a minute. His voice ebbed away when he realized that she was not paying attention.

'You're not listening,' he said indignantly.

She looked at him and placed her finger against her lips.

'Listen!'

Samir fell silent and after a few seconds, he could hear the rasping of the cicadas.

She smiled.

'There's something other than bacteria here, Samir.'

He felt a hand on his shoulder and jumped. He looked into Adil's grave face.

'Are you sad, brother?' the other asked.

'What? No. Not at all.'

Samir put his hand on his empty stomach.

'I'm hungry. I'm just dreaming.'

'But are you ready?' Adil asked him anxiously.

Samir looked with some displeasure at the younger, very earnest and correct Adil, who was technically below him in the hierarchy.

'Are *you* ready, brother?'

Adil nodded.

'More than that, I'm looking forward to it,' he said.

36

'Hello?'

A white box van from the Department of Forensics was parked outside Irene Adler's house, and Lene presumed that the CSOs were still busy inside, even though there was not a sound to be heard when she pushed open the front door.

She walked through the hall, opened the door to the two living rooms, which took up most of the ground floor, and nearly jumped out of her skin when she discovered an immobile figure in a white overall sitting in an armchair right inside the door.

'Arne? Hi. I didn't think anyone was here.'

There was a whoosh of nylon as the chief forensic officer turned his head and looked at her. He nodded minimally.

'Lene,' he greeted her gravely.

She frowned. She had known Arne for eighteen years and they had always got on well together. Whenever she put forward her steep and unreasonable demands, he would tease her gently, and she would listen when he talked about his wife, who suffered from multiple sclerosis, and his children, who had all the problems children tend to have. He was a passionate bridge player, kept saltwater aquariums and had a certain, paternal affection for her.

But today Arne's grey-bearded and bespectacled countenance was introverted and stern.

A younger CSO whom Lene did not know appeared in the doorway to the kitchen, holding a Hoover. Arne looked at him.

'Andreas. Put that in the car, then drive down to the petrol station and buy me a tin of red Orlik pipe tobacco, do you hear? Don't hurry back.'

'But—'

'Goodbye, Andreas.'

The young man shuffled through the living room with his tail between his legs, and Lene heard the front door slam behind him.

Arne pointed to the armchair next to his, and Lene sat down with her knees together and her hands folded in her lap like a schoolgirl in the headmaster's office. She studied the floor, which was lit up in broad stripes by the morning sun, and for the first time in donkey's years, she felt quite refreshed and energetic.

She looked at the strange circular trail of blood beginning and ending by Irene Adler's beautiful antique desk.

'Where was the body found?' she asked.

There was a dangerous pale glow behind Arne's spectacles. His face contorted as if he was tasting something bitter. He pointed.

'Just over there. On her back, in the centre of the circle. Half naked. But you already know that.'

'How on earth could I know that?'

Lene smiled and tried to catch his eye.

'What's wrong, Arne? Has someone died?'

'I don't think that's funny, Lene. Not at all.'

'It was a joke, for Christ's sake. All right. How many toothbrushes?'

This question was the first in their customary exchange at every crime scene.

'Two,' he muttered reluctantly.

'One pink and one pale-blue? A boy and a girl? A razor and a lady shaver?'

'One mint-green and one pale-blue toothbrush,' he said wearily. 'A girl and a girl, would be my guess.'

Of course. A girl and a girl, she thought, and closed her eyes while feeling as if the ceiling had collapsed on her. Of course. It was obvious now. Of course, of course, of course!

'And two hairbrushes, one with long blonde hairs and one with long dark ones,' he continued. 'The latter are unusual. I'm able to make out oval cross-sections with a magnifying glass. They're Semitic. Arab, for example.'

'Of course,' she whispered, without listening to him.

Lene remembered the shadow behind the curtains on the first floor on the day she had threatened Irene Adler with all sorts of terrible consequences. She remembered the scent that was different from the one Irene normally preferred, and she remembered the hand luggage with the plane ticket in the hallway. She had assumed that it was the psychiatrist herself who was going away. But the bag just as easily could have belonged to the unknown woman.

Arne said something again.

'Sorry?'

'I was just saying there's an abundance of hairs in this house,' he repeated. 'If you look properly.'

'Is there? Hairs?'

'Irene Adler's blonde hair and black Arabic hair – like from this woman, for example.'

'Who?'

Arne took out a slim volume from the bookcase next to him and passed the book to her. *Classic Arabic Love Poems* by Abu Nuwa.

'Oxford University Press, 1967,' he said. 'Fine poetry from the twelfth century. Erotic poems, and a picture of a more recent date.'

Lene flicked slowly through the book. Arne was right. If the poems matched the beautiful illustrations in any way, they had to be pretty salacious.

'Unbelievable,' she mumbled, turning the book ninety degrees. The positions depicted seemed to her physically impossible unless you were one of those Chinese artistes who could jump into a jar without touching the sides. Then again, people were smaller in those days.

'Probably not something practised on a daily basis in a

suburban swingers' club,' Arne conceded with a glimpse of his usual and quite well-developed sense of humour.

'Unless it's a sub-branch for chiropractors,' she said.

'Quite, but just before you get too carried away, on a purely professional basis, may I suggest that you keep on looking,' he said.

Lene did as she was told, and discovered a shiny black-and-white photo.

It was taken in natural light, either early in the morning or at dusk. The light must have come from a window on the left side of the room. A naked woman was lying on a dishevelled double bed. The soft grey light caressed her long legs, domed hips and drew a deeper, darker cleft between her rounded buttocks and muscles from her lower back and up to the long black hair which concealed most of her face. The photographer must have been standing diagonally behind the woman. Her slim left arm lay along her side with her palm resting on the perfect curve of her hip, while the other was bent at the elbow joint so that her hand was near her face. Her fingers were relaxed, and Lene wondered if she was asleep. The leg underneath had been pulled up.

It was an infatuated person's depiction of a deeply desired body. There was a sense of tranquillity in the picture, which suggested that the photographer had planned this shoot, waiting for the right light, knowing when the beloved was most likely to assume a favoured sleeping position.

Nazeera Gamil.

Here, there and everywhere.

She wondered if Nazeera sometimes mistook Ain's flat for Irene's town house, but then realized that Nazeera always knew exactly where she was going, who she was with – and why.

She lowered the picture and looked at Arne, who was absorbed in the study of his nails.

'The bed looks remarkably like the one upstairs,' he said, without looking at her.

'That doesn't surprise me.'

She was about to get up, but there was a strange gravity in Arne's presence that made her sit down again.

'We were talking about hairs, Lene. As you'll undoubtedly be aware, no two people have the same hair.'

'That's right.'

'The same applies to dogs, incidentally.'

'Dogs?'

Arne found a transparent plastic bag in his chest pocket and handed it to her. It was filled with dark short hairs.

'From the Hoover,' he explained.

'Dog hair?'

'Yes.'

'The woman in the photograph owns a dog,' she said. 'A cross between a Dobermann and Rottweiler. The size of a pony. Rudolf. It's a kind of bodyguard, I believe.'

'I think you're right. There is a bag of food for big-breed dogs in the basement, and we found a bowl on the floor in the kitchen.'

'But then it all adds up, Arne. So why the hell are you so grumpy? Lesbian couple, a dog, dog food. Surely a woman could have bashed that thing into her brain, couldn't she? I mean, it doesn't take great physical strength.'

Arne smiled lethally at her, and Lene did not like the look on his face.

'A woman could easily have done it,' he said ominously.

'Are we done with the hairs, Arne?'

She thought about how quiet Copenhagen had seemed this morning. Half of the city had been cordoned off for Foreign Office motorcades. When she drove to Irene Adler's address after having been reunited with her beloved little blue car, the city had seemed mute and dead with the exception of the ever-present patrol cars, police motorbikes and surveillance helicopters. The buses were almost empty, and though it was a weekday, you would think it was a Sunday afternoon or that Denmark was playing in the World Cup final. No one wanted to be in the wrong place at the wrong time. Communal fear exuded from the pores of the city.

'Not quite,' he said.

Again Arne's hand moved to his breast pocket. Then it hesitated, and Lene watched the technician's face attentively. It expressed doubt and a kind of . . . grief?

Then he fished out another plastic bag from his pocket and handed it to her. Lene held it up against the light from the living room windows. Long red hairs coiled into a small circle, dried blood gluing some of them together. Arne leaned forward and swiftly plucked a single hair from her head and placed it carefully on his white sleeve.

'I found a small handful of hairs in the victim's right hand, Lene. It looks as if they were pulled out by the root, and it was terribly familiar. In fact, I have always thought it was one of the finest gifts the fairies gave you. Your beautiful red hair.'

'Thank you,' she muttered.

She said nothing more, and it was Arne who broke the silence. He flung out his hands.

'Is that it? Thanks a bunch! Lene, you're in seriously deep shit. I mean, you do know that, don't you? Please explain to me how a handful of your hair ends up in the hand of a murdered woman.'

Lene stole a glance at him. He was ashen with rage.

'I don't know,' she said. 'I simply don't know. But I didn't do it, Arne. Why . . . why the hell would I?'

Her voice faded away as she realised how it must look to him. It was common knowledge that she had hated Irene Adler.

She squatted down on her haunches in front of Arne and tried taking one of his hands, but he snatched it away. She reached out for it again, as if it were a lifebuoy. Finally he let her hold his large hand, but leaned back in the chair as far as he could.

She looked into his grey eyes behind the thick spectacles.

'I didn't do it, Arne. But let's pretend that I did. No, I didn't like her, Arne. In fact, I hated her. Or . . . I did once, for a long time after Josefine died, but I don't hate her any more. Really I don't. I've spoken to her a couple of times. I've been to this house before and I discovered that I still found her to be an arrogant, spoiled woman who thought too much of herself, but I didn't hate her. Sometimes I feel exactly the same way about Charlotte Falster – and my mother, for that matter – but I wouldn't dream of killing either of them, would I?'

He raised the bag until it dangled between their faces.

'But this, Lene. Curly red hair, torn out by its roots, in her hand. You don't need to be a rocket scientist to join the dots.'

Lene stared at the bag as the explanation dawned on her. That night in Ain's flat. Someone had put a bag over her head. And Kim had kicked her. Possibly more than once.

She bowed her head, parted her hair over the short gash and pointed at it with both index fingers.

'Look, Arne! Take a good look, for God's sake! Someone kicked me in the head and put a sack over my head. The hairs and the blood are from that sack.'

Reluctantly he leaned forward, and she felt his probing fingertips against her scalp.

He grunted something incomprehensible and took his hand away.

'That doesn't prove anything,' he said, but she heard a tiny note of uncertainty, which had not been there before.

'You can see that it's not a fresh wound, can't you, Arne? Please? You've seen millions of injuries.'

'Who did it?' he wanted to know.

'It doesn't matter. What matters is that you give me a miracle. A little miracle. Just a tiny one.'

Everything was hanging in the balance right now, she thought. Arne was old-fashioned. Grey was not on his scale of things; decency, honesty and doing your duty were the values that mattered.

'Have you told Charlotte?' she asked.

'Not yet. But I will.'

'Forty-eight hours, Arne,' she pleaded.

He rubbed his face with the palms of his hands and watched her through splayed fingers.

'Twenty-four.'

'Forty-eight. Arne? Come on, for God's sake. What the hell do you think I can achieve in—'

He got up abruptly.

'Take your twenty-four hours, Lene, or I swear that you'll be wanted for murder in five minutes.'

'Okay then. Thank you,' she said.

Andreas, the assistant, popped his head into the living room.

'I'm back,' he said unnecessarily.

'Did you get my pipe tobacco?'

The young man showed him the round red tin.

'Let's go,' Arne said. 'We're done here.'

'What about her computer?'

'Are you hard of hearing?' Arne asked, sounding genuinely concerned.

'No . . .'

'All right then, so let us leave the scene to the red-headed genius over there. And, Andreas . . .'

'Yes?'

'If you should ever have the misfortune of bumping into her at a crime scene, then do exactly what she tells you. Immediately. It'll save you immeasurable amounts of pain, grief and anguish. I'm just telling you.'

The assistant looked at her over Arne's shoulder and smiled. He had very nice teeth, Lene thought.

'I will,' he said.

She smiled back at him.

Arne watched them both with disgust.

He had herded the young man out of the living room when he turned in the doorway, ran his finger across his throat and mouthed the number *twenty-four*.

37

Lene looked at the bed where Irene had photographed her lover. It was untouched, so the psychiatrist had not been asleep when the killer arrived. A bedside lamp was lit and the room was fragrant with the scent of incense. A Buddha on a camphor chest below the window displayed a partly enigmatic, partly idiotic smile. One of the prince's chubby hands held a burned-down incense stick, and he had probably seen a bit of everything, she thought. She opened the built-in cupboards without disturbing the technicians' red fingerprint powder, pushed aside the clothes and examined the joints and backs of the wardrobes.

But Arne had already checked them and he rarely missed anything.

She spent the next hour exploring the town house. There was a number of family portraits on the walls along the stairs, and carefully framed black-and-white photographs from happier times between the Great Wars had been arranged on tables and windowsills: carefree afternoons, long summer dresses, big hats, greyhounds, children in sailor suits or lace dresses, waving Adlers on the railings of ocean liners, cigar-smoking men with narrow shoulders, moustaches and monocles, nannies on huge lawns in front of white, feudal houses.

She drummed her fingers on the shiny walnut case of an old radio while she surveyed the office on the second floor. There was a desk larger than the one in the living room overflowing with articles, texts and papers. There were books, reports and dissertations on bookcases from floor to ceiling. The Arabic influence was absent. This was the psychiatrist's workspace; it was not designed to impress, or to signal anything other than a busy working life.

There was, however, no computer despite a flashing Internet router in the corner.

Irene Adler's shoulder bag was leaning against the leg of the desk and it contained keys for the car and the house, her mobile phone, tissues, sunglasses and other items usually found in a woman's handbag.

Lene took a seat on the office chair and looked down at the birds visiting the neighbour's feeding tray. Had Ain and Irene known about each other through Nazeera? Were the murders really a tragic love triangle with no connection to international terrorism, foreign ministers or Israeli professors?

She fished the keys out of the psychiatrist's shoulder bag and popped them into her own pocket. She had closed the front door behind her and was about to lock it when something, a half-forgotten memory, came back to her. The beautiful antique Koran in the glass showcase.

The psychiatrist had said something about the showcase containing a great deal of truth. Lene unlocked the door and stood in front of the display a few seconds later. There was a switch on the wall and the yellowing pages of the Koran were illuminated by an indirect source of light. There were no visible locks or bolts.

The glass showcase rested on four delicate legs, and Lene pulled it out from the wall. From the back, two cables led into the wall and she identified one as an Internet cable.

'Arne,' she mumbled. 'You and I are a pair of miserable idiots.'

She kneeled down, running a nail along the piano hinge at the front of the showcase. It was artfully sunk into the wood and practically invisible to the naked eye. Lene grabbed hold of the back edge with both hands and was able to tip the upper half of the showcase up and over the hinge.

In a space below the sacred book was a pearl-grey laptop guarding its secrets like an oyster.

Bjarne might not have looked like one of life's most successful individuals, but there was an indefatigable, quiet obstinacy about him. In only a few hours he had managed to reconstruct their small office after Kim's berserker trip. The enclosure looked like its former self, with scattered cheesy Wotsits, piles of mysterious electronic equipment, a spluttering kettle, desks and chairs and computers the right way up, all back in their rightful places. Apart from the jagged hole in the partition wall, which Michael had stuck his foot through, the PET agent's visit might just have been a bad dream.

He had connected Irene Adler's laptop to his own computers, and was busy breaking encryptions and passwords while Lene drank poor-quality coffee and checked her mail. There was nothing of immediate interest and she was about to call Michael to bring him up to speed with the latest development when Bjarne raised his head.

'I think you'll find what you're looking for now,' he said.

'Super, Bjarne. Thank you so much.'

He cracked his knuckles and looked away.

'Don't mention it.'

Lene started searching the computer's hard drive, but a constant presence hovering at the edge of her field of vision made her look up at the technician, who was stubbornly studying a spot on the floor and had yet to move.

'What is it, Bjarne? Are you okay? I mean, I know that Kim . . . well, the guy is a total arsehole, he really is, but try to forget him, won't you?'

He held up a hand and his face contorted; the heavy features changed gravity and readjusted to their new position. Bjarne smiled.

'That's all right, Lene. But the other guy . . . Michael? Now, he was really . . . *wow!*'

His smile broadened. Bjarne had found himself a new idol to join Han Solo, Luke Skywalker and Obi-Wan Kenobi.

Lene returned his smile half-heartedly, while her eyes lingered on the screen.

'He has his uses,' she mumbled. 'He really does.'

Bjarne stayed where he was.

Lene looked up again and tugged a stray lock behind her ear.

'What is it? I'm sorry, I'm just—'

Wanted for murder, she was on the verge of saying, but changed her mind at the last minute.

'Do you remember me telling you about the Polish ship, the *Kazimierz Pulaski*, which sailed up through Øresund last year on the night between the 13th and 14th September and had an engine stop outside Vedbæk?'

'No, not really.'

'Kaliningrad to Oslo?'

'What about it?'

'She's coming back,' the technician informed her. 'Taking engine parts from Rostock to Göteborg, allegedly.'

Lene heaved a sigh.

'How many times has she been up and down Øresund since last September?'

Bjarne consulted a yellow Post-it note.

'Eleven times.'

She flung out her hands.

'Bjarne, sometimes I wonder if you and I live on the same planet.'

She stopped when she saw the expression on his face.

'I'm sorry,' she said.

'I don't mind. You're probably right.'

'Those poor Polish seamen are probably just doing their job. They're not dropping off terrorists around the Baltic on a monthly basis like some kind of Al-Qaeda courier service, are they?'

'Probably not,' he conceded.

'All right, then.'

Once again she turned her attention to Irene Adler's computer and Bjarne rolled his chair back to his desk.

It proved relatively easy to get an overview of the contents. Most files were recordings of the LSD experiments carried out at Rigshospitalet. Ain had been one of six young non-ethnic Danes who had been treated with LSD from November to February; two young men and four young women who, as it turned out, attended the same mosques and study groups and knew each other fairly well. All had been diagnosed with moderate to severe depression.

In Ain's case, there were also several audio files and video recordings from her home, picked up by hidden miniature cameras and microphones. It looked as if the exchange of information between Irene and PET had been all-inclusive, that their partnership had extended beyond an academic observation on one side and a strict intelligence application of these observations on the other. Otherwise why would PET have given her access to their surveillance footage of Ain? Lene wondered if Irene and Kim had known each other before the Tivoli bomb. They undoubtedly had, and their partnership had strengthened and expanded after the terror attack. Besides, it was a convenient arrangement, both for her and for PET. They got information and she got several new guinea pigs. They would see it as a win-win situation. And someone, probably some secret Interior Ministry committee, had funded the project.

Lene began to see what terror did to a nation: the dehumanization. In an attempt to protect itself, a country would start to kill parts of its own organism. Decency was one of the first casualties.

She clicked on random files. The films showed everything, from Ain soft-boiling her breakfast egg, to putting on make-up in front of the mirror above the sink in the bathroom; from lavatory visits, to lengthy night-time love-making sessions with Nazeera Gamil.

The video recordings from the sessions at Rigshospitalet initially appeared to be quite innocent. It was rarely Irene herself who conducted the interviews with the young people, but doctors and PhD students the same age who led the conversations and administered the LSD tablets, which were called something completely different: a new generation of happy pills without the side effects of the old ones. The room was bright and harmless; there was no stethoscope, blood pressure monitor or white coat in sight. Everything seemed very peaceful.

Until the drug kicked in.

Some started pacing up and down the room, waving their hands in the air, while their mouths uttered more or less coherent sentences non-stop; others became introverted and fearful, they curled up and hugged themselves, stopped making eye contact with the interviewer and became lost in brooding self-pity, confusion or silence.

On one occasion the interviewer had to summon help using a hidden panic button under the desk when a strong young Arab man came too close, incomprehensible curses flowing from his lips and his fists clenched. He was overpowered and dragged into an adjacent room containing a bed with a duvet, pillows and broad leather straps for his waist, wrists and ankles.

The doctor administered a sedative into a vein, and eventually the young guinea pig dozed off, still mumbling to himself.

The most fascinating section of the recordings was a post-treatment area with soft armchairs, carpets on the floor, flat screens, coffee, juice and mineral water along with plates of cakes and sandwiches for when the young people came round after the trip. Hidden speakers played soft classical music. Everyone was offered something to drink and eat, and all showed signs of great thirst after the experiment. Lene was convinced that the food and beverages contained a kind of antidote. Their tense bodies slowly loosened up, the anxiety and restlessness lifted and even the aggressive young man looked unaffected thirty minutes later, as if he had no memory of what had happened earlier.

They addressed the lovely nurse by her first name, were given a card with the date and time for their next interview and left the reception looking almost exalted.

The extent to which you could manipulate someone's mind was terrifying, Lene thought. What made them come back? Did they feel understood and listened to? Forgiven? Cleansed?

Or was the reconstructed LSD in fact addictive? In all likelihood. Helle Englund had said as much.

She clicked through a handful of sequences showing the same narrative: a thorough but unprejudiced exploration of the patient's political convictions, their role models and ambitions, the ideologies and beliefs of their friends, their family relationships, places they had visited and their travel patterns. Their likes and dislikes.

Finally, she found Ain, who was just as strangely devoid of willpower as the others. But it was that passivity in particular which appeared to get on Irene Adler's nerves. The psychiatrist herself conducted all five interviews with Ain, and Lene would bet that Kim had sat in a room not far away, from where he could prompt her.

Lene had spotted a small, flesh-coloured ear piece in one of Irene's ears.

The conversation flowed relatively freely when Ain talked about her childhood in refugee camps in Tunisia and her early years in Denmark, her time at sixth form college, her friends and lovers. However, she showed an insurmountable resistance when it came to her acquaintances from the immigrant women's club in Møllegade and friends from the mosques of outer Nørrebro. Her body language was natural and relaxed when she talked about her parents, growing up and going to school in Værløse. But she blushed, red and anguished, when the psychiatrist asked about her first sexual experiences.

Ain was totally uncommunicative when it came to political sympathies or involvement with radical political acquaintances, and she would appear not to remember very well the names of other participants in the Koran study circles she would occasionally attend. And no, she knew no Danish fundamentalists, no one who had travelled to Syria, who had fought there and had returned home. No one. Ultimately, she expressed no interest at all in the conflicts of the Middle East and Irene's veiled hints at terror organizations ran into a blank wall.

Lene caught herself smiling triumphantly when Irene once again found herself at a dead end. She grew increasingly pushy, irritable, but her exasperated tone of voice bounced off the young girl, who withdrew deeper and deeper inside herself.

Irene Adler spent most of the time during the last interview staring ostentatiously out of the window in the hope of putting pressure on Ain so that she would say something. But the girl did not pick up on the psychiatrist's mood – or if she did, she did not care. She spent the whole time staring at her polished fingernails, seeing God knows what visions behind her retinas, induced by the LSD intoxication.

Lene made herself a cup of Nescafé in Bjarne's miniature galley.

She watched the raindrops trickle down the windowpane. The first of the EU's foreign delegations would have landed in Copenhagen Airport two hours ago, and the El Al flight from Tel Aviv would land in one hour with Ehud Berezowsky on board.

There was no more time.

She opened the last, innocent-looking yellow folder on the computer's desktop, which Irene had given the cryptic title: *Notes on LAD-S3-25: individual cases, ex. Protocol*. Lene interpreted it as a file note about the use of reconstructed LSD in individual cases outside the overall experiment protocol. There were no videos or sound files in the folder, just the names of four female patients whom Irene Adler, personally and without the knowledge of those patients, had treated or considered treating with LSD: two middle-aged women with severe anxiety, one a famous actress who had abandoned her career due to stage fright, the other married to a well-known businessman. There was also a thirty-year-old woman with severe schizophrenia whose name meant nothing to Lene. And finally a twenty-three-year-old woman with life-threatening depression who had responded to anti-depressants and ECT treatment, but whom the psychiatrist assessed as very vulnerable and at serious risk of a relapse.

Her own daughter, Josefine.

Pt. has been admitted for almost six months, but in the last three weeks has shown some improvement after ECT. On several occasions it has been possible to engage the pt. in normal conversation. She makes eye contact, but when left alone she quickly becomes introverted, tormented and blames herself.

The trauma she suffered was of a brutal and sadistic nature and the memory of it will always be associated with imminent disaster and a belief that her life is at risk. Because she is fundamentally healthy and normal, her ability to suppress is very poor. I see no other option than a lifetime of heavy medication and probably several readmissions in the pt.'s future, and she will present a constant suicide risk. The pt. has been affected in several vital areas: her sexuality, her fundamental trust in the world, her loss of body confidence, and a great sense of shame towards her mother. She feels that she acted irresponsibly and thoughtlessly when she was kidnapped and that she placed her mother in an impossible situation. She constantly blames herself, which is the very core of her depression. There are, of course, no rational grounds for this. She could never

have prevented what happened to her. In fact, I have
not witnessed such cynical cruelty since we treated rape
victims from Bosnia. It is a very extensive, psychological
disaster ..

Lene read on through a veil of tears. She had no tissues
within reach, so she wiped her nose on her sleeve.

... As always, we are short of beds on this ward and it
is my responsibility to allocate limited resources. We
cannot keep up after the Tivoli bomb. In my opinion,
the pt. is well enough to be transferred to an outpatient
clinic. She would like to move home with her mother
initially, and I have no objection to that. Her mother
seems to me to be a sensible, wise and resourceful
person, with her daughter's best interests at heart.
Of course, the tragedy will be ever present through
association in this proposed move, but I have weighed
up the pros and cons, and I believe it is the only way
forward. She has been a patient here longer than anybody else I can think of. I hope that the two of them
can find each other, and perhaps it can be a part of
their mutual healing process. The mother is almost
as hard hit as the daughter, with a perpetual if futile
sense of self-recrimination, but she shows no clinical
symptoms of insanity. She has a strong, extroverted and
individualized personality, in contrast to her daughter,

who is still too young to process and externalize an assault of this nature.

Praise and respect from Irene. Lene closed her eyes when she had finished reading the extract.

There was not much more to be found. Irene had considered treating Josefine with LSD in the hope of pulling her nightmares up by the root, but it had stayed a thought. It was too risky.

Lene left the office with Bjarne's eyes following her, walked through the Mosaic Hall with its bowed, grey heads, found an empty lavatory just off the corridor, and sat on it with her chin in her hands.

Her emotions were an impossible mix of relief and shame: relief that someone – everyone, in fact – had taken good care of her daughter; and profound shame at her suspicions, accusations and the threats she had heaped upon Irene.

38

She stayed in the cubicle for a long time before she got out, splashed cold water on her face and started pacing up and down the corridor outside. She walked with her arms folded across her chest, staring at the floor. Everyone instinctively avoided her.

She remembered what Charlotte had said about looking beyond her own private tragedy and bearing in mind that some people had lost everything that day in September. Whole families had been wiped out.

She returned to the office and Bjarne greeted her as if she had come back from a war.

'She's outside Skanör,' he said eagerly, pointing to a green icon on the electronic naval chart which he had hacked into on SOK, the headquarters of the Royal Danish Navy.

'What is?'

'The coaster. The *Kazimierz Pulaski*.'

'Bjarne, for Christ's sake! Forget about that bloody ship right now and start doing something worthwhile, okay? Like finding out if Nazeera Gamil left the country by plane on Monday afternoon or evening from Copenhagen Airport. Do you think you can do that?'

Bjarne's eyes were wounded, but he clicked obediently away from his naval chart and into another province of his strictly illegal hacker universe.

'Bjarne?'

'Mmm.'

'What happens if the Civil Aviation Authority or SOK find out that you've hacked into their systems? I mean, would you be able to direct air traffic in Copenhagen Airport from here?'

'Are you asking if I can overrule instructions from air traffic controllers? Make planes crash?'

'Yes, for example.'

Lene had asked in jest, but now she detected a dangerous glint in the technician's brown eyes. She placed her hand on his shoulder, even though she knew he didn't like it, and gave it a warning squeeze.

'Forget it, Bjarne. Okay?'

The glint was extinguished.

'Lufthansa Monday afternoon to Amman,' he mumbled a little later. 'Nazeera Gamil. She landed in Jordan at 13:42 exactly according to schedule. I love Lufthansa.'

Lene studied the green digits on the screen.

'When did she return?'

'Same evening at 23:19.'

'Thank you, Bjarne,' she said gravely. 'She's the one. That's

Kim's mole. His agent with Safar Khan. I would bet a million on it.'

'Who?' he asked, but he was talking to an empty room.

She half ran towards the stairwell. Everything added up. Nazeera Gamil was Kim's mole in Khan's organization. That had to be how it was. It was her identity he was trying to protect. And Nazeera had used Ain to prove her loyalty to Khan.

It added up with the footage from Nørreport Station: Ain had raised her head and detected a scent that shouldn't be around skateboarding boys. The scent of a woman she knew. Two seconds later, Ain had felt a hard push to her back, a dizzying feeling of disaster and the air pressure from the train only a few metres away.

It was all about scents.

Lene remembered the dark, sensual perfume Nazeera had trailed in her wake. An invisible presence in the corridor behind the restaurant kitchen. It was the same scent she had registered in Irene Adler's hallway, without recognizing it when she ought to.

She ran towards the reception area and out through the swing doors. The rain was cold against her skin, but rather than curse it she closed her eyes and raised her face. She thought clearly for the first time since Josefine's death. She remembered what it used to feel like. Well-organized rows of thoughts, marching towards their inevitable conclusion. She had not expected to ever experience it again.

Her mobile vibrated in the pocket of her jeans.

'Yes.'

'It's Bjarne. I'm sorry.'

'Don't apologize, Bjarne.'

'Sorry.'

She closed her eyes.

'What?'

'Nazeera Gamil. She went to Amman four times last year,' he said.

'Four?'

'Yes, and to Limassol, Cyprus, three times, Beirut once, and two years ago she spent three months in Pakistan. In the hot season. Islamabad and Karachi. Incidentally, she travelled with Kim Thomsen. Same plane.'

Lene lowered her mobile. Three months in Pakistan? With Kim? And in the lowlands, during the months when all sensible people travelled to the highlands? This was not a place you visited for recreational reasons, that much was certain. And Limassol. Since the creation of the state of Israel in 1948, every Middle Eastern faction had staff, an office or a media platform in Cyprus. Anyone who did not sell honey or rent out scooters on that island was mixed up in Middle Eastern conflicts.

She raised the mobile to her ear.

'Thank you, Bjarne.'

'Don't mention it. I'll call you if anything happens with that Polish ship, all right?'

'You do that,' she said.

She reached her car, got into the driver's seat and was about to call Michael just as he called her.

'Michael! I know the identity of the retriever,' she began breathlessly. 'I'm one hundred per cent sure. And I've found Irene Adler's—'

'Nazeera. I know. Now shut up and listen. Please would you just shut up and listen?'

She could hear a strange snarling in the background.

'Michael?'

'Wait, just wait a moment, please let me . . .'

His voice disappeared and was replaced by a low growl. Then she heard a sharp sound like dry pasta snapping. Michael screamed out loud and Lene jumped out of her car and started walking around in sheer agitation.

'It bites harder when I shout,' he whispered.

'Who?'

'The dog! That bloody dog. That bitch's bodyguard. It doesn't like people shouting.'

'Rudolf? Nazeera's dog? Why . . .? I don't understand, Michael, what are you doing? Have you taken something from it? Have you hurt it? Where are you?'

Michael was silent for a few seconds.

'What do you mean, have I hurt it?' he hissed with forced calm. 'And what the hell could I have taken from it? Its bone? I *am* its fucking bone!'

The dog growled ominously as he raised his voice.

'Where are you?'

'In the yard behind Le Crocodile Vert. I'm lying on the grass, there's not a living soul within three light years and that sodding dog is about to eat my leg. Do you have your gun on you?'

'Of course. But why haven't you called the police?'

'That's exactly what I am doing. Now get a move on, for pity's sake.'

39

Nazeera was standing by the window with her back to Kim and her arms folded across her chest. The faint light in the almost empty warehouse with the high ceiling softened her silhouette. A long, graceful curve ran through her body, from the top of her head to the tip of her toe, which balanced behind her other foot. Her hair was scraped back and gathered at the neck. She wore a long grey cardigan, black jeans, no make-up, and she watched the man and the dog on the lawn below without expression.

She had never seen him before.

The dark stranger was currently lying with his face pressed against the grass and his eyes squeezed shut. One hand was still clutching the mobile he had just used and Rudy was a motionless black ridge behind him. The dog's eyes were half closed in concentration and the only movement were small twitches rippling through its black lips. Its jaws were closed around the man's right lower leg, and long bloody trails of saliva ran from his knees.

The building had once served as the storeroom for an

art auction house which had gone bankrupt. The windows were barred and the steel doors massive. It was a good venue for their rare meetings. In the corner was a large mattress covered by a red bedspread. A champagne cooler half full of water and an empty bottle of Veuve Clicquot were standing on the filthy concrete floor, along with two champagne flutes.

It was impossible to imagine Nazeera far away from a good bed, Kim thought, who had himself tried the mattress out in other, happier times. He wondered vaguely with whom she had shared the champagne. There were several candidates.

'Perhaps we should make tracks, Nazeera. I don't suppose he has just called his wife to tell her he'll be home late.'

Nervously she chewed a nail.

'No, but who is he?' she asked.

Kim rubbed his throat. He had trouble swallowing, and his voice was an octave lower than it had been before the man on the lawn had floored him with such frightening ease in Glostrup, but he saw no reason to worry Nazeera more. Irene Adler's death had hit her surprisingly hard.

'I've no idea,' he lied. 'I've never seen him before. Perhaps he's an estate agent. After all, the building is up for sale.'

'He doesn't look like an estate agent,' she said, without turning around. 'He looks like something else.'

'Does he?'

'Yes, Kim, he frightens me. We're so close! Who is he?'

She gave up biting her nails and folded her arms tightly across her chest again.

He wanted to hold her, but knew that she would withdraw with that glassy, hard stare she reserved just for him.

'You're not scared of anything,' he said with a smile. 'You're Zebra, don't forget.'

'Zebras get eaten, Kim. They're a bloody long way down the food chain.'

'Yes, but they can never be tamed.'

'Yes . . . sorry. I'll . . .'

'What has happened to your friends from Jordan? Are they coming or aren't they?'

'They're coming. They'll never get a better chance, and they know it. Safar Khan knows it. They'll get the ID cards that you have obtained. Was it difficult?'

He shrugged his shoulders. It made no difference. The suicide bombers would praise Zebra's skill and efficiency. They would think that she had surpassed herself. Dressed as waiters from the international catering company, supplying the service and the food during Ehud Berezowsky's visit, they would be able to walk all the way up to the high table in the university's Festival Hall at the lunch after the award ceremony, without anyone stopping them.

Denmark would never recover from it, he thought.

The Swiss catering company had the highest international security clearance, and the Israelis had insisted on using it. It had cooked for and served the Sultan of Brunei, Vladimir Putin, Hugo Chávez and Fidel Castro's brother, Raúl. The company employed only staff vetted by intelligence services across the world. The lives of their staff were scrutinized from kindergarten onwards.

The owner of the company had protested vociferously before he finally – and in return for all sorts of written guarantees – had handed over the specialist ID cards which the chefs and waiters would wear at the event. The cards were laminated and issued with sophisticated holograms. They showed a colour photograph of the wearers, which Nazeera had provided him with, and a print of their right index finger. They were only valid for twenty-four hours, and it was universally agreed that they were impossible to fake.

'Not really,' he replied.

'You're lying,' she said, turning to look at him. Her face lay in shadow and was impossible to read.

'Then tell them that it was really difficult. Anything to keep them happy, all right?'

'Don't underestimate them, Kim,' she said gravely.

'If there's one thing I don't . . . If there's one thing I would never, ever dream of, then it's underestimating them. I've thought of nothing other than not underestimating them for the last seven months, just so you know.'

'And afterwards, Kim. When your clever, devious trap has shut and everyone is dead or arrested, then what?'

'Afterwards?'

He stroked his face. He had no idea. All along he had presumed that he would commit suicide afterwards. But perhaps not. Perhaps there was another way. Perhaps with her?

'I haven't thought about it,' he said. 'What's he doing?'

'Nothing. He's just lying there. He's very still and patient. I think he's a dangerous man.'

Kim could not agree more. Where the hell had that eternally cursed Lene Jensen found him? And why had he yet to hear that she was wanted for the murder of Irene Adler? Police radio channels should be red hot by now; they should have crackled with sensational gossip about the red-headed superintendent. Lene Jensen had finally run amok and murdered the psychiatrist who had failed to save her daughter.

Nazeera started to cry. Her shoulders trembled when he carefully placed his fingertips on them, but she did not shy away from him.

'Is it Irene?' he asked.

'Yes! Yes, it is.'

'I'm the one who is sorry,' he said. 'I don't think I fully realized that . . . that . . .'

'That we weren't just using each other?'

'Yes.'

She withdrew from him and wandered further into the room, which smelled of emptiness and dust.

'I loved Irene, Kim,' she said. 'She was my equal, do you understand?'

I understand that you were equally screwed up, he thought with a dart of jealousy.

'Perhaps you'll get a chance to take revenge,' he said.

'On Lene?'

'Yes.'

She scrutinized him and he looked away.

'Because I don't suppose you did it, Kim? To make Lene disappear, I mean. So she won't ruin anything for you. Your clever trap. That would be an outrageous suggestion, wouldn't it?'

'I liked Irene,' he protested. 'We had a fantastic partnership.'

'Fantastic . . . only it never led to anything, did it? Everyone you interviewed turned out to be duds, didn't they? There was nothing to be gained. They were all normal young people. I tried telling you that Safar Khan only uses people from outside the country.'

Her eyes flashed.

'And if I don't know, then who the hell would?' she continued. 'Have you any idea how many times I've risked my life for you and this ridiculous little country, which is only interested in food and the next royal baby? Do you know what it's like not knowing if the next second is your last when something very close to you makes an incredibly loud noise – like, for example, when you're shot through the head? Give me the sales pitch once more, Kim, the one about being a patriot, making a difference, being the best version of yourself, that the only thing necessary for the triumph of evil is for good men to do nothing? Because I've forgotten why the hell I'm doing this. Imagine, there was a time I actually thought I was doing it for you.'

'I'm flattered. Thank you.'

'Fuck you! Then I thought I was doing it for all the people who sit in the Crocodile every day eating with their friends and families, for mothers with their buggies who drink coffee in the morning, for students with their laptops making a latte last two hours between lectures, for people walking their dogs in the park, for the little boy from Mozambique who lives on the ground floor with his Danish adoptive parents and is named after Lionel Messi – something his father, who always greets me, probably insisted on.'

Kim held up both hands to placate her.

'But you do, Nazeera. We all do, for Christ's sake! We do it so that Lionel and his parents won't be blown to bits if they happen to be in the wrong place at the wrong time. I would have thought that was obvious.'

He wanted to hit her. He wanted to hold her. He wanted to take her to the mattress in the corner and make love to her until the whole world disappeared – and stayed away.

He looked at her.

'When they called me, I went there,' he said slowly. 'I can't remember very much of it. Even when I was standing in the middle of Tivoli, I still couldn't believe it. I kept thinking it was a film.'

'Poor Kim,' she mumbled, but whether it was said with irony or compassion, he gave up trying to understand.

'Christian had come with me, but I didn't realize until later that he had been there all the time. That's why I have a special relationship with Christian. He took care of me when I needed it. I slept on his sofa for fourteen days. Drank his overcomplicated coffee.'

'I've fucked him. Several times. Did you know that?' she asked in order to maintain the upper hand. 'Your best friend,' she stressed, in case he had forgotten.

Kim smiled and shrugged his shoulders.

'Of course you have, Nazeera,' he said affably. 'Your cunt is like a revolving door, we all have to go through it at some point. It's natural. Forget it . . . Anyway, it was impossible to get close to the Star Flyer itself. It lay in two pieces like a heavy ruler that had crashed through all the stalls and cardboard buildings, amusement arcades and restaurants. All that made-up fairy-tale crap. There were fires everywhere. All the gas pipes had been severed, I think. It started to rain and the rain was black.'

She nodded indifferently. If he had started telling her this in the hope of igniting a spark of compassion in her, he now gave up on the idea. Perhaps it was his remark about her cunt and revolving doors.

'You think there will be intact bodies lying around with peaceful faces. As if they're asleep. But there aren't,' he went on. 'You can't find them at all! Everything is levelled and covered with a thick layer of dust – and where the hell does all that dust come from? Everything bounces under your feet, and it is only when you look down that you start to make out objects which belong to the bodies or *are* the bodies.

It's like walking on a glass floor with the street from hell below you. People were crushed under the rubble. Everything is one-dimensional, and they assume all sorts of positions which you quite simply would not believe possible. There is no up or down. You almost can't see them, even though you know there are hundreds of them right below you. Did you know that they found my daughter's left foot two hundred metres away? Still with her sandal on? It had been flung through a third-floor window of the town hall and ended up in their finance department. It was lying on the conference table the next morning in between mineral water, coffee, sugar and cream.'

'Stop it, Kim, please.'

But he could not stop. He knew it was the last time he would ever describe it. It was important to him.

'In one place, I stood for a long time staring before I realized that I was practically standing on top of a young man. I thought he might be Chinese. Then I saw that he had his arms around a woman. She was wearing a summer dress with a pattern. Her head and legs were stretched backwards and it looked as if he had caught her mid-air in a leap or a dance. Who the hell has time to do something like this, I thought? Who the hell has time to grab her and hold her close when you know that death will exterminate you in a second? Did he even know her? Or did he just know that he did not want to die without holding someone?'

'Lene Jensen is downstairs,' she said from the window.

He took a couple of quick steps over to her and had time to see the gate close behind the superintendent. She walked with long, determined strides across the yard, with a pistol in her right hand, looking only at the dog and the man.

Nazeera produced the whistle from her pocket and put it to her lips. The sound was much higher than the human ear could detect, but the dog immediately released the man's leg. It glanced indifferently at the red-haired woman approaching it with her pistol in her outstretched hand, padded through a hole in the fence into the next backyard, and disappeared.

The superintendent stopped and looked up at the warehouse.

'I think it's time we got going,' Kim said.

He pressed the button to call the old goods elevator and they stood shoulder to shoulder like random guests in a hotel.

'Why is she here, Kim?'

'I suppose he called her.'

'So he's probably not an estate agent?'

'I guess not.'

'That wasn't what I meant.'

The elevator reached the ground floor and he opened the heavy doors.

'What did you mean?'

'Why has she not been arrested if she killed Irene? I mean, she's here, isn't she? Right in the middle of Copenhagen, and she's not someone you tend to overlook. She's not acting like someone trying to keep a low profile.'

He shook his head.

'I don't understand it either.'

'No, I can see that.'

He tried to catch her eye, but she refused to look at him.

40

'Ouch, that hurts! Bloody dog.'

Michael slowly rose to his feet, like a deckchair unfolding. Lene tried to help, but he bashed her hands away.

'What the hell kept you?'

She stuck her unwelcome hands into the pockets of her jacket, and stared up at the warehouse.

'It probably felt longer than it really was,' she said calmly. 'What are you doing here?'

'Fuck!'

'Fuck? Is that supposed to be an explanation?'

He finally straightened up and looked glumly at his bleeding, maltreated lower leg. Would it take his weight? Would it ever support anything ever again?

'That woman, Nazeera . . . I thought I'd take a closer look at her.'

'A closer look at her?'

'Find out who she was talking to, dammit.'

'And did you?'

'No!'

Putting his weight on his left foot hurt insanely. He had not even seen the animal coming. It had been like walking through a dark forest and suddenly putting your foot into a bear trap.

He had watched Nazeera for a couple of hours.

Today she would appear to be on barista duty. It was a slow day at the bistro. A couple of students perched on the tall stools by the window with their Macs and a group of mothers sitting at a table in a booth which looked like something out of an American diner. Red plastic seat covers, a square Formica table with a steel edge, bottles of tomato ketchup and Worcester sauce.

The Arab woman had great posture and moved deftly and smoothly, but when she was not serving customers, she stared pensively into eternity. She would smile when someone addressed her, but afterwards her face would return to concerned introspection. After a couple of hours, she had taken out a mobile from the pocket of her apron and checked the display. She had taken off the apron, folded it, placed it under the counter and called out something over her shoulder. A fat, melancholic man with dark bags under his doggy eyes appeared from the kitchen regions and took over the shiny coffee machine. Nazeera Gamil walked through the passage behind the counter and disappeared.

Michael left the car, crossed the street diagonally and examined the lock on the gate next to the restaurant. He knew from his map studies that the area behind the building was divided into several yards and that behind Le Crocodile Vert was a bike shed, a square patch of grass and an empty warehouse, which was for sale. He had picked the gate lock and entered.

On the lawn were a teak garden table and four folding garden chairs. There were no sandpits, climbing frames or prams. Along the fence was a series of neglected bushes where the monster must live. It must have been watching him in silence.

Most of the warehouse windows had been whitewashed. There was a rusty loading beam up under the roof, with a winch that had undoubtedly not been in use for years. He was halfway across the lawn and had started sizing up the lock on the solitary white metal door when, without warning, his left shin was locked in a painful vice. He fell over and tried yanking his leg out of the dog's jaws, but its mouth was as immobile as a gravestone.

He had read once that you could strangle an aggressive dog with your belt, but when he had finally managed to unbuckle it and pull it out of the belt loops on his trousers, the animal had given him a look which suggested that it too had read the article; it growled menacingly and increased the pressure from its jaws until Michael heard his shinbone creak and knew that it was a matter of seconds before something irreversible happened. He had tossed aside the belt, and felt the pressure of the jaws diminish, as a kind of concession to his common sense.

But the dog had not minded him ringing Lene.

41

Four hours later, Michael had to acknowledge that there had been times when he had felt worse. His optimism had started to return.

This change in outlook was mostly down to his visit to Rigshospitalet's casualty department, where he was treated by a female doctor who had listened with scepticism to Lene's story about how Michael had been injured while pretending to be the villain at the Danish Police Dog Championships.

The beast had been disqualified, Lene informed the doctor, but by then the damage had already been done.

The doctor had taken a long, hard look at Michael's expensive suit and black, handmade shoes but said nothing. The deep bite to his shin had been injected with wonderful local anaesthetic, cleaned and bandaged. The doctor had administered a broad-spectrum antibiotic into one vein, and her examination suggested that no important nerves, tendons or blood vessels had been damaged.

He was given a tetanus injection and a leaflet about rabies. He was told to read the leaflet thoroughly, which Michael solemnly promised that he would do. The symptoms sounded medieval and horrific. The hospital would have liked to keep him overnight for observation for potential pressure sores, but Lene assured the doctor that she would take good care of him.

Right now he was lying in his hotel bed with pillows and blankets under his injured leg. He had a glass of whisky in his hand and was watching two ice cubes float around lazily in the liquid.

'How about another Ketogan, Lene?' he mumbled. 'They're divine.'

'Your pupils are the size of pinheads,' she said sternly from the armchair by the French balcony. 'You can have a cold flannel on your forehead and some more penicillin, but no more morphine. I need you to be able to think straight.'

He watched her through half-closed eyelids. The afternoon light – or the morphine – cast a soft pastel glow across her face and neck. Her eyes had never been greener.

She looked up at him when she noticed his scrutiny.

'Lene?'

'Mmm?'

'I want you to promise that you'll shoot me if I get rabies – I mean, if I start cramping, foaming at the mouth. That kind of thing. If I start turning my head like a bloody owl.'

'Nothing would give me greater pleasure, Michael. But to my knowledge, we don't have rabies in Denmark, and Rudolf undoubtedly lives on a diet of foie gras, Argentinian beef and marshmallows, and has had every jab known to man.'

'I do hope so. By the way, are you aware how incredibly beautiful you are?' he said, and was overcome by a sudden urge to cry.

'Oh, shut up, Michael. So, what did you discover?'

He gritted his teeth, sat up, rubbed his eyes and put down the glass.

'All right then, if you insist! The pictures of Ain and Nabil Maroun were not taken by a Swedish civil engineer and wildlife photographer. He and his wife were already dead when the pictures were uploaded. They died in their home in Södertälje in an electrical fire. But the photographs were sent in his name to Rigspolitiet's Tivoli server. No one would appear to have verified the details, such as the sender's IP address. They were too busy congratulating themselves.'

'I knew it,' Lene muttered under her breath. 'I knew those pictures were too good to be true.'

'Yes, but they were just a small part of it,' he said. 'Don't forget the drone in Iran and the recordings from Newark Airport. I think the pictures were taken by Nabil Maroun's friends. They watched him, they followed him at a distance around Tivoli to make sure that his courage didn't fail him, or that he was overpowered. It's normal procedure with suicide bombers. They discovered who Elsa Valerius-Klüver was, I'm guessing by stealing her purse, or simply by following the couple.'

'But why?'

'To keep PET chasing the wrong suspect, in case they got too close. Too close to whom or what, I don't yet know, but I hope to work that out in the next twenty-four hours. I've asked a friend of mine in London to do a little research. PET was given Ain gift-wrapped, but they were sold a pup. She had no idea what she had done, but she could be used to keep them occupied. They followed her, bugged her flat, put up cameras, and dragged all her friends and acquaintances into those dubious LSD experiments.'

'I found Irene's private computer,' she said. 'It was hidden in a showcase with an antique copy of the Koran.'

'Was there anything about Ain?'

'Everything! There were recordings from the LSD treatments of her and five other depressed young people, but there was nothing to be obtained from it. They were just ordinary young people with an immigrant background. Not one of them expressed political radicalization. Not one of them had been a war tourist in Syria. There were also tons of films and sound recordings from her home.'

'I'm glad, Lene,' he said.

'That I found them?'

'No, that the young people were the way they were.'

She got up, poured him some coffee, carried the cup over to him and sat down on the edge of the bed.

'I thought that maybe I loved Ain like you love a hopeless baby sister,' she said. 'But Ain really was vacuous. Utterly self-obsessed.'

'Like most people her age.'

She interlaced her fingers in her lap.

'I've spoken to a senior CSO at Irene's house. His name is Arne. He likes me. He's old school. Very honest.'

'Go on?'

'He showed me some hair he found in Irene's hand. There was blood too.'

'I imagine she fought for her life,' he said.

'Except that it was my hair and my blood, Michael. Arne has given me twenty-four hours to prove that I didn't kill her. It's common knowledge that I hated her.'

Michael said nothing.

Lene grabbed his upper arm hard and the coffee sloshed onto the duvet.

'Say something! You know that I'm not capable of killing.'

He calmly freed his arm and put down the cup on the bedside table.

'What do you want me to say, Lene? I believe you. If you tell me that you didn't kill her, that's all I need to know. I know that you wouldn't just kill another human being. She might have been guilty of professional misconduct when treating your daughter, or maybe she wasn't, but I know that you can tell the difference. Bloody hell. You're not . . . '

'What?'

'Twisted. Insane.'

Lene delivered the first genuine, broad smile he

remembered ever having received from her. The corners of her eyes crinkled, as did her nose.

'So where does the hair come from?' he wanted to know.

'The night PET attacked me in Ain's flat, they put a sack over my head and then they kicked me in the head. I was unconscious most of the time.'

Lene bowed her head, parted her hair and showed him the scab on her scalp.

'Kim,' he muttered.

'Of course.'

'He really is one of a kind,' he said.

'He certainly is. But then it occurred to me that I might have done the same if I had been in his shoes. He lost his wife and two little girls that day in Tivoli.'

'But Irene didn't set off the bomb. She has never hurt a fly, has she? Kim has no excuse or reason to kill her. Try thinking straight, would you?'

'That's rich coming from you,' she smiled. 'A moment ago you told me I was beautiful. Yesterday you said that I looked like shit. Make up your mind.'

'I'm under the influence of medication.'

'Yes, I can hear that. Kim wants me out of the way, no matter what it takes. Even if it meant him killing Irene.'

'That means that he's desperate, Lene.'

'Of course it does.'

'It also means that he doesn't give a damn what happens to him.'

42

She had only gone as far as the hall, but Michael felt strangely abandoned while he listened out for her movements.

She returned with something in her hand.

'What are you thinking about?' she said when she saw his face.

'My leg. I was thinking about my leg. What's that?'

'A photo from Irene Adler's bedroom.'

Michael looked at the soft-focus black-and-white photograph of the sleeping naked woman.

'Is there anyone she hasn't slept with?' he asked.

'Probably, Michael, but I think that she practically lived with Irene. Toothbrush. Dog food. Dog bowl.'

'Please don't mention the dog. She's a very busy girl, isn't she?'

'Definitely. She visited Amman four times last year, she has been to Cyprus dozens of times, and she has spent periods of up to three months in Pakistan.'

'And not because she's interested in their culture, I presume?'

'Unlikely. In fact, she travelled to Pakistan with Kim.'

'Cyprus is the nearest you can get to Istanbul as far as the number of intelligence agents per square kilometre is concerned. Every jihadist cell has an office on Cyprus.'

Michael gazed up at the ceiling. They were undoubtedly thinking the same thing. Nazeera Gamil was PET's retriever with Ebrahim Safar Khan, and she was balancing on the same knife's edge as Kim. There was probably nothing the two of them would not do for each other right now.

'Perhaps there is a happy ending after all,' he said. 'Perhaps the two of them really know what they're doing.'

'And perhaps the moon really is made of cheese.'

'But you clearly don't believe that?'

'Of course not. I don't think Kim can control her. I think she has her own agenda.'

'Perhaps. But you can't be sure. What is tomorrow's programme?' he asked.

'Ehud Berezowsky is giving a lecture about historical Judaism at eleven o'clock at the old university campus on Vor Frue Plads. Afterwards he'll be presented with an award and made an honorary doctor. The crown prince and princess will be attending. Lunch will be served.'

'*Coelestem adspicit lucem*,' he quoted.

'Sorry?'

'*The eagle watches the celestial light*. It's the inscription above the main entrance to the university. I read law for a year before I joined the army.'

'Really? I'm impressed.'

'There's absolutely no reason for you to be. I slept through every lecture. Let's hope no one ends up watching the celestial light tomorrow. What about the foreign ministers?'

'They start early. Negotiations and presentations kick off at eight and continue until eleven, after which lunch will be served. Everything takes place in Eigtveds Pakhus on Christianshavn. There will be press briefings in the evening.'

'No light entertainment?'

'They've cancelled a planned gala performance at the Opera House followed by an official dinner at Amalienborg Palace, for security reasons.'

'Very sensible. But the Foreign Ministry is a nightmare,' he said. 'There are numerous access roads which are difficult to secure, and at the same time it's a strangely claustrophobic place. For example, there is no park you can close off, or where people can go for a quiet walk to think, make phone calls or negotiate confidentially. There's only one car park and there will inevitably be problems with ministerial cars going in and out of it. There will also be vehicles belonging to the police, the press and catering companies. What's the weather forecast?'

'Hang on.' She got up to fetch his laptop, but stopped halfway. 'Perhaps they'll ferry people back and forth in water taxis across the harbour from Havnepromenaden. That way they wouldn't have to drive motorcades through the city.'

'Let's hope no one has had that brilliant idea,' Michael

said. 'The temperature of the water is only twelve degrees. A single grenade tossed from the promenade, and that's the end of that.'

'Fair point.'

She rested the laptop on a blanket and Michael checked the homepage of the Danish Meteorological Institute.

'Sunny. A light breeze,' he said. 'No significant precipitation. By the way, does Charlotte Falster know about Irene Adler and your hair?'

'If she did, I definitely wouldn't be sitting here now,' Lene said. 'She would have had me arrested. She always plays it by the book.'

'Does she?'

She looked at him.

'Doesn't she? Have *you* spoken to her? I imagine she must know your number.'

'Of course not.'

He leaned back in the bed. His leg was starting to wake up.

'It hurts like hell, Lene. Just a half? Half a measly Ketogan? Please! I got sleeping pills for you!'

'I really don't think it's a good idea, Michael. Honestly. What if something happens and you just lie there unconscious and useless?'

'Then a whisky. It bloody hurts!'

She fetched a miniature of Famous Grouse and poured it with a sigh.

'It's the last one,' she said.

'Of course.'

'She took good care of Josefine,' Lene said after a pause. 'What she did was good enough. It was okay.'

'Who?'

'Irene. I found a kind of diary on her computer. She even sang my praises! Wrote that I was strong . . . good for my daughter, but that she had to discharge her. There weren't enough beds on the ward, and Josefine had been admitted for longer than most people.'

'That's good,' he said. 'That she was given proper treatment, I mean.'

'Even so, I feel as if I have lost something. Of course I'm pleased to have seen what she wrote about Josefine and me, but now I don't know . . .'

'What to do with your anger? Give it time, Lene. You have all sorts of other things on your mind, but in my experience it can be just as hard to lose an enemy as to lose a friend . . . or . . . something like that.'

'Try getting some sleep,' she said.

'It hurts too much.'

She smiled and got up. She stood by the balcony door with her back to him and her arms folded across her chest for a long time.

'Which one would you pick?' she asked at length.

Michael raised his leg and pushed yet another pillow under it. Then he lowered it, as delicately as dandelion seeds.

'Berezowsky. If the attack succeeds, the assassination

won't be as sensational as the extermination of Europe's foreign ministers, obviously, but it'll definitely make waves where it matters: at home in Lebanon, Jordan, the Yemen and on the West Bank.'

'So that's where we're going tomorrow?' she asked.

He nodded. 'A fat lot of good that will do. I can't walk and you'll be arrested for Irene's murder by the first police cadet you meet. What a team we'll make.'

She massaged her temples without saying anything.

'Have you thought about just calling Kim?' he asked. 'Tell him what you know and hope that he'll see sense? It might be that he's aware of what's about to happen.'

'If he knows that, he definitely won't listen to me. Besides . . .'

'What?'

She turned around.

'He killed Irene. You haven't forgotten that, have you? If he finds out where I am, he'll trigger an arrest order under some pretext, or he might come after me himself. Might as well be hung for a sheep as a . . .'

Michael heaved a sigh.

'You're right.'

'Now try to get some sleep.'

'Impossible,' he mumbled, yawned and fell asleep instantly.

Lene watched his sleeping face. Michael's features moved incessantly; they stretched, expanded and contracted. He whimpered a little, furrowed his brow and Lene presumed that Rudolf was leaping through his subconscious right now. A one-legged security consultant and a superintendent on the run from her own officers, with a charge of murder hanging over her head. Impossible. The whole thing was impossible. That had been Michael's last word before he nodded off.

Lene felt bone tired and on the verge of throwing in the towel. She sat down in one of the armchairs, pulled over the other one and tried curling into a foetal position on the two seats, but she had never been good at sleeping in anything other than a bed. Finally she gave up and carefully lay down next to Michael in the big double bed. She rolled onto her side and watched his face, which even in sleep was concerned and restless. She felt like placing a hand on his chest or arm to reassure him, but decided against it.

What was his game? He had told her she was beautiful and actually sounded as if he meant it. He had taken far more photographs of her than of Nazeera outside Værløse Church, even though Nazeera looked like every teenage boy's fantasy.

He was probably just lonely and homesick, Lene decided. It made him reach out for the nearest and most convenient.

Touching him would be a huge mistake, she thought, turned over onto her back and gazed at the ceiling.

43

The sound of her new mobile woke her up. She scrambled to her feet, nearly tripping over a chair, found the mobile, dropped it and found it again.

'Hello?' she grunted in a thick voice.

'She's doing it again, Lene!'

'Bjarne? What time is it?'

'One-thirty. Is it not a good time?'

She located a light switch and heard Michael wake up, stretch out and gasp in pain when he discovered that Rudolf had been more than just a bad dream.

She squinted against the light and looked out into the darkness on the other side of the balcony door. The water in the port was smooth and reflective like oil.

'What in God's name are you talking about, Bjarne, and why aren't you in bed?'

Even she wondered at the latter part of her question the moment it had left her lips. Bjarne was at least forty-five years old and could surely do whatever he wanted to at night.

The technician swallowed a mouthful of air in frustration.

'The *Kazimierz Pulaski*! The ship. I've followed her all the way up the Øresund, and she's deviating from the international sailing channel again. I've spoken to my friends from the Coastguard, and she's following exactly the same route as last year . . . three days before . . . you know.'

He paused to let Lene process these obvious and ominous facts.

She watched Michael's hand waving from the alcove, but ignored it. It slumped despondently to the floor.

'Where is she right now?' she asked.

'Off the coast of Klampenborg. She's 5.4 nautical miles from the position where she dropped anchor last autumn.'

Lene glanced at her watch while an excited Bjarne talked about the Navy, overflying, Coastguard vessels and thermal cameras.

'Bjarne? . . . Bjarne!!'

'What?'

'We don't want to start World War Three, do we? We're not about to sink the *Bismarck*. When will she reach that position?'

'If she keeps the same course and speed, she'll be there in three-quarters of an hour.'

'Right. I'll look into it. Call me the moment something happens, will you?'

'Roger that.'

Lene sighed. She could imagine the technician hunched over his ghostly glowing computer screens, tensely following the enemy sneaking up through Danish waters, without any awareness of Bjarne's suspicious eyes following their journey from his home in Vanløse.

'Goodbye, Bjarne. And, for God's sake, take it easy, will you?'

'Sure will.'

Lene thought like crazy. Three-quarters of an hour? She looked towards the alcove. Was Michael at all useful? It would take at least an hour to get him on his feet and dressed.

44

It took less than ten minutes. She had forgotten that Michael had that third, fourth and possibly even fifth gear she had seen him demonstrate a couple of years ago above the Arctic Circle in Norway, where he had set a merciless pace across the endless, snow-covered expanse. He would appear to be able to eat his pain and exhaustion. It was probably something they learned where he came from.

As it happened, he found her information about the Polish coaster extremely relevant.

'Why the hell didn't you say so right away?' he ranted at her from the edge of the bed while he flexed and pointed his injured leg, then with considerable effort pulled on a pair of black jeans. 'It's bloody obvious, Lene!'

'Is it?'

'Of course it is! It's discreet. Anyone can wander in and out of a port without being asked for anything other than a discharge book, which is the easiest document in the world to fake. Any thirteen-year-old with a colour laser printer and a graphics program can make one in five minutes. And a coaster like that has a crew of no more than five people, so not many people need to keep their mouths shut.'

He gritted his teeth, put on dark-grey trainers and got up.

Lene held out a hand ready to catch him, but he did not look at her. He took one step and then another.

'You okay?'

'Yes!'

A black roll-necked sweater and a dark anorak completed his outfit. He limped about the room, but the leg appeared to support his weight relatively effortlessly.

They left the hotel and walked through the empty, rainswept streets towards the underground car park.

He tossed her the keys when they reached the Mercedes.

'You drive,' he said. 'But be careful, won't you? It's new, and everything ... almost everything was customized specifically for that car.'

She rolled her eyes.

'I've had a driving licence for several years, Michael. More years than I care to remember, in fact. And I do have a car of my own.'

He did not seem impressed.

'Comparing this car with your Citroën is like comparing a Riva speedboat with a hollowed-out tree trunk,' he said.

'A what?'

'Forget it.'

He wasn't wrong, she thought, as she stepped on the

accelerator, heading up the Helsingør motorway. They were alone on the tarmac strip and it felt like being kicked in the back by a horse. Michael did not comment on her driving but pulled a face when, taken by surprise by the car's colossal acceleration, she swerved a little too close to the crash barrier. He entered a number on a keypad under the dashboard and a panel slid aside silently. An illuminated compartment appeared by one of his knees. It was empty except for a large grey pistol.

He took it out, clicked the magazine into his hand and pressed the top brass cartridge down. The magazine was apparently loaded to his satisfaction because he slammed it back in the handle before he stuck the pistol under his belt on his right hip. His hands were assured and routine like a violin builder.

'What's that?' she asked.

'A Sig Sauer with Teflon-coated 9mm bullets. Very illegal.'

'Cool, Michael. But what does that mean?'

'That the bullet will go through you even if you're wearing a bullet-proof vest, and if your identical twin was standing behind you, it would go through her as well.'

'Really? And here was I thinking you hated guns.'

He looked at her.

'I really do, but if our theory is correct and a tactical confrontation occurs, I don't see why we shouldn't be able to defend ourselves effectively.'

'A tactical confrontation? Jeez, Michael . . .'

'What?'

'You're talking about killing people with your special bullets, aren't you? I mean that is what you're talking about?'

'Of course. I guess so. In one way. A confrontation.'

She overtook a North Sjælland teenager in daddy's Porsche, which looked as if it was stationary.

Her mobile rang.

'Bjarne?'

'The skipper of the *Kazimierz Pulaski* has contacted SUNDREP on channel 16 to say that they have engine failure,' the technician said solemnly. 'Just like the last time.'

'Same location?'

'Exactly. They think they can fix it themselves, they say. That's what they said the last time as well.'

'Excellent, Bjarne.'

She looked at Michael who mouthed the word *hello*.

'Michael says hello. We're on our way. He thinks that you're right. Sorry.'

There was a moment of silence before Bjarne cleared his throat.

'You're on your way? You and Michael? Shouldn't I call . . .?'

'We have advised PET and North Sjælland Police,' she lied, to reassure him. 'You don't need to do anything at all. Communications will get muddled if you start making calls as well. You can see that, can't you?'

'Of course,' he said humbly. 'I understand.'

'What are the coordinates?' Michael asked, pulling out an iPad.

Bjarne supplied them to Lene, and Michael located the position on an electronic chart.

'Faster,' he said, sounding worried.

45

Hard, cold showers of rain accompanied by flat, long banks
of fog moved down the Øresund. The rain made the deck
of the coaster treacherously slippery and the fog distorted
all sounds. Samir put his mouth close to Adil's ear with the
final instructions. The boy's hair was sticking to his pale
face.

He nodded, but said nothing.

Adil was ready, Samir thought. Sombre, but vigilant. As
always, Ebrahim Safar Khan had made a good choice.

The anchor chain clattered out of the hawse hole with
a muted clonk, and the engine fell silent. Samir turned
and saw the captain's shadow behind the dark windows of
the bridge. The anchor lantern above the bows was turned
on, but looked strangely distant and blurred. The *Kazimierz
Pulaski* floated quietly around in her own length and found
a new balance, tethered to the anchor under the bows and
determined by the northbound current. The coast south of
Vedbæk was invisible, but it lay one nautical mile behind the
port side. There would be no flashing torch to guide them,

but the coordinates on Samir's handheld GPS receiver would be exactly the same as last time.

The captain's square figure appeared in the illuminated doorway. He passed the two young men without looking at them and continued to the gunwale on the port side to watch two able seamen lower a rubber dinghy into the water. They steadied the dinghy while the captain kicked the ladder over the side of the ship. He waved the two boys over.

They hitched up their rucksacks and quickly crossed the deck. Samir waited by the gunwale, while Adil climbed nimbly into the Zodiac and sat down in the stern.

Samir looked at the Polish captain. His red hair and sideburns had been pulled into watery strands and his large freckled hands rested on the gunwale. Samir held out his hand, but the Pole's hands remained where they were. The Syrian shrugged, swung one leg over the gunwale and found his footing on the narrow, dangling ladder. He took a final look into the shadows under the captain's oilskin hood.

The bearded face moved. 'I don't expect to see you again, young man,' the captain said in perfect English.

Despite the rain, Samir could feel his face grow hot.

'Our euros no longer good enough, Captain?'

'These ones?'

The captain unbuttoned the top of his oilskin jacket and fished out an envelope from his inside pocket. He pulled out the fat bundle of euros, ripped off the rubber band and let the banknotes flutter into the dark, quiet water.

STEFFEN JACOBSEN • 408

He spat after them. 'Just so happens they're not, mister.'

The ladder was pulled up the moment Samir reached the rubber dinghy, and the white moorings floated through the air and hit the water.

Samir pulled the ropes on board and started the outboard motor with an angry movement.

Adil watched the banknotes float along the side of the ship.

'Do you think he'll report us?' he asked.

Samir shook his head.

'He has a family.'

He checked the GPS receiver and turned the prow of the rubber dinghy towards the coast. The few scattered lights he could see looked as if they were swimming in the rain and the fog.

Samir was furious and humiliated. But he was feeling something else as well.

A slippery, restless feeling of doom.

46

'I can't see a bloody thing,' Michael complained as he took the binoculars from his eyes and dried the lenses on the hem of his T-shirt. It made little difference; his clothes were drenched.

They were currently standing under a tree in bud in a well-kept garden behind an elegant residential villa on Strandvejen. The house was quiet and dark, but the garden had a view of the Øresund between its tall trees. At times he could also see lights along the Swedish coastline and on the island of Hven, and he was fairly certain that on one occasion he had seen the dark outline of a ship and an anchor lantern, which might be that of the Polish ship. But a few seconds later another bank of fog had enveloped the view and it was impossible to see if anybody left.

The surface of the sea was at least thirty metres below them, at the foot of a steep, muddy slope. They had no way of knowing where exactly the terrorists would land. His best guess was that it would be at the end of the small park that bordered the villa's garden. The park reached all the way down to the water, but in the darkness it was an impenetrable maze of dense shrubs and narrow, winding paths. His bad leg would not be able to manage it. Besides, they would lose sight of Strandvejen, the road which was the only way out of the area, and they would be unprotected on the beach.

They had parked the Mercedes in a public car park, a few hundred metres from the park. It had been deserted apart from a trailer carrying building materials and a white box van. Michael had examined the van. All the doors were locked, there were no windows in the back, and he could see nothing unusual at the front. He had placed his hand on the bonnet and the headlights, but they had the same temperature as the rest of the van. It could have been parked there for a day or a year.

'Why would they embark right here?' Lene asked, her teeth chattering.

She too looked like a drowned rat. Michael had banned all speech, noise and sudden movements, but Lene appeared to think that his complaint about the visibility cancelled out his ban. The ghostly grey veils that constantly drifted in from the sea intensified certain sounds – passing cars and buses up on Strandvejen, for example – but muted most others. There was an ominous, fatalistic atmosphere in the old garden, which was heightened by the mournful hooting of foghorns on invisible ships. Closer to them was the constant splashing, dripping and gurgling of rainwater.

'In theory, they might as well sail the dinghy down to

Copenhagen or Vedbæk or Rungsted Marina,' she said. 'No one would bat an eyelid. Marinas are unguarded, and they would be closer to taxis, buses and trains.'

Michael had drawn a right angle to the coast from the assumed position of the *Kazimierz Pulaski*. It ended exactly by the beaches to their left; the shortest, but not necessarily the most sensible route ashore. Then again, the suicide bombers were from the desert. The sea was a hostile element, and he assumed they would seek land as quickly as possible.

'I don't think they want to be on the open sea longer than absolutely necessary,' he said. 'And I can't imagine that they're responsible for their own onward transport.'

He winced as the pain once more shot through his injured leg. He gritted his teeth and shifted his weight to his other foot.

'Are you all right?' she asked, placing her hand on his arm.

What the hell do you think? he thought, and nearly uttered an angry remark, but controlled himself. She probably meant well . . .

'I'll manage,' he grunted and raised the binoculars to his eyes once more.

Nothing between the drifting widow's veils. Only glimpses of the black water far below them between the tall, bare trees.

'It's as if the Devil himself is keeping them safe,' he said. 'They could not have wished for better conditions.'

She made no reply and he licked raindrops off his lips and

looked at her. Lene's face bore the slightly vacuous expression of someone listening closely. Her hand was still resting on his arm as if she had forgotten about it.

'I can hear them,' she then said. 'An engine of some sort.'

Michael closed his eyes and tilted his head. The rain was now falling straight and hard, and the only sound he could hear was water hitting thousands of surfaces before draining away.

'I can't hear it,' he said.

She straightened up and became present.

'That's because it has stopped.'

'This is hopeless,' he said. 'They could walk right past us at less than five metres without us seeing them. Let's go back to the road.'

He tried taking a step forward, but he had been standing still for too long and his leg refused to obey him. It felt as if it was concreted into the lawn. He grabbed hold of his knee and lifted it forward, while Lene looked at him.

'Bloody brilliant,' he groaned, looking up at her. 'I can't walk. I'm sorry.'

He tried smiling, but failed. He looked down at his foot. The cramps came and went and his leg twitched impotently and without coordination.

She took his arm, slung it over her shoulder and slipped her right arm around his waist. She was almost as tall as he was, and she was upright and strong.

'Come on, Michael. We can't stay here. So let's get going!'

She must have seen something desperate in his face because she looked away and chewed her lip.

After a few steps of Lene practically carrying him, things started to improve. He was able to feel his foot touch the ground once more. They crossed the lawn, which had seemed like an insurmountable wasteland, and reached a flagstone path that led them out between the house and a separate garage.

An old man who had been unable to sleep was dragging a fat, tired golden retriever after him. He looked at them with alarm when they squeezed themselves through the garden gate, holding each other tightly. Lene flashed him a beaming wet smile.

'Good evening!' she exclaimed.

The man said nothing, but yanked the flexible lead, which made the old dog sigh asthmatically and set off at a pathetic trot.

They looked after the pair.

'You almost gave him – and the dog – a heart attack,' Michael said.

'Did I? I always think it's important to mind your manners, don't you?'

'Most certainly.'

They looked up and down Strandvejen, which appeared empty, and glistened in the faint light from the interspersed streetlamps.

'What do we do now?' she asked.

He bent down and stretched out his injured leg.

'Nothing. Maybe you heard something, maybe you didn't. We're going back to the hotel.'

'I did hear something, Michael.'

'Okay, you heard something.' He gestured impotently towards the road. 'But where? It's hopeless. They could be anywhere.'

A taxi whooshed passed them.

She nodded. 'You're right. Let's go back to the hotel and have a brainstorming session.'

The red hair stuck in long strands to her white face and neck. It looked very dramatic, he thought. She looked like a film star . . . in a horror movie.

He stomped the paralysed, obstinate foot hard against the tarmac. The pain shot up his spine and into his head, but he did not care.

'Sod it! They *are* here. I can feel it!'

'Come on,' she said. 'We'll find them tomorrow.'

They reached the deserted car park at the same time as the terrorists, but from opposite directions. The rain was lashing hard and straight down and bounced back knee-high from the tarmac. Their heads were bowed against the rain, and Michael had the car keys in his hand when instinct made him look up. The trailer with its drenched building materials was still there. Fifty metres away, the white box van was parked with the engine off and he could hear the rain drumming with a hollow sound against its roof. A few metres from the box van, two shapeless figures emerged from the darkness and the rain, dark grey against the faint glow from the sole light in the car park. They walked hunched under the weight of their rucksacks. Michael blinked water from his eyelashes and raised his hands to his face to shield himself against the rain. The two figures could have been anyone, but he had no doubts. He turned his head and looked at Lene, who was standing on the other side of the Mercedes.

'Lene . . .'

He moved his hand to his hip and gripped the butt of his gun. Lene squinted against the rain and lifted her head.

'What?'

The two figures had stopped at the back of the box van and were looking in their direction. Michael watched the white face of the man at the front, framed by long black strands of hair. Tall. Young. Calm. Michael narrowed his eyes against the rain, while his hand was still in the process of pulling out the pistol and his thumb slid aside the safety catch. He dangled the gun by his left side. Then he hobbled a couple of steps forward and raised his left hand.

'*Salaam, sadíki!*' Michael called out, smiling at the young man in front. '*Marhaba*, welcome!'

He took a couple more steps, while the first of the two young men swung his rucksack from his shoulders and put it on the ground so that his hands were free. His face was completely devoid of expression.

'Michael!' Lene called out. 'The van! Watch the door, for Christ's sake!'

But he had already heard the loading door of the box van slide back on its tracks.

He stared at the gap while a small smile spread on the face of the young Arab. Slowly he raised his hand to Michael.

The extended middle finger was a universal up yours gesture which needed no translation. Michael was about to raise his gun and aim at the man's head, when the loading door opened even further and something narrow, black and pipe-shaped appeared.

Like the barrel of an AK-47, for example.

'Michael!'

The gunshots sounded very loud and very close, and Michael could feel the air pressure against his ear. He spun around on his good foot and saw in a flash Lene's face screwed up in concentration, half hidden by her service pistol. Her eyes were open and focused, she did not narrow them like so many amateurs when she fired the gun. He heard the projectiles hit metal and presumed that she was aiming at the door opening in the box van.

He rolled over the bonnet head first and swept her down onto the ground. He remained on top of her with his face close to hers, looking into her eyes. They were furious, and she tried wriggling out and away, but he pinned her down as a long salvo from an automatic carbine rocked the Mercedes on its shock absorbers. The projectiles from the Kalashnikov went through the steel plating of the car as if it were paper and ricocheted off the tarmac and the kerb. Michael heard the air leave the tyres in explosive coughs. The car sank a couple of inches and offered them greater protection. In theory. Or at least until the unknown sniper left the box van and approached them in an arc. Then they would be at his or her mercy.

Shards of glass rained over them and settled like tiny, glittering crystals in Lene's hair. He placed a protective hand over her face and narrowed his eyes. It took three or possibly four seconds before the magazine of the automatic rifle had been emptied, that was all, but it felt like forever. Then he dragged Lene up from the tarmac and across the crash barrier in the car park. He hoped that he had remembered correctly. Behind it there was supposed to be a low slope, leading down to dense evergreen shrubs.

His memory had been correct. He kicked her feet away from under her, and they rolled into cover behind the slope. Then he lifted his head slightly and caught a glimpse of the white box van, whose side door was now wide open. He saw the tall young Arab again. His companion had climbed inside the van while the young man walked across the tarmac with a close combat weapon in his hands that Michael recognized as a baby Kalashnikov. The boy went through the loading motions and approached the silver Mercedes. Ten metres from the car he stopped and opened fire.

'Oh, Christ!' Michael mumbled and rolled onto his back.

He stuck his hand up above the crash barrier and fired blindly at the position where he believed the terrorist to be. He fired six shots in quick succession, which were answered by brief, accurate salvos that ricocheted off the crash barrier or hit the ground with soft, squelchy plops.

He lowered his weapon and pressed his lips against Lene's ear.

'Come on, we're leaving!'

She stared at him.

'Leaving? Where?! We're done for, Michael . . . We're going to die now! We're going to *die*!'

Her lips were quivering. The noise from the two automatic weapons was indescribable. They sounded like nail guns working overtime. Water, soil and plant fragments rained down around them.

'Then we die. *Now come on!*' he shouted.

He forced her deeper in between the bushes. Like blind moles, they moved on their stomachs between slender tree trunks while projectiles lacerated branches right above their heads.

Even in the midst of the terror and the adrenaline rush, there was a small, forensic part of Michael's mind which assessed the situation from an elevated position, like a tennis referee. He was familiar with this part of his mind, and loathed it intensely. It did not care whether he lived or died; it just wanted to be right. Right now it concluded that everything depended on the terrorists' need to eliminate them as witnesses. After all, they were not here to kill a couple of infidels, but to send hundreds of Christians to the special hell reserved for the infidels. They were here to write history.

It was a balancing act.

Unfortunately, his theory presumed that his attackers shared his informed tactical overview and sense of priorities, which was debatable. Young warriors in the grip of blood rush were not known for their logical reasoning. Quite the contrary.

With a colossal effort of will, Michael shut down the logical referee and rose to his full height to confront his enemy. He took a deep breath, wondering if it was his last in this lifetime, breathed out halfway and placed his foot between Lene's shoulder blades to keep her on the ground. He rested his full weight on his foot and frantically searched for a head, an upper body – some worthy target for his cross hairs – one of the young devils whom he could blast out of his undoubtedly stinking socks.

There was no one there.

The car park was deserted. Which was weird, he had time to think, before he was caught in the box van's headlights. It skidded across the wet tarmac, straightened up with light-ning speed and its powerful engine was revved up to first or second gear. It accelerated towards them, then turned at the last moment and pulled out onto Strandvejen. It passed him less than a metre away, its back end swerving wildly with every gear change as it roared up Strandvejen's next southbound bend, and then it was gone.

Slowly, Michael lowered his gun.

He heard a voice that had probably been talking to him for some time while his ears echoed with gun salvos.

He also thought he could hear . . . music?

47

'Please would you remove your foot now?' she asked him for the second time as she looked at a snail's shell just under her nose. Was there a snail inside it? she wondered like an idiot and tried again to push herself off the ground, but he was too heavy.

'Sorry,' Michael mumbled. He lifted his foot, reached down and helped her to her feet.

The heavy shower of rain had ended as suddenly as it had begun and a slim moon appeared between the torn clouds. There was something comforting about seeing its friendly yellow crescent again, she decided, but frowned when she also heard the music.

They walked together hand in hand, like two children who have survived an earthquake, towards the sad remains of Michael's German masterpiece. The radiator must be perforated, she thought; thin columns of steam rose through the bullet holes in the bonnet.

Some kind of electric malfunction must have turned the radio on too, because the crisp, tinny version of Cock

Robin's 'Just Around The Corner' drifted through the broken windows.

> *Things aren't quite as they seem inside my domain.*
> *You can't know about everything, only pleasure and pain.*
> *You wonder why I come here with head to my hands . . .*

She might be imagining it, but Lene thought she saw a shiny film of tears in Michael's eyes.

Emergency sirens were approaching; the coastal villa owners had woken up.

She looked to her right. A man in stripy silk pyjamas was standing on a raised terrace on the far side of Strandvejen, staring at them. He had a mobile pressed to his ear.

Michael finally blinked. Tiny fragments of glass dropped from his black hair and onto his shoulders. She had not noticed it earlier, but his temples were starting to go grey. She thought it gave him a distinguished look, which inspired confidence: like a consultant surgeon or a bank manager. Besides, he had just done the bravest thing she had ever seen or heard about. He had stood up in a hail of bullets to defend her.

It was both unreal and real at the same time, and she knew that she would never forget it.

'Good song,' she mumbled, half expecting him to slap her.

'Yes, it is a good song.'

Michael hobbled to the car and stuck his finger through

one of the holes torn in the bonnet as if he was searching for a pulse. A painful spasm crossed his face and his body shook.

'It's finished,' he said emptily. 'Dead.'

She placed her hand on his shoulder.

By now they could see the reflection of blue emergency lights on their way from Skodsborg.

'Perhaps we should get out of here,' she suggested. 'Besides, it was insured, wasn't it?'

'It was customized,' he mumbled. 'You can only insure standard cars. In this case, that would be the wheels and the ashtray.'

'I'm sorry.'

He merely nodded, ran his palms across his face and looked miserably at the wreckage.

There was a flash of light from the other side of Strand-vejen. The concerned citizen on the terrace was taking pictures of them with his smartphone.

She nodded in the direction of the man, who had now been joined by his somewhat younger, negligee-wearing, equally outraged wife.

Michael followed her gaze.

'In my capacity as superintendent and an officer with Rigspolitiet, I hereby give you permission – indeed, I order you – to shoot that moron over there,' she said. 'And his wife.'

He broke out in a smile.

'It's a very tempting offer,' he said.

She tugged at him, but it was like trying to move a house.

'Come on,' she said, getting increasingly desperate.

'You okay?' he asked.

'I'm great. Now come on, for God's sake.'

48

The mobile rang.

Charlotte didn't know if she was asleep or awake when the blasted mobile beeped on her bedside table. It no longer made any difference. Everything melded together.

She pulled a pillow out from under her head and pressed it against her face. It was lovely and cool. She could hardly hear the mobile now, and the darkness behind the pillow was deep and friendly.

She was nodding off again when her husband stuck out his hand and shook her in a manner which would have been unthinkable one month ago.

She was well aware that it was her life and her job that were wrecking their marriage, but she had no idea how to fix it. She removed the pillow, but did not have the energy to turn over.

'Bloody answer it,' her husband hissed.

His tone of voice would also have been unthinkable one month ago.

She was on the verge of tears when she swung her legs

over the bedside, switched on the lamp and answered the phone.

'Yes?' she mumbled wearily.

'It's Lene. They're here, Charlotte.'

'Lene? What . . .'

Her mobile buzzed to indicate another incoming call. And then another.

She wanted to scream.

'What's happened?' she demanded to know.

Their landline started to ring in the living room downstairs.

Her husband got out of bed, flung his duvet around himself like a toga and stomped across the floor like a Roman senator walking towards a beaker of hemlock.

'That's it! I'm sleeping in Gitte's room,' he shouted at her from the door. 'This is insane, Charlotte! Our life has become insane, do you hear me? I can't live in this house!'

She blinked as the door was slammed shut behind him with a bang.

'Otto?' she muttered helplessly.

'What's going on?' Lene asked.

Charlotte closed her eyes and took a deep breath. One more day. Just one day. She could do that, she told herself. The truth was, she had to. There was no one else. Afterwards, she and Otto would take that trip to Paris they were always talking about. Stay at Hotel Castille in Rue Cambon behind the Grand Palais, where they had stayed during their honeymoon almost thirty years ago. They would dine out every night, stroll around the Luxembourg Gardens, go to the Crazy Horse, get drunk . . . forget everything and find each other again. She remembered the Russian Blue cat at the hotel.

'That's exactly what I want to know, Lene,' she snarled and opened her eyes.

Just one more day.

'There has been a . . . fracas just south of Vedbæk,' Lene informed her. 'You'll hear about it soon.'

Charlotte looked at the list of incoming calls on her mobile before pressing it to her ear again.

'So I gather,' she said. 'Half the world is trying to contact me right now. A fracas, you say? What's your definition of that word, Lene, and who are they?'

Charlotte could hear traffic in the background and the sound of more than one pair of feet. She presumed that Michael Sander was with Lene. She sincerely hoped so. She had always regarded him as a safe pair of hands.

'Terrorists, Charlotte. Two of them. They arrived from the sea in a rubber dinghy from that Polish ship, the *Kazimierz Pulaski*, and were picked up by somebody waiting for them in a white box van.'

'Hang on.' She pulled a notebook towards her. 'How do you spell that?'

Lene spelled out the name of the ship and gave her the registration number of the box van.

'But you were there as well?' she said, still not

understanding. 'Alone? And how did you know that the terrorists would arrive at Vedbæk at this time? And what exactly was the . . . fracas?'

'A tactical confrontation.'

Charlotte frowned, got up and started pacing up and down the bedroom.

'In Danish, damn you,' she hissed.

'An exchange of fire. They had Kalashnikovs, Charlotte. We barely had time to say anything before they opened fire.'

'And what would you have said to them? Go home? Surrender? What?'

'I don't know. But they're here now. You have to cancel Ehud Berezowsky and the foreign ministers' summit. It's too risky. They're heavily armed, at large, and they won't give up.'

Charlotte felt like shouting that they were not talking about cancelling a parents' evening, but a meeting of European foreign ministers which had been more than one year in the planning, debating some of the most important foreign policy dilemmas since the Second World War. But she gave up.

'I'm aware of it,' she managed to say. 'But I don't understand why and how a superintendent whom I, God knows how many times, have told to back off, suddenly features in an exchange of fire with Islamic terrorists in the middle of the night, in North Sjælland, of all places. I thought you were investigating the murder of Irene Adler, and that was the purpose and scope of our agreement.'

Lene started to say something, but Charlotte cut her off.

'Stop! I don't want to know; from now on I want you to keep a bloody low profile, Lene! And this time I mean it! I told you to assist with the Adler enquiry, but now you're messing with things you don't understand. PET deal with terrorists. PET and no one else.'

'But—'

'Now be quiet! And let me get one thing straight: you're saying they got away?'

'Yes.'

'Unhurt?'

'I would think so, but I can't be sure.'

'Good, go home and stay there, understand? Ideally I would like you to go away somewhere until it's all over. Alaska would be good.'

'Charlotte? I don't think you quite understand . . . A group of armed terrorists has just arrived, for God's sake! Presumably the same group who bombed Tivoli. Bjarne was right.'

'Who?'

'My technician, Bjarne. He said we should keep an eye on that ship. That it also deviated from the international sailing route and dropped anchor off the coast of Vedbæk three days before the Tivoli bomb. That's what you told us to investigate.'

'Yes, but as far as I recall, you yourself dismissed his suppositions as irrelevant,' she said harshly. 'But I'll give him an apology and a pay rise the next time I see him. I promise. Goodbye.'

'Charlotte . . .'

She clicked to take the next call. North Sjælland Police. Very upset indeed.

It went on and on.

It was not until half an hour later that she was able to call the duty officer at SOK and ask them to pursue the Polish coaster, both at sea and from the air. The man was remarkably helpful, competent and proactive. He had already found the *Kazimierz Pulaski* on the AIS live ship map and radar, and he would make sure that the ship was boarded and searched.

She put on her dressing gown and went out into the passage. She could hear her husband snoring in their daughter's old bedroom and wondered if she should knock, but decided against it. He needed all the sleep he could get. His minister was driving him crazy and he was seriously, and not for the first time in his career, considering handing in his resignation.

Perhaps that would not be such a bad idea after all, she thought, to her own great surprise. They had enough money. And they could sell the house. It was too big for them now anyway. Both of them could just quit. A warm feeling spread through her. It was an option, wasn't it? Yes, it was! They had both been delivering the goods for decades without anything other than lukewarm thanks and a medal in return.

She went downstairs to the kitchen and made herself a mug of hot chocolate with a dash of rum. She carried it into the study, sat down in an armchair and lit one of her rare cigarettes.

Her mobile vibrated in the pocket of her dressing gown with a text message. She took it out and watched the display pensively as she smoked. The message was as brief as it was crucial.

Zebra says EH. They are alive and unharmed.

Charlotte smiled and let out a long sigh of relief.

The sender was Kim and EH was Ehud Berezowsky. So not the foreign ministers in Eigtveds Pakhus. Thank God! Kim was still delivering, and the trap had been set.

She knocked superstitiously on the wooden desk and was about to pop the mobile in her pocket when another text message arrived from the same sender.

And if I see Lene Jensen, I will shoot her on the spot.

She did not reply, nor would he be expecting her to. As far as Lene was concerned, she understood exactly where he was coming from. Lene was a thorn in his side. Seen from his point of view.

Exactly as Charlotte had hoped she would be.

In contrast to what practically everyone thought, Charlotte Falster had not enjoyed a privileged upbringing in the upper echelons of society. She came from a lower-middle-class background on Amager, but she had learned to play the game at university, in the ministries and on North Sjælland, where they now lived.

Her father had been a self-employed bookbinder and her mother a housewife. Her father had added a small, draughty conservatory to their house and it was here that Charlotte remembered sitting with her father every Saturday with their pools coupon, watching Premier League football matches. Her memory was a long row of rainy days, ill-tempered games between teams such as Wolverhampton, Nottingham Forest, Norwich, Leeds, Sunderland and Stoke City that inevitably ended in a nil–nil draw or one–nil at best. She was not there for the football, but to be with her father. They always filled in their pools coupons, but they rarely won anything.

However, her father had taught her one thing: when you were unsure of the outcome of a match, it paid to bet on both sides.

It was a lesson she never forgot.

49

Kim was lying fully dressed on the narrow, messy bed, staring at the ceiling. He turned over onto his side and looked out of the bedroom window.

Dawn was breaking.

He felt nothing. He had spent too long in his private corner of the war. Those people who did not think that it was a war, knew nothing. They included most politicians, the press and his superiors, who wandered around in a Photoshop universe, a Disney-produced la-la land which bore no resemblance to his reality. About seventy young Danish Muslims had fought on the side of the alliance in Syria, in factions born out of Al-Qaeda. When they returned home, they would be radicalized, ready for violence and well trained. It would be mayhem, but he would not be there to see it.

There was a half-empty bottle of mineral water on his bedside table next to the ticking wristwatch. Beside the watch was a bottle of Johnnie Walker Black Label, also half empty. On the floor an electronic multi-charger was flashing. He was charging several mobiles; he didn't want to be without a fully charged phone today. His service pistol was lying beside them.

He was sweating though the room was cool, and he pulled his shirt away from his armpits. His eyes stung from lack of sleep, but he was used to that.

Despite Lene Jensen's meddling, Nazeera had picked up the boys in one piece, and that was the most important thing. That, along with her confirmation that today's terror target would be Ehud Berezowsky. Of course Safar Khan had picked the eminent Israeli professor. The meeting of the EU foreign ministers was too big a mouthful for the small but lethal terror cell in Amman. He smiled in the darkness.

Nazeera had delivered as he knew she would. She was as reliable as a Swiss watch, and he was ashamed that he had ever doubted her.

He swung his feet out onto the floor and rubbed his stubbled cheeks.

He could sleep later. When everything was over, he would hit the town with Christian. They would celebrate their victory without saying very much to each other. They would drink themselves into a stupor with grit and determination and become good friends again. They always did, somehow.

He considered inviting Lene along. Her and her mysterious bodyguard. He did not want to bear her a grudge.

He walked through the first living room and looked at the double doors which led to the other living room in the flat on Vesterbro. It was a room that must never be entered. Behind the white doors was his old life, which he had not visited for almost seven months. The day after Anne and the girls were killed, he had carried everything in there. Their clothes, their toys, posters, drawings, books, DVDs, Anne's kitchen utensils, her sewing machine and fabrics, the furniture she had brought with her from college. The living room was stuffed full of the three of them.

He would never be able to enter it; Christian had offered to clear the room one day when he was out, and now he was ready. When this day was over.

He turned on the tap in the kitchen and almost threw up from hunger and nerves, but steeled himself and drank two glasses of tepid water.

He looked at his right hand holding the water glass. The rain had lashed against the windows all night, but right now everything was quiet. The city was holding its breath. The glass trembled and he put it down and bit into his knuckles hard. The blood tasted salty, but his hand had stopped shaking.

One. They only needed one of the two boys. And quickly. Ehud Berezowsky was accompanied by Mossad agents. Some were close protection officers, but the more important ones were a couple of older, scarred, expressionless interrogators of whom it was said that they could make an oyster speak Swahili in thirty minutes. You did not want to know how they did that. He had an agreement with Jerusalem about one of the two Arab boys. No questions. No formalities.

Kim had made it a condition that he would accompany the team back to Jerusalem, where he would personally witness the destruction of Sheikh Ebrahim Safar Khan. Mossad and the Royal Jordanian Mukhabarat would dispatch a team of specialists to the sheikh's house. The very best.

Lene. He shook his head. He had hated her more than he had thought he could hate another person, but in recent times this hatred had given way to a different emotion. Not exactly admiration, more a kind of awe. Her stubbornness was superhuman. A force of nature.

The cold shower spray drummed against his scalp. He stayed under the icy water until his skin turned blue and he started to shake. Afterwards, he carefully combed his hair, cleaned his teeth until his gums bled, and shaved with a new razor.

He pulled out a new white shirt from its plastic bag, chose his finest tie and a dark suit, which had just been cleaned, put his pistol in the belt holster above his right hip and, for the first time in seven months, he slipped on his wedding ring. Then he put on black socks, newly polished black shoes, slotted keys, mobiles, extra cartridges and his wallet into various pockets and sat straight up on a chair in the kitchen with his hands on his knees, even though Christian would not be there to pick him up for another hour and a half.

He wondered what Nazeera was doing right now. Resting? Reviewing the architects' plans of the old university on Vor Frue Plads with the two suicide bombers? Making them tea? Showering? He had personally given her the bland powder with the light sedative that Irene Adler had recommended. It would not make them fall asleep, but it would lower their spatial awareness and slow down their reactions. She would send him a text message if she succeeded in deactivating the explosive vest. They had practised the procedure for hours with experts from the USA, so she should be able to do it with her eyes closed.

Green was the code word meaning that the explosive vest had been defused, and *red* was the code to say that Nazeera had not had the chance and that the vest was still armed.

Where were the terrorists now? Were they just driving around at random until it was time? Were they staying with a new, ignorant Ain, recruited through the international network? Nazeera did not know, nor did it matter.

What mattered was to capture one of them alive and convince Safar Khan that the attack in Copenhagen had been successful. Nazeera would contact him when Kim and the Israelis were airborne. The media would confirm the story – the edited version that PET would give them – and the old man would gather his fanatical, lethal congregation around him. They would cheer and embrace each other and watch the two boys' goodbye videos with their families. The news would spread like wildfire through refugee camps and slums from Benghazi to Homs, and the usual anti-USA demonstrations would be ignited.

Kim heard a car sound its horn downstairs and looked out of the kitchen window.

Christian was on time. The dark-blue Mondeo was parked alongside the kerb.

He got up and stood for a moment in front of the tall mirror in the hallway. He looked like an undertaker, which seemed appropriate. He locked the door behind him and wondered if he would ever be back here again.

Christian smiled and opened the door on the passenger side.

'Did you manage to get some sleep?' he asked.

Christian himself looked relatively refreshed despite the still-swollen lips.

'I've had my teeth fixed,' he said, putting the car into gear. 'Temporary solution. Was that Lene up in Vedbæk? The shooting?'

'Of course it was,' Kim said with a sigh. 'But they got away. They weren't harmed.'

'Where are they?' Christian asked.

'No idea. Nor do I give a toss. We know where they'll be in six hours.'

'Of course.'

'Coffee?'

There was a steaming mug in the cup holder behind the gear stick.

'No, thank you.'

If suicide bombers could go without food, then so could he.

Kim stirred in his seat when a text message arrived. He

picked up the mobile, took a deep breath with his eyes closed, but then clicked on the message.

Green. Repeat, green.

He smiled, then he stretched out his hand to show Christian the display.

His partner also smiled happily.

'She's done it?'

Kim sank back into the car seat and folded his hands on his lap with a heartfelt sigh.

'Yes. She's done it. It couldn't be better,' he said. 'Do you want to come with me to Jerusalem?'

Christian looked at him.

'Would you like me to?'

'Of course,' he said. 'Yes, of course I would.'

'Okay, then let's go get the bastards. I'd like to. I mean . . .'

'They're finished,' Kim said. 'One of them took part in the Tivoli bombing. Samir. Syrian. Long hair, white scar to his left temple. He's the one I want. I don't care about the other one. If you see him, then shoot him. Here.'

He pointed to the knot on his tie; the hollow between the collarbones. It was the scientifically agreed way to take out a suicide bomber: the bullet would go through the cervical vertebrae, sever the top of the spinal cord and activate every extensor in the body. In theory.

'I'm actually looking forward to it,' Christian said.

50

Several taxis on Skodsborgvej went past them, but no one fancied the fare. The cars would slow down when they saw Michael's hand wave in the fog, but one look at the couple made them hit the accelerator and disappear.

'What's wrong with us?' Michael asked, as yet another taxi did a runner.

'It has to be you,' she said.

He looked at her.

'You're the one who is as white as a ghost, with blood and glass in your face, looking like you've just crawled through a fresh mass grave.'

She raised her hands to her face.

'I have? Do I?'

'Not to worry, it's my blood. Do you know anyone who might want to pick us up?' he asked, and she was about to reply in the negative when she remembered Bjarne.

He arrived twenty minutes later in his beige Fiat. He gazed awestruck at Michael and glowed with pride at being included in the operation.

'We have very little time, Bjarne,' Lene said. 'But please would you drive us to the Admiral Hotel?'

'Of course. Is that where you're staying?'

'Yes.'

He looked at them and articulated the fantasy of the lonely man.

'Together?'

'Yes.'

The technician sighed and opened the door to the back.

They sat next to each other on the back seat. Michael tried finding a comfortable position for his injured leg in the small car, but had to give up. Lene looked at her watch.

'It's almost six o'clock, Michael. Six hours left on planet earth for Ehud Berezowsky or a lot of European foreign ministers. It's about time we got devious. And proactive. We need to make a choice.'

He looked out of the window.

'Don't I know it!'

'How about your friend in London? What was he meant to be finding out?'

'Sandy? Cross-referencing. I remembered that Nazeera's father is a Professor of Economics at the University of Copenhagen. The award ceremony is taking place at the university, and I'm assuming that Nazeera knows the place inside out. Her brother and sister live and work in London. One for a film company, the other as an investment consultant, so it must be reasonable to assume that the family has links to the UK. Wouldn't you agree?'

'I guess so. And then what?'

Again he lifted his knee with both hands. The night's excesses had not been exactly what the doctor had prescribed, she thought.

'Before Sheikh Ebrahim Safar Khan became a mass murderer, he spent fifteen or sixteen years as an ordinary Professor of Middle Eastern Studies at the London School of Economics. I thought there might be some ties between the families. Parallel developments. Perhaps Gamil and Safar Khan knew each other when they were young.'

'But surely everyone must have investigated that, Michael,' she said. 'The Brits, Mossad and the CIA must have gone over Safar Khan's London past with a fine-tooth comb.'

'Yes, *his* past. Of course they have. But there has never been any reason to focus on Khalid Gamil. I'm sure he's as pure as the driven snow. Or at least I would think so. It's more likely to be his elder daughter who is about to get famous.'

Lene nodded. She thought it sounded quite far-fetched. If Nazeera really was Kim's agent, she could not possibly be a blank page. Her past must have been mapped and every aspect given security clearance.

She half turned in her seat.

'The FET, Danish Army Intelligence. They're the ones who recruit and train informants, am I right?'

'Yes.'

'If Nazeera is what we think she is, that's where Kim found her, isn't it? He must have been given a complete file on her. They must have checked her background, Michael.'

'Of course. But she's a star, Lene. She probably speaks half a dozen languages. She's charming, beautiful and super bright. She can mix with people in all kinds of environments, both here and in the Middle East, without standing out. So what if her father worked in London at the same time as Safar Khan? It's not enough to disqualify her. London is a bloody great big city. I lived there myself for twelve years and I met hundreds of people. Half of them could easily have been international terrorists without me being any the wiser.'

Lene sank back in the seat. She could see from Bjarne's slightly hunched shoulders that he was following their conversation.

'Okay,' she mumbled, absent-mindedly picking more shards of glass out of her hair and dropping them on the floor. She smiled at Bjarne's swimming eyes in the rear-view mirror to reassure him. 'But when is your London friend getting back to you? Can't you call him? Can't he speed things up a bit? Did you tell him it was urgent?'

Michael laughed a mirthless laughter.

'Sandy Huffington is . . . different. Barely human, in fact. If I tried pressing him, he would never speak to me again.'

'But you're paying him?'

'A princely sum, Lene. But that's not the point.' He flung

out his hands. 'I can't explain it. It's the equivalent of asking Daniel Barenboim to play the second movement of Beethoven's Fourth Piano Concerto a little faster. You just don't do it.'

Michael gave up on his leg and stared out of the window.

'But we don't have any time, Michael! Did you see anything? Did you recognize anyone?'

He closed his eyes.

'Young guy. Early twenties. Long black hair. Looked like a film star. Johnny Depp, perhaps, but stronger. Taller. Strange star-shaped white scar to his left temple. He was cold as ice, Lene. He smiled at me and gave me the finger.'

'I saw it,' she said. 'You're right. Or at least, he's not the nervous type.'

They looked at each other. He blinked first.

'But apart from that I saw nothing useful. I got no impression of his partner at all. How the hell did they get here? Into Europe, I mean?'

'No idea. You didn't see who was inside the box van either?'

'No.'

'He or she was there all along.'

'Of course. They're very good.'

She looked down. Her eyelids were stinging.

'What was going through your mind when you stood up in the middle of the shooting, Michael? I have to know. It was insane. And brave.'

He put a hand on her knee, squeezed it and then withdrew his hand.

'Later. Perhaps. Okay?'

'Okay.'

They would never get any closer, she thought. It was impossible.

'We're here,' Bjarne said.

He made a U-turn across the deserted Toldbodgade and looked at the hotel's main entrance.

'Thank you so much, Bjarne,' Lene said.

'You're welcome. Do you want me to wait for you? I don't have anything else, I . . .'

'Go home, Bjarne. Get some sleep. I'll call you as soon as I know anything.'

He turned in his seat and looked at her.

'Do you promise?'

51

They mulled over the case while they had breakfast brought to the room by a crumpled, sleepy waiter, but it got them nowhere. Lene had a burning need to do something, no matter what, and paced up and down the room while she ate scrambled eggs and croissants and drank black coffee.

It had been Michael's young friend, the Swiss-trained concierge, who had been behind the counter. She had given Lene a look that clearly indicated she did not think that Lene was good enough for him, and Lene had felt a bizarre and awkward stab of jealousy to which she didn't know how to respond.

Lene changed the dressing on Michael's shin. She was getting quite good at this. Everything she knew about first aid came from being with Michael. He had a unique ability to be maimed. In a few years there was not likely to be much left of him.

The bites looked neither better nor worse than yesterday.

There was no fax from London and the computer's inbox was empty.

Michael got up, limped to the balcony door, opened it and lit the first cigarette of the day.

'There's nothing we can do, Lene,' he said. 'We're going around in circles, we're too tired and I feel as if I've been lobotomized.'

'Same here,' she said with a yawn.

'I'm loath to admit it, but we just have to hope that PET has everything under control. Kim killed your psychiatrist. That must present something of a dilemma for you, I would have thought? At first you think that Irene is the very Devil. And then you discover that she was a saint, and now you have to hope that her killer has a really good day today. That's something of an unlikely twist, isn't it?'

At that moment in time she hated him with all her might. But then she realized that his sarcasm was born out of sheer frustration. Michael was used to being in control. Being reduced to a mere spectator was just as unbearable for him as it was for her. Deep down, they did not trust anyone but themselves. Other people were either not careful or not skilled enough.

'What do you think?' she said. 'Of course it's a dilemma. Tell me, have you ever relied on anyone but yourself?'

He turned around with the cigarette dangling from the corner of his mouth and scrutinized her for a long time. But then he smiled.

'You're right,' he said. 'I'm sorry. No, I've never trusted anyone. Not seriously. Not with important matters. I think that's why I'm still alive. And that's the reason, of course, why I . . . why the two of us . . . Christ.'

'What, Michael?'

'Oh, just shut up, will you?'

But she refused to give up.

'"Of course that's why the two of us" . . . what?'

'What do you want?'

'A little bit of honesty.'

'Then take a good look at yourself in the mirror,' he said. 'I don't think I can make it any clearer. You and I . . . the two of us are . . . What does your ex-husband do for a living?'

'He's an accountant.'

'Of course he is!' He flung out his hands. 'An accountant. And my wife gets ecstatic when she finds a first edition of one of B. S. Ingemann's historical novels. We need people like them, Lene. Normal people. They haven't got a clue what's really going on in the world, but we've learned to live with that, and besides, we don't want anyone to understand us because we think we're so bloody special! But if two people like us found each another . . . It would be a rocky foundation, wouldn't it? Two idiots . . . am I right?'

She got up and went over to the bed. She was wearing only her underwear, a fluffy hotel dressing gown and slippers with the hotel logo.

'I'm going to lie down,' she said.

'Good idea. May I lie down next to you?'

'It's your bed.'

They lay down on opposite sides of the bed. It was a big bed with two separate duvets, which was good, Lene thought. She closed her eyes and she could smell him: Michael always smelled of nice things. Things that did not come out of an aerosol.

The bed creaked when he turned onto his side. He suppressed a groan as he lowered his leg. Then there was silence.

She too turned onto her side with her elbow under her cheek. Facing away from him, yet still surrounded by his presence.

A few quiet minutes passed, until she opened her eyes in alarm: Michael was not breathing.

She counted to ten in her head before the air was finally drawn into his lungs with a gasp that tugged at her heart-strings. He was not invulnerable. He did have a limit. Of course he did.

She turned over and looked at his shape under the duvet. The broad back with the terrible scars and a hideous Homer Simpson tattoo was bared to the shoulder blades and she wanted to reach out her hand and touch the scars with her fingertip, like a child trailing a raindrop down a window-pane. She would very much like to erase them.

She looked at her watch. Seven thirty. Four and a half hours to go to the ceremony at the university. It was either very little or a great deal of time, depending on how you looked at it.

Then she could not take it any longer and slipped out of the bed and got up.

She was standing by the balcony door, looking across the harbour when she heard him behind her. From the room they had an excellent view of Eigtveds Pakhus, the old converted warehouse next to the Danish Foreign Ministry where the EU summit was being held.

'Michael?'

'Mmm . . .'

'This is driving me crazy. We have to do something, do you hear?'

He positioned himself next to her.

'Why don't we try finding her?' he suggested.

'Yes! Let's start with where she lives.'

'In a luxury apartment on Grønningen with a view of Kastellet.'

'Let's go there.'

Again she looked at her watch.

'My time is up in four hours, Michael. Arne will sound the alarm and I'll be wanted for murder. He's very punctual, and he means it. He would do it even if I were his own daughter.'

'So what are we waiting for?'

They left the taxi a few hundred metres from Nazeera Gamil's address. The well-kept apartment block on Grønningen presented itself elegantly with a clean, sandblasted façade. The entrance was all polished brass and dark mahogany. A brass plate above the entryphone stated that GAMIL lived on the third floor above Caspian Sea Trading Company, Ltd.

Nazeera's flat and the company each took up a whole floor.

The double doors were inlaid with lightly frosted, engraved glass, which offered a blurred preview of the marbled foyer and royal-blue carpet runners. Lene almost felt regretful when Michael smashed one of the windowpanes with his elbow, slipped his hand through and opened the door.

The door closed behind them and they stood for a moment, side by side in the foyer, which was as quiet as a library. It was the kind of place that made you whisper.

Michael looked at her.

'What if she's upstairs with the two bastards? What if we screw everything up? What if she's one of the good guys?'

Lene walked past him.

'She's not,' she said.

'You can't know that for sure.'

'I know it.'

They walked up the stairs as quickly as Michael's injured leg allowed them. The runner muffled their footsteps. They found the same exquisite decorations outside Nazeera Gamil's front door and listened closely, but there were no sounds coming from inside the flat.

Michael kneeled on the coconut doormat with the wording *Welcome, Bienvenue, Willkommen* and fished out his lock picks from his inside pocket. He eased open the old-fashioned letter flap, but could see nothing but a polished parquet floor in a herringbone pattern, an old Persian runner and the base of a coat stand. He pressed his ear against the gap, but still heard nothing. He looked up at Lene and nodded. She took out her service pistol and cocked it, then held it in the approved two-handed grip and looked at him.

There might be a security chain on the inside of the door, but the main lock was an old Ruko model, which was like putty in Michael's hands. He pulled back the latch and nodded at Lene, who rang the doorbell.

For thirty endless seconds nothing happened, and Lene had reached out her hand to try the bell again when she saw Michael shake his head. Very, very carefully he let the letter flap close as they heard a woman's high heels. He took out his gun, slipped a bullet into the chamber and took a step back.

An unsuspecting Nazeera would think that the door was

still locked, while in reality it could be opened with a light push.

The footsteps stopped in front of the door. There was no spy hole.

They heard a click as the woman started turning the lock, and Michael balanced on his bad leg and kicked the door as hard as he could just above the handle. The heavy front door jumped on its well-oiled hinges and was stopped by the woman's body and face with a hard smack.

Her scream was loud and shrill.

They forced their way through the doorway simultaneously and got stuck comically, shoulder to shoulder, but wiggled free and Lene was the first to enter the hallway. There were white, panelled doors on both sides, and a large painting of a desert on the end wall, which lit up the hallway with shades of red, ochre and yellow.

A young woman was squirming on the floor in front of them. She was wearing jeans, high-heeled sandals and a freshly blood-stained white silk T-shirt. Her neatly manicured hands clutched her face and her long black hair spilled across the floor.

They heard agonized groaning behind the hands.

Lene kneeled down and forced the woman's hands apart. Two dazed, wide-open brown eyes stared at the ceiling. They were veiled with pain. Her nose had been broken and Lene could see a black hole where her front teeth used to be. She let go of the girl's wrists and got up. The unknown woman whimpered and buried her face in her hands again. She curled up on her side, pulled up her knees and rocked from side to side.

'It's not her,' Lene hissed.

'Inaya?'

The voice was coming from a doorway through which daylight fell in a long beam and it was accompanied by the sound of running footsteps. A slim young man quickly appeared from around the corner, but stopped as if he had run into a glass wall. Michael was a fraction of a second away from pulling the trigger when he aimed his gun at the young man's smooth forehead, but Lene stuck out her hand, put it on the gun and forced the barrel towards the floor.

The young man's brown eyes widened. His face was drained of colour and his hand was still on the doorframe he had used to swing himself out into the hallway. He was too tall, too well groomed, as well as being clean shaven and well dressed. He looked nothing like the two terrorists.

Lene held up her warrant card at eye level, but the man was not interested. He looked only at the squirming girl on the floor, who was still groggy and incapable of finding a position that eased her intense pain.

He kneeled down by her head.

'Inaya? It's me, Zaki. What happened? It's me, sweetheart.'

He spoke a mixture of English and unaccented Danish.

He sat down, lifted up the girl and placed her head in his lap.

'Get me a towel and some ice,' Lene said to Michael, 'and check if there's anyone else in the flat.'

With a kind of apologetic smile, Michael edged his way around the couple on the floor.

The handsome young man raised his head and stared at him with hatred.

It was not a good day to make new friends, Michael thought as he walked through the flat, which had high ceilings and was airy and comfortable. It was meant to be lived in. He might have furnished it in exactly the same style, and the view across the ramparts of Kastellet and the Old Mill were amazing. He walked through two adjacent living rooms and along the way admired a blue-and-red-striped FC Barcelona shirt with the number 10 on the back and the undoubtedly genuine black felt-tip autograph of the Argentinian football god Lionel Messi. The shirt was behind glass in a mahogany frame and was hanging over a pleasantly messy desk. A large glass cabinet containing old Leica cameras, which must be worth a fortune, was mounted on the wall next to the desk.

He opened the door to a large, well-appointed kitchen, and stopped in his tracks.

The dog. Rudolf. The bloody animal which had maimed him was lying in a huge basket in the middle of the attractive black and red chequered marble floor, staring at his feet through half-closed lids. His jaws were open, baring a row of large, pearly teeth. Michael felt a long, agonizing shoot of pain in his leg and he raised his pistol.

Not again. Not ever.

Then he exhaled and decided to take a closer look at the monster, which was remarkably passive. He bent down and poked him warily with the muzzle of his gun before beating a hasty retreat.

Rudolf's black rubbery lips did not even twitch. He wore a broad collar of rhinestones and golden studs as if he was dressed to perform in Las Vegas. His rear was covered by thick plaid of the finest Scottish wool. He had been a much-loved dog, there was no doubt about it, but Rudolf was now running around in the eternal hunting grounds in the sky, looking for people to maul.

On the kitchen table were two capped vials and he picked them up carefully so as not to smear possible fingerprints: an almost empty vial of Nembutal, an anaesthetic that would knock out even Rudolf. It had been injected through the folds of his neck, he thought, because a syringe with a larger needle was lying on the table. The other vial contained potassium chloride in a high concentration, which had undoubtedly been injected directly into the heart of the unconscious animal and caused it to stop beating.

Reluctantly, he placed a wary hand on the animal's enormous head and closed his eyes. He patted his broad chest, which was as cold and as hard as wood. It must have been dead for hours.

'*Auf wiedersehen*, Rudolf,' he mumbled.

53

Lene and the young man had carried the girl into the living room and placed her on a sofa with a towel between her bloody head and the man's lap. She was now fully conscious and watching Michael with pale-brown eyes that expressed confusion and pain. The man glowered at him with disgust.

Michael placed the bowl of ice cubes on the floor, put a few handfuls in a towel and bashed it hard against the floor. The girl jumped at the sound, and her knuckles around the young man's arm whitened.

'Ice?' Michael offered.

The girl nodded and carefully pressed the icepack against her face.

'Who the hell are you?' the angry young man demanded to know.

Michael could clearly see the family resemblance between him, the young woman and Nazeera. He moved to one of the windows to leave the stage to Lene.

'I'm Superintendent Lene Jensen from Rigspolitiet,' she said calmly. She sat down on the edge of a chair close to the sofa.

'I'm happy to show you my warrant card again, but we have very little time. So who are you and what are you doing here?'

Her face was perfectly welcoming, but her voice was authoritative and hard.

The young woman looked up at her brother and nodded.

'I'm Zaki Gamil, and this is . . . the woman you've just beaten up is my baby sister, Inaya.'

Lene maintained eye contact with the outraged young man.

'And we're very sorry about that, Zaki. We really are. But we had good intelligence to suggest that terrorists were planning an attack from this address.'

'Zaki . . . what is she talking about?' the girl mumbled and her distraught brother looked down at her. He ran his hand over her thick dark-brown hair.

'Easy now, sweetheart.'

He glared at Lene.

'Terrorists? Really? So where are the dogs and the helicopters, then? Or is it just the two of you? I'm sorry, but it all sounds a bit weak. Very weak indeed.'

Fair point, thought Michael, who was sorely tempted to break something in the young man's face. He was too handsome, his shirt and shoes were too handmade, and he was too pleased with himself.

Lene's smile was imperturbable. She leaned forward in the chair, but kept her elbows on her knees. She exuded empathy with every feature.

'The dog is dead,' Michael interjected. 'Put down in a kind and compassionate manner it so absolutely did not deserve.'

Lene smiled apologetically at the two siblings.

'Please ignore my colleague,' she said with an irate, sideways glance at Michael. 'He has been under a lot of stress recently—'

'And dog bites,' Michael said.

'And dog bites. But I really need to know why you're here. It's important. Inaya?'

The girl watched her brother over the blood-soaked tea towel.

'Tell them, Zaki. All of it.'

There was a hateful, defiant expression around the young man's mouth, and Michael moved from the window. He was more than willing to beat the information out of him. It did not matter. All that mattered was Nazeera. She had put down her undoubtedly much-loved pet; she was not coming back.

Zaki looked down at his sister, his expression softened, and Michael knew that he would talk. There was something other than defiance in the man's eyes now.

Michael went back to the window.

'She called us yesterday morning,' he said, still looking at his sister. 'We – Inaya and I – work in London and share a flat in Knightsbridge. Nazeera asked us to fly home to Copenhagen. It was important. Very important, she said.'

'When did you arrive?' Michael asked, looking out of the

window. A police helicopter was about to land by Kastellet and the rotor sounds rattled the windows.

'Last night,' the girl mumbled. 'We went to the Admiral Hotel where we spent the night. We were told not to come here until early the next morning. Nazeera herself would not be here until seven o'clock. Nor were we to be any later than that. She was adamant . . . and she sounded weird. Solemn, in fact. She's usually so happy.'

Michael and Lene exchanged glances. The Admiral Hotel? Michael looked at his watch. Nazeera had been here, right here, less than two hours ago. If they had asked Bjarne to drive them directly to Grønningen rather than to the hotel, they might already have found her and incapacitated her. Instead, they had wasted time having breakfast, showering and lying about in bed. It didn't bear thinking about, so he didn't.

'Very happy,' the young man echoed.

'What did she want?' Lene asked.

Zaki looked down and wiped an angry tear from the corner of his eye. He refused to look at them. If anyone were to provide them with an explanation, it would be the sister.

'To say goodbye,' Inaya whispered in despair. 'That's what I think. She had put down Rudolf. Rudy. That was the reason she wanted us here. We were to take him away and bury him. She had planned everything. She had even bought two spades. He's to be buried in his basket.'

'Have you spoken to your parents?' Michael asked.

'My mother is ill,' Zaki said. 'Gravely. Leukaemia. She's in a hospice in Gentofte. She's going to die there.'

'Zaki!'

'It's the truth, Inaya.' He looked at Michael and Lene. 'I think Nazeera went there yesterday afternoon. I believe that she spoke to my mother, but I don't know how much she understands. My father is in the USA on a visiting professorship.'

Michael watched a bleed the colour of red nail polish form under the white mucous membrane in the girl's left eye. It grew bigger and bigger.

'Did she give you a letter, a film, anything?' Lene wanted to know.

'No. She just told us to turn on the TV around noon.'

'Did she mention Ehud Berezowsky?' she asked.

'Berezowsky? Is he here?' What they could see of the girl's face lit up. 'He's amazing! He's an amazing man, isn't he, Zaki? Insanely brave. And important. The most important man in the Middle East right now.'

Zaki nodded.

'Everyone appears to agree that he's perfectly wonderful,' Michael interjected. 'Including the people who keep trying to kill him.'

The two siblings looked blankly at him.

The helicopter over by FET's headquarters took off.

'She didn't happen to mention where she was going after that, did she?' he shouted over the noise.

'What do you want with her?' Inaya asked. 'What has she done?'

'Do you know what she really does?' he asked. 'What she does for a living, I mean.'

'She's a waitress,' the girl said.

'With incredibly good tips,' Michael said, with a sweeping gesture, taking in the ceramic stove, the high panels and the stuccoed ceilings. 'The Leica cameras in there alone must be worth a fortune. No waitress makes that kind of money.'

'The cameras belong to me, and we share the flat,' Zaki said stiffly. 'We take turns using it when we're in Copenhagen. We have separate bedrooms. It's an investment, if you know what that means.'

'She was going to a warehouse behind the restaurant,' Inaya informed them without guile. 'There was something she had to do. It's empty, I believe, and we were supposed to take care of Rudolf and then fly home to London, if we didn't hear from her.'

Lene got up from the chair and headed for the door. She was no longer looking at the two young people.

'Come on, Michael!'

'Hang on.'

He looked at the girl.

'Did she say or do anything unusual?'

'No. Nothing . . . except that she has started wearing the hijab, you know, a scarf around her hair and face. She never used to do that before. She has always despised it. She used to say that it was oppressive and medieval. Now that is strange, isn't it, Zaki?'

'Yes.'

'Michael!'

Lene was shouting from the hallway and had apparently opened the door already, because her voice echoed in the stairwell.

'Women!' Michael smiled at Zaki. 'You can't live with them and you're not allowed to shoot them. Take your sister to casualty now, Zaki. And hurry up, or I can guarantee that you'll be at the back of a bloody great big queue.'

For the first time he got through to him. He now had Zaki's full attention.

'Why? What's going on?'

'Like your sister said: turn on the television around noon. You're going to be very famous. The whole family. Have a good day!'

54

'A hijab,' Lene muttered when they sat in the back of the cab. 'Finally she has shown her true colours. What the hell next?'

'Suicide vests,' Michael replied. 'Goodbye videos on YouTube.' He shook his head in despair.

'I want my brain back,' he said. 'Why the hell didn't I ask them about Safar Khan and London? If he came round to their house every Tuesday for dinner, if the arch terrorist bounced their sister on his lap? The good old days. They were there, for heaven's sake!'

Lene squeezed his hand.

'It didn't cross my mind either, Michael. Even you can't remember everything all of the time.'

'Palm trees,' he mumbled.

'Sorry?'

'I want palm trees. Somewhere very quiet, with lots of palm trees. And the moon, lots of stars and a beach. After this. Somewhere hot.'

Perhaps she wasn't listening, he thought. Or she didn't

have the heart to tell him that they were unlikely to still be alive at the end of the day.

Then she smiled.

'That sounds great, Michael. It really does. Wonderful.'

His hand was still in hers. Forgotten, but warm.

She remembered it when the taxi turned a corner and entered Østerbrogade. She withdrew her hand, so he interlaced his fingers in his lap instead.

'Did she know that we were going to raid her flat?' Lene asked.

'If she's half as smart as I think she is, then of course she knew,' he said.

'Then she would probably also have known that they would tell us about the warehouse.'

'Most likely. They knew nothing about her double life.'

'We're walking right into a trap,' she said.

'Of course we are.'

She turned to look at him.

'What do we do?' she asked.

'Keep on walking. What else? Unless you have a cunning plan, like calling Charlotte Falster and asking her to divert half the armed response unit from the university and the Foreign Ministry and send them our way.'

'They wouldn't stand a chance,' she said with a small smile. 'They would never get out alive. The terrorists would just set off their crap and blow us all to high heaven. It would be a victory of sorts.'

He grinned.

'And they won't do that when they discover us?'

'Of course they won't. We're completely harmless,' she said.

'So it's a repeat of Norway,' he said. 'We walk into the trap and get ourselves shot.'

'As far as I remember, nobody shot you,' Lene corrected him. 'I was the one who got shot!'

'A minor, superficial flesh wound.'

She snorted with derision, but said nothing.

Michael took the pistol from his belt and checked the magazine behind the driver's seat, even though he knew that it was full.

It was a ritual.

The taxi stopped a hundred metres from the warehouse and Michael paid the driver with his MasterCard.

There would appear to be no one in the street.

'It's a strange day,' the driver said gravely. He was a Sikh and had a photograph of his wife and their three children taped to the dashboard. There were rugged, snow-covered mountains on the horizon, behind a small, gloomy-looking concrete house with a flat roof. In the foreground two scrawny hens were pecking the ground by the side of the road. The photograph looked as if it had been taken in the Punjab near Kashmir, a place where they had no cause to love either Afghanistan or Pakistan. Quite the opposite, in fact.

He was a tall, stately man with the clear eyes of a bird of prey. Michael had an idea.

'Yes, it is a strange day, but God has blessed you with beautiful, healthy children, *baba*,' he said softly in English, pointing to the black-and-white photograph.

In a friendly manner he leaned forward between the seats and the Sikh flashed him a golden smile in the rear-view mirror. A considerable part of the family fortune lay in those gold teeth. But although he was smiling, his deep-set eyes were narrow and reserved.

He placed a long brown finger on the children. 'Balhaan, Iskander, Kashmiri,' he said.

Kashmiri was the girl.

'She's a princess,' Michael said.

'She's the sun who will shine on our old age,' the Sikh nodded proudly. 'But the boys are devils.'

'They are now. But they will grow into good, sensible men under your guidance,' Michael said.

'God be willing, *sahib*.'

Michael noticed with considerable interest a faded blue tattoo under the driver's right wrist, the insignia of an Anglo-Indian regiment. This was better; it was much, much better than he had dared hope for. Perhaps.

Lene stirred restlessly, but the two men ignored her.

'We don't have the time,' she began, and Michael and the driver exchanged glances.

Michael had practically wedged himself between the front

seats, in order to be as close as possible to his new friend.

'Royal Indian Rifles?' he asked, pointing to the tattoo.

The man straightened up. The snow-white turban touched the roof of the car, and the gaunt, aristocratic features were charged with pride.

'*Better to die . . .*' he began, and sought out Michael's eyes in the rear-view mirror.

'*. . . than to live like a coward,*' Michael completed the motto of the elite regiment.

'Michael . . .'

He did not look at her.

'You go watch the road, sweetheart,' he said and closed his eyes as the door slammed shut behind her.

The cab driver grinned.

'When did you last go home?' Michael asked as a shadow passed across the man's narrow face. The long dark hands were raised until the pink palms were facing the sky.

'Far too long ago. I send money home every month, and the money gets there, *sahib*, but without me. Do you understand? It's either that or me.'

'I understand,' Michael said, exploiting the opening. He had a chequebook in his inside pocket and he slowly produced it while wishing he had time for more delicate negotiations. The Sikh was a proud man whose services he could not simply buy. One careless word could mean the end of the dialogue.

'I don't wish to offend you,' he said, without looking up,

'but I need your help, and I will pay you for a favour which is not without risk. Like you said, it is a strange day. It's strange, my friend, because the air is pregnant with death. You're a warrior and you know it.'

The man did not stir. His gaze was hanging on Michael's lips in the rear-view mirror.

'Sons should see their father,' Michael said, tearing a blank cheque from his chequebook and writing five digits on it. 'Their father should not be a stranger to them.'

He handed it to the driver, who studied it.

'British pounds,' Michael said.

The gold teeth glittered.

'For this amount I would burn my brother-in-law's house to the ground while he was sleeping inside it and piss on the embers.'

'Or your mother-in-law's?'

'For half that amount, *sahib*.'

The driver laughed out loud while Michael signed the cheque. The driver's name was on his ID card on the dashboard: Gurpal Singh. He folded the cheque in the middle, and it disappeared inside his leather jacket.

'You don't have to kill anyone, Gurpal. Unless you absolutely insist.'

Michael pointed to the warehouse across the street.

'In exactly forty-five minutes, I want you to knock on the blue door in the white building over there. Hard. And keep knocking. If no one opens, then kick the door down, make a hell of a racket and then disappear. If anyone opens, that person will be an armed jihadist, Gurpal. Holy warriors for Islam, do you understand? But they will also be careful because they plan to blow up half of Copenhagen a little later today – but somewhere else, not here. So he might be polite.'

'And then I ask him what the time is? Or if someone ordered a cab? Or a pizza?'

Michael grinned. He stuck out his hand and patted the cab driver on top of his inside pocket.

'That's a lot of money, *baba*,' he said. 'But you will earn it. Ask him whatever you like. Walk away. Or knock him out if you can do so safely.'

The cab driver nodded.

Lene was glaring at him when he got out of the car and bent and stretched his injured leg.

'Making new friends? Now?'

'Don't you think we need friends?'

Behind them, the cab driver turned off the engine.

They walked across to the warehouse and Lene looked back over her shoulder. The cab driver was sitting perfectly still behind the wheel. She thought she saw a golden smile behind the tinted windscreen.

'Did you pay him?' she asked.

'Yes, of course I did. A fortune.'

'What for?'

'To knock on a door.'

'What's stopping him from just driving away?'

Michael stopped and looked at her.

'Nothing. But he's not like us, Lene. He's a proud man. He has served with one of the finest regiments in the world. He's a Sikh and he has no love for Muslim extremism. Sikhs are the Jews of India. The Hindus destroyed their greatest shrine in Amritsar in 1985. The Pakistanis don't exactly love them, and the Taliban have attacked them repeatedly since 2010. He's as tough as old boots, don't you worry.'

They were fifty metres from the four-storey building with its blind white windows facing the street.

Windows like eyes with cataracts, he thought. There was something menacing about the building.

'What do we do?' she asked.

'I walk around the block and enter through the gate by the restaurant, like I did last time,' Michael said. 'I know the way and the dog is dead. You enter from the front. Five minutes?'

She nodded. Michael smiled and placed his hand on her shoulder.

'Don't say anything,' she mumbled.

He looked down the street.

'The Sikh is still there,' he said.

'Excellent.'

He turned to leave.

'Michael?'

'Yes?'

'The pregnant girl . . . in Somalia.'

'What about her?'

His eyes darkened, and he stared at the pavement.

'It wasn't your fault. You couldn't know that she was pregnant, and she would undoubtedly have called for backup. You would never have made it out alive.'

'See you inside,' he said.

He was only a few metres away when she called out again.

'What?'

'Why are you doing this?' she asked.

'I don't really know. Okay?'

'But what do I tell your wife, Sara? In case you don't . . . I mean, should anything happen?'

'She'll want for nothing.'

'She'll want you.'

'I've hardly been at home these last four or five years. I don't think it'll make much difference.'

'You're an idiot, Michael.'

'Now let's go inside and act like proper ninjas, okay?'

'Okay.'

'Michael!'

The warning sounded loud and clear inside her own head, but was obviously nothing but a muffled roar behind the gaffer tape which the tall young Arab with the long black hair and the white scar on his temple had wrapped around her lower face. The tears were squeezed from her eyes as she crashed onto the floor. She had let herself and the chair to which she was taped fall sideways when she heard noises on the other side of the wall by the stairs and knew that Michael had walked into the trap.

As had she.

The door to the street had not been locked and they had been waiting for her in the deep shadows. She didn't see her attacker before her pistol was bashed out of her hand and she was grabbed in a chokehold from behind by an arm as hard as iron. She was reaching for her attacker's fingers in order to break them when another attacker slipped out of the darkness and kicked her in the solar plexus. Exactly where Kim's knee had hit her a few nights ago.

The attacker in front of her was wearing the same perfume as she was.

When she was finally able to breathe again and make out her surroundings, she found herself taped to a solid wooden chair in the middle of the room, with a view of a mattress on the floor covered by a red bedspread.

Then she had raised her head and looked right at herself.

A spitting image of her, right down to the scuffed toes of her boots, the faded Levi's, the silver snake ring she had worn on her left thumb ever since she had bought it at a market in Turkey, aged seventeen, and which could probably no longer be taken off, her small silver studs, her ponytail, her body language, her gaze. And her smile, which was currently tender and tinged with regret. Her lipstick. Her perfume. She blinked hard, but the doppelgänger did not disappear. It remained standing right in front of her while the handsome Arab boy wrapped gaffer tape around her.

'Nazeera?' she had said with stunned incomprehension, and the copy had nodded gravely.

'Yes, darling. I'm you, and you're me. It's just for today, sweetie. It's necessary,' the Arab woman said quietly and without hostility. 'It's a good idea, isn't it? That's why you survived the car park last night. I really need you.'

She bent down and raised Lene's chin with the tip of her finger so that they could look each other in the eye.

'I like you, Lene,' she said gravely. 'I really do. Unless you have hurt my brother or my sister. If you have, then I don't like you quite so much.'

'We didn't hurt them.'

The woman narrowed her eyes.

'Do you promise?'

'Yes, but your dog is dead,' Lene said and looked hard at the other woman in the hope of seeing rage or grief, but there was nothing. Only immobile black pupils in the middle of the green irises exactly the same shade as hers.

'Rudolf,' Nazeera said. 'He was a good dog. And the two of you are very brave coming here all on your own. But perhaps you didn't have a choice? I'm guessing you're on the run after that business with Irene.'

She glanced at a table with a radio scanner. It was undoubtedly tuned to police frequencies, but it was currently silent except for a low buzzing.

'You killed Ain,' Lene said.

Nazeera made to turn around, but changed her mind.

'You don't understand, Lene. It's not that simple. Yes! Yes. She's dead. I did it. Arrest me! It was necessary.'

'So she died for the cause?'

The woman smiled as one would smile at a dim-witted child.

'Let's call it that, darling.'

'But she was innocent. She hadn't joined your stupid cause!'

Lene never saw the blow, Nazeera was as quick as that, and it felt as if a firework had exploded by her ear and blown her head off. The Arab woman was incredibly strong. She was white around her lips now, and her eyes were glittering, green cracks.

'You don't know that, Lene! And Islam isn't . . . Islam . . . Our path is not what you just called it. I was fond of Ain. I really was, but there was no other way. She's happier where she is now than she ever was here on earth!'

'You keep telling yourself that, you twisted bitch. How did you get her to do it?'

Nazeera pulled herself together and the rage left her beautiful face.

'Do what?'

'All of it. Letting Nabil Maroun into Tivoli. Letting other people use her flat.'

Nazeera blinked. Then she smiled.

'Do you really not know? Nabil meant nothing to Ain. I told her the guy was a student with no money who might turn up looking for something to do. That he was a bit eccentric, the religious type, and she should just let him into Tivoli and then forget about him.'

'And her flat?'

Nazeera glanced over her shoulder to check on the men's preparations.

'She stayed over at my place for a couple of days in September, and she was grateful for it. She was in love with me. She was thrilled to have me almost to herself. It was all very simple.'

Then she slipped her hand inside Lene's jacket and pulled out her purse. Lene's warrant card disappeared into Nazeera's own jacket pocket.

'I'm going to need this. Thank you, sweetie.'

Lene closed her eyes. Nazeera was an exact copy of her, and with her warrant card, she would have access everywhere. It was a nightmare.

'Why are you doing this, Nazeera? If you stop it now, right now, we can work something out, I promise. I can talk to someone. You don't have to do this.'

Nazeera smiled.

'You have no idea what you're talking about, Lene,' she said in a steady, normal tone of voice. 'You see . . . this is what I want. I was born for this. I believe, Lene!'

'In what? Innocent dead people?'

The other woman looked away.

'Yes. Innocent dead people in their hundreds of thousands. From Damascus to Tripoli and Benghazi. During the last hundred years, and the next hundred years. You've never seen them. I have. There is nothing in this world where I live with my friends, my parents and my siblings that I truly love. And that was the point. It was all an act. I learned my lines. I walked from a white mark to a red one on the stage in Act One, from a green to blue in Act Two and have ended up where we're supposed to be now, Lene. I sat in a house in Jordan with my real brothers and sisters, even when I was right here in Copenhagen. How would you ever be able to understand that? You can't. It's not your history, or your faith, or the path you have to walk! It's not your people's history. Don't even try.'

'And Irene?' Lene said.

'Yes! I loved her. She was good to your daughter,' the woman said, pensively. 'Did you know that?'

Lene nodded.

'But you accused her of all sorts of crap she didn't do,' she said.

'Yes. I'm sorry.'

'Killing Irene was stupid. Kim is an idiot. He can't think straight, and he was obsessed with you. Made you out to be much bigger and more dangerous than you are. I'm the one who should apologize. I'll think of something. Don't worry about him. He killed Irene because he can't think straight.'

'You don't want me to worry about Kim?'

'Absolutely not,' the other said definitively. 'Forget about him. He's history, only he doesn't know it yet.'

Lene looked past Nazeera at the taller of the two young Arabs who had now changed into a white jacket with golden buttons and epaulettes that made him look like a naval officer. A green ID card was clipped to his chest pocket; he wore a grey tie, black trousers and shiny black shoes.

The catering company, she thought in anguish, which would be serving lunch for Ehud Berezowsky and the bigwigs from the university. His disguise was perfect, and he and Nazeera would both be as unavoidable as death.

The two young men moved around calmly and silently. There was a sleepwalker's assurance and remoteness about the trio. It was almost impossible to provoke Nazeera, and Lene realized that the three of them genuinely regarded themselves as dead, already in the next world.

A video camera was mounted on a tripod by the end wall and a folded black banner with embroidered golden characters was lying on a windowsill. They had undoubtedly already recorded their goodbye messages and sent them home via the Internet.

The taller of the young men took his jacket off again so his partner could help him put on a tight-fitting vest. It was dark grey and made from a smooth material like neoprene, like a wet suit, and closed with Velcro straps. The craftsmanship was very sophisticated, far from the clumsy, home-made canvas vests Lene had seen ad nauseam at the seminars after Tivoli. On the front and back of the vest were a series of wide pockets, which now – one after the other – were filled with flat black bags and plastic bags containing transparent balls.

'You'll never make it past the metal detectors and the dogs,' she objected desperately.

'It doesn't contain any metal, darling,' her doppelgänger said without looking at her. 'We've put our clocks forward to the twenty-first century, like you. We use fibre optics and reinforced glass bullets rather than cables, batteries and steel.'

The young man buttoned his jacket over the suicide vest. No one would notice anything until it was too late, Lene thought, and she felt nauseous.

She instinctively flinched when Nazeera bowed down and cupped her head between her own strong hands. The green eyes smiled a few centimetres from her own and she planted a lingering kiss on Lene's mouth. She tried prising Lene's lips open with the tip of her tongue, but Lene gritted her teeth.

The cool hands released her face and Nazeera watched her with a strange expression.

'What a shame,' she said. 'It would have been amazing, don't you think? We're twins! Can't you see it? Your mouth tastes good, and I'm sure your cunt is delicious, Lene. I think it would have blown your mind.'

Lene closed her eyes. Had she been able to, she would have shot Nazeera dead on the spot.

The younger boy came over to them and started wrapping tape around Lene's lower face. The other terrorist, the man with the pale face and the inscrutable eyes, raised a finger in warning.

Nazeera Gamil playfully pressed her finger to her lips and smiled at Lene.

'Your friend is coming up the stairs. Infrared photocells. Brilliant, aren't they? He'll think I'm you, I hope!'

An anguished Lene watched her disappear through an open doorway. The two young men turned off the police scanner and melted noiselessly into the shadows.

56

The restaurant was closed and the gate to the back had been left open, which was in itself suspicious.

Michael checked his watch. One minute to go. The warehouse windows overlooking the back had also been painted over, so any number of terrorists could have a clear view of the yard, the garden and him, without him being any the wiser.

'Come on . . . come on, woman,' he muttered to himself.

As far as he was aware, Lene was not a born lock picker – and he had no idea how she had gained access to the building. She would probably knock and improvise. With her gun.

Perhaps he should make his move now. Beat her to it and draw their attention to him.

The adrenaline dulled the pain in his leg, which was a relief. The second hand reached twelve, he made the sign of the cross and strode through the gate, crossing the lawn without looking up. Then he positioned himself flat against the warehouse and looked down some steps leading to a basement. At the end of the five steps, there was a decaying door with no windows. The steps were covered with mould and would not appear to have been in use recently. Michael walked down them and pressed his ear to the door. There was no sound coming from inside.

He removed some sticky cobweb from his face and examined the lock. The door did not look as if it had been opened since the Flood. He tried it, painfully aware that time was passing and that Lene might be in trouble on the other side. The door did not budge. He took a deep breath, grabbed the banisters on both sides of the steps, and kicked down the door. It did not swing fully open on its groaning hinges, but hit something after thirty centimetres.

Michael squeezed through the gap and into the darkness with his pistol raised and discovered a stack of car tyres on the other side. He let his eyes adjust to the darkness, knowing that right now it was a case of less haste, more speed. The light was grey and dim. There was a faint trickle of water, but he could not locate the source. Crates of shrivelled, sprouting onions were stacked up against the wall, and that was all. He moved to the next empty basement room and the one after that.

He eventually reached the bottom of the stairwell where worn, grey-painted concrete steps led up to the different floors of the warehouse. He walked up to the ground floor, keeping himself pressed against the wall and letting the pistol follow his sightlines around the corners.

The front door to the street was ajar, and Michael risked a

quick glance through the crack. The Sikh's taxi was exactly where they had left it. A young woman with a pram passed by without noticing him. Michael kneeled down and examined the floor. There was nothing. No scraping marks in the dust. No bloodstains.

He pulled aside the latch and closed the door with a small click, opened it and closed it again. If his new friend, Gurpal, stuck to his part of the deal, he would be able to open the door himself even if a potential guard believed it to be locked. That little trick had already worked once today.

The air did not move on the stairs; the tiny hairs on the backs of his hands stood still. Michael walked swiftly through the high-ceilinged, abandoned rooms on the ground floor without finding anything or anyone of interest. Below a window was a foil cup from a tea light which had been used as an ashtray. He picked up two cigarette butts and sniffed them. They were relatively fresh, and there was a faint imprint of red lipstick on one of them.

A small patch had been scraped clear in the thin white paint covering the windows, so he had an excellent view of the backyard. Michael was about to leave the ground floor when his mobile pinged as loudly as if he had run into a cathedral bell. He swore and retreated. He waited for the sound of safety catches being flicked aside on Kalashnikovs, heavy boots stomping, agitated voices, but nothing happened.

The entrance to the first floor was a black hole in a filthy whitewashed wall. Michael stopped in the first room. The hairs on the backs of his hands were now undulating in the air current that was not picked up by his other senses. He went to the right. Here was the same hazy darkness as in the rest of the building. After the first empty room, he thought he could hear a distant electric hum. He closed his eyes and listened with all his being.

There was another living creature nearby, he sensed. Quietly, he slipped through the next doorway with the tips of his fingers trailing along the almost invisible wall. He rounded a corner and saw Lene's figure faintly outlined against the grey light from the tall, painted windows. She stood perfectly still, her left shoulder pressed against the wall, and when he came closer, he could see the deep, reddish glow of her hair. She was resting the barrel of her gun against her forehead in deep concentration. Michael passed a few metres behind her, but did not dare to say anything.

What could be around the next corner to make her so tense?

Michael thought he was moving in complete silence, but Lene's body froze suddenly, and she reached one hand back in a slow downward gesture which meant: Wait! Quiet!

He could see her profile now, but then she turned her face back into the shadows and waved him forward, while at the same time placing a warning finger on her lips.

Michael sidled up alongside her. Another fifty centimetres and he would be able to see what it was she was looking at.

He was parallel with her and was watching one of her neatly shaped ears, when she turned to him. There was a long hall with a high ceiling to their left, and he stuck out his head.

There was a crash and a suppressed scream followed nearby, and Michael nearly jumped out of his skin. When the pistol in Lene's hand started describing a short, angry arc towards his head, he took a long step forward. The shock of the attack arrived at the same time as the realization that something was terribly, terribly wrong.

He got no further with the thought before the butt of her gun hit the top of his scalp with a thud. The picture keeled over, and his knees disappeared underneath him. It sounded as if someone had knocked down a house inside his head.

A few seconds later, he opened his eyes and discovered that he was slumped on the floor staring at his own gun, which was now several metres away. The blood was dripping warm and evenly onto one of his hands. He raised his gaze at Lene's long legs, which were slightly parted.

Up in those foggy heights he could make out a white smile. He whirred his head like a wounded animal and tried crawling towards his gun, when one of her boots was pulled backwards and slowly, terribly slowly, floated through the air like a derailed train in a nightmare. Then everything turned into an empty darkness.

57

Michael lunged forward in the chair and threw up, and the young man with the baby Kalashnikov and the rock star hair had to jump aside so as not to ruin his socks and shoes.

He had tried suppressing the nausea, but knew that the body was merely evacuating itself in reaction to the concussion. He closed his eyes, but the world kept expanding and contracting. It was like horizontal bungee jumping. His arms were skilfully twisted behind the back of the chair, taped together and fixed to it. Then it was the turn of his thighs. When they were about to attach his feet to the legs of the chair, the roll of gaffer tape ran out, so they left his feet alone.

He dribbled onto his chest and despised his own weakness.

Then he opened his eyes and shook the sweat from his hair. His body did not like him shaking his head and new waves of nausea rose up through him, but this time he managed to keep them down.

The clone was standing nearby, watching him dispassionately. He peered at Lene in the chair next to his and looked at the woman again. The likeness was eerie. It was almost impossible to tell them apart. Next to the video camera a pale young man was unfolding a table. He spread out the black banner and hung it from hooks on the wall. Then he got busy adjusting the camera, while frequently glancing at his watch. Finally he placed something that looked like a fabric hood with eyeholes on the table next to several butcher's knives, a meat cleaver and a stainless-steel meat saw. Everything was done neatly but with the same passion, as if he was putting out crisps and beer for his friends before a football match.

The woman watched Michael's face with her head slightly tilted, as if she was looking for something. But Michael refused to give her anything, even if it was the last thing he did. He returned her gaze without blinking. Suddenly the nausea disappeared and only a roar of adrenaline was left in his ears. Nazeera Gamil kept looking at him until the handsome young man in the waiter's jacket whispered something in her ear. He pointed to his wristwatch. She nodded silently, walked over to the mattress with the sinful red bedspread and let the young man help her put on the tight-fitting grey neoprene vest. He closed the Velcro straps over her lower back and shoulders and pushed clear bags of glass balls into the pockets at the front and back.

It was every anti-terror unit's worst nightmare, Michael thought. Heavy hardened glass balls, just as lethal at close range as steel or lead bullets. He could not see any electrical cables or batteries, and the explosive cells were undoubtedly connected with optical fibres. The vest was a possibility people had talked about in his world, but everyone had thought that the technology still lay somewhere in the future.

With the extremely irritating part of his mind that was always factual and dispassionate, while the rest of him was five minutes away from a ritual beheading and ten minutes from being uploaded to YouTube, he started to wonder about the explosive. That too would have to be a new material, reserved for specialist construction tasks. It would have no smell and would have to expand at about 4,000m/s. Sniffer dogs would not recognize it and it was not something you could outrun.

Not even if you were Usain Bolt.

The woman put on a copy of Lene's scruffy leather jacket over her vest and zipped it up.

At least they now knew that it had not been PET that had searched Lene's flat, but Nazeera Gamil, who had gone to check out Lene's limited wardrobe. Michael had never seen her wear anything but jeans, T-shirts, a man's white shirt and two different leather jackets. In winter she might occasionally wear a dark-blue duffel coat. And that was it. She owned a pair of low-heeled Spanish leather boots, which was also what Nazeera wore today, and a pair of Fred Perry tennis shoes. That was all.

'Where are you from?' the woman asked.

He merely smiled at her. It was not easy, but he succeeded.

She looked as if she was considering hitting him. Then she glanced over her shoulder at the pale young Arab's preparations. A pair of black leather gloves was now lying next to the hood with the eyeholes and the butcher's tools.

'Jerusalem?' she ventured.

'Close. Fåborg.'

She did not believe him.

'They do not make people like you in Fåborg,' she said.

Michael shrugged his shoulders.

'You have things to do,' he reminded her, while he recalled a small, dusty house in the Punjab, two hens and a flat roof, and three children with white teeth: the boys Balhaan and Iskander and the girl Kashmiri, the sun over Gurpal's old age.

'Give my best to Ehud Berezowsky,' he added.

The room fell silent. Even the trainee executioner at the table interrupted his work and lifted his head. He looked at them distractedly.

Nazeera pointed to her heart and forehead, and made a small bow with her hands pressed together.

'Assalamu alaikum,' she muttered.

'Ma'assalam, fi aman Allah,' Michael replied automatically and regretted it immediately.

Nazeera and the terrorist in the waiter's jacket left the room after having exchanged a few quiet words with the executioner.

They made a handsome couple, Michael thought.

He heard a door slam shut downstairs and prayed that they did not check to see if it had locked behind them.

He looked at Lene, but her gaze was remote and glum. She sat slumped in the chair, a long way from her usually straight posture and her combative attitude; she appeared to look only inwards, as if she was concentrating on recalling the most important moments from her life. With her daughter, Josefine, no doubt. Day by day. Year by year.

She was taken first. The young man cut the gaffer tape from her face and then pulled off the strips – to ensure her identity could be confirmed on the recording, Michael thought. The chair was tipped backwards and the boy dragged it across the smooth painted floor. Lene ended up facing the table with the banner on the wall behind her.

Then the young man walked behind Michael and tipped his chair backwards. Something gave with a crisp crack, but it withstood being hauled across the room.

He ended up half a metre from Lene, who was still studying the floor through half-closed eyes. The boy paused between them to make sure that everything was in place. Then he went behind the table and put his eye to the viewfinder. A small light on the camera started flashing green. He turned the camera slightly and adjusted the zoom function. Then he switched it off and checked the connection to a computer at his feet. He seemed content.

He picked up the hood from the table, pulled it over his head and adjusted the holes over his eyes. Then he tied a black band with white characters tightly around his forehead and put on the leather gloves. There was nothing sadistic or lingering about his movements, and he was not spitting curses at their faces. He barely seemed to notice them. He was simply trying to remember every detail, which was more terrifying than anything else he could have done. He went back to the camera and observed them through the viewfinder. The light started glowing again.

'Lene? . . . Lene! Look at me, damn you!'

Slowly, she raised her head and aimed her bottomless gaze at him.

'What?'

'Look at me.'

'I don't have the time, Michael. Really, I don't.'

'For my sake.'

He breathed three times before she opened her mouth again.

'All right then. Just for you.'

The glittering dark eyes inside the hood followed their exchange. Then the boy shrugged his shoulders and picked up a long carving knife. He sized it up, rejected it, chose the meat cleaver instead and weighed it in his hand. Lene's eyes did not leave Michael's, but she took a deep breath and held it.

The boy had taken a couple of steps towards them when three loud, metallic booms echoed through the building. Michael tried his hardest not to react and Lene's facial expression didn't change either. Perhaps she had not heard anything.

But the boy had. He froze in midstride. The banging resumed. The front door was an enormous white steel plate, Michael remembered, and it made one hell of a racket.

They could hear muted Arabic curses coming from inside the hood.

The camera was turned off and the gloves, the bandanna and the hood were quickly and carefully returned to their original locations on the table. It sounded as if the front door was being subjected to a medieval battering ram.

The boy ran to the windows. There would appear to be no visible threat in the street in the form of cordons, armoured vehicles, anti-terror troops dressed in black with laser sights, gas masks, dogs and snipers because a deep, perplexed furrow formed between his thick eyebrows. He muttered something incomprehensible, spun around and stared at them wildly. Michael did not meet his gaze, but understood his dilemma. Should he quickly turn on the camera and behead them, and thus get the ritual out of the way as evidence of the almightiness of Sheikh Ebrahim Safar Khan, or should he seek out the source of the noise and silence it?

Their lives were balancing on a knife's edge.

He found it hard to suppress a sigh of relief when the boy chose the latter, grabbed one of the small Kalashnikovs and disappeared towards the stairs.

Michael almost felt sorry for him.

58

He wasted no more time feeling sorry for the terrorist who would have decapitated him, but rose instead like a tortoise with an ill-fitting carapace, hobbled through the room past Lene's wide eyes and hurled himself at the wall, chair first. It splintered under him and he landed on his back. He was able to wriggle his arms free from the remains of the chair. He got to his feet and jumped to the table, where he grabbed one of the knives.

There was not a sound to be heard from the stairwell. By kneeling down, he managed to cut through the gaffer tape around his thighs. Then he turned the knife between his fingers, sawing blindly through the tape around his forearms behind his back.

He ignored Lene, who was shouting something at him, snatched his pistol from the windowsill where Nazeera Gamil had left it and sprinted towards the stairwell. As he ran, blood and sensation returned to his legs, and he could run more smoothly and confidently. He took the stairs three at a time with suicidal recklessness, while at any second expecting to hear a crackling salvo from his would-be executioner's Kalashnikov.

He reached the last landing before street level and turned sharply around the corner with his pistol at eye level. Then he stopped in his tracks and lowered the weapon.

The tall Sikh watched him calmly from the door. The snow-white turban was askew, and a lot of his long plaited hair and beard were hanging over one shoulder. There was a gash over one of his cheekbones and blood was dripping onto his leather jacket. He held the Kalashnikov in one hand and was completely in control of the situation.

Michael looked at the boy lying in a pile by the wall. He looked dead, but then they heard a faint whimper and saw his eyelids twitch. Michael stuck his pistol into his belt at the small of his back.

'You came, mighty Gurpal.'

'As you see.'

'And the boy . . .'

The tall, gaunt ex-sergeant shrugged his shoulders.

'. . . was a boy, *sahib*. He never realized that you can also bang on a metal door with a cobblestone from the inside.'

Michael grinned and pointed to the Sikh's cheekbone.

'You're bleeding,' he said.

'Am I?' The Sikh looked at his wet fingertips. 'A scratch. Do you want me to kill him for you? I would be happy to do so. Al-Qaeda?'

'Kind of. But no, thank you,' Michael said.

He bent down, picking up the boy by his belt and swinging him up over his shoulder in one movement. He weighed nothing.

'I'm indebted to you,' Michael said. 'But perhaps there is something else you can do for us? In return for a suitable fee, of course. Can you drive a car? I mean, really drive a car?'

The question received a cold, minimalist nod.

'Will you drive us, Gurpal? Really, really fast. Fast like the wind?'

'Perhaps . . . You mentioned a fee, *sahib*. Same as earlier?'

Michael stared at him.

'I don't want to buy your car and your garage, for Pete's sake. Just borrow it for one hour. A third perhaps, but only because my generosity knows no bounds.'

'I might lose my licence,' the Sikh began with downcast eyes and a mournful expression. 'Then what would happen to my family?'

Michael was tempted to say that his family could live like royalty in the Punjab for the next hundred years on the cheque he had already written them.

'You would steal the begging bowl from a blind beggar,' he muttered instead. 'Half?'

Another nod.

'I'll carry the machine gun even though it's heavy, *sahib*. Lead the way.'

Lene glared at him furiously when he returned and dropped the boy on the mattress.

'Tie him up. Very, very thoroughly,' he said to the Sikh before he started freeing Lene. She tore the last tape off her ankles and wrists herself, stood up, took a step and nearly fell over.

'Be patient, dammit,' he scolded her. 'Give your circulation a chance to get going again.'

She nodded and started massaging her forearms.

Michael found their things, checked the magazine in Lene's service pistol and stuffed it into her shoulder holster. He looked at his watch. In twenty minutes, the waiters from the catering company would start to carry dishes into the university's Festival Hall, and everyone would be killed when the long-haired terrorist with the scar arrived. He would walk right through every metal detector and the sniffer dogs would not even deign to look at him.

Behind him, Gurpal had finished binding and gagging the terrorist. For extra safety the Sikh dragged him across the floor by his feet and tied him to a pillar in the middle of the room.

He brushed the dust off his hands and spat at the boy, who was now fully conscious.

Lene tried to squat down on her haunches, got up and took a couple of steps. She was almost moving normally.

'We're running out of time, Michael,' she said.

He nodded in the direction of the stairwell.

'Come on, Gurpal,' he called out.

'What about him?' Lene asked. 'Are you just going to leave him there?'

'If everything goes tits up, we might use him to barter with,' he said.

'They don't give a toss about him! They regard themselves as dead, Michael. They don't have anything to lose! Don't you understand?'

He overtook her and started running down the stairs. She was almost keeping up with him.

'But he knows where Safar Khan is,' he called out over his shoulder. 'And that's worth something.'

Even though there was little traffic in the streets, Gurpal proved that he really did know how to drive a car, and Michael aged with every second. He regarded himself as a skilled driver and his natural talent had been honed on several courses in offensive driving on various redundant airfields in southern England. But the Sikh was a natural who should have been driving Formula One cars. Lene did not open her eyes at any point.

While the car was skidding, Michael remembered that his mobile had pinged earlier. He managed to pull it out, despite the centrifugal force, and click it open. The email from Sandy Huffington had arrived at last. He skipped the main section of the document and zoomed in on the short, concise conclusion.

'Bloody hell,' he mumbled and looked at Lene.

'What?' she asked, without opening her eyes.

'The email from London,' he said. 'Before Safar Khan became the godfather of all terrorists, he was a professor at the London School of Economics.'

'But we already knew that!'

'Yes, but he lost his wife in 1982. She was visiting her parents in Lebanon. She died on the 17th September, Lene.'

'Oh, God. Are you saying . . .?'

He nodded sadly.

'Yes. The rest of her family were staying in the Shatila refugee camp. God knows how she got inside it or why, but she was executed by the Phalangists, along with her elderly parents and younger brother.'

'A never-ending cycle,' she muttered.

'What?'

'An American terror expert gave a lecture at Police Head-quarters on the day Ain . . . Forget it.'

'How old is Nazeera?' he asked.

'Don't know. Mid-thirties, I would have thought.'

'Almost,' he said. 'She was born on the 14th March 1983 at St Mary's Hospital.'

He screamed silently when Gurpal, in the absolutely last fraction of a second, swung the heavy Mercedes up on the cycle path in Sølvgade to avoid colliding with an oncoming HT bus, swerving to avoid some roadworks.

Michael turned in his seat and saw the bus driver's mouth

turn into a shocked black hole. The man stood on the brakes, the whole bus rocked, and he could almost hear the bones of the elderly passengers snap like dry twigs at the rear of the bus.

Then he turned back and glanced at the face of the Sikh, which was carved in dark, smooth rock.

'Good. And then what, Michael?'

'What . . .?

The bus driver's mouth had been big enough to swallow a container ship.

'Her name was Nazeera. It's not a common girl's name.'

'I know she's called Nazeera.'

'No, dammit! The wife. Safar Khan's wife, Lene!'

'So you're saying that—'

'Exactly. Khan and Gamil worked at the same faculty and the two families lived three doors from each other from 1972 to the late 1990s when international Islamic fundamentalism really took root. Safar Khan sold his house, travelled to Jordan on his holy quest and became radicalized. His neighbour and good colleague Gamil named his newborn daughter after Khan's murdered wife, and she was chosen by Khan to be a weapon and a mole in a European coalition forces country. It could have been any country, but it happened to be Denmark. She was schooled and indoctrinated on her travels to Amman.'

Lene digested the intelligence, while Michael tried desperately to read Sandy's long email.

'But if she was practically born into the organization and had known Safar Khan her entire life, did she really have to kill Ain?' she wanted to know.

'Not at all! But Kim would have expected something like it. Khan had no doubts about her loyalty, but Kim believed that Nazeera would have to prove it at some point because it says so in PET's introductory guide to Middle Eastern terrorism for beginners. Kim ... everyone ... everyone thought that she had to prove that she had what it took. So it was for *their* benefit, not Khan's. He could not care less; he knew that she was trustworthy and irresistible to every intelligence service. It happened to be the Danish one that snatched her up. She was a sleeper and Khan planted her.'

A few near-death experiences later they reached Krystalgade. Gurpal slowed down and Lene opened her eyes.

'Listen to the midday bells, Michael!'

Gurpal pulled over on Nørregade. The street was blocked off. A few curious onlookers with time to kill were standing in front of the barriers, but most people would have little idea why the street was now inaccessible.

He turned to Michael.

'*Sahib?*'

Michael looked at Vor Frue Cathedral a couple of hundred metres away. The pale sandstone façade looked timeless and indestructible. Behind the cathedral tower he could make out three pointed garrets on either side of the columns framing the main entrance to the university. He had sat on those steps many times smoking cigarettes with the other law students while they discussed girls, the future and exams.

Behind the tall interlinked barriers, black-clad officers from the armed response unit were clustered in small groups. White pavilions had been put up. They undoubtedly concealed the vans of the catering company. There were plenty of sniffer dogs around, but no long-haired young men in white jackets.

'We can't just stay here, Michael,' Lene said, opening the door. 'Let's try Skindergade instead.'

Lene entered a number on her mobile while she ran.

Someone would appear to have picked up because she stopped in her tracks, grabbed Michael by the arm and forced him to stop.

'Charlotte? Thank God! Charlotte, you have to listen to me. It's a matter of life and death. I mean it!'

It sounded as if her boss was speaking from inside a diving bell.

'Lene! Now what? I really, I mean really, don't have time to talk to you. Hang up this instant! I'm turning my mobile off now!'

'WAIT! They're inside, Charlotte! A young man in a waiter's uniform. Long straight black hair, 1.85 metres tall, white scar to his left temple and he's carrying a genuine, valid ID card from the catering company. He's wearing some kind of high-tech explosive vest and he's going to kill you all, do you hear me? Are you inside now?'

'. . . inside . . . I know . . .'

Lene crouched, clutched the mobile and closed her eyes in concentration. Michael dragged her along like an obstinate teenager. She opened her eyes and lashed out after him without hitting.

Then Charlotte's voice came through clearly.

'We know! We've known all along. I'm looking at him right now, Lene! Samir El-Shennawi from Homs in Syria, twenty-five years old. I know everything about him! We all do! I'll talk to you later. I'm hanging up now. We're not even allowed to use mobiles in here.'

Lene straightened up and stared at her mobile as if it had just bitten her ear.

'But what about Berezowsky? He's going to be killed!'

'He was here yesterday, at midnight, he got his award and a handshake from the Crown Prince and now he's back in Tel Aviv. I spoke to him thirty minutes ago. He was very happy, proud and grateful, and he's in excellent health.'

'What?'

'Later, okay?'

Lene stamped her feet, and Michael looked at her as if he wanted to slap her.

'But you don't understand,' she tried again. 'He's wearing a kind of suicide vest with fibre-optic cables and glass balls. The dogs can't detect it, and he's going through the detectors.'

'. . .I know. It's been defused. It's fine. It really is!'

'Defused? Who by?'

But Charlotte had rung off and turned off her mobile as well, as Lene discovered because her call went straight to voicemail when she pressed speed dial.

'What did she say?' Michael asked.

She blinked and squinted at the sun, which had broken through the clouds.

'That they had everything under control,' she muttered, bewildered. 'That they already knew about him. Samir El . . . El-Shennawi, aged twenty-five and from Homs in Syria. Berezowsky is not even there, Michael. He's not there! He was given his award last night and flown home, and Charlotte knew all about the suicide vest and told me it was harmless. That it had been defused.'

Fiolstræde had also been cordoned off near the cathedral. There were several police officers with dogs around. There was a crowd of onlookers in front of the barriers, but there were no disturbances. It was mostly made up of people heading for Nørreport Station, now looking for an alternative route, Lene concluded. Michael dragged her along to a wall. They could see the eastern part of the university's main entrance with steps, busts and the large copper pots that could be lit on special occasions such as graduation ceremonies.

He pointed and Lene spotted the white box vans of the Swiss catering company among the pavilions and police vans. The tall, arched windows of the university were dark.

Michael asked something, but her legs were about to buckle underneath her.

'Sorry? What?'

'Who defused the vest?'

'She didn't say.'

'Both of them? Nazeera's too?'

Lene shook her head.

'I've no idea.'

She looked at Michael when the same thought occurred to them simultaneously.

'If they think Nazeera has defused that vest, they're going to get one hell of a—'

At that moment the whole street shifted sideways. A wave which started inside the university rippled quickly in every direction like water after a stone's throw, and Michael nearly fell over. Lene could actually see the paving rising up and falling back down again. It was as if a huge beast had woken up and turned over underground. Then the sound; a suppressed roar close to the lowest audible frequency of the human ear.

People around them were lifted towards the sky like swimmers on the surf, before being set down and resuming their normal height. An old woman landed on her backside and looked around, confused, while a child in a bicycle trailer started to cry. For a brief second the walls of the university seemed to expand and contract, and the bust of Niels Bohr toppled from its plinth outside the main entrance. His serious but sympathetic head rolled down the steps, and ended up at the paws of a police dog which had slumped to its knees. It stood up, shook its hind legs and urinated while it sniffed the bronze head.

'—surprise,' Michael completed his sentence.

Lene grabbed his hand and dragged him towards the barrier. The regular police officers and members of the armed response unit were running around like headless chickens between the cathedral and the university and no one was watching the barrier.

'We have to get inside, Michael!'

But he stood rooted to the spot.

'Something is wrong,' he said.

'What do you mean something is wrong? Of course it is, they've just blown that building and everyone inside it to high heaven, you moron!'

He pointed to the dark windows at the front of the university.

'Then why didn't the windows break? Not one of them is even cracked. It's impossible.'

'Whatever, we have to get inside. Now come on!'

59

'Do you remember the cicadas by the sea, Samir?' she had asked him when they sat in the car she had rented in her own name, because she no longer needed discretion.

'Of course,' he had said. 'Bacteria. A tourist who couldn't sink. He was reading his newspaper.'

'You wanted to kiss me,' she said. 'Make love to me.'

'I always did.'

It was easy for him to say it out loud now. It no longer mattered.

'Watch your face in there,' she said. 'Your expression, I mean.'

'Of course.'

They looked across to the barriers outside Vor Frue Cathedral.

'Go with God, Samir,' she said, and gave him an awkward embrace.

'And you, Nazeera.'

'You're our father Safar Khan's chosen one.'

He looked at her, smiled, and shook his head. 'You're

wrong, sister. I might be the sword, but you'll always be the jewel. He loves you. You're his daughter.'

He opened the door.

'You should have done it,' she said with her hands on the steering wheel.

'What?'

'Kissed me. Loved me.'

'I wasn't brave enough.'

He didn't look back. He walked upright, but not stiffly. He smiled at the female police officer at the barrier, showed her his ID card and held out his arms while she ran a hand-held metal detector through the air a few centimetres away from his body. He started saying something about being late, but the young woman just nodded and let him through.

A few metres inside the barrier he pretended to tie his shoelaces and glanced at the officer. She did not look at him, but nor did she look away from him, and she was speaking into her walkie-talkie.

It was difficult now. He was faint with hunger. The shirt stuck to his skin between the shoulder blades. The girl ran her eyes up and down him indifferently. She was good. Really good. But he knew that he had been recognized.

He joined the queue at the biggest catering van; a truck whose sides opened up so the cooks could pass the heated dishes into the waiters' hands or onto their shoulders. Half a dozen other young men were waiting in line in front of him, and some were walking across the cathedral square.

It was Samir's turn. A chef in a tall white chef's hat pushed a silver tray covered by a dome, which gleamed in the sunlight, across the counter and Samir took it. The chef smiled and gestured for the next waiter.

Seventy metres.

It felt as if the famous scientists in front of the university stared suspiciously at him from their granite plinths. A Labrador dragged its handler towards Samir.

In theory, he could still change his mind. He could toss the tray aside, sprint across the square and leap across the barrier, flee. The only problem was the miniature camera made to look like a uniform button in his jacket. It transmitted everything he saw to Nazeera's smartphone less than two hundred metres away. If he tore it off the jacket or deviated from the plan in any way, she would detonate the vest, even though she cared about him. She would expect that he would have done the same to her, if the situation were reversed. Besides, he would never dream of betraying her and the sheikh.

The dog sniffed his knee and looked up at the tray.

'It's just hungry,' the handler said amicably.

'Of course,' he muttered.

The dog salivated and whined as the handler dragged it away.

He reached the tall double doors. A slim, upright, middle-aged woman with a grey bob and glasses was walking in front of him. She was wearing trousers and a grey anorak, and the bulge on her left hip suggested she carried a gun. She turned as if she noticed that he was looking at her, and smiled.

'It's just inside, to the right,' she said in English and Samir nodded.

'Thank you,' he mumbled.

The other waiters had disappeared.

He entered a tunnel formed by dark-blue velvet curtains. There were black rubber mats on the floor. The tunnel was unlit and behind its next corner, it was almost entirely dark. Ten metres further ahead the tunnel was closed with another curtain and, behind this, he could hear numerous people engaged in cultivated conversation, the clatter of cutlery against china and the sound of wine bottles being uncorked. The smell of food threatened to overpower him.

Someone took over the microphone, speaking in slow but perfect English. The other voices died down. Samir spotted two young short-haired men in jeans and leather jackets with machine guns hanging from shoulder straps.

Although he had been expecting them, he was gripped by a kind of instinctive fear. They had anti-terror unit written all over them, but the two young men just looked at him and held aside the curtain.

He passed them and walked towards the next curtain a few metres away as the voice on the other side grew clearer. He was there. He had arrived.

Something heavy moved behind him. It sounded as if a large truck was being rolled across the rubber mat, but he did not look back.

Suddenly the curtains were pulled back and he shielded his hand against a sharp white light from a spotlight that nailed him to the strange black floor.

The voices fell silent.

Samir narrowed his eyes and looked around. He had spent many hours memorizing photographs and blueprints from the university's beautiful Festival Hall, but whereas there ought to be at least twelve metres to the ornate ceiling, with a gallery, huge wall paintings and rich, carved dark wooden panels, he found himself standing inside something that looked like a recording studio. The ceiling was less than four metres above his head and consisted of heavy dark-grey pyramid-shaped blocks and huge fire- and explosion-proof blankets hanging from thick steel wires. The same type of pyramid-shaped blocks covered the walls, except in places where stacks of metre-thick sandbags had been piled up. Behind him there was now a sliding wall, which looked as if it could stop an armoured tank. There were no other living human beings in here; only video cameras behind Plexiglas.

He was trapped in an explosion containment chamber with a tape recorder on a trolley and four loudspeakers which had played the soundtrack from an official lunch.

He set down the tray on the floor and took the mobile phone out of his pocket. He put his thumb on the green ring button, raised his hands above his head and kept them in full view as he turned around as if he was expecting applause.

No one clapped. In fact, there was not a sound to be heard.

Samir smiled at his invisible audience. Then he let his arms sink. He kneeled down and pressed his forehead against the rubber floor, but he did not let go of the mobile.

'Let me go in there, Christian,' Kim said to his partner, who had grabbed hold of his arm. 'I trust Nazeera, I've chosen to trust her, and I want to look him in the eye.'

Christian looked at Charlotte Falster for help; she was sitting in front of a console of TV screens, along with police and army technicians.

A couple of middle-aged sunburned men in ill-fitting suits were leaning against the wall. They spoke Hebrew to each other and they were unarmed. They whispered like valets and seemed impressed, almost awestruck, at PET's trap and the excellent precautions taken by the Danes. The two friendly Mossad officers were the last two members of Ehud Berezowsky's close protection team.

Charlotte studied Kim, but could not make eye contact with him.

'I'm not sure that's a particularly good idea, Kim,' she began. 'When did you last speak to Zebra? How do you know if she actually managed to defuse that vest? And anyway, where is she?'

His jaw muscles looked like knots under his too-tight skin.

'That's irrelevant,' he said. 'It's just a matter of replacing one mobile with another. Besides, all she had to do was squash a fibre-optic cable against the edge of a table. They're made from plate glass. It takes no effort to break them. It's not rocket science, is it?'

Charlotte took a deep and long-suffering breath.

'But where is she?'

Finally he looked at her with his deep, grieving eyes.

'I don't know, okay? But I'm sure she's somewhere being useful.'

He pointed at the row of TV screens, which showed that the terrorist had got up from his kneeling position, and was now standing with his hands dangling by his side and his head bowed.

As if he awaited the result of their discussion. The verdict.

'After all, he's here! He's right there. She has delivered him to us exactly as we agreed. She has done everything for us! It's not like he can just hold his breath in there, is it? Or hang himself with his shoelaces. Jerusalem is welcome to him. In fact, that's the deal. And once we have him, then we'll have Safar Khan.'

The older Israeli watched him with eyes like dark pearls when he heard the name of his arch-enemy.

'Then let *them* enter,' Christian pleaded with him. 'They're the experts, Kim.'

The older PET agent shook his head stubbornly.

'They were *my* children and *my* wife, Christian,' he said. 'That bastard was there. He planned it. He made it happen, damn you. Get it into your thick skull!'

Charlotte and Christian exchanged a look. Then she nodded and chewed her lip.

'Two minutes,' she said. 'Max. And don't you dare touch him, Kim! If he does anything at all which you don't like, shoot him down.'

Kim nodded and signalled to the two explosive experts who were dressed in what looked like deep-sea diving suits. Their facial features were blurred, as if they were under-water, and coloured green by the inch-thick safety glass of their helmets. They rolled one of the reinforced wall sections aside and let him slip through the crack.

'Oh, God,' Charlotte muttered as she watched the screens. They saw Kim Thomsen enter the claustrophobic arena. 'This is not going to end well, Christian.'

Christian said nothing. He looked like someone who was holding his breath.

It was not until then that she noticed he had got rid of the ponytail in favour of a sober, conservative hairstyle. Perhaps as a concession to the gravity of the occasion.

60

Samir raised his head and saw a slim man in his early forties in a dark suit cross the rubber floor.

He held up his hand with the mobile phone and the man stopped respectfully three metres away.

'Are you quite sure?' the man asked him gravely and in English.

'Sure? Sure about what?'

He gestured towards the explosive blankets and the pyramid walls.

'You won't even break the windows in here, my friend.'

'You don't think so?'

The man pointed to Samir's chest.

'Isopropyl nitrate and glass balls,' he said. 'Had it been old-fashioned Semtex, I would have been worried. Really worried. Then this old building would have ended up on Mars, but the clever thing about your fine new designer vest from Russia isn't the explosive, is it?'

Samir could barely keep his eyes open. He was dead tired. He thought about ending it all right there and then, but a fire was burning in the eyes of the police officer. He had suffered. There was no doubt about it. He had taken care when dressing for the occasion and somehow it would be rude to interrupt him.

'The balls?'

'Exactly. It's a close combat weapon, Samir, isn't it?'

'You know my name?'

The man nodded gravely. His hands were empty.

'Samir El-Shennawi. Homs. Syria. We've been expecting you, Samir, and you'll be in Jerusalem tonight. Trust me.'

'I don't think so, stranger. But you can come with me to Paradise instead. Perhaps they will let you in, even though you are an infidel dog.'

He closed his eyes, raised the mobile phone and pressed the button hard.

Then he opened his eyes again. He was still on earth. The walls were there. The ceiling. The tall, serious-looking Dane had not even blinked. Samir looked at his mobile and pressed the button with the green telephone icon once more.

'You can press that button until your thumb drops off,' the man said, calmly. 'Nazeera shafted you. She's good at that.'

Samir watched him. He had personally checked everything. Not once, but dozens of times with the test circuit, and every time the light had flashed green as a sign that the circuit of the vest was intact.

'Who are you?' he asked in despair.

'One of those whose life you ruined in Tivoli. My children. My wife.'

Samir stared at the floor. He could not look the other man in the eye.

Jerusalem . . .

The man came closer. He was within arm's reach.

Samir lifted his head and smiled at him.

'You're forgetting something, policeman. You're forgetting the most important thing.'

The man frowned and his hand moved towards the pistol in his shoulder holster.

'Am I?'

Samir pointed to the second button from the top on his white jacket.

'That, my friend, is not a button,' he said. 'That's a camera and Safar Khan is watching everything.'

The man leaned forward and his eyes widened when he saw the small black pupil of the lens.

Two hundred metres away, Nazeera watched Kim's face on the screen of her mobile. It grew bigger as he leaned closer.

'Samir, say hello to Irene,' she muttered and remote triggered Samir El-Shennawi's suicide vest.

She lifted her head. The screen went black and the car rocked on its shock absorbers as the underground pressure wave travelled past.

The alarm in the car behind her started to howl.

61

'There's Charlotte,' Michael shouted.

No one had taken any notice of them or challenged them as they climbed over the barrier. People were running in all directions across the square. A dog handler was lying on his back defending himself while his own dog, momentarily psychotic, stood bent over him with salivating jaws, trying to bite his throat.

There was an infernal noise when every helicopter in the airspace above Copenhagen congregated above the university. From near and far they could hear the emergency vehicles, which had been on high alert just in case this very event should happen.

The chief superintendent looked as if she was walking on hot coals. Strangely stiff and very carefully, she walked down the university steps one at a time. She looked at Niels Bohr's upturned countenance before she heard Lene's voice.

Lene ran up to her and put her arm around her superior's shoulder.

'Are you okay? What happened inside, Charlotte?'

The chief superintendent looked at Lene in stunned incomprehension, as if she had never seen her before. And then she stared at Michael, who was bursting with impatience.

'That's not important right now . . .' he began, but received a furious glare from Lene.

'Shut up for a moment, Michael. Can't you see she's in shock?'

'Yes, but . . .'

'What?' Charlotte mumbled.

She closed her eyes and made a determined effort to pull herself together. When she opened them again, there was some sign of life behind the lenses.

'We miscalculated,' she said. 'Or underestimated them. Kim bore the brunt of it. He went in.'

'In where, for heaven's sake?!'

Lene shook her boss's arm, but discovered that it was not a very good idea, so she stopped.

'We did know that he was coming. The terrorist. We had been told. We had turned the Festival Hall into an explosion containment chamber. We thought it would be the best solution. Isolate him, get him inside it, into a controlled environment. We thought that the vest—'

'Had been defused by Nazeera Gamil,' Michael completed her sentence.

Charlotte stopped and stared at him and Michael firmly but carefully ushered the two women towards Nørregade, where he prayed that Gurpal would still be waiting.

'Yes!'

Then she looked at Lene.

'How did he know that . . .?'

Lene smiled tenderly.

'Are you listening, Charlotte?'

Red spots blossomed on the chief superintendent's cheekbones.

'Of course I'm listening! Stop treating me like an imbecile . . .'

'Nazeera is named after Ebrahim Safar Khan's late wife,' Lene explained. 'She died in Shatila in Lebanon on the 17th September 1982. Butchered by Christian Phalangists or the Lebanese army. The families were neighbours in London. Safar Khan and Nazeera's father were colleagues and close friends before he was radicalized and went to Jordan and formed his cell. He has known Nazeera all his life. He made her. He moulded her beliefs.'

'Are you sure?'

They were approaching the barriers on Nørregade and Michael could see Gurpal's green Mercedes waiting faithfully where they had left it.

'Totally,' Lene assured her. 'Michael has actually spent a great deal of time and money on this, Charlotte. Nazeera is a rotten apple. And while we're on the subject of rotten apples, Kim murdered Irene Adler to get me arrested, so I wouldn't get in the way of his grand scheme.'

Charlotte nodded.

'I thought as much,' she mumbled. 'Unbelievable. Unforgivable.'

She looked at the car door, which Michael was holding open for her.

The Sikh half turned in the driver's seat and sent her a golden smile. Michael noticed that he had managed to get the stray hair and beard back under his turban.

'What are we doing? Where do you think you're going? I have to stay here and take care of things. Christ Almighty! What a nightmare!'

'It is, Charlotte,' Michael said gently while he placed his hand on her head and pushed her into the back. 'But I'm afraid that was just the beginning. The first course.'

Lene squeezed her boss's hand, but she shook off their hands in irritation.

'What are you talking about?'

Michael closed the door after her and slipped into the passenger seat himself.

'Drive, Gurpal, for Pete's sake! Drive like . . .'

'The wind?'

'Exactly. The Foreign Ministry. Use the pavements.' He pointed to Charlotte. 'She's a chief superintendent. Everything will be forgiven.'

The heavy car started with a jolt and white smoke poured from the screeching tyres. It did not look as if Gurpal found it necessary to use the pavements. Instead, he started driving against the one-way traffic in Nørregade, pressing one hand against the horn and switching on the emergency flashers.

Michael turned to Charlotte.

'Fasten your seatbelt and close your eyes. It's for your own good.'

Charlotte glanced at Lene, whose eyes were already firmly shut. Her knuckles, gripping the handle above the door, were white.

'What did you mean when you said it was just the beginning?' she asked a little later through gritted teeth, as Gurpal threw the taxi around the corner and swept through the private car park behind Copenhagen Town Hall. At the very last minute he avoided a fire engine about to pull out of the fire station and skidded out on H. C. Andersens Boulevard. The outbound traffic was too heavy for his taste, so he used the overtaking lane on the left instead.

'Nazeera,' Michael said. 'She has turned herself into an exact copy of Lene. Right down to the scuffed boots. She's in possession of Lene's warrant card. I don't suppose you've issued an arrest order for her in connection with the murder of Irene Adler?'

'Arne found some of my hair in Irene's hand,' Lene explained. 'But it came from the sack they put over my head in Ain's flat. Before they kicked me.'

'We haven't issued a warrant for you,' Charlotte said firmly. 'It wouldn't cross my mind, even if thirty sober press photographers had seen you do it and had the pictures to prove it.'

'Thank you,' Lene said.

Michael checked his gun again, this time not so discreetly. He unloaded it, skilfully caught the cartridge when it was ejected from the chamber and examined it carefully from all angles. He kissed it furtively, took out the magazine and replaced the cartridge. Then he reloaded it and put on the safety catch.

It was a good cartridge. He was sure of it.

'There were two undetectable high-tech suicide vests,' he said. 'One for Samir and one for Nazeera herself.'

'Two?!'

Lene opened her eyes narrowly, saw a truck loom in front of them and closed them again. She gulped fiercely.

'Nazeera is wearing the other one,' he said, 'and I don't think she has gone to Amager Common in despair, to blow herself to bits and take a couple of flashers and a few seagulls with her. I think Khan intended all along for her to kill the EU foreign ministers in Eigtveds Pakhus. That was his goal from the beginning. The university and Ehud Berezowsky's award ceremony was only ever a smokescreen, diversion, camouflage . . . so that Nazeera could exploit her likeness to Lene. To gain access.'

'I understand,' Charlotte said.

'She has been watching Lene. She ransacked her home, took photographs and copied her wardrobe.'

'Then again, your style is very easy to copy,' Charlotte said.

Lene turned red.

Michael looked from one woman to the other.

'The result is,' he continued, 'that dressed as Lene, she can stroll unchallenged right up to the podium in the conference hall, past sniffer dogs and metal detectors. And while all your colleagues are busy at the university, congratulating each other, she'll have the floor for a brief remark and then will eliminate every single European foreign minister and their delegations. That's worth killing your dog for. It's worth everything.'

Charlotte started rummaging around for her mobile phone, but Michael placed his hand over hers.

'I have to stop her. I have to warn them—' she began.

'Charlotte, I don't think you quite understand. She's an exact copy of Lene. If you stop her and we then turn up, people will get confused. Shoot the wrong person. And anyway, we're there now!'

The taxi pulled up in front of the barriers where Asiatisk Plads met Strandgade.

'Come on!' he called out, opened the door and started running.

62

It was the sunny weather and a strict chair that would save the lives of the ministers, Michael thought, as they ran across the square in front of the beautiful, four-storey, thoroughly renovated Eigtveds Pakhus. The person in question had carefully stuck to the programme, which right now decreed a fifteen-minute coffee and cigarette break, and the sun had tempted most people out into the open.

Michael looked at his watch: 13:12. In three minutes the ministers would be called back inside. They would return to the conference room on the second floor to discuss the next item on the agenda: the rise in illegal immigration from Africa. In the previous week, another three young Angolans had fallen out of the sky above London's northern suburbs, when the plane in whose wheel bays they had hidden themselves lowered the wheels prior to landing at Heathrow Airport. One of the frozen young men had pulverized the glass roof above a wedding to which several members of the House of Commons had been invited. It had become intolerable.

The conference room would be densely packed and Nazeera Gamil's suicide vest was designed for this very purpose: to kill everything and everyone within a radius of fifty metres. Everyone in that room would die.

They were met at the barrier by police officers armed with machine guns. One was just taking off her helmet and shaking free her long hair.

Lene stopped.

'I know her. She was at Nørreport Station when Ain was killed.'

The girl looked up, spotted them and her face darkened. Slowly she took a few steps forward, and Lene whispered something in Charlotte's ear. The chief superintendent summoned the young officer.

Lene smiled at the young woman.

'It *is* me,' she reassured her. 'Nørreport Station the other day. Ain Ghazzawi Rasmussen.'

The girl frowned and looked over her shoulder.

'But . . . you just . . . I mean . . .'

'It *is* confusing,' Charlotte Falster said, 'we know, but we have everything under control. Please let us through. It's very, very important. Extremely important, in fact.'

The officer nodded at her colleagues, who also looked as if they had seen a ghost.

Lene went up to the girl.

'Incidentally, when did I walk past? I mean, when did you let me through?'

'What?'

Michael looked over the officer's shoulder and spotted the Danish foreign minister, a withered but gregarious man with a big grey head of hair. He was entertaining his German counterpart, who laughed politely at the Dane's stories.

The girl looked at her colleagues.

'Three minutes ago,' one of them said. 'Maybe four.'

'Thank you.'

They quickly walked up the wide steps on the waterfront side and past a well-maintained, three-mast schooner which was moored in front of the warehouse. The flags of the participating countries were flapping from the rigging of the ship and all doors to the warehouse were thrown open to let in the spring.

Michael's eyes scanned the entrances to the building.

'There are too many entrances. I'll take the back,' Lene said.

Michael looked at her. He did not like letting her out of his sight. Then he glanced at Charlotte.

'We have to split up,' the chief superintendent agreed, 'there are still only three of us who have the full picture. If you find her, shoot her.'

Michael raised his eyebrows. Behind her academic, quietly correct appearance, the chief superintendent was unforgiving and merciless.

He turned around to give his okay to Lene, but she had already disappeared.

'Bloody stubborn bit—' he started angrily.

'You should try having her around forty hours a week,' Charlotte said.

'Then why do you keep rehiring her?'

'Because she's the best.'

A young woman in a dark suit that resembled a uniform appeared outside the main entrance, raised an antique ship's bell and summoned the delegates.

Ministers, spin doctors, secretaries and civil servants drained their coffee cups, extinguished their cigarettes, finished their various conversations and started milling back inside the warehouse. They used all available entrances.

'Should we warn them?' Michael asked. 'Should we tell them to stay outside until we have found Nazeera?'

Charlotte looked up at the front of the building.

'We don't know if she's watching us right now. People will congregate. They won't just do as they are told, Michael. And while we're standing here, speaking our best school English, French and German, she'll come down and kill everybody. The result will be the same.'

'You're right,' he said. 'I'll take the west side and you take the east. Okay?'

Charlotte mingled with a group of Italians in beautiful suits who were making their way through one of the arched doors. They gallantly stepped aside for her, probably commenting on her figure as she walked past.

Michael himself attracted no attention when he walked up

the stairs. He thought like crazy. What would he have done if he had been Nazeera? The answer was simple. He would have hidden in a lavatory cubicle until the meeting was well under way and everyone was busy.

He wound his way through civil servants from the Czech Republic, while he thought about what drove Nazeera to do it.

She had it all. A good family, looks, brains, money. But she had given it all up, and for what? An overdeveloped sense of justice, maybe? The Middle East bred paradoxes and extreme fanaticism. It had done so for centuries . . . millennia: the Son of Man, the Old Man from the mountain and his *hashashins*, Saladin, Mohamed al-Amir Atta.

He pushed aside a female secretary who started talking to him. A gallant civil servant grabbed his arm and protested on the woman's behalf. Michael knocked him down and started running. Mayhem erupted behind him. It was fine. He considered triggering the fire alarm on the wall, but knew that it would be only a brief respite.

Nazeera might not get all of them, but she would get a stairwell full of innocent people.

He pulled out his gun and flicked aside the safety catch, holding it along his thigh as he reached the second floor. Halfway down the corridor, people were walking through doors into what had to be the great conference hall with room for 250 people.

Why didn't they hold these things at military airbases?

he thought in despair. He walked down the corridor, having tuned his eyes to any sighting of Lene's hair colour and tall, upright figure.

He thought about Sara, his wife, but with a wistful distance, before his thoughts returned to the enigma that was Nazeera Gamil and her loyalty to a crazy old sheikh in Amman.

Where was she and why the hell had he not told Lene to take off a ring, do her hair differently, turn her jacket inside out? Anything so that he could tell the difference. The sweat was dripping into his eyes even though it was cool behind the thick walls. The last delegates arrived and a ministerial officer in a suit came out, looked around and smiled at Michael.

'We are closing the doors, sir,' he said in English.

The man's gaze automatically searched for the shiny ID card with a photograph, a hologram and the EU stars against a blue background, which ought to dangle from Michael's neck.

The man was no longer smiling and had produced a walkie-talkie from his inside pocket when Michael reached him. He put almost full force behind the edge-of-hand blow which he delivered to the man's throat, and the officer crashed like a felled tree. Michael caught him and was about to place him gently on the tiled floor when a hand reached out for his arm.

He was starting to tire of this.

He let the man fall. The back of his head hit the floor

with a sickening thud and Michael aimed his pistol at the new threat, when he discovered that it was Charlotte. He kept his gun pointing at her face for a long moment, and studied her eyes either side of the cross hairs. His gun was cocked. She was only a very light push from eternity. Then he lowered his weapon.

'May I suggest that you say something the next time you creep up on me,' he grunted. 'Clear your throat, cough, anything.'

'I will,' she said.

Her face was as white as the walls.

The ministers were taking their seats around the enormous horseshoe-shaped conference table at the centre of the hall. The microphones glowed red, and projectors showed the EU flag on a screen towards the rear. Interpreters, civil servants and secretaries had spread out. The Danish foreign minister studied his cue cards, ready to welcome the participants to the next session.

The voices died down as the room slowly filled with people. No one took any particular notice of Michael and Charlotte, who remained standing right inside the doors. She elbowed him, and he pulled the doors closed and started locking them. He stared gloomily at the other entrances to the hall. There were far too many. He moved to the end of the hall while Charlotte remained where she was. The Danish foreign minister got up and started his short walk to the podium.

The heavy blue curtain which concealed the end wall twitched, or perhaps it was all in his mind. Michael frowned and stared at Charlotte until she turned her head towards him. He pointed to the curtain and signalled with two walking fingers that he would take a closer look at the room behind it.

The voice of the Danish foreign minister filled the room. He opened with a short, improvised account of the failed attack at the university, but otherwise stuck to general, reassuring phrases and offered his congratulations to the police.

Michael used his pistol to pull aside the heavy velvet drapes. Behind them was a room almost five metres deep, with a whitewashed end wall and a door leading to the kitchen. There were trolleys with Thermos flasks and used cups and saucers. The room was dark and shadowy. He could smell fruit, coffee and pastries.

For the second time within a few minutes he stared into terrified eyes over his gun sight. This time they belonged to a young woman in a white waiter's jacket, dark trousers and a tight ponytail, who was holding a cinnamon swirl in her hand. She froze mid mouthful.

Michael lowered his gun.

'Are you alone?'

The girl nodded mutely.

'Have you seen anyone who shouldn't be here?'

She shook her head. The girl had tears in her eyes.

'Then get out,' he said. 'And take everyone else with you, but be quick.'

'There's no one else but me. They've had their last service. There won't be any more,' she stuttered.

'Super. Now get out, okay?'

The girl stood rooted to the spot, incapable of movement. He wanted to slap her, but restricted himself to shoving her hard towards the door to the kitchen.

'Out!'

She disappeared through the swing door, which squealed on its rubber hinges, and he caught a glimpse of a dark, empty kitchen behind it.

'Dammit . . .'

Michael lowered his pistol. The sweat was pouring into his eyes and the floor felt weird. When he closed his eyes, strange patterns zigzagged across his retinas. He gagged, but supressed the urge to throw up. It's just the concussion, he told himself. It was natural. It was nothing.

Then he heard a bump and a frightened outburst from the kitchen. Michael rolled his eyes: that poor, terrified girl was probably knocking down half the catering equipment as she ran.

He was about to go back when a second thud from the kitchen made him turn around. He placed his hand on the swing door and pushed it open.

The kitchen was far bigger than he had expected. There were long, stainless-steel tables, industrial cookers, rows of dangling kitchen utensils that obstructed his view, and a dim light from frosted windows positioned high up. The young girl was lying on her back about ten metres away, slumped against a cooker with a rapidly growing pool of blood underneath her. The blood poured down her white jacket from a large, dark smile under her chin. A blood-stained filleting knife was lying on the floor, and Nazeera Gamil kneeled by her side with a pistol in her hand. Her other hand was resting on the girl's chest and it was red and wet, like everything else.

Michael's hands shook and the foresight of his gun swung in small arcs over Nazeera's head, chest and neck. He had sent the girl to the kitchen himself, right into the arms of the terrorist.

How old was she? Nineteen? Early twenties perhaps, but no more.

'Don't you dare touch her, you murdering bitch, do you hear me?'

Nazeera looked up at him with a frown. She made to get up.

And Michael shot her.

63

He was not up to the job, he realized, as he saw the bullet penetrate her left shoulder – far, far away from its intended target between her eyes.

Gurpal Singh would not have missed, he thought.

She turned back to face him after being struck. Michael looked straight into her luminous green eyes and adjusted his aim. His hands were suddenly as calm as a statue's and he knew his next shot would kill her instantly.

Despite her wound and the pain, she managed to raise her own weapon and pull the trigger. The bullet knocked Michael's already injured leg aside like a sledgehammer and he fell slowly backwards into a towering shelving unit filled with kitchen equipment and stacks of stainless-steel trays. He heard only his own heartbeat.

Time stopped. But he kept on falling.

The noise was indescribable. He flailed his arms to get up and free himself, but was hopelessly entangled in shelves, heavy mixers and beaters. Michael searched frantically for his gun, which had disappeared under all the kitchen equipment.

Then he looked back at Nazeera Gamil and knew that he had been horribly, fatally wrong: by now he had expected her face to be glowing with religious ecstasy. Or triumph, at least. But it showed only pale concentration, and she was not even looking at him.

It was not her.

It was Lene, and all her energy was focused on raising the undoubtedly heavy gun further up and out to the right.

Michael lifted his head and followed her gaze to the doppelgänger who had appeared a short distance away as the heavy door to a freezer room closed behind her. Nazeera stood with her legs slightly apart, concentrating only on entering a code into her mobile. Then she walked quickly to the door to the main hall without sensing their presence. She was no more than twenty metres from the conference table, and he knew that no power on earth would be able to save them.

Nazeera was halfway through the door when the first of Lene's bullets hit her spine and her legs disappeared from underneath her.

She lay still for a few seconds, and Michael was halfway through a sigh of relief when she raised her head and dragged herself onwards on her hands and elbows across the smooth, bloody floor.

He had once hit a fox with his car and broken its back. He had got out of the car and seen the same thing he was looking at now: a dying creature whose blind instincts made it keep going.

Then Nazeera's face was slammed forward and into the floor tiles by Lene's next bullet, which hit the back of her head. Her mobile lay next to her right hand. Her fingers opened and closed one last time.

Lene's breathing was whistling, fast and strained. Her hand unclenched and she pushed the pistol away as if she did not want to know of it. Then she put her hand back on the young girl's chest. The bleeding from the long, open gash across the girl's neck had stopped.

Michael closed his eyes and did not open them until he heard Charlotte Falster's voice very close to him.

64

The boy opened his eyes and looked around. Perhaps he had been asleep, perhaps he had been dreaming. It was growing dark and the neon sign above the restaurant cast green and orange flashes of light across the empty floor. He heard slow footsteps coming up the stairs.

'Samir?'

A wave of hope surged through him, and he tried pushing himself up into a sitting position against the pillar. Then the feeling of relief was replaced by despair. If it was Samir coming, it would mean that he was still alive, and if he was alive, their mission had failed horribly.

His hands were asleep under the gaffer tape.

'Samir?'

He called out softly in the darkness.

He stared towards the stairwell, trying to penetrate the darkness by sheer force of will. The darkness merged and turned into two . . . no, three figures. They switched on their flashlights and the beams swept across the floor until they found him by the pillar. Defenceless and tethered.

The torches pointed down and lit up the men's shoes: two

pairs of worn and scuffed brown shoes, which had probably been expensive once. Grey socks and trousers. The original creases had long since given up the ghost. The last set of feet were wearing black trainers. No socks, jeans. A young man. From the Danish intelligence service, no doubt.

He caught a glimpse of a metal wristwatch as one of the men in the down-at-heel shoes squatted down on his haunches and twisted back the sleeve of his jacket.

The man's face was furrowed, sandblasted, red from the sun, and he was very nearly bald. There were dark spots and freckles on his scalp, but he had a wide, amicable, Slavic smile. His small dark eyes almost disappeared in laughter lines when he studied Adil, as if he were a much-loved son. He smelled of the desert and Adil's bladder emptied when he realized who the two men were. He stared at the dark stain spreading along his thighs with shame.

The older man had undoubtedly noticed it, but had the good manners to ignore it.

'Who are you? Where are you from?' Adil asked, but did not really want to know the answer.

The man smiled his best, most reassuring smile.

'Jerusalem. You're going home, my boy.'

He closed his eyes and so did not see the syringe in the man's left hand.

He felt a sharp prick to his shoulder and looked up in surprise before being swallowed up by the darkness.

*

The two Israelis looked down at the boy while Christian wished he had had time to drink a cup of coffee. He got a headache when the intervals between coffees were too long. Or perhaps his headache was the after-effect of the explosion and the sight of Kim dissolving in a red mist.

'He's a fine boy,' one of the Israelis muttered in English.

'Very fine,' the other man said, 'but you wouldn't want him to marry your daughter, Gabi.'

Christian was no longer listening to the two men. He walked across to the window and looked down at the ambulance waiting below. The emergency lights had been turned off, and the two paramedics were smoking by the kerb. He took out a walkie-talkie from his pocket and pressed the *send* button twice. One of the paramedics looked up at the window and tossed aside his cigarette.

The boy would be strapped to a stretcher and taken directly to a discreet corner of Copenhagen Airport, where one of the Royal Danish Air Force's Challenger aircrafts would be waiting. No formalities.

One of the two Israelis was an army doctor who would keep an eye on the patient all the way to Jerusalem.

Christian took out a pocketknife and cut the rope and the gaffer tape. To be on the safe side, they put the boy in the recovery position, but his breathing was fine and unobstructed. He was in good shape.

For a moment Christian considered slitting his throat. It would save the boy so much.

Then he looked across to the table with the butcher's tools, the video camera and the banner; at the table and chairs where Michael Sander and Lene Jensen had been bound, convinced that their lives were about to end.

The older of the two men placed his hand on Christian's shoulder.

'So will you be coming with us? Have you made up your mind?'

Christian nodded.

'I would be honoured,' he said.

No matter what they did to the boy, it would not be enough, he thought.

65

The coffee machine was out of order. Michael's crutches careered across the floor and he had to wait until someone's kind-hearted relative in the waiting room picked them up for him. Everyone's head turned each time a nurse or a doctor in blue scrubs appeared in the doorway to the trauma centre.

Lene's bullet had drawn a deep furrow across the large muscle on the front of his thigh, and Michael had been treated by the same doctor who had cleaned and bandaged the dog bites. She could not help herself and had asked if he was still the playing the villain at the Danish Police Dog Championships. Were the dogs now carrying guns? she said. The wound was not serious. It needed to heal from the bottom, she said. He would get yet another fine scar to add to his already impressive collection. He had asked for morphine, but been given only a small amount of over-the-counter painkillers.

The door to Casualty opened and Charlotte appeared. Michael hobbled towards her. It was impossible to read anything from her face.

'Why don't we go outside?' she suggested.

'How . . .?'

'Outside.'

They stood in the car park and Charlotte turned her face to the sun.

'Do you have a cigarette?' she asked.

Michael lit one for her.

She blew out a long, thin stream of smoke and squinted at him.

'She'll make it,' she said. 'But it's not just the shoulder. The bullet hit a bone and continued through her left lung. She has lost a lot of blood. They have inserted a drainage tube into her chest cavity, as far as I can gather. She's in intensive care, but she is awake. But they say she'll make it.'

'Can I see her? Talk to her?'

'She doesn't want to see you, Michael.'

'What do you mean?'

'That she doesn't want to see you, under any circumstances. She was very clear. Very.'

He stared at the chief superintendent. His leg hurt more than ever.

Charlotte placed her hand on his arm.

'She doesn't understand how you could have mistaken her. Hopefully she'll understand in time . . .'

'For Christ's sake! They resembled each other like two drops of water!'

'You're right, they did.'

Her hand left a little heat. Then it dropped along her side.

'It's not rational, Michael. Give her time.'

'Time doesn't help,' he said. 'Not with her.'

'You're probably right, but she saved your life. Everyone's lives.'

He straightened out and looked up at the hospital façade.

'Yes. Yes, she did. I hope she'll save her own life too.'

'She will.'

Michael made his way to the nearest exit. He had never felt so alone in his life.

The Sikh studied him in the rear-view mirror when he got into the back of the taxi. Gurpal had waited patiently for him on the cab rank outside Rigshospitalet all afternoon.

'Did it go well, *sahib*?'

'Brilliant, Gurpal. Absolutely brilliant. Bloody brilliant. Thank you.'

The gold teeth lit up the inside of the car.

'Where to, *sahib*?'

Michael said nothing.

His eyelids stung and he pinched the bridge of his nose hard. The Sikh never took his eyes off him, but the man said nothing.

Michael leaned back.

'Gurpal . . . palm trees. Do you understand? Find me a beach and some palm trees,' he said.

'Are we waiting for anyone? The woman with the red hair?'

'No.'

'Is she alive?'

'Yes.'

'It's going to be a long trip, *sahib*. To the palm trees, I mean.'

'The further the better, Gurpal.'

EPILOGUE

One month later

Charlotte spotted Michael from far away. As arranged, he was sitting at a picnic table on a windswept motorway layby and was the only living being around. The swings on the playground squeaked mournfully in the wind, which swept in from the fields. He looked as if he was cold inside his black overcoat. He watched her without expression as she approached, flicked a cigarette butt onto the playground and lit another one.

A rented Opel was parked behind him.

She sat down on the bench opposite him, leaned across the table so that they could hear each other above the roar of the motorway traffic, and smiled.

He looked past her.

'How is she?' he asked.

'She's doing well. She has started exercising and stopped drinking. She looks good, Michael. I'm very grateful. Very. We all are.'

He turned up the collar of his coat.

'I've been asked to tell you that you can become a Knight of Dannebrog, if you . . . I mean . . . well, your real name and so on . . . they'll want to know that,' she said.

He didn't appear to be listening. The expression on his face and in his eyes remained unchanged. Instead, he took out an envelope from the inside pocket of his overcoat, opened it and handed her two densely typed pages.

'My account number is at the bottom,' he said.

Charlotte stared at the total amount and her jaw dropped. The sum exceeded her wildest imagination. How on earth would she ever get . . .

'Is anything wrong?' he asked her calmly.

'What? No . . . I just think . . . Does it really say 1,253,000 kroner for the car, here?'

She pointed to the middle of the paper.

'They perforated my customized Mercedes,' he said flatly. 'It wasn't just a scratch. It's not something you can fix with a bit of wax and a damp cloth.'

'No, no . . . but . . .'

'Is it a problem? They can save some money by keeping their knighthood.'

She folded the papers and tucked them into her jacket pocket.

'Not at all,' she said, sounding considerably more optimistic than she felt. 'Just over three million? Not a problem.